HOWL OF THE GOLDEN JACKAL

(BABYLON/PERSIA #1)

KRISTIN SWENSON

PG
B

First published in the United States in 2025 by Pretty Good Books, Charlottesville, Virginia

Identifiers: ISBN 979-8-9989339-0-5 (ebook); 979-8-9989339-8-1 (trade paper)

~ for those wild women
who are women of the wild ~

PROLOGUE (ASHUR CITY, 614 B.C.E.)

The king of the Medes leaned over the neck of his warhorse. Blood and sweat slicked under his hands. He squinted. Out of the smoke of Ashur's ruin, twin chargers, black as a moonless night, galloped toward him. The robes of their riders gave them wings. Behind them, an army emerged. Babylonians. They were late.

The riders pulled up – King Nabopolassar and beside him, like an avenging shadow, crown prince Nebuchadnezzar. The Babylonian king looked around the field. He took in the sight of Ashur's defeat and of the battered Median king before him.

"Well done," Nabopolassar said.

Cyaxares bit back the complaint on his tongue. His Medes had done it alone.

That evening, after King Cyaxares had regained a sense of equanimity -- after his attendant had cleaned the wounds of the day and Cyaxares had eaten and drunk the fare of soldiers, after he recalled how the hero-king Nabopolassar had led a popular uprising to found a Babylonian state independent of Assyria -- he was ready. He was ready to discuss strategy with these allies whose strength Cyaxares knew had already met and might soon surpass Media's own.

Nabopolassar congratulated Cyaxares again on the Medes' victory that day. "Together we are indomitable," Nabopolassar said.

"It's not over yet."

"It will be. Then, when Assyria is no more, we shall wed our houses, my son to your daughter. An alliance to last the generations."

"I have no daughters," Cyaxares said, suddenly conscious of his speech -- so crude compared to the Babylonian's polished dialect. "I have but one son."

"Then we wait. If that son has a daughter before you do, she shall be the one to marry Nebuchadnezzar."

Assyria did fall to the alliance of Babylonians and Medes; but still the Medes had no princess. Nebuchadnezzar married a Babylonian slave from the temple of the goddess Ishtar. She had already born him a bastard. It was she who then bore Babylon's crown prince, and she who was put to death for the boy's insanity. So it was that years later, King Nebuchadnezzar would finally honor the agreement to wed the princess from Media.

The great Cyaxares never did have a daughter. But he lived long enough to see his son Astyages, a disappointment in every other way, have two. Nearly identical the girls were, but in appearance only. One was born to the queen. The other was gotten on a slave. The regal child – Mandane by name – was a timid girl, protected from birth to become a linchpin of peace, Media's key to protection from Babylonian encroachment in its rapacious hunger for resources. The other girl, Amytis, uncivilized and all but wild never knew a moment when she wasn't responsible for the wellbeing of her half-sister. And that was fine with her. Amytis had no interest in a Babylon with all its material glory, or a throne of any sort. Rather Media, with its mountains of forest, clear streams, and high meadows, with its wolf packs and hawks, oaks and pine would always be Amytis's home.

That was all she ever wanted. Until.

It's a terrible thing to discover that in order to keep what you love the most, you have to leave it behind.

PART I

CHAPTER 1

I am a bastard. It's no secret. The king is my father, but my mother was a slave. Or so I'm told. They say she took the first opportunity to run.

No matter. I'm a legitimate daughter of this land, and I love her with all that I am – her old forests, mountains, and rivers; her meadows and the grasslands that are nursemaid to the world's most impressive steeds. Over her rocky crags and cliffs mountain goats climb; under them, badgers hide. And all around, yet rarely seen, the golden jackal ghosts the deep shade, broad snowy expanses, and sun-dappled thickets in hunt and love. I hear its howl as much by the rush of life in my blood as by the ears on my head. Svelte and small, the jackal will stop at nothing to protect her home.

Mine is a story of trying ever and always to protect Media.

So, in the face of Babylonia's rapacious need and my own father's groveling weakness, I could not stand by and do nothing. That's how I'll defend myself to the gods, when it's all over. Besides, who's to say finally what the gods intend? Mazda, the great creator and transformer still needs our help. Mithra urges covenant. And Anahita... well, I thought I understood her words.

Maybe I was wrong. I often am. Gods or no, for some of what happened, I'll never forgive myself.

IT WAS SPRING, but still cold. In this land, the sun takes its golden-honeyed time getting up over the mountain peaks. At the time, I didn't think much of the quiet -- no jackals' morning howl to signal good fortune for my sister's journey. After all, she wasn't supposed to leave that day. A few feet away, my horse pawed at the loosening ground, nuzzling out the early shoots. Of the thousands of steeds, raised half-wild on Media's magic grass, Bepti was the most magnificent. And that's saying a lot. My favorite. I'd nursed him as a foal - abandoned or orphaned, I don't know. He needed me then. I needed him, too, I guess. From him I learned how to accept the loneliness of my position. Hence his name, "'rebel'-times-two." After Bepti had grown, I was the only one who could ride him, though he'd let Mandane on his back, too. Of course. He snorted frost off his whiskers. A few paces east, the river bounded and crashed, swollen with melt, lusty.

Inside a ring of broad evergreens, I finished my prayers. These days, they were all about clinching that damn treaty. We were finally so close to getting it done. I stood up, adjusted the sheepskin under my course wool robe, and brushed the dirt and leaves off the knees of my trousers. Beneath gnarled branches, I laid my palms against the bark of an Ancient One. Some prayers don't need words.

Mandane emerged from the woods, her ermine stole a bright counterpoint to the browns and evergreens.

"How did it go?" I asked.

Mandane shook her head.

I gave my sister a few moments of silence. "You can't save every one." I said, wishing I could reassure her more than that.

"At least the mother survived." Mandane sniffed back tears –

she took even an infant's death hard – and adjusted her satchel. "Can you believe, they call her 'Dog'?"

"A childless slave? I can believe it. Not everyone's a princess." I bent to catch her downcast eyes. "And not everyone wants to be," which made Mandane smile, which made me happy.

For all the ways I might have resented or even hated my half-sister, I couldn't. No one could. She was lightness itself and goodness all the way through. What's more, she had manners. She'd been trained from birth to join the world's most sophisticated elite – Babylonian royalty – and it became her. As for me, my entire worth was tied up in keeping her safe until the marriage was done. Finally, today, the Babylonians would arrive in Media. There'd be feasting and music and hunts and dancing. And Mandane would marry the king. Best of all, with the marriage of Mandane to King Nebuchadnezzar, he and our father King Astyages would establish the treaty their fathers had promised years and years ago – parity, brotherhood. Equals. What relief that would be. While Babylonia had become ever bigger and more powerful in the years since that verbal agreement, we'd become, due to my father's cowardice and failings, ever weaker. And we had so much to lose. I had so much to lose.

It wasn't only the Babylonians' myriad conquests or their wish to control the most valuable trade routes, which ran through our capital, but King Nebuchadnezzar's endless building that put my land at risk. In short, they needed what we had. To get it – timber and minerals (we had silver and gold enough to gild our palace walls) – they'd ruin wild Media. They'd sully Anahita's sacred streams, throw off the delicate balance of bird and forest and animal – and who knows? even kill her gods. Based on pure might, they could do it. They could take and subdue and ruin. The only thing stopping them was the promise Nabopolassar and Cyaxares made to each other – that a daughter, or granddaughter if it came to that, of Cyaxares's would marry then crown prince, now king Nebuchadnezzar.

Well, it had come to that. And it was finally time. This meant everything.

"He's old enough to be our grandfather," Mandane said, accepting my boost onto the horse's back. I handed her her basket of medicinal plants.

"All the more reason to marry now." I twisted goldenrod into a wreath. "He cannot die before the treaty is set," I said.

"A little sympathy would be good here."

I vaulted up behind her and set the wreath on her head. "But you'll be a queen."

We followed the river back toward the palace. The sun was high enough now to set off the colors of its seven rings of walls, each taller than the outer and topped by increasingly valuable materials until the inner, highest – circling the royal palace – dazzled in yellow gold. In front of me, Mandane's hair fell in perfect waves, one lovely length, held here and there by tiny golden clasps. Brushed every night by a palace slave, her hair shone. My own hair I'd hacked in uneven bits where it had knotted into mats or caught a burr. Or simply to keep it out of my eyes. I put a hand to the feathers I'd strung, the talons I'd made into clasps of my own, and secured a wayward lock.

"Astragalus!" Mandane exclaimed, pointing to a leggy plant waving leafy fronds from the river bank. "I'll just quick get some, and then we can go." She slipped off, even before I'd stopped the horse.

We were already late. The Babylonians were due to arrive today. But in this, this one thing alone – a particular kind of healing – Mandane would break the rules, challenge authority. As for me, I couldn't seem to help it. I was always in trouble, one way or another.

The creek bounded and babbled as carefree as any other day. Mandane's leaving didn't change that, didn't change the snow on the mountains or the alfalfa in the valley, heavy with seed. But it would change everything for me. The thought made me antsy with conflicting emotion. "I'll be right back," I said.

Mandane was focused on that swath of green on the river's bank. Her lower lip extended in a concentrating pout. I squeezed my eyes shut. Kara, our nurse from infancy, had said that as infants the subtle dip in my half-sister's lower lip had been the only feature distinguishing us. To me, it had become everything – the difference between importance and irrelevance, precious hope and the lengths one went to protect it. Mandane mattered; I did not. Or rather only as I kept my half-sister, the true princess, safe. Some days I almost hated Mandane for it – for the dip, for the difference, for everything. But finally, affection won out. I couldn't help loving Mandane any more than I could help loving home – Media in its wild wonder, its beauty, and savage grace. Besides, everyone loved Mandane.

I leaned forward and nudged the horse's flanks. I grabbed a hunk of mane as he dropped his haunches and plunged into a gallop across the meadow toward a bank of trees. The morning sun on my back and neck held the first hint of spring warmth. My muscles loosened with the rhythm of the horse. A fallen oak loomed ahead. The horse rose up, its mane sweeping my cheek as we soared over, then down, and on.

It was a distance and growing, but nothing like the miles between Ecbatana and Babylon. I'd miss Mandane. But I would have Media. Always. And that was more than enough. When the burden of caring for Mandane had felt too heavy or my own worthlessness in the face of her value dulled my limbs, I'd found comfort in the wildness of this land, in the burble of ice-topped streams, the shriek of a hawk, Media's animals fierce and fragile, and the odd-angled posture of mountains – witness to ages whose secrets they kept.

"No contact." It was something our father had drilled into us. Once married and gone, Mandane's commitment to Babylon must never be questioned, he said. I couldn't see the reasoning (his paranoia was frequently illogic), but we all agreed that the treaty must hold.

Speaking of – the treaty, Mandane!… My horse tossed his head against the rein, frustrated at the restraint, the turning. We raced back. And just in time.

Mandane stood, thigh deep, in the middle of the river, reaching for a particularly tall plant. What she didn't see was a heavy log spiked with thick branches, torn from the bank by the swollen stream, and heading straight for her.

"Get back!" I leapt from the horse. "Mandane! Get back!" My throat frayed with the effort. Mandane, fixed as she was on the spindly plant, bending in the current, didn't heed my warning. I tore off my robe and threw myself into the water, upstream.

"Anahita," I prayed, "Turn the tree, I beg. Save my sister. Save this, your land." But the gods have rules of their own, and the current ran a certain way. The log bore down mercilessly.

I fought my way upstream toward it. "Get back!" I yelled again. I didn't turn to see Mandane's expression turn from annoyance to horror or see her start back to the shore. I planted my feet against the current. I stood, right where I'd wanted, directly in the tree's path. Icy water eddied around my waist. I tapped the scabbard at my hip. Habit. But I left the weapon, my only possession of any value, there. It'd be no use here. I leaned into the river and focused – a fifteen-year-old slip of a warrior. I bent my knees. "Anahita, give me strength equal to this river."

The log tore into me. Its heft spun me half around. I went under. The cold clamped my lungs. Something slashed my face. I came up sputtering and grabbed a branch as it swung. It flipped me. Down again. My feet scrabbled for, and found, purchase on the river bottom. I dug in and hung on. My fingers cramped around the limb, my hands already numbed. I got my head back up to air, but only barely. Water sloshed my face again and again.

I needed to hold only long enough for Mandane to get to

safety. Had she? My shoulder ached. It was ever my concern – Mandane's security – ever my preoccupation.

But I couldn't hold on – not the branch, not my breath, not any longer. But in a final act, I let Anahita's force twist my body and with it the tree to launch the log away from Mandane and myself free. I rose and gulped air. But as the log turned, another branch slammed against my back, knocking the breath from my lungs even as I went under again. Specks like white ash flickered in my eyes. "For Media," I prayed, "Let me rise." I gave in. And from the smooth stone bottom of the rushing stream, I felt the river goddess lift my body and carry it to a still point near the shore. Maybe it was merely the whoosh of water passing my head I turned my face to the clean air, but I thought I heard the river say, "Finish the thing."

Even as I vomited churning river water, I took it as blessing. I rolled onto my knees and stood. Mandane was safe on the shore, her stole still as bright as the snow on Mount Alvand. She worried over the gash in my arm, the cut across my cheek, my limp. But I was fine. She was alive.

I whistled for Bepti, stripped quickly, and wrung out my clothes – my riding trousers, linen blouse, the sheepskin – as well as I could, put them back on and gratefully shrugged into the rough-spun wool cape, still dry on the bank. I pulled the hood over my hair and tucked in the feather clasps now matted and limp. While Mandane gathered her things, I selected one smooth stone from the bank. There was a thing that never failed to calm me. Cool, real in my palm, I eyed the stream and cocked my arm. I faltered once on my injured ankle, then, lifting that foot off the ground, I sent the stone skittering across the river's surface. Ripples spun out in all directions and disappeared back into that greater whole.

I boosted Mandane and gingerly eased my body up behind. The warmth of the horse's back under my legs was a welcome comfort. We rode quietly for a while my body tallying its fresh injuries. "I heard a cougar wandered into cottage yards in the near valley last week," I said, to take my mind off my aching ankle. "Took a ewe before anyone knew it. And bear cubs were up an apple tree. They say spring may be hard this year." In front of me, Mandane shivered. "But you, you'll be in Babylon – all warm and wearing..." I knew virtually nothing about Babylon, only that it was nothing like here. "All sorts of nice things. I suppose you'll have a crown. Maybe a whole bunch of them."

I felt Mandane shiver again.

"Get down," I said, stopping the horse. I slid down to stand, hopping on one foot, beside her. I put my cape over Mandane's shoulders, took the wreath off her head and seeing nowhere else to lay it, set it on my own to pull the hood over Mandane's head. Behind me, Bepti's breath blew a question on the flowers in my hair.

Mandane dabbed a handkerchief against my cheek. It came back bloody. "That's a bad cut," she said. "Deep."

"It's fine." But I took the cloth from her and pressed it against my skin.

A rumble in the ground made us both look to the road. Bepti stomped a hoof.

"Nebuchadnezzar," Mandane said. From the south, a small caravan approached, eddies of dust rising and falling behind like spirits dragged in its wake. Mandane's voice rose with anxiety. "We should have been back by now." She tugged the robe's hood forward.

"We'll still beat them," I said. The road winds, but we didn't have to follow it. We could take a shortcut and make it back before the caravan. "We've got time." I wanted to see these Babylonians, the caravan and great king I'd heard so much about. I led Bepti off the road. Mandane followed.

Four mounted men passed first, ahead of the lead carriage. Heavily armed, their glinting shields bore in blood-red paint the image of a spade - "the god Marduk's sign." Mandane said. From inside the carriage, a man, his pale skin offset by a sharp goatee looked out. He squinted at me, red lips drawn into a thin, disapproving line. He didn't look all that old. The man next to him – dark, square-jawed and quiet – seemed younger still. A second carriage, fully closed – a blue wool curtain with Marduk's spade in black – pulled along behind. That must be the one with Nebuchadnezzar.

Suddenly, the carriage horses cried out and reared, their sharp hooves clawing the air. When they came down, they bolted our way. Without thinking I pushed Mandane behind me, and leapt forward to grab the reins. Furred shadows on the far side of the road disappeared back into the dark woods.

The horse I held shuddered but stilled. "Wolves," I said to the driver. Across the horse's back, lines of blood betrayed a profligate whip. "Probably drawn by that. You can see the city's outer walls ahead. You don't have to whip the horses anymore."

"...this barbarous wild...." I heard from the carriage, "Babylon will make it better."

It echoed in my head – Babylon still to impose itself on wild Media? – shocking me over and over again. But there was more.

"Such a waste. All these trees." The goateed man looked out again. His face was tight with disgust. I felt my bile rise. His eyes passed over Mandane, hidden in my brown robe, and settled on me. Suddenly conscious of how sheer my blouse was, I adjusted the damp sheepskin shawl over my shoulder, tucked it more tightly into my belt. "No need to worry young women –" one corner of the man's mouth raised, as if amused by incongruity of the word to the rough image in front of him. "On!"

I released the reins. Shocked, I turned to Mandane as the carriages lurched forward. "Did you hear that?" Alarm made my voice tight. "Does Babylonia think they can take from here even after you marry Nebuchadnezzar?"

"I'm sure it's nothing," Mandane said.

That troubled me at least as much as what I'd heard. "It's

everything." But there wasn't time to talk about it. We had to get back to the palace before the Babylonians. I boosted Mandane onto Bepti, swung up behind, and urged the stallion to canter off the road, then gallop along footpaths herders had made through the trees, along a ridge, and then climbing a last hill, straight up to the palace gates.

Familiar with my coming and going, the guards at the gates of each successive wall made room for us, and well before the Babylonians could have taken another of the road's switchback turns, we had dismounted – Mandane to her rooms to get ready and I, to face our father and the inevitable rebuke. Bepti tossed his head, rejecting the stable boy's reach until I patted the stallion's neck and passed the reins. I was still troubled by that remark by the goateed Babylonian. Surely Nebuchadnezzar didn't think he could take from Media with the treaty in place. But what else could it mean?

CHAPTER 2

The hall passing into in the king's wing was lofty – high-ceilinged, and brisk. Mountain breezes swept through the second-story portico. I opened a door to the wide anteroom and stepped inside. My ankle had swelled, and the gash on my arm wasn't pretty. But I lifted my chin, inhaled pungent cedar from the hall's rough columns – strength for the conflict ahead – and limped up to the door.

The guard, with whom I'd shared games of dice, shot me a sympathetic look. I twisted to undo the scabbard at my belt. "Agh." It hurt.

"Here," the guard bent forward to remove the weapon. "Trouble in the hills?"

I hated to part with my tiny dagger, but I let him take it. "Just the gods reminding me to be strong." More ceremonial than true weapon, Ziwiye metal workers had given the dagger, a work of art and its scabbard, equally ornate, to King Cyaxares. Astyages disparaged it for its size and chipped a notch in its blade. "See? Mere iron underneath," he'd said, focused only on its gold-plate and not the quality of the ironwork, too. Some time ago,

Harpagus told Astyages that I needed it to defend Mandane. I treasured it.

The guard grinned and opened the door. "Amytis, your grace," he called into the weak-lit room.

I stepped inside and heard the door clank shut behind me. My eyes were still adjusting to the dark when the king's voice hit me like a jagged rock.

"Where is she?" Even in his private quarters, my father sat on a throne. This, a gaudy, exaggerated replica of the sturdy oak that grateful tribesmen had carved for my grandfather years earlier. That other remained in the throne room, gilt in gold, its seat cushioned with flamingo down and covered in finely woven wool. My father thought it unimpressive.

"The princess is fine, in her rooms, now."

Like everything of King Astyages's the room was an ostentatious display of the empire's former power and reach. Dim light masked its decay. I wished my father would at least leave the door open. By contrast to the airy hall, the room was heavy with dank as if its woolen tapestries – once bright with the colors of lands far to the east – never dried. Tallow candles exhaled sooty ribbons of smoke from thick wicks, their flames spurred to stirring by my advance. I stopped in front of the king's throne. How many times had I approached like this, the penitent protector, called into question yet again? Well, this would be the last. Mandane was surely preparing her wedding finery now.

Out of a matted lion's-mane cowl, my father shoved his face, a splotchy red, toward mine. "How many times --?"

I bit my lip, forgetting its injury. I tipped up my head to hold in the quick tears. I'd lost count the number of times my father reminded me of Mandane's importance and my duty to protect her.

"Look at me."

I did, and swiped away the tears, angry that they might make me appear to be sorry. "She was with me."

"Then-" Astyages gestured in disgust at my broken and disheveled state. "She was involved in this, too?"

I wasn't sorry. "In the middle of the river, there was a plant that Mandane wanted." My head began to throb. "A log broke loose upstream. I –"

He waved his hand impatiently. "She's fine?"

I straightened my back, proud at least in this – I'd deflected the log, wrested it away from Mandane, never mind the slash across my hand and arm, the branch that slammed into my face, or the that with each breath came the searing report of a broken rib. "Not a scratch." I tried to stand evenly on my feet, despite a distinct light-headedness.

He narrowed his eyes. "One daughter. That's all I need. All I've ever needed to secure Media. I have made allowances for your sister's –"

"Yes, sir," I made myself say. It was true, after all. In everything else, Mandane had conformed to the princess that she was, except in her obsession with a certain midwifery, which took her to where ordinary guards would never let her go. So it was I who attended her to cottages, tents, and hovels deep in Media's wild countryside.

Astyages slapped an arm of his throne. "Over there," he waved a hand, "Babylonia has just kept growing. To the Great Sea. Judah, last I heard." Astyages railed on, seeming to forget that they'd soon be here. "Building, building, building. While I..."

It was true Babylonia could crush us, *would* crush us, but for Mandane.

"I have suffered!" the king's shouting brought me back. "*We* were the stronger. Media was the greater, when my father and Babylonia's king made that promise."

Mandane must marry Nebuchadnezzar. I knew the story by heart: the decisive battle against Assyria that my grandfather's Medes had won, all alone, without the help that Babylonia had promised. The Babylonian king, who arrived late but while the

ashes still fell had pledged that his son, crown prince Nebuchadnezzar, would marry a Median princess. They would make their
nations equals in a binding treaty alliance. A marriage would
clinch the treaty. But my grandfather had no daughter – only a
son, Astyages. So the Medes waited until Astyages had a daughter
suitable to marry. But Nebuchadnezzar hadn't waited. Against
his father's word and wishes, he married a Babylonian, low class,
and already had a son – Babylonia's crown prince. Now, that
woman, the queen mother was dead – killed, I had heard, but not
the details. It didn't matter to us that Babylonia already had a
crown prince. What mattered was simply that Mandane could
now marry Nebuchadnezzar. That was all they needed to clinch a
treaty that would last even beyond the lifespans of Nebuchadnezzar and Mandane, a treaty to last for all time, granting Media
her own autonomy and protection against Babylonian encroachment and even, with Babylonian help, against any assault.

Astyages leaned forward. His face bore an angry intensity
and… was it fear? "Do you know what they did to its king, to the
king of Judah?" He lowered his voice. "They dragged him, bound
and beaten out of his burning Jerusalem, to King Nebuchadnezzar's pavilion. They made him watch as they killed his sons.
Then, they tore out his eyes." Astyages blinked furiously. "They
tore out his eyes!"

I believed it.

"And you." My father stabbed his finger at me as if he could
poke in sense like the cooks poked garlic into raw meat. "All you
had to do was keep her safe until Nebuchadnezzar marries her."

"I have," I said, more loudly than I needed. "As for your part –"
Remembering the Babylonian's words, I couldn't help myself,
"you need to make the treaty terms clear – that Media cannot be
exploited for Babylonian purposes."

"Impertinence!" Astyages leapt up. "Go!"

I knew he'd forget about me just as soon as I was out of sight.
I just hoped he wouldn't forget what I said. He had to clarify the

treaty's terms. I walked toward the door as fast as my ankle would allow. But before I reached it, I remembered Anahita's words whispered from the river. I turned back. "Finish the thing," I said, and walked out.

The guard buckled my scabbard gently around my waist. "Protect him well," I said. "For all his faults, my father cares about Media more than anything."

He nodded, but as I started down the hall, I heard him mutter, "Throne, you mean. Cares about his throne."

I WENT to check on Mandane, who was nervous, of course, but not so much that she hadn't remembered to pack the astragalus - "for long life," she explained – into the box of medicinal herbs and such that she would take to Babylon. By now, the Babylonian caravan must have arrived. Nebuchadnezzar would soon call for his bride. Mandane anxiously talked about this and that – Babylon, the king... But I was preoccupied by the comment that goateed man had made. I needed answers. I excused myself and stepped out.

"Harpagus," I called to the straight-backed figure ahead trodding the stone floor of toward the throne room. Astyages's steward had always been good to me... despite his code of obedience to my father. I'd asked him once how he could bear serving my father. He didn't answer. Not exactly, but spoke instead of patience – that things are always changing, to be prepared, clear about the truth of circumstances and of who you are. "Harpagus," I called again. He turned, his face as straight as his back. His eyes warmed when they settled on me. I hopped my limping gait to catch him. Familiar with my mishaps, he gave me a crooked smile. Patience. It was he who told me that when Mandane finally married the king of Babylonia, I could live free and as I wished in this place that I loved. Now, Harpagus gestured not to my injuries but to my head. "It suits you."

I grimaced, remembering the sorry state of my hair, its clasps.
I put a hand to my head. "Oh," I said, surprised. I'd forgotten the
crown of goldenrod, preoccupied with bigger things. Much
bigger things. "Can Babylonia still build," I asked. "I mean, after
Mandane marries Nebuchadnezzar, can they come here, take our
rocks and trees, make changes?"

"No." He gave me a long look.

"But is there more to the treaty than simply Mandane's
marrying?"

He considered. "I suppose the Babylonians will want the
terms written down."

"Are they?" We Medians didn't put so much stock in the
written word. "Written down?"

"I don't know." Harpagus scowled.

Voices from behind the throne room door reached us in the
hall. I had to hurry. "You'll see to it, then?" I asked.

"I'll do my best."

I slipped to the side as Harpagus entered and the door shut
again.

My stomach growled. The smell of roasting meat, rich stews,
breads, and cakes – hints of the coming feast – wafted up from
the kitchen below. I swallowed hard. The guard, another of my
off-duty dice buddies, grinned at me. He gestured me forward to
listen at the gap in the door.

I pressed my ear to the crack. Impatient to get closer, I pulled
off the flower wreath. My father's voice was high, solicitous. I
winced. It was the sound of desperation. But did he have to
show it?

"Fancies herself something of the sort –" I heard him say, but
didn't understand.

I couldn't catch the Babylonian's reply. But the voice I recognized. The man's tone was high and nasal, slow, like a tutor's with
a dull but sensitive student.

"Of course." My father Astyages again, as the distinctly

Median idiom confirmed. "That stupid woman... you'd have to..." His voice dropped to something indecipherable.

Then, Harpagus's voice, crisp. "... King Nebuchadnezzar. We expected... formalize the terms. But you're saying the treaty –"

So, Nebuchadnezzar was not there. My heart sank. There'd be no wedding in Media.

"- will be finalized in Babylon," the Babylonian said.

Harpagus cleared his throat loudly. "In writing?" he asked.

"For certain," the Babylonian replied.

"Then it will be," (Astyages again), "just as we expect, yes?"

Had my father no courage to demand explicitly the terms? I wanted to scream but held my tongue.

"For certain." There was that tone again. Slippery. I wished I trusted this stranger from the south. "Which will bring definite improvements to Media," he said. My stomach dropped. The circlet of goldenrod fell from my hand. "You'll see." The man's voice was getting louder, closer. "A place like this... wild dangers on merchants' roads. And all those trees just going to waste..."

My face grew hot. I pulled away from the door as the guard moved to open it and ducked into the shadow of a pillar to let the men pass. It was all I could do not to jump out and accost them then and there. My father a sniveling coward; Harpagus, his hands all but tied in this treaty business; and that goateed Babylonian – who was he? so smug and self-righteous. His nose high in the air, the man kicked, unwittingly, the limpid ring of flowers. It seemed decades ago that I'd strung it for Mandane. It slid across the floor and stopped. The other Babylonian, the younger, alone saw it. He hadn't said a thing. Now he looked my way. I couldn't tell if he saw me – his eyes were deep, inscrutable – before he looked away again.

Harpagus trailed enough that I could step out and catch his sleeve. He slipped into the shadow next to me.

"What happened in there?"

"That man, Igliss - " Harpagus grabbed me by the shoulders.

He glanced down the hall at the figures getting father away, then back at me again. "You must tell Mandane to leave healing to the priests."

I shook my head, bewildered. I couldn't understand what that had to do with anything, much less the intensity of Harpagus's reaction.

"I can't. You know that."

"She was a *baby*."

I'd told Mandane a thousand times, if I'd told her once, that just because her mother died bringing Mandane into the world didn't make her death Mandane's fault. But Mandane wouldn't hear it. Helping birthing mothers in crisis eased the guilt.

"But who is he?"

"The king's proxy. Neriglissar. A distinguished war veteran, they say."

Hard to imagine, with that reedy frame and slick from head to toe.

"Something about the west," Harpagus continued, "Jerusalem, maybe."

"And the other man?" I asked.

Harpagus released my shoulders. "Managing the dowry, I suppose. Didn't say much."

"But what about --?"

"Tell Mandane." Harpagus glanced ahead, then bent to my face. "No midwifery. Now, go!" He straightened. "They're taking her to Babylon today."

"Today?! But the treaty," I said.

"Exactly!" Harpagus's whisper had the intensity of a shout. He hurried after the others.

I had to find out, had to get assurance of Media's autonomy and security against *any* encroachment. It seemed the only one who could answer my questions was the Babylonian Igliss.

. . .

IN THE COURTYARD, the caravan assembled under a cloud-darkened sky. Men and women, Babylonian and Mede bustled about packing the boxes and carts that would carry Mandane, her dowry and gifts away to Babylon. Igliss stood in front of a carriage, issuing orders. I hustled toward him as fast as my ankle allowed. "Sir," I said. He waved away an ox-cart blocking the vehicle. "The treaty –" I raised my voice. "Sir."

Igliss looked at me, then. His gaze sliding down the sharp ridge of his nose. It took in my dirty trousers, the damp sheepskin and my blood-streaked blouse, the gash in my cheek. Recognition flashed across his unsmiling face. "I might have known they'd let grooms – girls, no less – into such a palace." His interest suddenly shifted to the man approaching – Astyages, my father, the king.

I stepped in front of Igliss again. "The treaty, sir, that goes with this marriage –"

Igliss glared at me. "Will be settled in Babylon."

"How?"

He shoved me aside and clutched his robe more tightly around his chest as Astyages stumbled up next to him. Behind them, the clouds had yielded to an uncompromising gray. A cold wind swirled eddies in the courtyard's dust and drove through my sleeves with a chill. From the corner of my eye, I saw Mandane step out from the gate.

Beside me, Astyages straightened his crown. "My daughter –" But it was I who held the Babylonian's gaze. So although Astyages gestured toward Mandane, Igliss didn't see.

I shivered but pulled my shoulders back, a rough girl in a slippery man's gaze. The Babylonian had heard my question. And his look fired up all the impulsive and rebellious tendencies I tried so hard to quell.

"My daughter," Astyages said again, his eyes on Mandane.

I lifted my chin. "Here."

Igliss, his eyes on me, said, "I see." He grabbed my elbow.

"Then you can take it up with the king yourself." I winced as his fingers sank into my arm. But I didn't pull away.

I braced myself for my father's protest – that Igliss had the wrong girl; the true princess, born to a queen, suitable and prepared, stood just over there. Igliss hurried me forward toward the carriage. I looked over my shoulder at Astyages, but he was backing away. Of course, I suddenly realized with a chill that had nothing to do with the weather, not only did Astyages want to avoid angering this Babylonian but he realized that it didn't matter which girl went, so long as Babylonians understood her to be the king's daughter. I watched his mouth form the words, "No contact." The sky began to drop a slushy rain. Under the archway across the courtyard, Mandane stood radiant in her finery. Igliss growled something about the sleet. I stumbled to keep up with him as I looked at Mandane and shook my head, willing her to understand, wishing I could explain. Finally, to my relief, she stepped back into the shadows.

I turned forward just in time to lift my feet. Igliss shoved me into the carriage, but his sleeve caught my scabbard. He wrenched his arm free. "Get rid of it. In Babylon, women have no need for such."

Harpagus alone ran to the carriage. He had Mandane's travel coat of golden jackal pelts draped over one arm. He called to Igliss but the Babylonian was already trotting toward his own carriage, sharp shoulders hunched. Harpagus put his hand on my carriage window. "What are you –" He looked frantically for Astyages. But my father stood in the shelter near the outer gate, his lips fixed in a tight line.

"The treaty," I said. "Harpagus, it's not drafted, not the terms, nothing." I peered out toward Igliss's carriage just as his door slammed shut. "And I don't trust them."

"But what are *you* --?"

"I'll send for Mandane as soon as I get it done." I shoved my scabbard with its tiny dagger into the steward's hand. "Tell Mandane to keep this with her. Always."

Harpagus took the weapon and pushed the fur coat in to me. "Take care of yourself."

"She has to marry Nebuchadnezzar." The carriage pulled forward. "Tell her," I said, leaning out the window. "It'll be soon."

CHAPTER 3

$\mathcal{A}$s the day's weather had shown, winters are long in our mile-high city. It snows in Ecbatana well into spring. I supposed the Babylonians were already unhappy, even before they reached the capital, even before Mandane and I saw them on the road. Igliss was cold, for sure, and probably sick from the altitude, which didn't make the situation any easier. I knew we'd gotten off on a bad foot, he and I, so I was grateful for the separate carriages, the chance to strategize. And I was grateful for the ride. My ankle ached.

I hadn't accounted for my heart. As we rode out of the palace, through the gates of its seven concentric walls, from gold to silver all the way to the outer ring of white mineral paint, then out – under a low grey sky, the dark forests rising up beyond, it was as if a mill stone were dropping slowly, inexorably its fierce weight on my chest.

What had I done? I'd never left Media before, never thought I would. Who was I to confront King Nebuchadnezzar, as I'd surely have to do, in order to lay out the treaty terms to last for all time? Who was I to stand up to Igliss, a man of obvious power and powerful interest in fleecing Media for her valuable resources, destroying her complex and elegant wildness?

Shivering, I wrapped Mandane's coat around my shoulders. I examined the gash in my arm. Anahita had given me strength in that river, strength to survive. I looked out. In a south-lit valley, sour cherry trees had begun to bloom – pale pink in a hint of green. Mithra expects a true covenant. I'd try, I thought, though I had to bend some rules to get there. Mazda, who made everything good and subject to change, who asks our help in sustaining what's right, couldn't be blamed for this rebellious streak that drives me to beat my head against power. Could he? The flat sky broke into thin sheets of clouds, letting the afternoon sun through in shining rays. Wild sheep watched our passing from rocky heights. Who was I to go to Babylon? High in the clean air, a hawk banked its wings. Damn the gods. All I wanted was here.

I PUT my head out the window. The cottages of palace slaves, each surrounded by its own small garden, sent up diaphanous scarves of smoke. Low limbs of apples, plums, and peaches grew both gnarled and straight, a harmony of domesticity with wildness all around. Wind lifted the feathers in my hair. I took a deep breath inhaling sharp cedar and the earthy funk of leaves turning over to fresh ferns and long needle pines. I opened my eyes again.

Behind me, our caravan of carts snaked along, loaded with Mandane's things and extravagant gifts from Astyages, gained as tax for Ecbatana's unparalleled access to trade. I squinted. There was more. The square-jawed Babylonian walked alongside an ox-cart carrying only timber – both massive and slender trunks of diverse trees – a wedding gift for Babylonia's wood-starved construction, I supposed. Behind that, eight or ten – a veritable herd – of our finest horses sashayed in their tethers. My stomach lurched. Among them, my stallion Bepti tossed his head in defiance. I hated seeing him there among dowry and gifts for the Babylonians. I told myself he'd make my return to Media that much swifter. Something else I'd have to negotiate with Nebuchadnezzar. The swarthy Babylonian – a palace recordkeeper, Harpagus had said, though he looked more like a laborer to me – nodded my way as if he'd seen me looking this whole time.

I started to duck back, lifting my feet onto the bench when I spotted Kara. Our nursemaid was unmistakable, her face so badly disfigured by a fire she suffered when we were infants that even at this distance, I could tell it was her.

"Hey, stop!" I called to the carriage driver. He did, and I bounded out. Then crumpled. I'd forgotten about my ankle. But Kara had seen. She trotted toward me. Up ahead, Igliss called out something in exasperation. I ignored him and waved her to hurry.

"Get in," I said. I climbed in behind her. Kara's lips were blue with cold, so I shrugged off my coat and wrapped it around her. I bounced once on the cushioned bench, appreciatively. She smiled. A box stowed under the bench caught my eye. I drew it out. Inside, neatly folded and arranged, was embroidery. I grimaced and quickly put it back. "On!" I called to the driver, like I'd heard Igliss command earlier.

But the carriage didn't move.

I leaned out the window and recoiled. Igliss glared in. "What's this?" He gestured to Kara, his tone sharp and demanding.

I looked from Igliss to Kara and back.

"This," I said, regaining my composure, "is Kara."

Igliss wrenched the door open. "Slaves walk."

"Is there some trouble here?" The Babylonian merchant stepped up.

I hadn't seen him coming. But I focused on Igliss. "She's my... personal attendant." I sidled forward to block the door.

"With a face like that?" Igliss ducked and wove to look around me at Kara. "Where are you from?" he asked her.

"Harran," Kara said, then realizing her mistake, shrank back.

Like the cat that caught the bird, Igliss smirked. "Just as I thought. A nobody." He glanced at the broader man beside him. "Khai, remind the princess of our history, of Harran. She appears to have forgotten."

Princess, he'd said - I had to resist the impulse to look around for Mandane.

"When our nations' coalition defeated Assyria..." The man spoke flatly, seeming to have no particular interest in the report. "... Harran's elite were taken to Babylon. Media took the under-class, laborers, and such for slaves. So, if she's from Harran and in Media, I guess she's a slave." He paused. "Kara did you say?" I couldn't read the man's eyes, set deep and wide. Khai. So that's his name.

"In Babylon," Igliss said, "we don't confuse slaves with nobles. She's a slave and will walk like any other."

Behind me, Kara slid out of the coat, pushed it onto my lap, and prepared to get out.

I shoved it back. "As you can see," I said, gesturing to my disheveled clothes, my hair tangled and loose. "I require my attendant in order to be ready for Babylon."

Igliss narrowed his eyes. "You could never match the grand-ness of Babylon."

"But," the man Khai said, "she obviously needs the help." His mouth turned up ever so slightly at the corners.

Igliss spat on the ground. "A Median marrying the great king..." But he shut the door. "Good thing you have time."

As soon as the wheels rolled again, Kara said, "You shouldn't have done that." The odd huskiness in her voice – due to throat damage from the flames that ravaged her face – was a peculiar comfort to me now.

"I shouldn't do a lot of things. This, probably."

She leaned forward. "What were you thinking?"

"I learned that the terms of the treaty haven't been formalized yet. Igliss has designs on Media's wild spaces, resources, trade routes, and who knows what else. And he seems to think he can get them. That Khai guy probably, too. You know, I swear I saw that man grin. 'Needs the help,' my foot."

"Speaking of," Kara gestured for my ankle.

I raised it gingerly to her lap. "I overheard Astyages making concessions, so I just –"

Kara massaged the ankle gently but skillfully. "Took it upon yourself to negotiate with the king of Babylon, pass yourself off as a princess, and marry him?"

"No. Ow! I mean, yes. And no." I pulled my leg away. "Listen, I didn't give it much thought. I didn't have time."

"It's not broken, your ankle," she said. "But that was a nasty twist. Keep it up and stay off it."

That'll be easy, I thought, stuck as we were inside this carriage for the two hundred fifty miles or so between Ecbatana and Babylon.

"Why are *you* here?" I asked. "I didn't think anyone from Media was going to Babylon – only Mandane, and only after marrying Nebuchadnezzar."

"When I saw you get in that carriage –" Kara looked out the window, then back at me. "I, too, thought you could use some help."

I looked more closely at Kara, then. This woman, whose name wasn't even a name but the lazy shortening of *karadara* meaning "slave," had always been a part of my life. It was she who had nursed both Mandane and me through infancy, despite her own fresh injury. No one else was hurt in the fire that destroyed her face, though people say that's how her own baby perished. I now recognized that like Harpagus (but without his power and cache), she had always been my advocate. Sure, she berated my impulsive idiocies and had no sympathy for my having to protect Mandane, but she had bound my wounds and thrust me back out, the better to learn how to survive. Her own disfigurements and scars were so familiar to me as to seem perfectly normal. I only noticed them when strangers reacted, seeing her for the first time.

"Well, Mandane will benefit from your company," I said. "As soon as I get the treaty formalized, Mandane will marry Nebuchadnezzar. By then, I'll be back here, back home."

"You do know they think you're the princess. Igliss will be even angrier to learn that you duped him."

"It couldn't be helped," I said. But Kara was right. "I'll tell him the truth next time we stop."

"No," Kara said sharply. "The king should be the first you tell. If you let on now, they'll just send you back."

I clenched my teeth and groaned. I'd made things even worse. As soon as I told the king, or worse if they found out before I came clean, the Babylonians would accuse Media of duplicity. "And *they're* the ones who can't be trusted." I felt miserable – leaving Media was bad enough, but if I'd undercut the whole point of it with my thoughtless actions... I could hardly ask the gods for help. They held truth to be the highest good. I lifted my head. I'd just have to wait until we reached Babylon, tell Nebuchadnezzar, and convince him that I acted alone. It was all my fault. What a mistake. I put my head down and groaned again.

Kara didn't say anything. She just started combing my hair with her fingers. One by one, she removed the hair clips I'd made until I raised my head. They lay next to me on the richly upholstered bench - the stiff quill of a jay I remembered finding on a summer morning when trout flashed their way upstream; downy fluff, muddied from my near drowning, I got climbing to a high eagle's nest, inexplicably abandoned... I reached out to touch the delicate feather of a rock partridge. Mandane had said that its many-hued browns and tawny gold mimicked my own hair. I'd strung the talon, somehow lodged in that abandoned eagle's nest, on red thread. It shone now like bare bone. From inside my shirt, I took the handkerchief Mandane had pressed against my cheek. I wondered how she was, hoped that Harpagus had explained... I spread the kerchief out wide, smoothed over the dark streak of blood, and set the clasps inside. I folded the edges. I drew out the embroidery box, opened it up, and laid the small packet of my old life on top.

AFTER WHAT SEEMED like an eternity of sitting, sitting, sitting, we finally stopped next to a spring-fed lake for the night. A man strode into the woods, bow slung over his shoulder. The first thing I did was check on Bepti. He'd already pawed angry divots into the ground around him.

Khai, untying the oxen, watched me. "Careful," he said.

"It's not like I'd hurt him." I lay my hand on the horse's neck.

"It's not him I'm worried about."

It took me off guard, this concern for my welfare. So I focused on Bepti. He nickered into my hair as I stroked his shoulder.

"I'm not accustomed to horses," Khai said.

I looked at him then. I wasn't accustomed to men expressing weakness. He leaned into the heft of the horned beast to lead it from its traces. I watched his broad back, the ox ambling beside him until he disappeared behind a tent. There didn't seem to be anything weak about Khai.

I turned back to the horse. Bepti was all right, if frustrated by the slow pace. He dipped his head. "We'll gallop to your heart's content just as soon as I get this thing done," I muttered into his furry ear. "All the way home."

I started to help unload, but Kara took the box from my hands and hissed for me to stop. "Unseemly," she said. So, despite the ache in my ankle, I walked off to stretch my legs along a hill studded with granite and shrubby blueberry plants. Before the day's bright light yielded to star-studded black, it settled with a sigh into shades of apricot and plum washed in rosehip tea. It was my favorite time of day, this ending to it, when the light transformed every object into something of incomparable importance, of shimmering worth.

Under Kara's supervision, the guards turned cooks and assembled a dinner of perishables sent from Media – a casserole of venison slow-cooked with dried apples, pears, and cherries, and plump farro, no doubt intended for the wedding that didn't happen. There was fresh cheese, honey, and flatbread, still soft. Water from the spring tasted cold, clear, and sweet. The men opened a barrel of spiced wine, which improved even Igliss's mood. At least for the time.

Since we ate as we did, I couldn't understand why the hunting. The man returned with a fallow deer – a small doe, shot dead. He hadn't field-dressed his kill, and no one moved to do so after he lowered it from his shoulders to the ground. I was thinking they'd forgotten about the animal – talk about waste – when Igliss summoned a couple soft-bodied men. He handed a knife to the man draped with a necklace of cut beads and bullae. The knife was carved with the strange symbols of Babylonia's gods. I tried to remember from what Mandane would tell me, which was which. The man cut the deer's belly wide and let her entrails spill out. They bent over the steaming pile and talked in low voices.

"Extispicy." Khai's voice made me jump. "They read the entrails to determine whether or not we have permission from the gods to travel another day."

I stepped a foot or two away from him. "Are they ever denied? Do you ever not travel?"

"Yes. The gods don't seem to like it if the weather's bad." A smile played at the edge of Khai's mouth. "Or if Igliss is tired."

I couldn't tell if he was being sarcastic or not and decided it best to keep my mouth shut. But when they launched the carcass into the woods, I couldn't help saying, "What a waste." I knew the wolves or vultures would eat the deer's remains, but still. It seemed an unnecessary Babylonian conceit.

No one asked or questioned my position. I guess they assumed that a place such as Media could only produce crude and unpolished women, no matter her station. What a surprise Mandane will be, I thought. Just wait until you see her in all her regal glory. I grinned to myself. After dinner, Khai helped set up the tents. It struck me how easily he moved between Igliss (who didn't lift a finger) and the lowest men in the camp, like there was no difference.

I was too wound up to rest, so while Kara reveled in the cozy finery inside, I limped to the lake's edge. I bent, selected a handful of smooth stones, and stood again. Slowly, finding my balance, I lifted my injured foot off the ground. Then, standing like the great, silent herons do on a single, steady leg, I sent first one stone and then another skipping across the water. Ripples spun out in rings that overlapping, found new direction, and rolled on. It eased me.

At the edge of the wood, not far from the camp, I knelt on the chilly ground. A mound of soft gray moss cushioned my knees. I buried my hands in the needles and leaves around, and held out a prayer – remorse, petition, gratitude too... The air was still. Then, from hills I couldn't see, a jackal howled. Another picked up its call. I lifted my chin. Footsteps in the leaves behind me brought me quickly to my feet.

Khai nodded toward the forest. "You seem all right."

I must have looked confused.

"I'm to keep things safe... For the king."

Things, I repeated to myself, strangely disappointed. I didn't expect to be anything more; but that was hardly the way to think about Mandane.

In one hand Khai carried a small chair. Crafted for Mandane, it was delicate and fine. Along its back of carved ivory placid animals – gazelles, goats, and ibex – walked in single file. He swung it to the ground. "They'd say it's more befitting a princess," he said.

Was he testing me, prodding for a reaction? Did he know?

Khai didn't wait for a reply.

After he left, I lowered myself onto the chair, conscious of its golden border, fashioned in the shape of a twisted rope, and how it lay over my shoulders. From there, I watched the stars blinker into a darkening sky.

THE NEXT DAY, I rode in clothes I had only ever seen. The fabric was soft and cut to fall in a way that flattered my sister's frame. I was skinnier, more sinewy than Mandane, so the clothes hung loose. The better to get accustomed to them, I thought. I missed my trousers.

Kara had spent a long time on my hair. When I finally lifted the polished brass mirror to my face, I started. I put a hand to my hair, held up in complicated twists – the Babylonian style, Kara had said. But for the cut across my cheek, it almost seemed to be Mandane looking back. Still, despite the image in the mirror, I'd never be Mandane. Nor did I want to be. She would become a queen in Babylonia, the most impressive and enviable empire in the world. I, no matter my appearance, would always be Amytis, acolyte of Media's mountains and stormy sky, its fields of horse-strengthening grass, its tall pines, wide oaks, lynx, badgers, quick lizards, and bright running water. And that was all I ever wanted.

DURING THE FIRST week or so, I took in the full landscape, the distant mountains, the foothills like ripples in a great animal's hide. At day's end, after visiting my horse, I sat in silence, all by myself. It was a bittersweet time. Each day took me farther from home, from everything I knew, and every day I missed it more. Yet the drama of the sky at day's end slowed my busy brain with its anticipations and anxieties. In that delicious hour between the pace of day and the dark of night, all that occupied me was this solitary vigil – to watch for the stars, emerging like shy cats, only after the light had gone. The hills went dark against the sky until they melted into it.

Apart from Khai's occasional appearances – checking on me, I supposed – the Babylonians left Kara and me alone. It was nice to be free of Igliss's constant judgment and simmering resentment, which he seemed unable to let go, even when we'd gotten out of the mountains and the air was softer, warmer. I focused on my goal. Whatever lay ahead in Babylon, as foreign as it was to me with its history of entitlement and plethora of gods, its urban sophistication, long-standing traditions, and elite families, I would let nothing dissuade or distract me from my purpose. I would get the king to agree to terms that honor Media's autonomy and protect her from any encroachment, including Babylonia's. If writing was what mattered, then in writing it would be. As for me, I would rely on the binding force of a promised word. I had to. I couldn't read.

Kara told me what she could, what she knew of Babylonia in an effort to make up for all that Mandane would have known. It was impossible, of course, even though Kara had been present for most of Mandane's lessons. My sister had spent her entire life at it and with the best tutors, no less. What I did understand was that in Babylonia, the gods determine everything. And the gods are all up in the sky. It made sense, then, that they wouldn't care about Media like I did – earth and air and water and all the flying, creeping, loping, buzzing, swimming, towering, flowering, and tiny things that lived within it. Just look at their nightly extispicy ritual. Every day another wild thing was killed and gutted for no reason that I could see except to say that we should hurry.

Hurry we did. I learned that the Babylonians wanted to be back in time for their annual New Year's festival. Kara explained that the Akitu, as they called it, was the most important national event. People gathered from all over the empire, the gods too, and it went on for days, recognizing the supremacy of Babylonia and seeking the gods' blessing on it for another year. Igliss seemed especially perturbed by our pace. He was always pushing to go faster.

I was in my own kind of hurry, of course. I'd decided the simplest thing was to tell Nebuchadnezzar immediately who I was and why I was there. I would take no concessions for Media but insist on complete autonomy and security. I was painfully aware that I didn't have any real leverage, merely to threaten that Mandane wouldn't marry him until it was so. And I could hardly enforce that. I tried not to listen to the voice in my head asking why he'd listen to me in the first place. Who was I, indeed?

CHAPTER 4

e turned south along the Tigris River. The land flattened, and the river ran wide, slow in places and tinged red with the soil of its banks. Just before we crossed from Media into Babylonia's greater territory, we stopped and set up camp. A small group of Babylonian men met us there. With their ring of tents, the ground cleared of foliage and worn dry all around them, it was clear they had been waiting awhile.

As eager as I was to get to Babylon, still many miles, to finish this business, passage out of the country I'd never imagined leaving felt like a breaking thing, like the hammer of cracking ice in spring – necessary, but a violence nonetheless. At nightfall, I grabbed my robe planning to walk out of the camp a way, where I could ask a parting blessing from the gods, our gods. From here on, it would be Marduk and Ishtar, Nanna Suen, and many others – Kara tried teaching me – the gods of Babylonia who inhabited the space beyond human seeing and determined earthly affairs. I threw the robe – Mandane's – over my shoulders. I choked back worry and sadness and straightened my back, determined to show the lady of our rivers – raging or sparkling and the gods of field and forest and all the wild things of the mountains that I could do this thing. That I would make Media secure from Babylonian despoiling and exploitation. I would make Nebuchadnezzar honor the treaty of our predecessors, make it easy for Mandane to do her part, to marry him and be the queen she'd been preparing all her life to be.

But when I stepped out of my tent, I was met by Igliss and two men I'd never seen before. One held a bulky satchel loosely at his side.

"Time to get rid of your demons," Igliss said. "Strip to the skin. It may take a while," he added with what looked like pure disgust.

I yanked my robe more tightly around me as Igliss walked away. I looked around for Khai. Wasn't he supposed to manage the dowry's security? He'd already shown he considered me part of that. But he was nowhere in sight. I was grateful for Kara's presence, so solid beside me.

The shorter of the two men stepped forward, bangles around his neck clanking with each footfall. "I'm the camp's doctor," he said, "appointed by the gods, for certain." His look was matter-of-fact, but what was this about demons? about stripping naked? "We need to do this before bringing you –"

"—a foreigner," the other man impatiently cut in, his words tinged with rebuke.

"—into the country of the gods…"

"*Your* gods," I said. Kara stuck her elbow into my side to silence me. I wanted to tell them I didn't need their religious nonsense. I'd be back home soon enough, and we have our own gods. Median magi subjected themselves to the intoxication of the gods' weed, haoma; they made offerings to Mazda and the other deities as required; and look, I was doing my part, honoring Mithra whose very name means "covenant," by ensuring that Nebuchadnezzar honor the promised treaty. But I knew it didn't matter. The men were busy gathering disparate things and laying them with great care on the ground. Already I'd seen enough – that daily animal-slaughtering ritual – to know that this would proceed, whether I liked it or not. My skin tingled with nerves.

"Do you know about this?" I whispered to Kara as the men began to busy themselves with the paraphernalia they'd brought.

She shook her head, then explained what she could. One man, the one now emptying his satchel, was the *ashipu*, she said, an astrologer-priest and exorcist. The other, the *ashu* doctor, filled a wide bronze vessel part way with water. "Holy water," Kara whispered. Into that, he put a dark brown wad "tamarisk paste, for purification." He stirred it with a reed until the tamarisk dissolved and then added a generous handful of "mastakal seeds, for absolution." From a white stone flask ("alabaster," Kara said), the *ashu* poured an oil. Its scent brought the cedar groves of Media to mind. If only I were there, I thought, and indulged an image of sauntering with Bepti among the tall trunks and soft branches. I couldn't hang on to the dream, though, for my anxiety at the strangeness of this. But whatever this was, whatever they did, surely won't kill me. The thought was a small comfort. And I'll be back in Media soon enough.

After he had stirred for a while, the doctor abandoned the reed to the mixture and set the pot on the ground in front of my tent. "Flour," he commanded. The *ashipu* handed him a linen pouch. The doctor walked around the pot, letting the flour trickle a dusty stream until he had gone full circle. The *ashipu* called out loudly in words I didn't understand. "He's asking the stars, the gods, to infuse the mixture with holiness," Kara explained.

Then, "Sleep well," the *ashu* said. "I will come for you at dawn."

I DID NOT SLEEP WELL. It was thanks only to Kara that I slept at all. Hearing my tossing and turning, Kara sat up. She told me stories of the gods that Kara's people shared with Babylon.

"To the Land of No Return," Kara began, "Ishtar, the moon-god's lovely daughter, determined to go. The daughter of Nanna-Suen set her mind on the house of darkness." Kara's voice grew richer as she recalled the old epic sung by gray-beards in the Harran of her childhood. "She took the one-way road, to the door from which no one can leave." I listened as Kara related the journey of the goddess Ishtar, full of vitality and bravado, to the land of the dead, where her sister ruled. Kara told how the earth above began to die, how the gods fretted as Ishtar suffered down below. "Only when the tortured goddess promised a substitution would her sister finally consent to release her," Kara said.

Kara had told me of Ishtar's romantic side manifest in the evening star that hung above them. And Kara told how the goddess's symbols – the white-petaled rosette and the lion she rode – balanced beauty with power. Whatever else happened with the *ashu,* tomorrow the morning star, Ishtar the warrior, lover, beauty and power would set us on our way, Kara said. And I'd be that much closer to finishing my work with Babylon.

Just before light, the *ashu* reappeared with an attendant, carrying folds of fabric in soft, fleshy arms. The *ashu* retrieved the pot he had set out the night before and summoned me to follow him. With the attendant shuffling behind, he led me to an area on the eastern edge of the camp. I could see Igliss watching from a distance. The sun was just cresting the horizon as the attendant layered linens on the ground behind a screen.

"This magic," the *ashu* said, "will rid you of any demons who may have taken up residence in your limbs."

I faced him and planted my feet. "I don't have any demons."

"Come. Take off your clothes."

"What?!" I looked around frantically.

"You have to be naked for this part." The man's voice was matter of fact. His attendant, mouth-breathing, stood beside him.

Where was Khai?

The attendant reached for the neck of my robe. I jerked away and clutched its edges more tightly together. "Touch me, and I will report it to – to Nebuchadnezzar himself."

I had always been comfortable in my body, taking it with animal-like acceptance, reveling in its flexibility and strength, favoring its injuries, and remaining generally unconcerned about its processes and appearance, even as it changed recently from girl to woman. I'd assumed, though I thought little about it, that I'd share my body with a man some day. But I hadn't desired it and certainly never imagined some stranger stripping me precisely in order to... what did he say, get rid of my demons?

The doctor sighed. "The king expects that we will do this. It is required." He signaled to one of his attendants. "Fetch the girl's nurse." We waited, unmoving until Kara hurried to my side. The doctor waved his hand for me to get on with it.

I looked at Kara. But I could tell from her eyes – one partly shuttered by scar – that there was nothing she could do. I thought about Media's vast untouched wilderness in the face of Babylonia's seemingly limitless power. For Media. I slowly removed my clothes, piece by piece and avoided the hungry eyes of the priest's attendant. Naked, I lay down on my back, face up as instructed. I shut my eyes and gripped the linen beneath me so tightly that my nails bit through the cloth and into my palms.

I could hear the doctor shuffling, the clang of the pot. Suddenly his fingers were at my head. I flinched. He rubbed my temples while he recited an incantation. Then he moved his hands down to my neck and began another poem, kneading the flesh behind my head and at my shoulders. He moved down each arm to my fingertips, prying loose my hands, all the while murmuring his incantations and massaging the heady mixture into my skin. With each touch, my muscles clenched. I tried not to think of my nakedness, tried not to think of the old man hovered over me, tried not to think of anything.

The *ashu*'s hands returned to my torso. "Relax," he said, suddenly kneading my breasts. I froze. He moved on, rubbing my belly and sides. Now the strange man's hands were massaging between my legs. I squeezed my eyes shut, ashamed to feel tears roll into my ears. Finally, he stopped. But then he told me to turn over. The *ashu* massaged my shoulder blades, my back, my buttocks. I took tiny breaths, thinking of Media's wild hares, how they panted with fright, otherwise perfectly still, to avoid a hungry hawk's aerial glare. Sometimes it worked. I willed myself to stay in place. Whatever he was going to do, I'd survive it. I had to. They thought I was Mandane, soon to be wife of their king. The *ashu* moved down my legs to my feet. He rubbed to the tips of my toes, rolled back on his heels, and stood. The attendant beside him breathed heavily.

"All done," the *ashu* said. "You may put your clothes back on."

I scrambled to sit, a mixture of relief and anger washing over me. Kara dropped my robe back over my shoulders. I pulled it close. The glare she gave the man could have shoved him clear back to Babylon, but he ignored her. He simply gathered his things, directed his attendant to follow, and left me to dress alone.

As I pulled the fine, fringed shift back over my head and wrapped the woven robe close around me, I wondered if Mandane knew about this ritual. It rattled me. I swiped my eyes dry. My legs still felt wobbly, disjointed. I realized I'd been shaking.

The first thing I did after getting my clothes back on was visit Bepti. His warm hide, the animal smell of him, and the brush of his mane between my fingers soothed me. He bent his big head around my back as I stroked the white hair of his shoulder. He snuffled warm breath against my side. "We're almost there," I said, "almost done. Then, you and I will be free and home in time for you to eat your fill of the lush spring grasses." Bepti jerked his head up, ears alert. From the distance I heard it, too – a golden jackal's howl. I nearly wept with relief. A good omen. I'd wondered if all this were mere folly and Mandane no better off than if I'd undertaken this in the first place. I worried what Mandane might be thinking and how I could get her here without damaging her reputation. But the land, saturated by its gods, called its wild blessing out to me.

OUR JOURNEY RESUMED JUST as it had every other morning. Khai took his place, steady on, in the caravan. The glance he shot me as we pulled out was impossible to read. As usual. But when we stopped for the night and Kara was busy helping prepare the evening meal, when I slipped away to visit Bepti, I saw the priest's attendant approach my tent. Khai suddenly appeared beside him. He took the man's shoulder roughly and said something that made the attendant hurry away.

I turned back to my horse. When the pounding in my chest had quieted, I heard Khai say, "Only a few more days, and we'll be there." He kept distance from the horses, but his eyes remained on them. "They're magnificent," he said.

I grinned. "Mithra's favorites." A gray mare stomped a forefoot, sending Khai back a few steps. She rubbed her face against her leg.

"Just an itch" I said. "See," explaining.

Khai nodded.

"Here." I waved him to the mare. "They're prey animals, easily spooked," I said. "So just let them know with your voice where you are."

With a gentle murmur, he stepped up. He stroked the horse's flank, and I could see that his caution came from unfamiliarity not fear. The mare, relaxed, could sense the strength of his ease.

"I'm sorry not to have more time to learn," Khai said, moving up to her shoulder. "From here on, I'll be doubly occupied." He patted the mare's neck.

I didn't know what he meant – "doubly occupied – " but as I watched Khai move away, an odd twinge that felt like regret – a wish that the journey were just a little longer – tugged in my chest. I counted it rather as anxiety. Soon, I'd not only need to reveal my true identity but also confront the king. I tried to focus not on all that could go wrong but on the anticipation of finalizing our treaty's terms so that Bepti and I could be on our way home again.

THE RUGGED MOUNTAINS WERE GONE, the hills too. We left the Tigris and tracked west to Babylonia's other great river – as broad as a mountain lake. But where Media's waters were clear and its surface reflected an ever-changing sky, this river was murky and busy with the barges and boats of human enterprise. We followed the Euphrates south again. The landscape stretched farther and farther. If I let go of my goal, my soul would wash out into that endless flat land, bereft and lost. So I clung to the plan. Flatter and flatter the land became and all around, it was empty of trees but for those on the river's banks. The clusters of houses got bigger and bigger. Farms laid out in green strips, carefully irrigated, became the only plants we saw. Gradually even the clumps of blue borage and gray-green shrubs that had silently witnessed my passing disappeared. I understood in ways I never had before why it was that Babylonia craved Media's forests. And with Babylonian strength only increasing… I looked back. Khai rode atop the load of timber from home. I shivered. Broadening space washed the land of only a few muted colors until I feared that it would tear me apart into a thousand pieces, dissolve my very self, scattered to evaporate in the vast expanse of beige and brown.

FINALLY, news traveled back: if you look just so, there in the distance, you can see Babylon. Sure enough, still many miles away the hazy outlines of its massive walls and over them, a great tower, "the temple of Marduk," Kara said, rose up out of the flat land to touch the sky. I'd never seen anything like it.

We stopped. I looked back and saw Khai rearranging the carts – now I understood, covering obvious valuables – and arranging their order to prioritize security through a more densely populated region. He seemed to be everywhere, but without hurry, addressing queries from several different directions. There'd be no more chatting among the horses.

I hopped out, surprised to find Igliss, with his nasal intonations, suddenly beside me. "Center of the world," he said with more cheer than I'd heard yet. Igliss gestured toward the city like a proud parent. "The Entemenanki, rising as it has from the beginning of time," his pinched voice grew louder as if declaring some great grand truth, "links every layer of the universe."

Says who?, I thought, but kept my mouth shut.

"And Marduk's tower – eighty meters wide at its base and getting taller – so great that only from a distance can one see the whole thing." Igliss all but swooned. "Ah, Babylon." He looked at me. "As you know, the god Ishmun said Babylon is 'like a gemstone on the neck of the sky.'" I didn't know. But he didn't care.

The next day, when it was still morning, the carriages stopped. "Babylon," Igliss said, opening my carriage door. "Thank the gods. Home." My stomach twisted like wet laundry. Igliss reached around and secured the tapestries of my carriage, shutting me in. He closed the door.

"Hey," I said, "I want to see." But there was no answer. The vehicle lurched forward, rolling into the city. I lifted a curtain's edge, but Kara pushed my hand away.

"Decorum, privacy, maybe," she said. "Maybe the king doesn't want to share the first sight of his new wife with anyone, least of all the city's masses."

New wife I was not. Well, he'd know soon enough. I huffed dissent but kept the curtain closed.

As we rattled over a stone-paved street, Kara put the last touches on my hair. She wound and rewound a lank of hair, finally snorting in frustration. "Speaking of masses," she muttered. Finally giving up, she simply pinned it up with a golden clip.

The closer we got, the louder it grew – the rush and rumble of vehicles passing, the increasing clamor of people's voices; and the smells so pungent – sweet rotting dates, the noxious odors of leather-working, the dung of pack animals, fish from the wharfs. I wondered if it was always like this, or only during the great festival. What was it called, again? Oh yes, the Akitu. I fidgeted in my new clothes, slid my feet in and out of the utterly unfamiliar open sandals. It was hot, but I raised Mandane's ermine stole to my cheek for the comfort of home. We rode in a stuffy silence.

The carriage turned. Distinct voices replaced the general street din. We slowed, then stopped. My stomach lurched with anxiety. I was excited – it had been a long wait to get to the business of the treaty – but beset by self-doubt, too. Who was I to negotiate for Media, to fight for her well-being against this most powerful empire? Well, Mandane would never do it. And my father obviously hadn't. I took a deep breath and pushed the door open. A collective gasp met me. The courtyard was crowded with personnel, each of whom stared, frozen. I had slammed the door into the king.

CHAPTER 5

I recoiled at the thunk, seeing my mistake immediately. Behind me, Kara muttered, "Oh, child." But King Nebuchadnezzar, unmistakable in his deep blue robe and jewel-studded golden crown, had caught the door. And coughed. Then the coughing turned more into a chuckle, and the crowd came back to life. I couldn't see Khai anywhere. Someone led Bepti – high-stepping his resistance, tail swishing and swatting dissent – away across the courtyard. I fought a reflex to follow. But here stood the king. I gulped, trying to find my words, to say something about who I was, something about the treaty. I stared at him. At best, I had expected a man like my father – fleshy, with florid pock-marks and few teeth – but even worse. Nebuchadnezzar was old enough to be my father's father. His hair – in tight ringlets like his beard – was gray, his face deeply lined. But his eyes could have ignited the carriage fabric, they burned with such intensity.

"Hah!" he said, his teeth full and white. "She's even pretty." He gestured to a middle-aged woman in a stiff, gray robe. "Get her settled." Then, he was off, striding across the courtyard in stiff but distance-gobbling steps.

"Sir!" I said, hopping out of the carriage. My ankle had healed, but I tripped in the sandals. I needed to catch Nebuchadnezzar, tell him the truth about who I was, settle the treaty... I slipped around the woman's reach, keeping the back of the king's robe in my sight. I ignored her call and focused on catching Nebuchadnezzar. Igliss cut me off.

"Go with Rdiya," he said, blocking my way. "Who do you think –"

The woman, Rdiya, tugged the stole off my shoulders and with a huff draped it over her arm. I let her take it, suddenly unsure.

Igliss turned and trotted after the king.

Kara got out of the carriage and stepped to my side.

Rdiya quickly controlled her surprise at seeing Kara's face. She shifted my stole from one arm to the other. "You can talk to the king later," she said sharply. "There'll be plenty of time after the Akitu. Only a few days left. Then your wedding."

I found my voice to protest, "But I'm not –"

Kara elbowed me into silence.

All around us, men unpacked the carriages and carts, carrying items – boxes, lumber, a great silver bowl filled with lapis lazuli – through the courtyard gates out of sight. Then I saw him – Khai walking away, a small sack over one shoulder, out into the street. Gone. I don't know why I cared – someone who'd become familiar, maybe, in all that was new. I turned away.

A person of indeterminate gender stepped up next to Rdiya. I studied him... her? A eunuch. Mandane had told me about these people – castrated men who assisted with the king's women. At the time I didn't believe her, couldn't imagine it. We saw so many different kinds of people traveling through Media's capital city, lingering to trade all sorts of goods and services. But never among them was such a person. Now I was staring at one. And as I looked around, he wasn't the most unusual thing I'd seen. We were in the middle of a city that I could see no end of and with buildings rising even higher than the palace walls.

"Follow me," Rdiya said.

The eunuch leaned in as we walked. "Rdiya is manager of the queen's household." His voice was high, thin. "And very good at it."

We stopped at one of the courtyard gates. Rdiya said, "Our palace serves many functions, both public and private. I suppose it's overwhelming, coming from Media as you do." I heard only judgment in her voice – a judgment that found me and all of Media wanting, inferior. I kept my face straight and my mouth shut. I hoped Kara appreciated the restraint. "King Nebuchadnezzar continues to build on an already most impressive architectural history. Now, follow me. Don't dawdle. We'll pass some of the most important public spaces, then into administrative and finally into the private wing – to your suite, as well as the greater women's section."

I bit back my comments and questions. She couldn't know that it didn't matter to me what went where, except as I might find the king. And there was no way I could make her understand that Media's forested mountains, waterfalls, and lakes were far more impressive than any hall or wall. Suddenly, Rdiya bent in to examine my face. She yanked a loose lock of hair from Kara's arrangement.

"Your work?" she asked Kara. But she didn't wait for an answer. "Let's hope," Rdiya said to the eunuch in a withering tone, "that the slave can be taught." She turned on her heel and strode on through the arched opening.

We had passed into a warren of halls with plaster walls painted in all manner of floral motifs offset by heavy wooden doors. People came and went around us. No one took any notice of me. Not that I wanted them to, but I wondered, if I were Mandane would it be different? I wanted to tell them that a true queen would arrive soon. Once I'd settled the treaty's terms... A short, squat man wearing a soft cap walked by, papyrus writing board under his arm. Rdiya stiffened and turned up her nose. The eunuch whispered to me, "Rdiya thinks foreigners, like that scribe there, should be in ghettoes, not incorporated into state affairs, much less in the palace."

I pulled back.

"Oh," he smiled solicitously. "Not you. That's different."

I couldn't see how.

We passed rooms shining with decorative tile and through an archway of brightly painted brick. My shoes felt flimsy on the stone floor, and I stumbled more than once. Thankfully, Rdiya ignored it, focused as she was on pointing out this and that, and at intersections – "to the public wing... to the administrative section... to the old palace... to the king's quarters..." The king. Where would Nebuchadnezzar be now? I'd find him just as soon as I got a break from Rdiya.

We threaded through a hall wider yet more crowded than the others. Everyone seemed to know where they were going and what they were about, moving with purpose, and quickly. I kept one eye on Rdiya. With the other I took in this impossibly sprawling palace. I grudgingly admitted to myself that it was indeed impressive, far bigger than the palace in Ecbatana and full of eye-dazzling details such as the gold-gilded lion statues outside this door and massive stone bulls outside another. Grand, yes. Impressive, for sure. But definitely not better. I missed the grand wooden columns, like an indoor forest, that graced the palace back home.

Rdiya officiously jostled us through the crowd up to double doors, fixed open. On either side, stone griffins, the size of mastiffs and covered in gold, reclined on feline legs. Slitted eyes of ivory with obsidian pupils looked out from eagle's heads. No one within a body's length of the door escaped their watch. Guards stood at attention next to them. "The king's public audience," Rdiya explained and pointed inside. The room was huge – even longer than it was wide and much longer than any room I'd ever seen. Images of stylized palms, orderly and straight, ran from floor to ceiling in shining tile on every inch of its walls. Mandane will love this, I thought. But what caught my breath was directly across the hall – the king's dais. I moved to approach, then felt Kara's grip on my arm. I stopped. Nebuchadnezzar sat on a high throne, listening to a couple of men in ordinary robes standing below.

"The king takes cases nearly every day, even during the Akitu," Rdiya said. "He's just back from Borsippa, matter of fact, called away to try a loyalty oath crime. Lying. The punishment, one's head."

I gulped. I had to explain, and soon. "Can I -?" I motioned to the room, could I enter and speak to the king immediately?

Rdiya scowled and shook her head, then continued with her lecture. "Right and honorable judgment is an important part of kingship. King Nebuchadnezzar takes this responsibility very seriously." I wondered how the people he conquered – the Judean king forced to watch his sons killed, for example – felt about that. Kara's grip tightened. I pinched my lips shut. I'd come back.

The dais held a second throne, empty. Rdiya saw me notice. "If the queen mother were alive, there would be three thrones on the dais," Rdiya said. "But since she proved a traitor to the gods and had to be killed, only the crown prince's throne remains."

"And where is he?" I asked.

The eunuch cleared his throat in that way people do who have nothing to clear but a lot not to say. In the pause, I thought maybe Rdiya hadn't heard me.

"Crown Prince Ean has been..." for the first time, Rdiya faltered. "... unable to attend the Akitu." Rdiya regained her iron spine and superiority and strode on as if to leave the rest of an answer behind. The rest of us hurried after her.

At the end of another long hall, we climbed a flight of stairs. We had taken so many twists and turns that I, who could find my way anywhere in Media, retracing paths through miles and miles of forest, fields, and mountains, had to admit I was lost. Finally, Rdiya stopped. "Your room," she said, stepping between a pair of granite and gold lions. She pushed the heavy oak door, and gestured me in. I caught my breath. It was actually a series of rooms and richly furnished with ornately carved chairs of burnished wood, sofas plush with down and covered in brightly colored cloth, a fine wooden table on which three oil lamps of a bright, beaten metal – each more elegant than the last – sat cold. At midday, it was bright enough already. Off to the right, through an archway was a long carved ivory bench. Off to the left another room contained a delicate table with three red pitchers, half a dozen small matching cups, and bowl of dates.

"These are your public rooms, as you can see," Rdiya said. "Spare. The queen mother had simple taste."

I wondered what Mandane would think. There was nothing obviously public or spare about what I saw, that's for sure.

"Through these," Rdiya tapped on heavy wooden doors carved with twining vines and and rosettes, "is the courtyard to the women's wing – living quarters for other of the king's women." She narrowed her eyes at me. "You may be his wife," Rdiya didn't see me shudder. "But you're not the only one."

"Of course," I said. "I mean, for certain." From these innocuous habits of speech to significant cultural practices, I could see why Mandane spent her life learning how to live here. This business of multiple wives was not the way in Media, not these days. Astyages declared that his seed was so exceptional that he had but one wife, Mandane's mother. Then again, in truth, he had made none of the alliances or conquests that would gain a king such resources. My own mother, a Harranian slave – admittedly never a wife – was there because of my grandfather Cyaxares's success, not Astyages's. The whole thing reminded me again of the urgency of my mission.

But Rdiya wasn't done. "The king's women have their own eunuchs, and they keep to themselves."

She had no idea how little I cared. "And there?" I nodded toward an archway blocked by a tightly woven curtain whose two halves met to complete a central rosette. A tiny beam of light shone from underneath.

"Your personal rooms, for certain." Rdiya walked in and pulled the curtains back. Light from a far window flooded the room. Boxes packed in Media long ago lay neatly stacked. But I hardly noticed, the suite so dazzled. Kara walked through. She put her hands on her hips and looked back, daring Rdiya to remark about how much better this must be than it was in Media. Rdiya said only, "I'll leave you to get settled while I see about dinner. With the Akitu underway, the cooks need extra time to prepare."

The eunuch helped Kara open one of the boxes from Media. He lifted out a pair of gem-studded golden cups and remarked at their weight.

"I'll be right back," I said. Before either the eunuch or Kara could stop me, I slipped back out into the hall and darted back the way we had come.

I FOUND the stairs and took them two by two until I met an aged eunuch coming up. I dropped my head, nodded quickly, and hurried on. I had tried to watch closely the turns we took on the way to Mandane's quarters, but the plethora of sights, the babble of strange languages, and my own excited anxiety had made it difficult to concentrate. Still, I kept moving. Remarkably, no one stopped me. Each seemed preoccupied with some important business or another. I came to a crossroads of hallways. I was pretty sure that I'd passed out of the private, royal section of the palace and had entered the administrative wing. But I couldn't remember – was it right or left here? Or had we come from the hall straight ahead? Voices raised in anger caught my attention.

They came from a room just ahead. I glanced around. The door was ajar.

"It was my idea." A man's voice, young-ish, quivered with energy.

"It was your grandmother's idea," another man, more measured, replied.

I quieted my steps, sidled up to the door, and peered inside. Across the room, two men faced off. Similarity in the structure of their faces, forehead and chin, suggested father and son. Age wasn't the only difference, though. The younger, plump, was dressed in layers of fine, fringed fabric and had more jewelry than I'd seen on even the far eastern traders. The elder didn't seem to care a whit about such luxuries. His robe hung straight and clean and his shoes were the practical leather sandal of an ordinary man. The younger man's soft chest thrust forward. The elder, lean and relaxed, stood with his arms at his side. "You were right to bring it to the king," he said, his voice firm. "Just be careful how eagerly you reach."

"I don't know what you mean." Though an adult, the younger was petulant.

"Yes, you do." The elder leaned in. "And there are high-born wolves all over these rooms and halls eager to sniff it out, wolves with better pedigrees than yours."

The younger man's face went red. He sputtered, "You may be some immigrant from the north; but my mother is Nebuchadnezzar's daughter."

"She is his absent, *bastard* daughter, Shazzi." I caught my breath and pulled back against the wall, feeling cool plaster against the back of my head, against my palms.

"A nobody." My father had been furious when he learned that Nebuchadnezzar had married. A slave, a servant? something scandalous. Word was that even before they married, she had born Nebuchadnezzar a child – like me, a king's daughter but bastard nonetheless. It must have been she, now a woman, who was the plump man's mother and elder man's wife. "Be satisfied with your position," the elder continued. "Don't pretend to anything higher." Apparently, only the children born after Nebuchadnezzar married his low-born love, now dead, counted. Any other was a mere bastard. I knew what that was like.

My legs twitched. I had to finish my business and get Mandane down here. I looked around quickly. The hallway was still empty. But they weren't done, and I was curious.

"Just because you," the young man's voice rose "have no vision, no ambition..."

I peered in again as the elder caught his son by the arm. The younger shook his sleeve free with disdain.

"Oh, I have ambition," the elder said. His voice was low. "It may not be to impress the peacocks," he plucked the sleeve that his son had jerked away, "that strut around this court full of their self-importance. My ambition is to serve -- this nation that has given us much, and its king, sure. But that's not all." His voice dropped so I could barely hear. "I serve my god. And one day I will see the great Nanna-Suen, god of our native land, return to Harran –"

So this man was from the same, defeated place as Kara, but held an important position here in Babylon.

"You've adopted your grandmother's ambition but missed the most pure and redeeming part – her piety for the god of all. Adad-guppi's successes in court, a success that gave you and me a place here, she achieved with the single goal of restoring Nanna-Suen to his temple home in Harran." When he said the god's name, the elder's voice deepened with a kind of awe-filled conviction.

The young man folded his arms across his chest.

"Nanna-Suen, who created and sustains, serene god of the tide-pulling moon, is Lord of the Heavens and redeemer of the earth."

The young man stomped his foot. "Marduk rules the gods."

The elder took no notice. "If it were up to me, Nanna-Suen, not Marduk would be the high god of all Babylonia."

The young man's jaw dropped open, then snapped shut again. "It is you who should be careful, father, and during this Akitu of all times. Marduk has been the high god of this city from the beginning of time as we know it."

"Not 'the beginning of time.'" The old man suddenly sounded tired. "Marduk was.... Never mind." His shoulders slumped. He reached out, his rough hand hovering for an instant over his son's soft shoulder and then dropped it back idle against his side. "I've said too much." The elder searched his son's face. "You're a fine young man, well-liked around here. That's worth something, I suppose."

The young man stiffened. "If you're done with your little speech, I suggest that we get on with honoring the gods. Marduk above all."

The elder paused, then started for the door.

I walked swiftly on. My thoughts churned, complicating the already difficult task of finding my way back to the throne room. What was this conflict? I didn't know much, but between snippets I learned from Mandane and my journey with Kara's tutelage along the way, I thought everyone believed Marduk to be not only god of the city Babylon but god of the gods of all Babylonia.

Well, it wasn't my problem to sort out. More of a problem was this hostility toward foreigners. I hoped that Mandane was truly prepared to fit in.

Up ahead, I recognized a particularly ostentatious door – those massive stone bulls – and went through. I found myself back in the broad and bustling hall leading to the throne room. My heart beat so fast it caught my breath. I set out along the stone floor, the slap of my sandals lost in the chatter of passing men and women. What would I say? Maybe: You do know that the intended treaty forbids Babylonian interference in Media.

No, too judgmental. Is it true that you plan to make use of Media's resources? No, too open-ended. Maybe: Igliss said something about cutting trees and subduing Media's wildness, though the treaty... I was at the door. Of course I'd tell him Mandane would marry him just as soon as we wrote down the terms. That would have to do.

Guards looked at me without saying anything. The door, open earlier, was closed. I hoped I wasn't too late.

"I'm here to see the king," I said.

The men didn't move. "The king's audience is over," one man said.

"I am King Astyages of Media's daughter..." I couldn't say "princess," and I certainly couldn't say "Nebuchadnezzar's new wife." The lie was bad enough already.

To my surprise, the men bowed and opened the doors. I barely heard them close it again behind me. Relieved, I saw that I wasn't too late. Nebuchadnezzar was still there.

Across the room ahead, the king bent over a table in conference with Igliss, who stood to Nebuchadnezzar's right. I walked straight forward, conscious to move swiftly but not hurriedly, and with purpose. I kept my head still, aware of the complicated arrangement Kara had made of my hair and tried to look every bit the polished and assured emissary.

Igliss looked up. His face flushed in anger. "Seize her!"

CHAPTER 6

Shocked, I froze, standing there, in the palatial throne room as Igliss's "Seize her!" reverberated off the tiled walls, I looked around quickly. But there was no one else. All I saw were the guards bursting through the doors and rushing at me. The men slammed into me, one on either side. I was too surprised and confused to resist. They grabbed my arms and yanked them behind me, forcing me to bend to relieve the sudden pain. For an instant, I almost laughed. I'd come all the way to Babylonia, all the way to the king's court only to be assaulted. Again. There had to be some mistake. My face burned. I resisted the urge to fight and felt a lock of hair swing loose against my cheek.

"Sir!" Igliss said.

I raised my head, awkward in the guards' grip. Nebuchadnezzar sat silently watching.

"This is a capital offense." Igliss's nasal tone trembled in the resonant room.

I tried to straighten, but the effort made me cough.

"Take her out," Nebuchadnezzar said.

"But –" I wriggled in a vain effort to free my arms. The guards yanked me around and pushed me toward the door.

I heard Igliss sputtering behind me. Nebuchadnezzar said something that quieted him, but the guards were already shoving me through the door. It slammed shut behind us. They let go of me then. I shook out my arms, angry now. "What was that?" I asked.

The men seemed startled. "Don't you know –?" They shared a glance.

"Obviously, I don't."

"You have to be invited – "

"Everyone does," the other added. "To approach the king."

"But you opened the door," I said.

The guards shuffled nervously. "You have to wait at the door until the king sees you –"

"-- and then motions you to come forward."

"Or not." The guards still seemed confused to be explaining this, like I was more stupid than they could imagine.

Well, I might not be the smartest young woman ever, but - "I have to wait for the king's invitation to approach?, to speak?" I asked.

The guards visibly relaxed, seeing that I was finally catching on. They nodded.

"Or you'd *kill* me?!"

They stiffened, uncomfortable again. The conversations of people passing by grew quiet. They stared at this girl carrying on with the guards. I stared back until they hurried along. I couldn't wait to get back to Media where even the palace made more sense to me.

"You did what?" Kara said, when I was back in Mandane's quarters.

By then, the shock of the whole thing had worn off and what

was left was just a pit of sick in my stomach. The eunuch had left, and Rdiya was blessedly absent. Kara stepped away from a vanity table arranged with all sorts of queenly things, some that I recognized from Media.

"Already," I said. "I've offended Nebuchadnezzar. And I still haven't even talked to him about the treaty." I threw one of the plush divan pillows across the room. It landed with an unsatisfying smack. "Or the truth about who I am." I took in the room, then. The boxes were mostly unpacked and gone, save one.

I recognized it as the box in which Mandane had been collecting and keeping the things she used to help child-birthing women in crisis. On top was the faded sprig of astragalus she'd been so happy to get from the river. I picked it up and sent a silent prayer, though Anahita couldn't possibly hear me so far from home. Still, I felt stronger, remembering the power of the river and my determination to get Mandane safely wed. I laid it back down.

"I need to find my horse," I said. "Tomorrow, by the grace of Marduk or Nanna-Suen or whoever – "

"What did you say? Nanna-Suen?"

"It was nothing. Something I overheard." Kara looked at me to go on. "One of those upper-class from Harran, who'd been taken here after the war. He seemed official."

Kara nodded. " I'd heard that Nebuchadnezzar uses even the people he conquered to the best of their abilities. Obviously, not every Babylonian is happy about that."

As if on cue, Rdiya strode in. "I heard about what you did in the throne room," she said. I couldn't imagine how. It had hardly been minutes. "Unacceptable." She rearranged things on the vanity. She sighed as if I presented a terrible burden. "You'll have opportunity soon enough to talk with the king. When the Akitu is over..."

I watched Kara bend over Mandane's box. Something had caught her good eye. She reached under the astragalus and straightened, a scrap of linen, stained with the lines and dots of writing, in her hand. She tucked it into her robe. Just in time. Rdiya scowled and rifled her fingers through the plants.

"Mementos from Media," I said. "Where are the stables?"

"Why ever would you want to go there?"

Kara coughed into her hand.

"Just curious, I guess," I said.

THE STABLES WOULD HAVE to wait, much to my chagrin. Rdiya had instead arranged a kind of tour of the city. She held out a robe. "There's a litter waiting in the courtyard." Fringes down the front fell soft and sumptuous. I hardly noticed as she slipped my arms through. "Babylon's greatness is unparalleled, as I'm sure you've heard." Rdiya hustled me out the door and shut it behind her. "But you must see first-hand."

"And Kara?" Amytis asked.

"What of her?"

"Shouldn't she come, too?"

Rdiya huffed. She opened the door again and gestured for Kara to hurry up. Rdiya said that now would be best for an introduction to the city, since the Akitu's activities for that day had concluded in the morning when Nebuchadnezzar had returned from Borsippa bearing the statue of the god Nabu. In the coming days the streets would be even more congested she said.

"We are in the Northern Palace," Rdiya said as we hustled along. "Nebuchadnezzar had it built on account of dampness in the Southern Palace – you may notice as we pass through. The Southern Palace is still entirely inhabitable, especially since Nebuchadnezzar raised the floors; but he prefers the Northern, in winter, anyway." I was glad to recognize some of the hallways we followed. Others were unfamiliar. I hoped they'd take us past the stables. "During the hottest months, when the city is... well...

less pleasant, we retreat to the Summer Palace, north a mile or so, for fresher air."

We reached the courtyard in time to see a couple of riders dismount. I noted where they led the horses even as Rdiya led me to the litter we'd ride. Four men, chests bare and bald heads shining in the sunshine, stood each at one end of the two long wooden poles that supported a wide platform holding cushioned benches. Curtains hung from posts on each corner. I was happy to see them fixed back, so that we could see. The men looked straight ahead, careful not to make eye contact as we stepped into the carriage.

The litter lifted and rolled. We trotted out the gate and onto a wide street. "Seven meters wide," Rdiya said. I couldn't imagine how many more people could fit on the road we traveled. Despite its width, it was packed with all manner of people, each so different and so busy that they hardly paid us any heed. Then I noticed the walls. "Procession Way," Rdiya said. Glazed tile brick rising up from the street on both sides caught the afternoon sun. Along each wall, lions of golden-orange against a deep blue strode eternal in tile the many meters of its length, their mouths frozen in wide snarls. "This is the street down which the gods will pass at the culmination of the Akitu, a most impressive occasion and auspicious time."

At perfectly regular intervals as far as I could see, doorways cut into the brick. High above, turrets jutted out. I could just make out men – archers – standing at the ready.

"Look behind you and you'll see the Ishtar gate through which they pass."

I turned around and caught my breath. The gate was no mere entryway, no simple passage, but a series of arches that disappeared one behind the other deep into what must be massively thick city walls. On either side of the opening, towers rose dizzyingly high. Every inch was decorated in glazed tile. A variegated blue, deep and rich, made a brilliant background to panels of figures – animals striding in ordered repetition across the same enchanting blue-green background. "Over 500 animals, if you count them inside and out," Rdiya said. "Marduk's dragons, Adad's bulls." Lanky yellow dragons – composite creatures with serpentine forked tongues alternated in rows with hefty horned bulls, the color of cream. "Nebuchadnezzar keeps rebuilding it. Maybe this version will stay," Rdiya said. "The road itself, as you can see, is paved with limestone."

Sure enough. Big squares carved flat and laid end to end. Rdiya was still looking at me. I must be missing something. "Limestone," Rdiya repeated meaningfully. Kara coughed and nodded discreetly to the ground. I trained her eyes on the road again, closer, harder. Still they were just stone slabs.

"Yes," I said. Then it occurred to me that all around was mud and brick. I tried to look impressed. "It must have taken a great deal of work –"

Rdiya sat back, satisfied in her pride again. "Carted in from many miles away. The underside of each is inscribed, 'Nebuchad-nezzar of Babylon, son of Nabopolassar, king of Babylon, I am...'"

My mind wandered to the treaty, to how I could broach the subject and get this ambitious king to agree to an agreement of equals.

Rdiya droned on, reciting, "...In the street of Babylon used for the procession of the great lord Marduk I made the road smooth with limestone slabs. May Marduk, my lord, give a long-lasting life...'" My eyes took in the scene.

So many people. Men and women, children, too, in all kinds of dress, crowded the streets. Some in rough tunics carried baskets of market goods – bread, onions, clusters of dates – and some strolled in soft sandals, beards neatly trimmed, engaged with earnest expressions in conversation with each other. A man hauling bricks over his shoulder called out to one of the men pulling the litter, who replied – a greeting, I assumed, but I couldn't understand the language. Few people paid any attention to us – just another vehicle, a noblewoman and her servants, on the busy street.

Rdiya noted my interest in the crowds. "With our king's success in subduing other nations, the truth of Babylonian superiority is spreading," Rdiya said. "Their people, defeated of course, work for us, now." I watched a young mother adjust an odd headpiece on her little boy. "I just can't understand why some people insist on clinging to their languages and silly old habits."

"You mean traditions?" I asked.

"*Babyloni*a has traditions," Rdiya said. "The foreigners are just stubborn. Or stupid. Or both." Thankfully, she kept talking. I let my retort die on my tongue. "On our left is the New Town neighborhood. To your right, the Ka-dingirra, Sumerian for 'Gate of the Gods.'"

Kara, otherwise silent, spoke up. "Isn't that the city as a whole – Babylon?"

Rdiya looked at her with a new, if fleeting, appreciation. "Bab-El, yes, 'Gate of the Gods,'" Rdiya said but didn't elaborate further. "Here we are. Stop," she called to the litter bearers.

A pair of bronze dragons each as big as a man sat guarding a cutaway in the brick wall, twice as wide as other doorways.

"The great temple complex," Rdiya said, stepping out.

I followed. "Marduk's, then." I tried to sound knowledgeable.

"Everything is Marduk's."

Of course it is, I thought.

"He has a separate temple, too, for certain, the Esagil."

I couldn't help but roll my eyes. Kara bumped me hard, a corrective, I knew. But it was all so ostentatious, so full of itself. So much. Rdiya didn't notice.

"You've seen the tower," Rdiya said. I resisted the impulse to pat a dragon's shoulder as we walked in. Rdiya pointed ahead. "Higher than anything else in Babylon." We walked through the wall's darkness into a plaza flooded with sunlight and bustling with people. "It rises directly out of the pure hill."

"What hill?" I asked, straining to see.

Rdiya looked at me as if I'd just crawled out of a hole. "The first land to rise out of the primordial sea, for certain." Rdiya waved toward the enormous ziggurat, tiers climbing one on top of the other behind yet another wall. "Babylon is, you know, the center of the world. And this is the center of the center."

I still couldn't see any hill. Barely a rise. Maybe. But Rdiya stood in a kind of awe before it. "This temple connects every level of the universe from the underworld to earth, clear up to heaven... though Nebuchadnezzar is still working on the top tiers. Thirty cubits it will be."

Men clambered up and down, mere specks on the highest levels, which, startlingly were completely tiled in a blue that nearly blended with the sky.

"There sure is a lot of blue," I said.

Rdiya inhaled sharply. She glared at me as if to determine if I *meant* to offend her, or if this were another accident. "Lapis lazuli is much prized here," she said. "But we don't have the kind of access to it... Yet."

My stomach flipped again. Media. We were drowning in lapis lazuli back home. It was pretty, sure, but it was cheap and plentiful, thanks to the highway of traders from all over the world that paraded in and out of Ecbatana. Our capital is the hub of east-west trade. So, Babylon wanted that, too.

I simply said, "the tile is lovely," which seemed to appease her somewhat.

Across the plaza, people purchased birds – doves, pigeons, geese – from men tending squawking cages. Goats and sheep bleated from a makeshift corral. A woman traded silver for a lamb, took its rope, and pulled it toward a gate in the wall around the ziggurat. Rdiya said, "You'll want to return to pay due obeisance later, I'm sure, pray, offer sacrifice..."

"Later, yes." I said, not sure what was appropriate or expected. Thank the gods it didn't matter. I'd be long gone.

Rdiya was off again, heading back to the litter. "To Kumar," Rdiya barked to the litter bearers. They trotted for a long way to the end of the temple complex and took a sharp right. The road – packed dirt, not stones this time – was narrower, though no less straight. On our right stood the south wall of the Entemenaki temple complex. Rdiya gestured left. "The Eridu neighborhood," she said. All I could see was the shorter wall of houses back to shoulder to back with no space between. "Do foreigners live there?" I asked.

"Conquered peoples? Exiles? Absolutely not," Rdiya said. "There is perfectly acceptable housing outside of the city proper, both before the far walls and beyond those, too. Jewtown, for instance, is somewhere east of the Zubaba Gate... or maybe south of the outer... It doesn't matter." They weaved through a cluster of boys wrangling an ox. "Marduk's temple, there," Rdiya pointed left. "And up ahead –"

Beyond another gate, past a dark archway, was a glitter of light. We trotted through. Suddenly it was so bright that I had to squint. Light shimmered off water to either side. We were crossing the Euphrates. It was the widest, slowest river that I had ever seen. Looking back, the city wall, rimmed by docks, seemed to rise directly out of the water.

"Bulwark of Enlil," Rdiya said, "Enlil being the high god."

"But isn't Marduk –?"

Rdiya looked at Kara. "Did no one teach her anything?" She shook her head in disgust. "'Enlil' *means* 'high god.' Marduk, for certain *is* Enlil."

"Of course," I said. But I remembered the argument I'd over-heard and wondered what she'd think about that man's desire to promote another god – who, again? Oh, yes. Nanna-Suen. It was all the same to me. Thank the gods, any old gods, I'd never have to keep all this straight.

I took in the scene around. The water itself was busy with

enterprise. All manner of boats and rafts, some empty, some loaded high, came and went.

"The inner city wall is square, like the world," Rdiya said. I suppose, if you really believe yourself to be the center of the universe... "The gap between its outer side, 'Bulwark of Enlil,' and its inner side, 'Enlil Shows Favor' is filled with rubble. It's wide enough so that at its top, two chariots can pass each other." She pointed up. "If you look just –"

We still weren't even midway across the river. On the other side, palms lined the shore. Beyond them lay a jumble of buildings.

"One of the oldest sections of Babylon," Rdiya said. "See how tightly temples to the other gods are clustered here."

Tight, yes. It felt as if the walls were closing in on me. Everywhere I turned, buildings and more buildings. Even the river – flat and muddy red – wasn't spared but covered with vessels and barges, coming and going. The soles of the litter bearers' feet slapped against the bridge.

"Where do you get the wood?" I asked, "For the bridge, for instance?"

"Babylonia includes the territories of defeated nations for certain. We simply float lumber down from forested areas, lands far north of here. I've heard it's quite remarkable, trees everywhere."

Through clenched teeth, I whispered to Kara, "I really need to speak with the king."

Kara pursed her lips and shook her head while Rdiya directed the litter-bearers into the warren of buildings. Rdiya pointed out one magnificent object or ancient building after another. But I could only think about Media and whatever plans Babylonia may have for its exploitation. Finally, we made our way back across the river, its docks buzzing with the work of men loading and unloading cargo from wide rafts and shallow boats. I could hardly wait to get off the litter.

As we passed through the gate, I caught a glimpse of mud brick steps inset in the rubble between walls. A ramp, presumably for the horse-drawn carriages, angled alongside.

"I'll walk from here," I said. "With Kara."

Rdiya sputtered, but she stopped the litter. The men lowered it to the ground, likely grateful for the rest. I stepped out, Kara behind me. I would have said something to the litter bearers, but they studiously avoided my gaze. Rdiya ordered the men back to the palace, and then they were gone. I darted into the darkness of the gate and up a few steps. Out of Rdiya's sight, I hopped up and down a few times to shake off the strain.

We climbed the stairs. We met no one along the way. At the top, we stepped into the wide sky. Kara wheezed and huffed. With a landscape flat as could be, I could see for miles. The city itself stretched out and out and out in endless blocks of brick structures and straight roads. I picked out one curving line, blue. "That must be one of the inner-city canals Rdiya mentioned." Palms planted by Nebuchadnezzar's father as one of his reclamation projects, according to Rdiya's report, had taken root and dotted the way, gangly trunks rising bare to tops that bore incongruously great drooping fronds.

"Mansions all along," Kara said.

The buildings against it were indeed spacious and elegant, with patios fronting on the canal and high pillared facades… each more grand than the last.

Beyond the city walls – inner and outer, was more of the same: people, people, and more people -- all kinds. Nothing wild. The only green and growing things were fiercely tended.

Overwhelmed, I closed my eyes. Everything clanged around me with reminders of Babylonia's reach–its bending every force to its will. Astyages hadn't exaggerated the effect. Everything was under construction, renovation, or expansion. Walls gleamed in painted plaster and colored tiles, stone slabs formed roads wide and straight, even the open land outside the city walls was ordered and tended in squares of cultivation dictated by human need and desires.

Well, I knew that the world is a whole lot bigger than this place. But. "If Babylonia wanted, they could decimate Media." Kara didn't argue. "I need to get back." Whether it was back to the palace to confront Nebuchadnezzar or back to Media's wilderness, I didn't know. But a pointed urgency had taken hold and drove me on.

In reality, the next best chance to talk to the king was tomorrow, when Rdiya said he'd lead the annual ceremony. She promised me a place near the king.

CHAPTER 7

$\mathcal{I}$ was far too restless to sleep. So after Rdiya had left, advising early bed – there were a lot of people for me to meet tomorrow, she'd said – I grabbed a tunic and robe, shoved a few carrots I'd saved from my dinner plate into a pouch along the tunic's side seam, and went to the door.

"Where are you going?" Kara asked from her pallet on the floor.

"It's not even dark outside. And you saw it out there." Noise from the palace halls outside and street below attested to plenty of activity still going on in and around the palace. "With this festival and everything,, no one will notice me."

Kara huffed. "Wait." From a pocket in her robe, she withdrew the scrap of linen I'd seen her take from Mandane's box of medicinal plants and such. "Find a scribe to read it. But be careful."

I nodded. Such a thing clearly meant for Mandane's eyes and done in haste had to be important. Writing, reading. I wished I'd learned this Babylonian custom alongside my sister.

I tucked the scrap into the bodice of my tunic and slipped out.

I was right, no one cared about me or my wanderings. I found my way back to the courtyard. The gate through which the horses had gone was on the far side. I wove my way through people still arriving – for the Akitu, or did they live here? A boy dashed through the wide gate near me. He had manure on his boots. I followed. It led to another courtyard. Along one side, I could make out vehicles neatly lined up, their traces empty but ready. The boy disappeared through another archway across the square. I ran to it and stopped. The passageway was dark. Very dark. Cautiously, I stepped inside.

This was it. The noise and smell of animals – of horse manure and, my heart raced, the tang of something wild – was unmistakable. My eyes adjusted, and my heart sank. I pulled my arms in tight against my sides. Flanking the hallway were cages of wild animals – lions, wild boar, true foxes, even a bear. So Babylonia did it, too – hunts with captured animals. Astyages did that, to prove his kingly prowess. I hated it. I willed myself forward, trying not to meet the sad and angry eyes of the desperate beasts, grunting and roaring and howling.

That hallway opened out into a smaller courtyard – quiet again – with a far doorway through which I hoped I'd find my horse. I fingered the carrots in my pocket, anticipating his nicker and nuzzle. I pushed open the heavy door. It was chaos inside. Barking and the scrapes and scuffle of struggle, a man's shouting. Something crashed. I inched forward.

Along one wall, spacious kennels, each with a run to the outside, housed mastiffs. Despite cushioned beds and bones, each dog stood barking at its gate. Across the hall, in an iron enclosure, a steel-gray dog nearly the size of a foal but three times as thick leapt snarling against a spiked collar. A red-faced man outside the fence hung onto the other end of a leather lead. "Hold the bitch!" a second man yelled. The mastiff lunged again, blood streaking her neck, her teats swinging against her belly.

"Don't let go!" Inside the gate, the second man stepped on a puppy, pinned it squirming against the dirt-packed floor. He raised a club and swung it over his head.

"No!" Unthinking, I leapt inside the gate and grabbed the man's arm, sending the club clattering to the ground. I scooped up the puppy. Suddenly, the bitch was loose and barreling toward us. I pulled the man away, taking him with me as I scrambled for the door. I felt the dog bite down on the hem of my robe. As the man dashed out, I slipped out of the robe and flung its edge over the dog, tangling her just long enough for me to get out and slam the gate shut.

The person who had been holding the dog stood wide-eyed. "What the --?"

"You could have gotten us killed!" the man standing next to me said.

On the other side of the gate, the dog paced, alternately growling and whining. "I'll take good care of your little one," I said. She couldn't understand the words, but I'd learned that a voice speaking true bore its own sense. She still paced, but more quietly. "A runt, isn't it?" I asked, taking in the pup's ribs, his shabby coat, patched with mud.

"Wily." The man huffed. "We got all the others out."

"I'll take him." I tucked stray hair behind my ears and bent my cheek to the warm fur.

"The puppy?"

"Not your friend, that's for sure," I said, angling my head toward the man across the room, his knuckles white against the bars.

"She can have it." A sonorous voice bounced off the walls. "The pup, that is."

The men dropped their heads. Nebuchadnezzar stood in the hall, a group of men behind him. "Clean it up and bring it to her," he said. "You." He fixed me with unyielding eyes. "Don't ever come down here again."

I caught my wits just before he disappeared around a bend, passed the puppy to one of the men, and ran to catch up. "Sir!" I called. Nebuchadnezzar and all the men turned. I recognized with a lift in my spirits Khai among his attendants, the doctor and astrologer-priest from the massage ritual (no attendant, to my relief), and the foreign scribe whom Rdiya had disparaged, too. "I'd like to talk with you about –"

"Come along then," he said.

With a glance at Khai, who shrugged, I scurried forward and fell into step beside him.

Nebuchadnezzar looked down at me. "You walk fast," he said.

"Do I?" We strode through the brick lined hall of kennels. Calmer.

"Most people can't keep up without jogging." He coughed once but kept up the pace.

We stepped through an archway. The smell of sweet hay and manure lifted my heart. Finally, the stables. through the far end, wide open, I could see a straw-strewn paddock where a pure white bull, bigger than any I'd ever seen, stalked the packed earth.

Walking ahead, Khai said, "He's here, sir."

The pounding of hooves against mudbrick shook a far stall. With a quick look at me, Khai led Nebuchadnezzar straight there. My nerves jangled. It was Bepti. What did they want with him? I felt my hands clench at my sides.

"Most magnificent, yes," Nebuchadnezzar said.

What was Khai doing?

Foam flecked Bepti's neck where lines of dusty sweat streaked his hide. He kicked at the door. Nebuchadnezzar stepped back. I hated that the Babylonians had gathered around him, hated that the horse was so upset. I had to settle this and get us out of Babylon.

"Hey," I said. I pushed past Khai and approached the stall. The horse stopped his banging. "Hey, you." Bepti whinnied high and happy, then dropped it to a soft nicker as I held out the carrots and rubbed his whisker-spiked muzzle. His presence gave me strength. Renewed clarity, too. I set aside my confusion – Khai, Bepti? – and focused.

"About the treaty, sir," I said, taking advantage of the shock among Nebuchadnezzar and his men. I couldn't think of a smooth segue. I needed to get right to it, the sooner to get out of Babylon. "It's come to my attention," turned to face the king, "that there's no written version of the terms."

"Your people don't care about writing." Nebuchadnezzar said. He looked suspicious.

"But you do," I said. "And I'm not sure we're in agreement about the details."

The men shuffled their feet nervously.

"It's a strange thing for the king's daughter to be taking this up."

I didn't have an answer to that. But I did have his attention, so I pressed on. "With her marrying you, the treaty would be fixed – Media granted full autonomy, security against threat, and no encroachment on her territory or resources."

Nebuchadnezzar narrowed his eyes. "Seems you've thought this through."

"Only all fifteen years of my life, sir."

Amusement passed over Nebuchadnezzar's face. "Well, we've got a scribe -" I fingered the linen in my pocket, remembering Kara's request. The king gestured around him, "and priests to summon witness of the gods..."

"But sir," The astrologer-priest broke in, "this is most unusual – here? Now?"

"Why *not* now?" Nebuchadnezzar said. "Why not here?"

The man sputtered. The others exchanged uncomfortable glances.

I held my ground. "A draft, to be finalized after the wedding, of course." That seemed to appease the administrators somewhat. I felt the horse nudge my shoulder. "How does this go?"

Nebuchadnezzar waved a hand, heavy with rings. "Write," the king said to the scribe. The man scrambled to affix fresh papyrus to his board. "I, Nebuchadnezzar, lord of all the great lands of Babylonia..."

What relief! Finally, we were going to settle this. I could hardly believe it. I struggled to pay attention.

"... who has so generously preserved the rights and lands of Media to the north,.."

I'd never heard one of these treaties before. Probably some similar statement from Media should follow. I tried to think how that would go.

But the king went on, " ... who has extended security and beneficence like a father, who by the standards of such agreement expects love and devotion –"

Khai coughed loudly, which startled me. What had Nebuchadnezzar just said? "...'a father'?... 'expects love and devotion'?"

"Wait," I said. "That's not right."

Nebuchadnezzar pulled back in surprise.

"It sounds... uneven."

Again the men looked at each other, even more taken-aback than they were before. Only Khai remained relaxed his deep eyes fixed on an indeterminate distance. He clasped his hands behind his back, patiently waiting for the negotiations to proceed.

Nebuchadnezzar huffed. "It's perfect," he said. Any amusement he'd had before was gone. "This is the form of any suzerainty treaty."

If there was one thing I knew from all the worry all my life, all the attention to this particular treaty, it was that there were two kinds of treaties – a covenant between parties unequal in power, a king and a commoner, for example; and a covenant between equals, which is exactly what had been the whole point of that agreement after the battle at Ashur and everything Mandane had been working toward – marrying Nebuchadnezzar. "Ours," I said, "is a *parity* treaty and should read as such."

Nebuchadnezzar's jaw clenched and unclenched. "Everyone knows that Babylonia is the stronger."

I couldn't argue that. Nebuchadnezzar waved to the scribe to continue – "Media will be subject to all –'

"That may be true," I said. Nebuchadnezzar stopped. "True that Babylonia is the stronger party. *Now*. But isn't a king's duty..." I tried to remember what Rdiya had said, "to honor justice, to see that promises are kept?"

Nebuchadnezzar's face was like stone.

"You were there when your father and my grandfather made an agreement. Whatever else they meant, and however else they saw the future when you'd marry a daughter of the Median king, it was to be the binding of equals to last forever." Out of the corner of my eye, I thought I saw Khai's mouth turn up at the corners. Or maybe he merely looked down at his boots, soiled from the stables and cracked from use.

In front of me, Nebuchadnezzar narrowed his eyes. I held mine steady on his. He pursed his lips together, then relaxed them into a small smile. I exhaled. "Parity, it is," Nebuchadnezzar said. He turned his head aside, momentarily overcome by a fit of coughing.

The scribe tore off the draft papyrus. Nebuchadnezzar, recovered, tossed it into a stall. A pure white goat picked it up and began to devour it.

Nebuchadnezzar and I negotiated together until it was clear that Media would have everything I wished for – peace and security, untouched in her wildness. It didn't take long. "Include also," I thought of Spaco, that Median shepherd slave and other women I knew who could not seem to have a child. "By way of clarification, that the treaty requires no offspring." I had no idea how things would go for Mandane. "And," I tried to ignore Nebuchadnezzar's wheezing – he was an old man, after all, "will continue in perpetuity after either party's death." Nebuchadnezzar nodded and waved the scribe to get it all down. At the end, according to protocol, the priests called on some gods as witnesses – Marduk among them. And a list of blessings and curses for keeping or breaking the treaty were said and written down.

Then, Nebuchadnezzar cleared his throat, "Bring out the goat."

"He is the one for tomorrow, sir," one of the priests said.

"Perfect," Nebuchadnezzar said.

"Yes," the priest replied. No one moved.

"Well, bring him out then."

The priests jumped to it. They led the goat, trotting out, a rope around its neck. Then, while one priest held the animal still, the other slit its neck. I caught my breath, as surprised as the animal. It all happened so quickly. Its knees buckled in death. Just as swiftly, the other priest stepped forward, withdrew a long sword from his side, and cut the goat lengthwise in half. "To cut the covenant," Nebuchadnezzar said. It took a while, sawing along the length of the animal's backbone. I swallowed hard and nodded. These Babylonians have the strangest customs, I thought. Were they always at the expense of some disinterested party? They left the goat's head in one piece but pulled the two parts, still steaming, away from each other.

Nebuchadnezzar nodded to me to walk forward, between the carcass halves. I stepped carefully. The fresh blood was slippery beneath my sandals. Nebuchadnezzar walked beside me as if he were merely walking his limestone pavers on an average day.

"Thus and so," one of the priests intoned, "shall be done to any one who breaks this treaty." I tried not to look at the goat, its tiny perfect hooves, the curly beard and already glassy eyes. I can't get out of this country fast enough, I thought.

Finally, we were through.

"Now," Nebuchadnezzar said, "nothing short of infidelity to the gods – acting with godlike presumption, or usurping the throne – yes, either throne – can break this treaty."

I nodded acceptance.

The process, so formal, legal and religious, seemed to rinse Nebuchadnezzar's mood of bitterness. "Scribes will compose a permanent version fired in clay," he said. "And our wedding, immediately after the Akitu concludes, will finalize it."

My stomach, already compromised, flip-flopped with new nerves. "About that," I said.

Just then, outside, something startled the bull to kick up its hind legs and plow around the paddock until blowing its nostrils wide, it threw out its forelegs and slid to a stop. My horse whinnied with strength and fury at the animal's display.

Nebuchadnezzar coughed and smiled. "A bull from Babylon and a horse from Media. So the gods favor."

"Listen," I said. "Sir. I'm sorry for any confusion. But while I am indeed a daughter of the king, it's my sister who's actually the princess." Even the animals seemed to freeze.

Nebuchadnezzar stared at me.

In the silence, I said, "I'll leave tomorrow and send her to you straightaway."

The king turned to his men. "The treaty says 'a daughter,' correct?"

The scribe looked down at the draft. He nodded.

A thin, dour looking man said, "Any daughter satisfies the treaty."

"But," I said, a frantic desperation creeping into my voice, "my mother –"

"Does maternity matter?" Nebuchadnezzar asked the dour lawyer.

"No. It does not."

"Sir. My sister, she's been preparing – " I steadied my voice. "Mandane is to be your wife."

"Well, get her then," Nebuchadnezzar said.

I was so relieved that I nearly threw my arms around the king. Instead, I kissed my horse on the nose -- I thought the dour man would faint on the spot. "Tomorrow," I whispered.

Filled with joy – the treaty done! – I flew out of the stables, through the kennels, and back into courtyard, hall, courtyard, hall, stairs, finally reaching Mandane's quarters, breathless with excitement and sheer amazement at what I'd accomplished.

Kara had left an oil lamp burning. But she was fast asleep, slumped on a chair.

"Kara," I whispered, "I did it!"

CHAPTER 8

I couldn't sleep, so I gathered together what things I would take on the journey home. There wasn't much. I found my trousers in a box that had carried Mandane's things, now unpacked. I made a bundle of clothes, wrapping the dirty shoulder pelt around my old blouse and fastening everything together with the thick leather belt I'd worn. I added Mandane's jackal fur coat to my things. Here in Babylonia it was hard to imagine being cold again, but I knew that Media had only begun wrestling free of winter's grip. I determined to secure food in the morning and a decent sword, too. Damn Igliss for insisting I remove mine back in Ecbatana.

I found myself wishing I might see Khai one last time, just to say goodbye. Then I put that out of my mind. I could hardly wait to see Mandane again, to explain all that had happened, and finally see her off, here to Babylon, while I remained forever in Media.

I don't remember falling asleep. But I dreamed of Media, riding my horse bareback in wide circles around a smiling Mandane dressed in bridal finery. Speed snatched happy laughter from my mouth as the horse devoured miles under flashing hooves. Then Mandane disappeared, the horse too, and I was turning in circles, trying to find them, trying to catch my breath. I woke tangled, nearly bound, in Mandane's fine bedclothes. The spring sun was already high, already hot.

At the sound of a eunuch's voice at the door, I hurried to get dressed. I pulled on my trousers and a Babylonian under-tunic that might come in handy as an extra layer up north. The over-tunic that I'd worn yesterday lay crumpled on a bench. I dropped that over my head, too. That's when I saw the linen note that Kara had given to me slide to the floor. I'd forgotten all about it. I tucked the fabric under my under-tunic, against my skin, and pushed through the curtain into the public rooms. Kara was there and Rdiya, too.

In Kara's arms was the puppy from the kennels.

"This –" Rdiya said, her face red with contained fury.

I reached for the pup. Rdiya couldn't get it away from her fast enough. I held the puppy for a sweet moment. "You'll stay with Kara," I whispered, "and be a good companion to Mandane. Protect her. You hear me?" He nibbled the tip of my nose.

Another knock on the door startled all of us. Rdiya rushed to open it.

My heart skipped. Mandane, I thought. In the doorway was a girl, about my age, her long hair held neatly by gold clips dangling with tiny yellow stones, a gold circlet around her brow. She smiled shyly, every bit an image of Mandane, standing with that sweetly eager, apologetic pose my sister took when she would ask me to go into the hills with her, knowing full well our visit to the remote birthing-room of some desperate woman would be trouble for me. Again. I went without hesitation every time. I swallowed the lump in my throat.

Even more striking, the sight of this young woman trans-formed Rdiya from a no-nonsense, humorless administrator into a soft and doting nurse. I could hardly believe it. Rdiya pulled the girl in, kissed her on both cheeks. Then smiling so widely I thought her face would break, Rdiya led the girl to us.

"This is Kassiya," Rdiya said, patting the girl's cheek, "the king's daughter."

The girl oohed with delight at the puppy while Rdiya smiled on.

"Rdiya was my nurse growing up," Kassiya said. "She told me you'd arrived." She stroked the pup's head and said in a soft voice, "I heard about what you did." Apparently, news travels fast in any palace. I wondered if she'd heard everything. "So," she continued brightly, "I thought I'd meet this new step-mother of mine." Nope, not everything.

"Actually –" I looked at Kara. I would miss my own nurse, but I was grateful that she would be here for Mandane. "I'm not –"

"Kassiya's mother is dead," Rdiya said.

Kara took the puppy from me and went into another room.

I said, "I'm so sorry." I looked through the doorway to my neat bundle, packed and ready.

"Don't be," Kassiya said. "No one in Babylon mourned her. It wasn't allowed." She sat down with a sigh.

Another of Babylonia's heartless traditions. I tried to figure out how to explain, with Rdiya here too, that I was not the princess and would be leaving as soon as I got a sword.

But Kassiya said, "It's my brother -"

"Ean, the crown prince," Rdiya said.

"-that led to our mother's death."

I gave up trying to correct my identity. They'd find out soon enough. After I'd gone. For now, I might as well learn more about what happened with the woman who'd born Babylonia's crown prince. I'd never heard that Kassiya's brother, the crown prince, had something to do with it.

"When my mother -"

Rdiya cut in. "She doesn't need to know everything."

Kassiya nodded. "Well, he lives in Uruk, where my mother is – was – from."

A eunuch summoned Rdiya to the door.

When she had gone, Kassiya bent forward to me. "There's nothing my father would like more than to get Ean to Babylon, especially now during the Akitu. But even after my mother interfered with the gods, even after she was killed trying to heal what she thought was –"

Ridya returned and stepped between us. "Igliss," she announced.

Kassiya froze. I hated the interruption. Kassiya's remarks – "trying to heal," did she say? – troubled me. "What did you mean –"

"I have to go," Kassiya said. "We'll talk after. I want to hear all about Media. It sounds so exotic, so thrilling!"

For the first time since I'd arrived, more than talking about Media, I wanted to know: what did it mean, "interfered with the gods," and "trying to heal"? All the gaps and unfinished snippets of Kassiya's remarks unsettled me. What did her brother have to do with their mother's death? Suspicion filled me with dread.

But Kassiya was gone, and Rdiya had already transformed back into the busy, bossy disdaining manager-of-the-queen's-household and was tugging at the clothes I'd just put on, clothes I intended to travel in. "No time for this," she muttered. "The ritual begins in minutes."

"But I'm not go–"

"Today's events will be over before you know it," she said. "Quickly. Nothing like the reading of the *Enuma Elish*."

"How quickly?" I asked. I let her pull off my outer tunic.

Rdiya held up my trousers. "You'll be back even before I can get rid of these," she said. I took them from her and shoved them back into the box. I needed to hear more from Kassiya. If today's whole religious Akitu business really did go quickly, I could still travel some miles with daylight... Ridya left my under-robe. The linen lay flat against my breast. So when she insisted I wear a fringed robe with clattering bracteates all down the sides and sandals stiff with precious stones, I let her drape me and shoved my feet into the sandals, too. I would not miss her.

A EUNUCH LED me through the palace, down new winding hallways and out a different gate than I'd seen yet. We crossed into an adjoining field. All Babylonia must be here, I thought. It was a huge crowd. The sun beat down on the flat plain, though it was barely mid-morning. Sweat pricked my temples where Rdiya had strung blue beads along a golden chain that wound around my head. No breeze lifted the heat. I looked around. No one else seemed to mind. Rather, the air fairly buzzed with excitement. The eunuch pulled me through the ever-closer crush of people. From all directions, people jostled and jockeyed forward. Finally, I could see. A huge pit was dug into the ground.

At its edge, "Ah, there," Nebuchadnezzar saw me and gestured the eunuch to bring me to him. On the king's other side, Igliss stood stiff, his eyes studiously avoiding me. From behind him, Kassiya smiled at me. In the rarified space around the king, there were a couple of men – priests, I figured from the layers of beaded necklaces and heavy symbols – star, spade... strung around their necks. I looked around for Khai but didn't see him anywhere. A scribe I didn't recognize – native Babylonian, judging from his swarthy looks and curled hair – held a tablet facing Nebuchadnezzar. Beside him was the scribe from yesterday, a foreigner, as Rdiya had made clear. The scrap of linen with its mysterious writing felt damp against my chest. I hoped it was still legible.

I stepped up next to the king. In the pit lay a pile of dry straw and over that, I caught my breath, the great timbers from Media.

"Why build with them," Nebuchadnezzar said, "when they can be put to this, even grander purpose?"

I thought about the stately trees that these had been these, cut and shorn as a gift from Media on the occasion of Mandane's marrying Nebuchadnezzar.

"Igliss's idea," Nebuchadnezzar said. He leaned on a gold-topped scepter. The courtier didn't meet my gaze. "It's a fitting recognition of the treaty we composed, to devote them like this to the gods, witnesses to the covenant our nations have cut."

I sent out my own silent thanks and apology to the gracious timbers and Media's gods who helped me get this far. The linen scratched against my skin, reminding me of the note I still needed someone to read.

Igliss whispered something to the king. Nebuchadnezzar turned and followed him around to the shorter end of the pit. I saw my opportunity and inched next to the foreign scribe. I leaned in close. "Read something for me?" I asked. He started, looked around, then back at me. "It's short," I said. Before he could refuse, I withdrew the cloth and pushed it into his hand. As I'd feared, the letters ran with my sweat. But their outlines remained.

He pushed it back. "You must leave it to the priests."

My stomach sank. "Why can't you tell me?" I slid the scrap back inside my tunic.

He glanced around again. "That's what it says."

Just then, one of the priests started up a deep, rolling melody. "Oh- oh- oh- oh," he sang.

The people quieted, but my mind clamored with the cryptic contents of this note written for Mandane.

Then things happened just as quickly as Rdiya had said they would. The crowd turned as one to look back toward the palace and parted. Between the ragged rows of people, walked the white bull, perfect, right down to the well groomed fetlocks above his hooves. A young man led him forward by a twisted, red rope. The great bull's lumbering steps shook the ground. A halter of thick red cord dangling multi-colored braids lay gold plated across the bull's forehead. His tail, too, swished with color and gold. Nebuchadnezzar and the priest began to sing in unison, "O bull, who burns in the heavens." But I didn't pay attention anymore. Because there, rearing and charging behind the bull, was Bepti. Four stable-boys could scarcely control him. My breath came quick and hard. Another red cord formed a halter and glinted with gold across his broad forehead. Multi-colored tassels swung from halter, mane and tail. His eyes rolled with fear and fury. Bull of Babylon, horse of Media, Nebuchadnezzar had said. They led the animals to the edge of the pit.

Someone, a priest I supposed, threw buckets of oil over the wood, and before I knew it the second priest pulled a fierce bronze sword across the bull's neck. Blood rushed out and ran down the edge of the pit. My horse screamed, piercing the crowd's roar. He reared up, punching his forelegs against the air and screamed again. The bull went down with a crash and fell, legs flailing, into the pit. Bepti saw me, then. My heart banged against my ribs. I held his eyes, big and white. Still snorting, he brought his legs down. Despite the king's singing and the crowd's roaring, I heard nothing except Bepti, hard breath heaving his nostrils and sides. His hide quivered. The priest, his sword still dripping with the bull's blood, turned to him. My throat seized with a scream. My horse's eyes rolled. He reared up again, higher as the priest parlayed his sword. It was a bad strike, cutting the horse across his chest and right foreleg.

I shouted, then, and rushed forward. Or tried. The foreign scribe had ahold of my arm. He pulled me back. "The gods," he said into my ear. "AGH!" The gods who witnessed the treaty we made, the gods who demanded what they would.... The priest readied his sword again. I saw it in slow motion, in my mind's eye – how the man would slash again and again and again because my horse would not be still. So, I raised my arms. From across the pit, my horse saw it. "Shush," I said, though he could not hear it. He blurred in my vision. "Shush." Slowly, I lowered my hands. He followed them to the ground, favoring the cut fore-leg. "Shush," from my cracking throat. His eyes on me, the horse stilled. The priest cut his jugular clean.

I closed my eyes.

Somehow I got back to Mandane's quarters. Kassiya was already there.

I staggered in.

"It was a great sacrifice," Kassiya said. There was sympathy in her voice. For that I was almost grateful. "The gods will surely smile on your marriage to my father."

I shook my head, but I couldn't form the words. Not me. And not this. What Kassiya saw as blessing, I saw as the Babylonian gods' ruthless demands. I felt so heavy. My arms, my legs, my head. The loss, the shock of it, slammed me hard as any tree in the river. And angry. So angry. Khai, whom I'd had the stupid inclination to trust... I'd even helped him - teaching him about horses. Then he led the king straight to Bepti. I burned inside.

Only in knowing that Media's security mattered most of all could I put the business with Bepti and Khai's betrayal of me aside and finally raise my face to this girl.

The linen scrap inside my tunic – that message meant for Mandane – burned like ice. "Leave it to the priests," the scribe had read.

I said only, "Tell me about your mother." Everything depended on this.

Kassiya asked Rdiya to get us some tea and honey cakes, too.

After Rdiya left, we sat side-by-side on the divan under the window. The sun, still high, shone in bright and bold as if nothing had happened, as if this were just another day. As if it were not the day I was going ride home on the horse I loved. Bepti, my rebel partner, who now was dead. Kara hovered while the puppy gamboled on the floor.

Kassiya took a deep breath. Despite my shock and grief, I focused on her words as if everything else I loved depended on what she would say. In truth, it did.

"My mother, our mother, was a temple slave from the south when she came, a long time ago, with Ishtar's barge to the Akitu. Nebuchadnezzar noticed her. They say she was very beautiful. When she returned home, she was pregnant. My grandfather wouldn't let Nebuchadnezzar marry her. He was supposed to marry –"

"A princess from Media." I tried to keep the impatience from my voice.

"Nebuchadnezzar loved my mother, I'm told. Sometime after my sister was born, Nebuchadnezzar became king and married my mother. After that, my brother Ean was born, legitimate, then me." Kassiya looked out the window. "But my mother and my older sister, too, hated Babylon. They were miserable. My mother wanted a purpose of her own. She had had purpose serving Ishtar in the goddess's Uruk temple. My father let them return there." She looked back at me. "But Ean stayed in Babylon, for certain. He was – is, the crown prince, after all. A few years ago, he started acting strange." Kassiya leaned forward. "He imagined he was other people – the legendary wild man Enkidu, even Dumuzi. My father tried everything – beating him, leaving him alone for weeks with nothing or no one to distract him... Still, it continued. My mother pleaded with Nebuchadnezzar. She said that Ean was ill. She -"

Rdiya returned. Kassiya sat back, quiet, while Rdiya set up our tea. I couldn't imagine drinking but bit my tongue. Finally, when we each held a minty cup, Kassiya continued. "My mother –" she glanced over at Rdiya, who sat straight-backed and tight-lipped.

"My mother said she was trying to heal him."

"Though he's not ill," Rdiya said again.

Kassiya laughed ruefully. "It's true. He's in great health. Strong. She brought him to Uruk, a sick house there." Kassiya looked again at Rdiya, who sat stone-faced. Kassiya seemed to weigh what to say and added simply, "Now, even as crown prince, he won't return to Babylon."

"Can't," Rdiya said.

"It's demons. That's what the test showed."

"The test?" I asked.

Kassiya sighed. "Babylonian doctor-magicians suspected that our mother was a witch, responsible for my brother's..." Kassiya looked at Rdiya. "She had presumed to do the work of doctor-priests." The words on the linen scrap seared my breast. "So they put her to the drinking ordeal."

In the doorway to the private suite, with the puppy tugging at her sandals, Kara paled.

"I don't know how much you know about such trials –"

I shook my head, a tight fist in my stomach.

Kassiya grimaced. "Well, she died. Which means she was guilty."

Kara stepped away, disappearing into the shadows beyond the doorway.

I didn't hear what else Kassiya said. I didn't need to hear more. I didn't know what happened with Ean. But it didn't matter. A woman presumed to act as healer, and for that, she was judged and killed. I wanted to destroy the warning note I held far, let it be trampled, evaporate, burn into bits, anything to make it irrelevant.

But I knew then what I hadn't wanted to see, what I wished more than anything not to accept.

"Leave it to the priests," the note read. Harpagus's, I was sure of it. But Mandane wouldn't. I was sure of that. She wouldn't leave healing to the priests. So, they would kill her. The treaty would be void, and Babylonia would move against Media with all its destructive and avaricious force. Mandane couldn't be the one to clinch the treaty. I knew with a sick despair that the only way I could save the thing I loved most was to lose it. The only way to preserve the only place I wanted more than anywhere else to be was to leave it for good.

I had to be the one to marry the king.

At some point, Kassiya said goodbye, and I guess Rdiya let her out. I dropped to my knees on the floor and let the puppy tug on my sleeves, tumble into my lap. I turned the options over and over but could find no other way. And oh, Mandane. Would Harpagus figure out what I had done, what had happened, and explain that to her? I felt sick. No one but me could really make her understand. And how little I wanted any of it!

By nighttime, I accepted that my only consolation was this: Nebuchadnezzar was an old man. Babylonia had its crown prince. As soon as the crown passed to Ean, I could return to Media, forever secure in the treaty I had forged.

I hadn't counted on Igliss.

PART II

CHAPTER 9

Once I had accepted that there really was no option for Media (and Mandane) except that I be the one to marry Nebuchadnezzar, I solicited help from a scribe to send notice back home. I only wished I could carry it there myself. I tried not to imagine how it would be received but I couldn't help picturing my father's anger, my sister's confusion, and Harpagus's relief. For surely it was he who had sent that note. I trusted he would explain to Mandane.

The puppy proved if not a comfort – that was impossible – then a distraction, though naming him had gotten me in trouble again. Rdiya and a eunuch were in my rooms when Kara asked what I would call him. My heart sank, one of the thousands of times it would break in the days after deciding that I must stay. I would name him something Babylonian, something right for this place and admission that I would be here... for as long as Nebuchadnezzar lived, anyway.

"Gula," I said.

"No!" Rdiya and the eunuch exclaimed in unison.

But "Gula is a dog, right? Babylonian?"

"Sacrilege," Rdiya turned her head as if spitting the word to the floor.

Kara rolled her eyes. "You'd better not."

"Gula is a god," Rdiya said.

"A god*dess*," the eunuch added, recovering his voice.

In my defense, Kara said, "She takes the shape of a dog, though."

"Gula-shuma-something, then," I said. "You have names like that, don't you?"

"Oh, for –" Rdiya said.

Kara said, "Gulash, for short."

"Gulash. I like that."

It seemed satisfactory to Rdiya and the eunuch, though nothing I did or said seemed to erase their general hostility toward me. At least my childhood had prepared me for this.

With few exceptions, like the misstep in naming the dog, the days following my devastating realization until the wedding itself are blur, a dark blot in my memory. Kassiya came regularly to Mandane's, now my, rooms. I remember that. Her softening effect on Rdiya helped to ease the trauma of those days. Plus, she was so like Mandane and genuinely interested in Media – not for its minerals and timber and access to trade routes but for how I experienced the land, its wildlife and horses, the weather. Snow was nearly impossible to explain. She asked question after question and exclaimed at my exploits. Or maybe it was simply that Kassiya could tell how talking about Media took me out of Babylon for a time, made me less miserable. And this unlikely daughter of Nebuchadnezzar was nothing if not kind. Gulash loved her.

WHEN THE NEWS GOT OUT, and it didn't take long, no one seemed the least bit surprised or concerned that I was not Mandane, the princess who had prepared her entire life to marry Nebuchadnezzar. They didn't care. Instead, I heard over and over, that of course - for certain, as they said in Babylon – I would stay, as if it were a foregone conclusion that only I hadn't seen. Nebuchadnezzar once already had made an unlikely woman his queen. And anyway, they already had a crown prince, born of a Babylonian, a crucial attribute for many native-born elites. Plus, if the treaty required simply "a daughter of the Median king," who were they to argue? But the most compelling reason to the high-born Babylonians around me seemed to be: who wouldn't want to trade a life in backwater Media, economically compromised by a weak and ineffectual king, for a place in the Babylonian royal court? They thought: so uncivilized, those wild lands to the north, so full of danger and dirty nature... any young woman would much prefer privileges of luxury and order, fine clothes and rooms and social sophisticates. With a royal title, no less? The king's primary wife?! "For certain," as they said in Babylon.

They didn't know me.

I couldn't explain how that wild land held my heart, how it meant everything to me, how it was the only home ever knew and the only one I ever wanted. I couldn't explain what privilege it was to live with wonder and awe at the natural beauty of a rugged place with beings I didn't control and who took little or no interest in me. Nor could I make them understand what skill and wisdom were required to live *with* rather than *against* a sometimes fierce and capricious natural world. I couldn't explain what a thrill it was to do so with joy. No one could understand why restraint in the face of great "resources," as Igliss called them, was more valuable than exploitation. They just thought it was stupid.

Besides, at the moment, people were far more preoccupied with the Akitu's grand culmination, the parade of gods, Nebuchadnezzar's great show of alliance with Marduk, and the gods' blessing Babylonia for another year than they cared about some bastard from Media.

I meant nothing.

Or so I'd thought, until we were seated mere days later at the wedding banquet.

THE DAY of the wedding felt no different than the others. In truth, I felt nothing at all. My shock and grief had morphed into numbness. Kara had talked about "the wedding night" as if I needed some special preparation, but even about that, I couldn't muster much concern. It was as though *I* was gone. I let Rdiya and Kara dress me, do whatever they needed to make me look like I should. I didn't care. When Rdiya left to find out when exactly to present me for the official ceremony, Kara slid open a vanity drawer, reached far to the back, and produced the handkerchief packet of my handmade hair clips. Something stirred in me then. Into the complicated up-do that Rdiya had fashioned of my hair (with much complaint, since my hair continually insisted on slipping loose), Kara tucked the partridge feather, camouflaged by the blond, beige, and brown of my hair. With that, the room and my whole situation snapped into focus.

I was here. And I would do this.

I understood from Kassiya's telling about her mother that I needed to live in Babylon to quell any suspicion that could compromise the treaty. But Nebuchadnezzar was older than my father, and Babylonia had its crown prince. So, not that I had any particular wish for Nebuchadnezzar to die – I didn't care one way or other about him – I began to hope with a fierce fervor that it wouldn't be long before I could return. That's what gave me the disposition to go through with things and the first blush of anxiety about how things would go when Nebuchadnezzar and I, newly wedded, were alone tonight. Thankfully, everything was so new to me, so unusual and happening fast that it was easy to put aside for the time being my worry about the night.

We gathered in a small chapel – half a dozen priests, about

that many courtiers including Igliss, and the elder I had over-heard with his son, a scribe, Kassiya, the king, and I, grateful to see not a hair of the hateful Khai. It was the shrine of Nabu, divine scribe and patron god of writers, Rdiya had said when she left me there. I sweated under layers of fine Babylonian weave. Inside, unglazed brick and bare stone, unusual among Babylon's buildings, tempered the harsh midday sun.

The ceremony was a formality. The gods were represented of course by priests who to my relief, read aloud the terms of treaty. I listened carefully. It was as we had worked out in the stables. Relief mixed with grief, as I remembered that moment with my horse's breath at my back – *that* I would take as a sweet blessing on the effort. The priests read from a clay tablet. Fired like pottery, it would outlast all of us and for centuries to come. I was grateful for that.

After the treaty was read and the requisite words recited, a priest with the jangling insignia of every Babylonian god hanging from a chain around his thick neck, settled a ring of gold on my head. And with it, a heavy relief. I sent out a quick thanks to this god of writing for the strange lines and dashes that would keep Media safe. Then, not that they could hear me at this distance, I set my mind on Anahita, Mazda, and Mithra. I willed that this be what they would want, that it would meet with their approval. And I willed that they not forget me here.

BACK IN THE PALACE, the banquet hall was packed, loud, and already soaked with beer by the time we arrived. I followed Nebuchadnezzar to a long table on the dais. An elderly woman indicated I should take the chair next to the king's in the center. Igliss sat on the king's other side, and Kassiya sat next to me. The others filled in, and the food arrived. There were pitchers of a sweet wine for our table, from which attendants poured liberally. A young man, "cupbearer to the king," Kassiya said approvingly, "from one of Babylonia's oldest and most prestigious families," poured only for Nebuchadnezzar. Before long, every inch of the table was covered with a platter, basket, or bowl of something – roasted meats, duck and geese in fragrant syrup, fish fried and flaky, wheels of bread, sweet fresh cheese, and fruits I'd never seen before. Kassiya put one of most everything on my plate. I didn't have the stomach for much.

My under tunic was tight at the chest, pushing my breasts in and up. I could hardly breathe, and the gold circlet atop Rdiya's fussy hair arrangement, slid with every turn of my head, reminding me that I was not entirely myself. I could feel sweat dampening the nicest clothes I'd ever worn. I pictured the partridge feather nestled in my hair and determined to make my own clothing decisions from here on out. As it was, I barely moved.

For his part, Nebuchadnezzar was hardly still. I had never seen anyone both seated and so constantly in motion. He wore a different kind of crown than I'd seen before – a crenellated ring of gold and silver and embedded with stones. It started at his brow and rose high above the top of his head. I couldn't imagine how much it weighed. But he swung his head as though it were nothing. He leaned back to issue orders to the head servers, as if they didn't already have everything in hand. To engineers at a nearby table, he called, "For all your formulas and equations... Ea and Marduk gave me the instructions. All you have do is carry them out. I want that tower done!" To an army general, sitting down the table to Nebuchadnezzar's left, he exclaimed, "Enjoy the food. You'll be back to Arvad with a thousand men on army rations next week."

"Adad-guppi," Nebuchadnezzar called. I recognized that name. Then to no one in particular, he said, "Where is that woman?" Nebuchadnezzar's breath caught in a wheeze. Finally, a reminder of his age.

"Here, my lord."

A small, wiry woman hurried up beside the king. She waited until Nebuchadnezzar had regained his breath. This was the woman who had seated me, and – I remembered where I'd heard the name – in that father and son argument I'd overheard. This was the woman who'd come from Harran – taken, but as an upper-class person of some kind of stature or position – and made a way in the court for her son and grandson after her.

"Where did you seat that Egibi boy?" Nebuchadnezzar asked.

"Among the other non-citizen men, sir. There to the back. Nabu-ahhe-iddin."

Nebuchadnezzar did not look, but my eyes followed the woman's finger to a table in the back populated by plain-dressed men. These I assumed, by location and dress, were Babylonians of a lower class – free, but unlike the noble "citizen" class obligated to pay taxes, do military service. No matter how old, they could never be elders. Rdiya had taught me more than I realized.

While most at the table gobbled off heaping plates, and swilled their beer with great gulps, a man – young, but no boy, judging from his shoulders; I couldn't see his face – at the table's end, sat relaxed. He had pushed his chair out at an angle turned away from us, stretched out long legs, and crossed his ankles loosely. His arm rested on the table. He nodded at a companion's comment and said something that made them all laugh. Then, perhaps feeling my eyes on him, he looked around. My face burned with a rush of anger. Khai. He grinned and lifted his cup to me in a subtle salute. How dare he, who sent my beloved horse to his execution, greet me now, here, with such nonchalance?!

Nebuchadnezzar said, "He'll serve as scribe tomorrow. Make sure he knows that."

"Yes, sir."

I gritted my teeth, and looked away, determined that if I couldn't throw him out of the hall, I'd put that Khai of some no-repute Egibi family out of my mind.

"And where's *your* boy?" Nebuchadnezzar asked.

Adad-guppi pulled her thin shoulders back. "Tending to the city's defenses, my lord."

"I know where your *son* is, woman. I meant your grandson, Belshazzar." Shazzi, his father had called him. "He wouldn't miss a banquet, and you'd be sure he had a good seat."

"For certain. Belshazzar is right over there. His friends wouldn't have it any other way." Adad-guppi pointed to a table only a short remove from the royal table. Young men and women, dressed in the latest fashion and dazzling with golden ornaments and jewels, laughed and smiled in lively conversation. Sure enough. There he was. Belshazzar's high, round cheeks were already flushed with the wine that had crossed his fleshy lips. He wore a necklace that I could see even from a distance hung with the spade of Marduk. Belshazzar looked over and bowed his head deeply to Nebuchadnezzar so deeply that the pendant clanked the table.

Nebuchadnezzar said, "All noblemen, I see."

"They're very fond of Belshazzar. He fits right in," Adad-guppi said and disappeared into the bustle of servers.

Kassiya broke my silence. She leaned over and said, "It's her son, Nabonidus, who's married to my bastard sister."

I nodded. "Nitocris… who lives in Uruk."

Kassiya smiled. "You remembered. Yes, Belshazzar is their son. He *loves* Babylon, nothing like his mother."

His mother, daughter of the woman Nebuchadnezzar took as his first queen… and killed for presuming the work of the gods. I shook my head. It was confusing. "And her?" I tried to nod discreetly toward the bustling servant.

"Adad-guppi, Nabonidus's mother." So I was right. "She's a force of her own," Kassiya went on, "a captive from Harran years ago. Nobility there, priestess or something. Indispensable to us now. She's very devoted. Nabonidus, too."

"No more devoted than I," said the voice on the king's other side. "And *I* am pure Babylonian."

Igliss. Kassiya cringed. He was dressed in the finest ensemble of under tunic and robe, exceeded only by Nebuchadnezzar, even I could see that. A broad strap hung with golden bracteates ran from his shoulder to his waist.

Recovering herself, Kassiya said, "Igliss is of the Nur-Sin family, one of Babylon's oldest and most venerable."

Despite Rdiya's effort to teach me, I couldn't keep the hierarchies of Babylonia straight, much less the esteemed families at the top. But I nodded as if I knew all about the Nur-Sins.

Igliss speared a bloody piece of meat. "We are well-acquainted, the Mede-ess and I."

I watched him transfer the flesh to his plate with a slap.

"Of course," I said.

Igliss flinched.

"Or as you say, 'for certain.'"

Igliss's eyes blazed at my blatant outsider reference.

"Ah, yes," Kassiya said, softening the air. "He headed the caravan to fetch you."

"Anything for my country and king," Igliss said, sawing at the meat.

"Igliss distinguished himself in a campaign to the west –"

"Jerusalem," Igliss chewed, "capital of Judah."

"—after which we were betrothed."

I choked on my wine. Kassiya and Igliss?!

Someone tapped Igliss on the shoulder. In the moment he turned away, Kassiya dared a grimace to me. Igliss wiped his mouth. "The king knows how important it is to ensure that Babylonia is in good hands."

Kassiya saw my bewilderment. "Igliss is to be Ean's regent... if my father should die before Ean... Before he is able to settle in Babylon."

My head spun. Igliss, as Nebuchadnezzar's son-in-law.

As regent, Igliss would, in effect, be king.

CHAPTER 10

So Igliss, this Babylonian courtier, who'd disparaged Media and elicited only suspicion in me was to be Kassiya's husband. Not only that, but the king entrusted the whole empire to him should Nebuchadnezzar die before the crown prince was ready to assume control. I reminded myself that with what I'd done, the treaty protecting Media would remain even after Nebuchadnezzar died. And as soon as he did, I'd be on my way back to Media. Nevertheless, the news troubled me.

Igliss said, "But such unhappy thoughts – our beloved king's passing – we shouldn't entertain on such a day!" The smile on Igliss's lips and narrow eyes belied his words. Igliss looked very happy.

Nebuchadnezzar stopped me from saying something I'd regret.

"So you decided to stay, after all," he said. "I knew you would."

How little he really knew – how near I had been to returning to Media, how much more suited Mandane was to this role, … except for that one, fatal thing.

Nebuchadnezzar tilted his head, appraising me. I clenched my teeth. I may be his wife, now, but I most certainly wasn't his.

But what the king said was, "That crown becomes you, girl. It's fashioned to represent a crenellated wall... not that emeralds, sapphires, and other such exist on that scale of course. I would have them if they did. Hah! But it's the city. You've got the city on your head!" He laughed. "And such a skinny neck!"

So, I guess my crown was a smaller version of his. I hadn't noticed.

His laughter turned to coughing. He reached for his wine. Then, "How do you find the city, our city?" He swallowed again, serious now, and I realized that this time he actually expected an answer. He repeated the question, louder this time. He waited, and the room grew quiet.

"Well," I said. "Sir." The sound of my voice echoed through the stone-paved room, tile walls reflecting my words as clearly as their vibrant colors shone out. I cleared my throat.

He waved me on, his face severe.

I shoved aside a rush of thoughts and feelings – the claustro-phobia of all this building, nothing but walls and streets and ceil-ings, the river so slow and brown and tame, the cruel demands of distant gods – my horse!... I caught the steady gaze of Khai at the back. Calm, clear. I looked away. It was hard enough just to be here. But I had to say something right, something that would put me a strong footing, maybe dispel the hostility that I sometimes felt bristled around me. I recalled the enormous tower in Marduk's temple's central courtyard, workmen bustling all around, shouting to each other even as the priests and people went about their religious activities, workmen so high they were tiny specks against the sky. "You've certainly given people some-thing to look at."

Wrong. I knew it as soon as the words left my mouth. For a moment, the air itself stopped. Wisps of steam seemed to freeze, hovering over the dishes from which they came. Nebuchad-nezzar stared at me. Wrong.

So, when I spoke again, it was if the voice belonged to someone else entirely. I couldn't believe that I was going to keep talking. "I mean to say, sir, that you've given remarkable elevation to a really flat place." With that, Nebuchadnezzar pushed back his chair. For an instant, I thought, that's it. He's going to demand Mandane, after all. At least I'd be dead when Babylonia conquered Media.

But he whacked his palms on the table and laughed.

The room erupted. Dishes jumped under slapping hands as people guffawed and pointed.

My face was so hot it felt tight. My eyes swung to the far table. Khai grinned. His chest expanded in a chuckle. But in contrast to the others, it seemed that his laughter was meant to be with, not *at* me. It was without malice, even conspiratorial. It loosened the knot in my stomach. I tore my eyes away and noticed that some people, despite laughing to match the king, did not appear amused. Belshazzar... was that hatred in his eyes? I glanced down the table. Igliss, too, glared at me...

Nebuchadnezzar wiped his eyes. "All that elevation, as you put it," he regained his voice, "takes a lot of people and a lot of skill." He pulled his chair close again, bit the last meat off a lamb shank. "I use the best – materials, men – no matter what." He waved the bone down the table. "Igliss and I differ on that."

Igliss, suddenly solicitous, bent forward and dipped his head toward the king.

"I employ the best men for any job, no matter where they come from." Nebuchadnezzar turned back to me. "It's a waste to ignore excellence. When we've conquered a country, I take the skilled people, the best, back here. Igliss would rather I leave them all."

"Or kill them," Igliss said. His tone was nonchalant, but my skin pricked.

"Yet on this we agree," Nebuchadnezzar said, "Everything always and only is for the betterment of Babylonia, Gate of the Gods."

Igliss raised his cup. "Babylonia first. The gods' gift to the world!"

I shivered, grateful yet again for having forged a strong treaty that would protect Media forever.

"Good man," Nebuchadnezzar said, and drank.

Igliss leaned forward, his eyes grabbing mine like an owl its prey. He narrowed them to slits. To my right, Kassiya stiffened. Igliss said, "Your father tells me that you fancy yourself a bit of a healer."

My heart quickened. "Not me."

"No," Igliss said, his voice low. "It was you. Definitely you."

"Well, here in Babylonia," I made sure my voice carried with clarity, "*great* Babylonia, it is the gods who prescribe treatment by the very best physician-priests." It pained me to say but cost nothing more than pride.

Nebuchadnezzar nodded. "As the gods wish and do."

Igliss may have hoped to rattle me, but instead he simply confirmed that in this, no matter what other missteps I may take and social blunders I would still commit, I'd made the right decision. I gulped my wine.

Igliss would have had Mandane's life within a month and Media's precious wilderness in the next.

Nebuchadnezzar shouted over his shoulder, "Music!"

Adad-guppi materialized behind Nebuchadnezzar again. "My lord," she said. "Your court musician..." She whispered something into his ear.

"Drunk?"

"We don't think so, sir."

"So?" Nebuchadnezzar said. "Who?"

"Overseers tell me that they're often amused by the songs of the Jews."

"Well, get some Jews, then," Nebuchadnezzar said.

Kassiya caught her breath. She dropped her eyes, but not before they set on Igliss. His jaw clenched and unclenched in silent fury. Unsure what that was about, I said, "So, when will you and Igliss marry?"

"Any time, now." Kassiya attempted an encouraging smile. "Igliss thinks the sooner the better." He turned away.

"And you?"

Kassiya's voice was so low I could barely hear. "It doesn't matter what I think."

"I'm asking."

In the hubbub, "I don't like him," Kassiya said so quietly that I wondered if I'd heard correctly.

"Me neither," I whispered back.

Nebuchadnezzar pushed his chair back and stood, shaking off an attendant's helping hand, and stepped down to confer with the noblemen. Igliss followed him, and they disappeared into the crowd, now milling about.

"Well," Kassiya said, serious again. "I'm glad you're here, no matter what others say."

"Oh?" I tried to sound nonchalant. "And what do others say?"

"You know."

I shook my head.

"That the greatness of Babylonia..." She shrunk her shoulders as if wishing she'd never said anything at all. I nodded encouragement for to her to go on. "That Babylonia is being overrun and diluted by foreigners."

"Ah, yes." I sat back. "And I'm Median."

Kassiya exhaled in relief that I understood. "And now you're the queen."

Kassiya didn't hear my groan. I was supposed to be on the road to Media, not here, dealing with court politics and Babylonian prejudice.

I looked out at the sea of revelers. Adad-guppi directed the musicians, what looked like a family of four – a woman and man, boy and girl – onto a dais against the far wall. They wore the plain, undyed linen of Babylonia's poor.

Nebuchadnezzar and Igliss resumed their seats while the musicians took the small stage with quiet grace.

From Belshazzar's table someone called, "Sing us one of the songs of Zion." Laughter rippled out from his companions. But Igliss slammed a meaty rib back onto his plate. "Foreign music," he hissed, "on the royal stage, no less." He snapped a cloth and made a show of looking away. I had meaning, all right. And it wasn't good.

I willed my eyes back to the musicians. Both the woman and girl had lined their eyes with dark black kohl. When the musicians looked up, unsmiling, toward the royal table, I felt as if the night sky had opened to pull me in.

That realization would have been enough to preoccupy me for the rest of the evening were it not for the music. The family began with a piece unaccompanied by instruments but knit with a tune that the youngsters hummed in harmony with their parents' singing. Guests, indifferent, went back to their talk and drink. But I was transfixed. I couldn't understand the words – not of that song, nor of the songs that followed. But the meaning was clear. The Jews sang of home. They sang of a place that transcended geography yet could be known intimately. They sang in strains that lifted and dipped, in rhythms simple and slow. They sang of loss. And they sang of love. My throat ached. For these were my songs, too, these songs of longing, of exile and home.

Too soon, their part ended, and the family stepped down.

I swiped a sleeve over my eyes and sipped my wine to steady my throat. Another set of performers took the stage – comic dancers, I think they were. By then, I was drunk. A first.

At some point, Rdiya materialized from somewhere and passed me off to Adad-guppi, who would establish Nebuchadnezzar's new wife in his bedroom. When the king arrived soon after, I felt frustratingly out of sorts. I could make neither my mind nor my body collect itself. This was why I never drank in Media, despite all those hours throwing dice with the stable-hands, swapping tales with off-duty guards, or even when I snuck off to celebrate holidays with the field and shepherd slaves. I had needed to be ready. Always I had kept something in me taut and watchful, prepared should anything threaten Mandane. Now, I wasn't ready. My head swam, and my limbs were loose. I wasn't ready. So, I tried to be Mandane.

Some time later, I woke, naked and tangled in sweaty linens, a strange room spinning around me. My head ached with a deep pulsing pain and my mouth felt like it had been swabbed of every drop of moisture. Then I remembered... some. I looked across the bed; but I was alone. I inched up to sitting. Streaks of blood under my legs momentarily shocked me into forgetting my aching head. It was no real surprise, of course.

I knew I'd have to sleep with Nebuchadnezzar this one night. I hoped it would be the last. In this, Igliss and I had a common goal: neither of us wanted me to get pregnant. The treaty didn't depend on it, and Igliss would hardly want a half-Median prince. My guess was that neither did Rdiya.

She bustled in, two eunuchs in tow. I pulled a sheet up over waist, but they kept their eyes on the floor. Rdiya shoved a jar of minted water into my hands. For the first time, Babylon's water tasted almost as sweet as the mountain water from home.

I downed the contents then examined the jar. Its top and shoulders were decorated in red and black with winged lions, rosettes, and tiers of geometric patterns. Two goats, one under each handle, stood in a standoff with the sphinxes that graced its sides.

"Soldiers drank the wine when they took the Phoenician palace," Rdiya said, taking it from me, "but the king insisted they keep the jar. It'll go into the museum rooms soon." She set it down and shook a lavender tunic at me. "You might as well get up," she said. "The king is on his building rounds. He won't be back anytime soon."

I slid the tunic over my head and stood. Too quickly. I sat back. Rdiya shoved my feet into sandals, then began to yank at my hair. The partridge feather, I thought. I pulled away, my head pounding worse than before. Rdiya stepped back, no feather in her hands. "Leave me," I said. To my surprise, they did. Gingerly, I ran my fingers through my hair. It was loose and tangled in places, still up in others. I let it all down. Still, I couldn't find the feather clasp. I searched the bedding and on the floor around. Nothing. It had to be here somewhere. Sure enough, from a table across the room, the glint of its bronze clasp caught morning light. I walked over. The feather curled up gently next to the crown I'd worn. I clipped the clasp above my ear and examined the crown. Its shape was as the king had said, like a crenellated wall. He certainly loved his buildings.

"Most unusual," Nebuchadnezzar said, striding into the room. He stopped in front of me and plucked at the feather clasp. "Median, I suppose." He grabbed my waist between his knob-knuckled hands, surprisingly strong. I resisted pulling away. "You know, I've seen your country," he said, "your mountains." He ran his hands over my breasts. I couldn't help flinching, but other-wise I stayed still. "Not so very large." He chuckled. I did not. I held his eyes until he dropped his hands.

He sat on the bed, wheezing again, then grinned. "You've given elevation to an otherwise flat place..." He laughed, remem-bering my stupid comment from the night before. I turned my head so he couldn't see me roll my eyes. At a knock, Nebuchad-nezzar opened the door. There stood Igliss, a girl on either arm. "I thought you might-" Judging from his expression, Igliss didn't like seeing me there any more than I him. The women dipped their heads and smiled coyly at the king. But Nebuchadnezzar shut the door on them and pulled me to the bed. I went as much to spite Igliss as anything. I had seen animals and wasn't surprised to find this to be pretty much as expected. I stared at the flimsy cloth draped overhead.

After, as Nebuchadnezzar buckled his belt over a sleeveless robe, he said, "You know that when it's done, my tower..." He slid a golden band up nearly to his shoulder. "... The great temple to Marduk will reach to the heavens. Its very top will be the blue of sky." He clipped a heavy rosette band around his wrist. "It should have been covered in lapis lazuli from trade through Media..." He looked at me, then, sitting up in the bed, fixed me with glinty eyes. "But we have the finest tile glazing artisans in the world."

I had meant to say something complimentary about the tower, something about how glazed tiles at the top will surely be even better, more like the sky, than lapis lazuli, or at least how no one could know the difference from the ground. But what came out of my mouth was, "The mountains are white on top."

Nebuchadnezzar stopped in his dressing, his feet bare.

"There's nothing like them here," I said.

I wasn't surprised when Nebuchadnezzar slapped the table. My crown there jumped. I figured I was next and braced myself. But instead, he said, "We should build them here!" Nebuchadnezzar grinned at me. "Your mountains. Of course you miss them. So," he rubbed his palms together eagerly, "we'll just build them here!"

Before I could protest, he was out the door.

DESPITE MY HOPING OTHERWISE and the women that Igliss and Rdiya made sure were presented to the king for his pleasure, I occupied the king's bed during those first weeks more nights than not and some days, too. Every morning, a doctor priest would apply the pessary test. "It might take some time," he explained, as if I was eager to become pregnant. I didn't say anything. Meanwhile, Nebuchadnezzar talked with me of nothing except how to make Media's mountains in Babylon.

Mostly it was about the engineering – Nebuchadnezzar relished every aspect of the challenge, raising and irrigating such an undertaking.

Once again, Nebuchadnezzar diverted workers from the tower of Marduk's temple to a new project. This one required a team of hydrological engineers, architects, and landscape designers. They identified a section of the city abutting the palace northwest, a wide strip of land next to the Euphrates, to build up in earthen tiers, irrigate from the canal, and plant with all manner of things. Trees, shrubs, flowers, and vines would tumble down in layers. Scholars assured the king that beautiful insects and birds would find their way to the place in short order and populate it with all manner of wildlife. Small animals could be introduced and tended as necessary. Word soon traveled that it was all for his wife, Amytis.

I told Kara that Nebuchadnezzar even asked me about the plants – shrubs and trees, groundcover, and even the fungi that we have in Media. I relished recounting them.

"There are too many powerful people who already hate you for being Median," Kara said. "Don't rub their faces in it."

"The king has said it's to mimic the northern mountains, meadows, and orchards," Amytis said. "I'm going to take advantage of it. Anyway, it'll never look like Media, for certain."

"That's my point," Kara said. "Let them fill it with their own things."

"No."

"Well, *you're* not going to be collecting the plants that will go into the garden."

Which got me thinking.

"How do you know?" I said to Kara's burn-scarred face.

"WE'LL   NEED   SEVERAL   WELL-STOCKED   CARAVANS..." Nebuchadnezzar tapped his ringed fingers on a heavy table in his administrative suite. I ignored Igliss's quivering fury. "Dozens of men with heavy tools, oxen to pull the specimens – with native dirt, I suppose..." Nebuchadnezzar thought aloud. He sat and rubbed his knees.

"Sir..." Igliss, unable to contain himself, blurted, "All this expense to make Babylon..." his voice rose, "... what... more *Median*?!" ending in a nasally squeal.

I was glad I'd chosen to wear my crown. I hadn't since the wedding banquet. Neither had I let Rdiya make up my hair in the Babylonian style since then. Until now. But I had never been present at the king's administrative deliberations, either. Kara said they would be sensitive. She was right.

"No, no," Nebuchadnezzar laughed, which turned into a cough that he silenced with a sip of water. "With this feat, we'll show how even in this, Babylon excels all other nations."

"Yet," Igliss said, leveling his voice, "We're soon leaving on campaign, important military endeavors. I'm sure you haven't forgotten. We'll need those men, the carts..."

"Nonsense," Nebuchadnezzar said. "I would have thought you more knowledgeable than that. Nabonidus," Nebuchadnezzar gestured to the older man who'd been standing straight and quiet at the other end of the table. "Explain."

Nabonidus rattled off numbers – of soldiers and slaves, of carts, of weapons, of tools...

"In other words," the king said, "we have more than enough to undertake both expeditions – both the martial and landscape engineering. And they can travel part-way together."

Judging from Igliss's expression, that hardly satisfied him. I didn't care. My goal was different. I saw a chance I'd never expected to get back to Media and explain everything, if not to Mandane, then to someone who could.

I cleared my throat. "You'll need someone knowledgeable about the Media's flora and fauna," I said, "for certain. Sir." I weighed whether or not to say more, to explain that of course they should include me, if not ask me to direct the Median expedition. But the king was savvy, and as he'd said and I'd seen – not afraid to use foreigners for what they knew or did best. Nebuchadnezzar nodded thoughtfully. My heart rose even as Igliss's glare sought to kick me clear to the Great Sea.

"Yes, to lead the Median tour..." Nebuchadnezzar leaned back. He wagged his index finger in the air. "I've got just the man."

My heart dropped. From the corner of my eye, I saw Nabonidus nod once. Right, I thought. His son. Obviously, Belshazzar was no soldier, so he wouldn't be going with the military. But from what I'd seen, I doubted he could lead a group in anything other than drinking. Still, I kept my mouth shut. If I asked the king to include me in the expedition, he'd say no. And that would be hard to overcome. So I said nothing. I'd learned long ago that for some things, it's best not to ask permission.

CHAPTER 11

*A*s it was, the king determined that the Median expedition, just a dozen or so people, should set out together with him and the Babylonian army. After all, their military campaign was also to the north (I can't remember exactly where – Babylonia was constantly exerting or re-exerting its might over others). But where the army would angle west, the Median expedition – its people tasked with gathering specimens for Nebuchadnezzar's great gardens project – would go east. The groups would part company north of Dur, the Median expedition following the Tigris north from there; the Babylonians keeping to the Euphrates. That complicated my plan to slip in among the Median expedition and only after we were well on our way, to excuse my presence as something the king approved. I'd simply have to adapt.

On the morning of departure, I dismissed Rdiya. I fastened the partridge hair clasp among the Babylonian gold and filigreed ornaments, then asked Kara to find my trousers. She shook her head but retrieved them from the travel chest. They were worn, even torn in places, I now noticed, but as wearable as ever.

Gulash had grown rapidly. With his big muzzle, he scoured every inch of the foreign clothes. I bent and took his head in my hands. "You'll have to stay here this time," I said, stroking the brow above his yellow eyes. "But one day, you'll come to Media with me, and oh the fun we'll have there." He swiped my face once with his broad tongue, then sat, fully ready to wait for as long as it took.

I stood. To Kara I said, "I'll be found out soon enough. I just want to get out of the city first. I'll figure out what to do after that." Normally, I could read Kara's disfigured face perfectly. But at that moment, even I couldn't tell what she thought. "It's not like their gods have forbidden me to go," I said. "So, the treaty will be fine." I took one of Kara's plain, hooded robes off its hook. "I just want to get to Media, explain for myself to Mandane... "

"You don't have to tell me," Kara said.

I shrugged. I pulled the robe on over my clothes, despite the heat. "Hold Rdiya off for as long as you can."

PEOPLE AND HORSES and oxen and carts of various shapes and sizes milled around the open courtyard. My heart raced with excitement and worry, too; but no one looked at me. It surprised me to see many women among the hundreds of men setting out. Then again, there are chores for an army on the move – from cooking and cleaning to tending wounds and other tasks at camp – that everyone believes women do best. It did make my presence even less conspicuous, which was good. I kept my head down and covered and said nothing. After a while and some sharp-barked commands, order emerged within the melee. I watched the women climb into carts. I did the same.

I found a spot wedged between sacks of something lumpy – onions, from the size and shape of them. Most of the food and supplies that took up much of the space in the open ox cart would be gone – used up – by the time it reached Media to make room for what trees and shrubs we could safely transport back to Babylon. I didn't particularly like the idea of digging things up from the hills, valleys, and mountainsides of home; but I could select with care and do my best to see that they survived the trip. Then, if they could adjust to such a different climate, they'd spread and proliferate back here.

I let images of Media occupy my imagination as the cart made its slow way through the dust of others. We'd assembled in a courtyard outside the city gates, so it wasn't long before the landscape opened up, flat and wide. I breathed through my sleeve and settled in for the ride. A few hours later, my back ached and the smell of onions had started to turn my stomach. Other riders had jumped out of the cart and back in, walking a while, relieving themselves off the side of the road. But I hadn't felt confident that I'd get far without recognition if I risked it. I shoved my hands against a sack, only to feel it fall back in on itself. Some new object pressed against my right kidney. I shifted my knees, hoping to ease my back. Then, we stopped.

I ducked my head deeper, willing myself to be invisible. Everyone else in the cart had left. I heard the clink and clatter of amphorae opening, the happy chatter of hungry people fed. "What, nothing for you?" I heard a woman's voice behind me. Then, someone pulled the hood back from my head. "Wait, aren't you –?" I turned.

"Hey!" the woman called, excitedly gesturing a friend over. "Isn't this the king's wife?" They gaped at me.

"Yes," I said and stood. I vaulted over the side. By then, the women had already drawn a crowd. I had to wait only another minute or two for Nebuchadnezzar. He didn't say anything, merely looked at me there. I straightened my aching back the best I could.

Igliss pushed his way forward, swaying into place beside the king. "What is she –?"

Before Nebuchadnezzar could say anything, I said, "In thinking about this great undertaking and how I might help in its success, I considered about how difficult it can be..." I chose my words quickly but carefully, hoping to sound formal enough to be taken seriously, "... when faced with a multiplicity of unfamiliar plants to identify what might grow best in Babylon and how to remove and transport specimens in such a way that they might be transplanted and thrive." I laid it on. "Not that Belshazzar isn't an intelligent and capable –"

"Belshazzar?"

"Leading the expedition," I said.

Nebuchadnezzar laughed. "No. Belshazzar has found much occupation in Babylon. He convinced his father he'd be of better use there. I didn't disagree. He wouldn't be any help here, though 'use' there may be overstating it."

Igliss stamped a foot. "Aren't you going to demand that she return?"

Nebuchadnezzar looked at him, then back at me, considering. Finally, he shrugged. "Who better to determine what to get and how? She can go if she wants."

My heart lifted like a bird from the brush. Someone called out for the king, and they were gone, disappearing back into the mass of people milling around eating and drinking, checking harnesses and rearranging cargo.

I was thrilled – to wander around the hillsides, taking in wild Media again. I'd already worked out exactly how I could explain things to Mandane.

"You'll be needing a carriage, I suppose," one of the women said. "And attendants," said her companion, elbowing the first woman in the ribs. I shook my head. "A horse would be nice, though."

I walked away. I didn't have to go far to see, over the heads of people, the gray mare who had come to Babylon with me. I pushed my way through to her. She was even more beautiful than I remembered and groomed so that her coat shone. Her mane flowed in perfect waves. Loosely tethered to a cart, she nibbled absently at the tough grasses that grew along the river. I stroked her neck and untied the rope. With a few turns, I'd fashioned a workable harness from it with enough length to serve as reins. Perfect. I seized a hunk of her mane and swung a leg over. I ignored the stares and whispered mutterings.

From the horse's back, I could see the hundreds, maybe a thousand people spread out around and behind me. A cloud of dust stirred all around. The horse shifted under me. It was possible from this vantage to make out a vague order – soldiers composing most all the men, carriages outfitted for battle, and carts of munitions – bows and arrows heaped high in one, another full of swords and another of shields to resupply men in battle. The thickest group of people stood around wagons distributing food. Other riders stayed mostly on the outskirts with what could only be cavalry – even in this heat wearing the leather vests of armor and slung with pikes and swords and shields. I urged the mare forward. It felt good to be on a horse again.

"We could at least get you a saddle."

A man rode up beside me. I felt my cheeks grow hot. "After what you did to my Median stallion...?!" Then it occurred to me: Khai was riding. This, his ease around horses now, too, only made the betrayal worse. "How dare you?!" I hissed. The mare fancy-stepped beneath me, the stomp of her feet a welcome counterpoint to my anger.

Khai's face was as open as ever, wounded. He opened his mouth to speak.

"No." I said. He pinched his lips together. "You had my horse, my Bepti –" I hated how my voice cracked, "cruelly killed. You showed them what a perfect horse he was." The mare, unnerved by the energy in my voice, stepped high. I held her in place.

"Never, *never* speak to me again." I didn't wait for him to try. I wheeled the mare away. We galloped to the periphery of the camp, where I eased her to a canter, a trot, a walk. I swiped at my eyes until they were dry, then rode back into the camp.

I didn't see Khai again. Not until I returned the mare to her gentle tether. When Nebuchadnezzar assigned a docile gelding to me, fully appointed with saddle and bridle, I didn't think it prudent to argue. Somehow, Khai was there. He appeared in time to take the mare's rope harness. But he didn't say a word and was quickly gone, the mare ambling beside him.

Now that I was heading to Media, and with the king's support, the pace of our caravan felt impossibly slow. In truth, it was faster than my trip south had been. When we stopped for the night, you could still see the Babylon's enormous city walls but barely. If we kept to this pace, we'd break away from the army tomorrow.

Nebuchadnezzar called me to his tent that night. I didn't care. I was on my way to Media. After this, I wouldn't see him for more than a month, maybe two. But in the morning, as I drew the light tunic over my head, a doctor-priest was escorted into the tent. Nebuchadnezzar went out. The man withdrew a swab from the packet at his side and motioned for me to sit back again. Even here they'd arranged to check me for a change of status. I huffed but did as expected.

"Oh!" he exclaimed. He straightened, smiling broadly, and held the swab for me to see. I groaned. It was green. I was pregnant. I sat up, my head in my hands.

When Nebuchadnezzar reentered, he told me to return to Babylon immediately.

"But women in Media ride long into their pregnancies," I said. True, but only of the small number of women who helped in the breeding, care, and keeping of the horses. "Or, I could ride in a carriage." I tried to find what reasoning would convince Nebuchadnezzar that I should continue north with the caravan.

"You need me for this. You said so yourself." But everything I said met with a "No." I considered slipping away again, hiding or following at a distance until it was better to keep me than to send me back.

"A carriage, yes," Nebuchadnezzar said. "But a team of guards with a doctor-priest will accompany you back to Babylon."

Ugh. I stood. So that was it. Back to Babylon to become heavier and heavier with a child I didn't want and that would make Igliss and Rdiya and all the other Babylonians hostile to foreigners hate me even more. "But the plants, who – ?" I tried once more.

"The Egibi will know what to do."

Another blow. So Khai was leading the Median expedition.

WHEN I THOUGHT it couldn't get any hotter, it did.

Kara promised that I'd feel more at home in Babylon with a baby on the way, but it was just the opposite. I couldn't stop thinking about Media. I missed everything about it. "Remember the wind there?" I asked Kara. "In an instant, fresh, cool. Here, the smell – ." I vomited into a pan. Kara handed me a damp towel, as usual. I, who was rarely if ever sick, could hardly stand this nausea, predictable as it was. I wiped my mouth and sat back. Gulash whined and nuzzled my hand. "And the heat. It's like the gods tossed an old, boiled rug on top of us."

Kara crossed her arms.

"The air here actually has *weight*. And all around? Flat." I fiddled with a scroll of Babylonian poetry that a tutor had left with me, trying to learn to read. "Static. Nothing changes." I threw out an arm, "The gods declare!" and let it drop again. "Brown, brown, brown. And flat, flat, flat. A big old river, and that's it. And it seems like everything here is made of mud." Kara gave me a look of rebuke but wisely kept her mouth shut. "I know," I said. "Nebuchadnezzar imported cedar and oak." I pointed to the doors of my room - a beautifully carved wood. "There's lapis lazuli, gold overlay tiles, and the palace, the city... I know. They're astonishing, wonderful. It's just that there's nothing wild. And no mountains."

I paced with heavy, awkward steps. "I wonder when they'll be back – the expedition."

Kara harrumphed. She'd heard me wonder that aloud too many times already. As much as I hated Khai and wished never to see him again, I couldn't help wishing he'd hurry up. I yearned to see plants from home and to hear whatever news there was. How I wished I could have explained myself to Mandane!

THE WEEKS PASSED, as they do, and to my surprise, the temperatures finally and truly cooled – a simple relief in my large and lumbering state.

In that time of waiting, my activities severely curtailed, the army returned – victorious of course. Igliss and Kassiya married and moved to a mansion on Babylon's most prestigious canal. Although I rarely saw Kassiya anymore, Igliss was still regularly at the palace, regularly at Nebuchadnezzar's side. He was there when I answered a summons from the king. I tried to ignore the courtier beside Nebuchadnezzar, but his displeasure was palpable.

"It'll be magnificent!" Nebuchadnezzar exclaimed. "Mountains right here – in Babylon! They'll be a kind of garden." As the king's excitement built, so did Igliss's anger, I could see. "Lush mountains just like Media." Nebuchadnezzar looked at me, expecting affirmation, I supposed..

"Any word?" I asked.

Nebuchadnezzar scowled.

"From the expedition," I said. "When we might expect them...?"

Nebuchadnezzar's face cleared with understanding. "No." He

turned back to the plans. "Here, look." He made space for me to stand and look at drawings laid out across the long table.

I tilted my head this way and that. "I'm not sure I see mountains, exactly," I said. Thankfully, Nebuchadnezzar wasn't listening. Of course, I thought. He'd brought me simply to have an audience who could fully appreciate the audacity of his project.

"...Covered with plants," the king went on, "but not flat like the farms. Elevated. The plants on tiers to a great height will appear almost to... hang!"

Igliss's already light face paled yet more, and the knuckles in his clenched hands turned white. "And the Akitu?" Igliss's voice shivered with strain.

Nebuchadnezzar looked up. "What of it?"

"At a time when we'll need considerable work preparing for Babylonia's greatest national ritual, Sir, the annual convention of gods, you would do this thing... for Media?!"

"We have months before the Akitu. Besides, this is for Babylonia," Nebuchadnezzar said. He stood back, admiring the drawings. "Who else but me could ever accomplish such a thing?" He bent over the plans again. "Here, here, and here, engineers will manufacture a pumping system. The tiers will go..." He continued, oblivious to Igliss's simmering fury and my silence.

I shifted on my feet. My back hurt.

When Nebuchadnezzar finally looked up again, he seemed surprised to see me still standing there. "You may leave," he said.

In my rooms again, "It has nothing to do with me, nothing to do with Media," I said to Kara. "He doesn't care about me or the mountains. If this spectacle – this hanging gardens – endures, people will no doubt say that he built them for me. But to presume that this *structure* is anything like Media's mountains, or that a man so obsessed with erecting ever higher or more complicated structures does so for anything other than his own pride, his hubris, is just wrong. Still, if he wants to identify the gardens as mimicking Media somehow," Gulash nudged my hands, so I absently scratched behind his ears, "I'll have more reason to tell this child I carry about home and how it's so very different from here. Who knows, we may be able to return to Media before my son or daughter even knows the difference." Gulash laid down, his head on my feet and whined. "You'll come, too. I promise."

CHAPTER 12

When the structure that Nebuchadnezzar had planned was done, I went to take a look. It was impressive, that much was true, representing countless hours of work and a cost impossible to calculate. As for mimicking beautiful, wild Media, nothing could have been further from the truth. High, yes, but nowhere near a mountain's height. Instead of craggy cliffs and jumbled boulders, the stone they'd imported was stacked into orderly walls. The paths they'd laid were anxiously straight. I couldn't see how the plants, whenever Khai returned with them, would change that.

With the discomfort of a pregnancy I hadn't wanted and construction of gardens I never asked for, I missed Kassiya's bright and gentle company. Besides, spending time with her took the edge off my anxiety about Mandane, what my sister must think of what I'd done... But my invitations had been met with Igliss's explanation that she was far too busy managing her own household, or feeling unwell, "we hope for productive reason." I didn't think much of it at the time.

And then Khai returned from Media.

It was Nebuchadnezzar who told me. Summoned to his quarters, I waited until the king had finished discussing details about renovating the quays, or something like that. The baby kicked in my belly, a liveliness I felt with mixed emotions. One more tether to Babylon.

"There you are," Nebuchadnezzar said and waved me in, as if I hadn't been standing, back aching for who knows how long. "I want you to meet the caravan – the group from Media." I forgot my back. Instead, a sudden desire to make this baby – my child – know and love Media as fiercely as I ignited warm in my chest. One day, she – or he – and I would return.

"Scouts say the Egibi will ride in soon," Nebuchadnezzar said. "Tell him where things should go."

Khai. Riding. The old fury at his betrayal displaced my excitement to hear about home. I tried keep the anger from my voice. "I didn't think someone of his class would ride a horse."

"They say he wouldn't let anyone else." Nebuchadnezzar looked at me then. "It's not just any horse." He gestured to a eunuch to bring a chair. I sat. "True. Unusual for someone of his position, to ride. But, ever since the Akitu sacrifice…" Nebuchadnezzar paused and shook his head. "Nearly lost his life over that stallion, arguing with me. Me!" I frowned. Hadn't Khai led Nebuchadnezzar to Bepti? "To deny the gods their right to such a perfect specimen and in such an auspicious moment…." I opened my mouth, but Nebuchadnezzar wasn't done. "He did convince me to breed the steed first."

"But didn't Khai didn't suggest you sacrifice Bep – I mean, that horse?"

Nebuchadnezzar laughed. "If by caring about that beast drew attention to its magnificence…" My mind spun. So Khai had been trying to protect Bepti? "They tell me he won't let anyone else handle the mare. You know, she's carrying that stallion's foal."

I stood. The horse I'd chosen to ride, that beautiful gray mare… My head swam. I felt the eunuch catch my elbow. He helped me toward the door until I felt steady enough again.

. . .

I watched from atop the city walls, working out what and how to speak, as the caravan snaked its way across the plain. Finally, I could just make out Khai, at the front. He rode the gray mare as if she were a part of himself. I remained rooted by the scene until they'd passed through the gate, out of view. I watched him gesture to the caravan behind, dismount, and lead the horse toward the stables. I hurried down, as fast as my belly would allow. I'd been so eager for news of Media, for news of Mandane; but clearing up this misunderstanding, my accusations, felt especially urgent. Thankfully, I didn't have to wait long.

Khai reappeared. His cheeks were ruddy from the mountain weather. It would be cold again there already.

"What are you doing?" Rdiya materialized next to me. "You should be back in your rooms."

"Not now." I walked past her.

When he saw me, Khai simply nodded a greeting, then let an engineer and construction foreman lead him through an arch into the acres of planned garden. I walked after them, leaving Rdiya behind.

Khai stepped aside to make room for me next to him. The men pointed out the irrigation system, braces and retaining walls, tiered to the top. Khai asked them to start bringing the specimens in.

"I'm sorry," I said.

He looked at me. Then turned to call out directions to a palace engineer.

"I didn't realize," I said.

Khai turned to me again, dipped his head to excuse himself, and walked off.

"Don't you want to know?" I called after him. He stopped. "Say something?" I asked. I could hear the pleading in my voice. "Please?"

Khai walked back to me. "Are you giving me permission to speak?"

"Of course I am," I nearly shouted with exasperation. "Though you're making me angry all over again."

But he didn't talk about the horse, didn't explain himself, didn't say anything about my apology. Instead, with the same easy manner I'd seen him have with everything, he swung his out arm to take in the gardens' layout, and grinned. "Not exactly Median mountains, are they?"

It was a kind of relief. It felt like acceptance.

Khai let his eyes trace the paths, the bouldered walls. He shook his head and looked back at me. "It's beautiful land, your home. And all those birds. So many different kinds, and calls." There was wonder in his voice and delight. "We saw animals of all sorts." Serious again, he said, "I understand why you'd miss it."

"I don't," I said, though why – except to be contrary – I couldn't say.

Khai just shook his head and laughed. "Well, I would. And I told your sister you didn't want to be here. I didn't think it was a lie."

Mandane! "How is she?" Finally, the news I'd been so hungry for, for so long, and without any of the anger I'd harbored for its messenger.

"Soon to be married herself," Khai said. "Some prince over in Parsa."

My heart sank. How will I see her or ever explain? Parsa is at least as far from Media's capital as from Babylon. Nearer Susa, if my geography was correct. Beyond that, I didn't know much.

As if reading my thoughts, "Not much of a place, Parsa," Khai said. He looked at me through long, dark lashes. "Anyone would say you got the better part."

I searched his eyes, fathomless as always. "And what would you say?"

Khai shrugged. "That it's up to you to determine."

A laborer arrived carrying one of Media's shrubs – cornelian cherry and already covered in tiny red berries, I recognized with a pang of homesickness. He asked where it should go. Khai looked at me. I pointed to a spot along one of the lower tiers.

"And remember," Khai called after the man, "keep the roots moist until you plant."

"Will you stay?" I asked, "to manage the gardens?"

Khai looked at me for a long time, as if counting the different colors in my eyes. Finally, "That's not a job for me," he said. With that, he turned his attention to the different plants.

I stood beside him and told what I could about each. "Mandane knows them better," I said, "for their human uses, anyway." But still I found I could talk longer than the time we had.

Never once did Khai comment on my size or condition as everyone else seemed these days to do. What he did say, after we'd finished walking the area, was, "Your mare is expecting, just as I'd hoped. Should drop the foal within a couple of weeks, if my calculations are correct." He smiled. "She's as strong and feisty as ever. Obviously Median."

With that, I felt we might be friends.

WALKING BACK TO MY QUARTERS, I noticed for the first time the way that the palace ceilings integrated with sturdy elegance broad beams of multicolored wood -- the reddish cedar from Lebanon, pale golden pine, and the warm brown of cypress. I looked at the heavy doors as I passed, likewise fashioned of the most beautiful wood of the empire -- cedar, violet-tinged Magan-wood from points east, and the sissoo ebony that shone dark as the shadows they cast. I slowed my steps and ran my hand across intricate designs of inlaid silver, gold, and ivory. Some doors had floral, some geometric patterns. Yet others were covered in beaten gold.

As I crossed the threshold into my quarters, I stopped and

looked up. The lapis lazuli that coated the ceiling made me feel that I could reach the sky. I walked across to the window, tossing my robe onto the soft leather divan as she passed. Nebuchadnezzar's private rooms on the corner of the northern palace gave him a view to the harbinger north as well as to the west. Mine looked simply west, out over the quay walls to the broad Euphrates, then orchards and fields beyond. I put my elbows on the cedar lintel. How many times had I compared that broad, slow river unfavorably to Media's clear and quick streams as an old cow to a sleek stag? Now I saw that it held its own kind of beauty -- serenity and strength.

IN THE DAYS remaining before my baby was born, and there were only a few, my body took over all my thoughts and feelings. Then it was time. If the contractions hadn't hurt so much, their coming would have been a relief – finally an end to this condition. I'd attended so many births with Mandane – problematic and diffi-cult births, some fatal to mother and/or child despite Mandane's ministrations – that my own pain, excruciating as it was, was manageable for its ordinariness. My labor began in the evening and was over while the sky was still dark with night. "A good omen," the doctor-priest said.

Kara had said that a baby would ground me and "soften my sharp edges." But the child himself, my healthy boy, made me feel not soft but fierce. "I would kill anyone who tried to hurt him," I said, as soon as he slipped from my body and I held my perfect, tiny son. True though it was, I just wish I hadn't said it out loud. Rdiya had listened with interest. To take someone's life like that would put at risk, even negate, the treaty protecting Media. I knew that she wouldn't do anything herself – too obvious. But.

I looked back at the tiny wrinkled red face in my arms. "I cannot imagine," I wondered aloud to Kara standing near, "how any mother – my own mother – could abandon her infant child."

Kara's lips pursed against her fire-scarred face as she turned to busy herself with the linens.

"A prince," Kara said when she returned.

"Unfortunately." I could hardly wait for the moment when the Babylonian Ean would assume the throne. Then, with the treaty protecting Media still firmly in place, I could take my son back home to Media.

I KEPT my mouth shut when Rdiya told me that I was not allowed to nurse. "That's how it's done."

Kara urged a shy young woman forward. "A Jewess," she said, "by the name of Rachel."

Temple magicians came before dawn to take the newborn to the city wall as was customary -- to recite the birth-prayer to the midwife goddess Ninmah, cast away any evil, and introduce the baby to the stars. "What god could think a baby is born with evil?" I said. Gulash growled his agreement. "Go with them," I said to Gulash. To my surprise, he did, his golden eyes fixed on the tiny bundle that was my son. And when they returned, Gulash heaved himself, satisfied, beside me again.

"Don't worry," Rachel stooped to pet the dog. "I'd never hand him over."

"What do you mean?" I clutched the baby tighter. Gulash, looking at the Jewess, tilted his head.

Flustered, the girl said, "Sometimes people want to hold a baby... like that man, the king's adviser maybe?... he asked to see the boy."

Igliss? Blood pounded in my head. "Never take the baby from these rooms without me."

"For certain." Rachel's face clouded briefly, troubled by some-thing. But she kept quiet. Gulash went to the girl and looked back at me.

. . .

FOR THE FIRST week or so, when my baby cried for food, my body ached. But I let Rachel take him, as long as she stayed near. She carried him to a seat under the window, and while he ate, she murmured to him a song. The sense and strain was like the music I'd heard at the wedding banquet. I leaned against the doorway and closed my eyes. Rachel's low voice poured notes like cool water over dry land. I swiped at my eyes.

Rachel tucked the baby's blankets tight around his sleeping form and handed him back to me. Then she gathered the small satchel of her belongings. "I'll return before he's hungry again, my lady," she said and walked toward the door.

"Where do you go?" I asked.

"Excuse me, my lady?"

"Where do you go when you leave?"

"Just out, if it please you."

"Yes, but where?"

Rachel ran her hands down the sides of her apron. "Usually I go back to see my own baby, even if only for a little while." She quickly added, "I don't feed her, though, of course. My sister-in-law has an infant four months older than mine. She feeds them both."

"And where is that?"

"Across town, my lady, in the neighborhood of my people."

"'Jewtown.' I've heard of it." I paused. "And do you tell your baby about home – Judah, right?"

The girl started, surprised, then nodded. "Jerusalem." She hesitated, glanced at Gulash standing patiently beside me. Then as if I had passed some test, she said, "My sister tells me I shouldn't, that the baby should know only Babylonia. It's easier that way. Besides, our god lost to Marduk. That's how it works, she says."

"But you?"

"There's a man, Ezekiel, a priest. He came with the first group of exiles. He says the ark – where our god could be – was empty when the Babylonians took it. And –" Her voice hushed with awe, or embarrassment, it was difficult to tell. "He's seen Yahweh here – the chariot of God, anyway." When I didn't say anything, her voice gained confidence. "Yahweh wasn't defeated, the priest-prophet-man says, but planned the whole thing. To teach us all a lesson." Rachel looked at me as if waiting for protest. I stayed quiet. "One day, Ezekiel says, the temple will be rebuilt. The holiness of God will return, and Jerusalem will shine again." There was a new defiance to Rachel's tone. I was hardly going to argue.

I said simply, "So many gods. Who can keep track?"

When Rachel had gone and I was alone except for Kara in another room, I whispered into the baby's tiny ear stories of my childhood, of Media. Unspoiled and wild, that land was all I'd ever needed of the gods.

"IT IS the king's prerogative to name the child." Rdiya looked askance at me. I had been talking to Kara about it, trying out some fairly common Median names, since he would live most of his life back there.

"Well," I said, "get me an audience with him, then." Rdiya huffed but did so.

I took our son to the king's rooms. I waited in the doorway. "Amytis, my lord," the guard announced. I saw with relief that Igliss was, uncharacteristically, absent. The steward Nabonidus stood over a large papyrus on the table. Nebuchadnezzar looked up and gestured me forward.

I shifted the baby from one arm to the other. "I'd like to name him after my grandfather, Cyaxares," I said, "who forged the agreement with your father that brought us here together."

Nebuchadnezzar looked at Nabonidus who remained silent, then back at me. "He's a prince of Babylon and will have a Babylonian name."

"But –" I bit back my words. I could hardly explain that I assumed Nebuchadnezzar would naturally die before much longer, that I could hardly wait to leave the Babylon of his pride and joy for the backwoods of Media, and that this boy – prince though he may be – would grow up and definitely grow old in his mother's land.

Nebuchadnezzar said, "A Marduk name, for certain."

The god of Babylon city and high god of all Babylonia. Anything but that, I thought. "But there are so many gods." I saw Nabonidus shift, glance at me. "Surely another?" I tried not to look at Nabonidus, remembering his passionate defense of another god – which one?... and how angry that had made his Babylonian devotee son, Belshazzar. His own name, Neb- I said, "Nabu. After all, we cut a treaty in writing. How about the god of scribes?" I asked.

"Fine." He turned to Nabonidus. "Now where were we?"

After ten days, Nebuchadnezzar officially named our son. Nabu-shuma-ukin. "A nice, modern Babylonian name," Rdiya said, "after Nabu, the great god of writing."

"For certain," I said, passing the hungry baby to Rachel. Rdiya didn't needn't to know that it was I who suggested it.

From her nursing stool, Rachel smiled. Since coming to us, she'd relaxed, talked a lot more. Their elders, she had told me – Jews highly educated in Judah, usually within the temple system – put a lot of store in writing, too, especially those who were determined to claim the authority of their invisible god, despite defeat. They recorded ancient traditions and spelled out practices that people could observe at home without a temple, changed some of the old stories in light of their defeat, and added more in the face of Jews assimilating to cosmopolitan Babylon.

Nabu, indeed. I called the boy "Bushu" for short. It stuck. I spent all the time I could with him, and Gulash never left my side. As I predicted, many of the Babylonians I met would rather he hadn't been born at all. How happy they'll be, I thought, and I too, when I take him back to Media, leaving Babylonia to Babylonian royalty.

Bushu was only a couple months old when the New Year festival rolled around. I felt sick remembering the sacrifice of my horse. Add to that the fact that I was still in Babylon, a full year after my arrival. Upper-class women were expected to retreat for weeks after giving birth, so no one asked when I begged off the festivities.

The talk rather was whether or not crown prince Ean would finally attend. The king had invited a Susian princess, Irdabama, to Babylon in hopes of betrothing them. "Turns out," Kara said to me, returning breathless from the kitchens, "Among other strange behaviors that no one will tell me about, he has refused to marry." Yet again, Ean wouldn't leave Uruk. And he wouldn't have anything to do with the Susian royal woman.

That was their problem, not mine. I only had to wait for Nebuchadnezzar to die.

CHAPTER 13

*D*espite Nebuchadnezzar's age and occasional frailties, time continued to pass for us in Babylon. After Bushu was born, the king rarely called for me again. Igliss kept him preoccupied with other women. Fine by me, the better to spend my time with Bushu and teach him everything I could about my home, our home far to the north.

I wanted above all for my son to be Median, to return with me there, and to love that land with the same fierce devotion as mine. I kept my Median clothing and hairstyle, to Rdiya's chagrin. The treaty didn't depend on my fitting in. And what with all the foreigners who lived and worked in Babylon, diverse peoples with diverse customs and dress, my clothing and hairstyle choices didn't seem to attract much attention. Admittedly most of the other foreigners were exiles – conquered peoples forced to relocate. Among those who weren't exiles, most were immigrants escaping worse conditions at home.

To Babylonians who cared, such as Igliss and Rdiya, suspicious or hostile toward foreigners, nothing I as a Median woman did could be good enough, anyway. It wouldn't have made a difference. I couldn't escape my foreignness. And I didn't want to.

I walked the city walls each evening, Gulash at my side.

I carried Bushu until he took his own steps. Then, the going was slow but sweet. "There," I'd point, "Far to the north is your home and mine." We walked to the quay to watch boats come and go and visited shrines of the gods and goddesses. Like me, Bushu's favorites were in the oldest part of the city, mainly because it took us over the long, broad bridge. We spent many days in the gardens, so he'd heard me talk all about the mountains. He'd even tasted cornelian cherries and wrinkled his nose at the bitter tang of juniper. Over time, most of the plants died and were replaced by Babylonian varieties. Those that hung on were a shadow of their Median selves. I tried to explain. But like everything else, he'd have to wait until we got to Media to see for himself to finally understand.

I'd been out with Bushu when the grey mare had her foal. Khai was present, I'd heard, in the stables as usual. He wiped the newborn down – a long legged filly – himself. I rushed to see the baby horse. She was grey like her mother, grey like Bepti was as a colt. I wanted to tell Khai, wonder with him, if she'd turn white like the stallion did. But he was already gone. And though I heard he tended the filly as carefully as he had her mother, and I visited the stable with Bushu as often as we could, I never saw Khai there. I hated to admit how I missed him. Then, some time after the filly was weaned, I heard that Khai had left the palace altogether – a surprise to abandon a position both hard-won and coveted – and for a commoner to do, no less. I found myself avoiding the stables after that. I felt locked out of something.

BUT TIME PASSED, and the weeks turned into years. Then, one day, while I was in my private rooms, fastening my sandals to walk the canals, Kara took a message at the door. She hurried to me. "Go. Right away. The king's administrative rooms. Rdiya is already there and others, too." I pulled on a fringed robe and told

Kara quickly to put my hair up in the Babylonian style as she talked. She said that Nebuchadnezzar was bent over in a coughing fit that wouldn't end. "He can hardly catch a breath. They can't even move him to his private rooms. People are worried that this might kill him." I'm still ashamed at excitement that leapt in my chest. Kara settled my crown over the golden clasps. I put Bushu's four-year-old hand in hers, told Gulash to stay, and ran out.

By the time I arrived, everything was back to normal. Doctor-priests passed me on their way out as the door guards announced my arrival. Nebuchadnezzar, his face a little flushed but other-wise fine, gestured for me to enter. Igliss was there, of course, and Nabonidus. Rdiya looked long and hard at my head and robe and left without a word.

"There's been a revolt in Judah," Nebuchadnezzar said, as if that explained it or as if the coughing fit had never happened at all. He tapped his finger on a map laid out across the table in front of him. "They killed Gedaliah, the governor we installed." He shifted a gold piece on the map. "We're sending troops."

Igliss rubbed one fist into the other palm. "We'll squash them like the vermin they are."

The courtier Nabonidus cleared his throat. "These things have a way of spreading."

"It already has, to Nippur at least." Nebuchadnezzar tapped another spot on the map. He leaned back. "I thought they liked him, Gedaliah." He sipped from the cup in front him and swiped his mouth. "Jerusalem's a ruin. They're only making it worse." Then, he looked at me as if startled to see me still there. "Why are you here? What do you want?"

Flustered, I said only, "I'd heard... Well, no reason. Nothing, sir."

Nebuchadnezzar moved another gold piece. "Foot soldiers here and here should be sufficient, don't you think, Nabonidus?"

I felt Igliss's eyes on my back as I left.

. . .

OUT IN THE bustling hall again, I stooped to catch my breath. What was that he said?: Why are you here, and what do you want? I knew what Nebuchadnezzar had been asking. But still... Those questions stayed with me as I worked my way down the broad hallway.

I had just turned the last corner before leaving the administrative wing when commotion – voices, the sound of a fierce scuffle got my attention. Up ahead, I could see the well-dressed backs of three youths, shoving and worrying at something they'd cornered.

"You couldn't do anything, even if you did have her!"

One danced back, and I caught a glimpse of their prey. A leathery old guard, sword swinging from its scabbard at his side, dodged a kick to his crotch. He stood, knees bent, arms forward, slapping away their advances.

"Her kind need taking down!" another youth cried as he lunged forward.

The guard pushed him back, but the third swung out with a punch that landed in the guard's belly. Gasping, the guard bent over. Blood dripped from his nose. Yet his sword remained sheathed. Behind him cowered a girl – Rachel. I ran forward. The first youth grabbed at Rachel, but the guard, already up, stopped his hand and flung it back.

"Give her up, worm-lover!"

One of the youths kicked the guard behind his knees while another caught his face with a smack. Rachel screamed, torn from the man's protection. The young man laughed an ugly humor.

"Leave off!" I said, finally reaching them. "Release her. Now!"

I could feel cold hatred in the young man's stare, sizing me up. Inwardly, I dared him to lunge, wanted him to come at me so that I could take him down and with no little pain to his high born ass. I knew exactly where the guard's sword hung, and *I'd* use it. My fingers itched. But the youth took in my robe, the crown... and dropped Rachel's arm. She darted back behind the guard. The youths straightened their clothes. As I watched them swagger off, jostling and jesting each other, I could have sworn I heard one say, "just another worm..."

I exhaled and turned back. Rachel, trembling, clutched her dress closed tight around her. The guard straightened slowly. I could tell it cost him. "Why didn't you draw your sword?" I asked.

"On citizens? It'd be the last time."

"What does it mean, 'worm-lover'?"

The man grimaced. He pushed his nose back with a crunch and a groan. "Foreigners. 'Eating us from the inside out,' they say. Like parasites."

"You don't agree?"

"People from other places? They're no different from us." He gingerly dabbed at the blood under his nose. "Oh, I'm Babylonian alright."

"But not citizen-class."

"We're all just trying to live. It's worse in other places – whole towns..."

I thought of what I'd just heard – a Jewish uprising, Babylonian troops probably already on their way... And I had an idea. "What's your name?"

"Shalam, ma'am."

"Come with me. You, too, Rachel."

At the door to Nebuchadnezzar's room, I stopped. "Wait here."

I raised a hand to my hair, so nicely arranged by Kara only a little while earlier. I unhinged a golden clip and worked free a lock. I let it fall, a single wave, to my shoulder. The guards shifted on their feet. "Open it," I said.

Igliss was still there. He scowled to see me in the doorway. I lifted my chin and waited. Finally, Nebuchadnezzar looked up. He raised an eyebrow and gestured me forward.

"What does Media want now?"

"For Babylonia," I said. "I understand that an uprising in Judah is causing trouble here, too. Nippur, did you say?"

"I am inclined simply to let the violence run its course."

"It's only right," Igliss said pointedly, "for citizens – true Babylonians, to remind these dirty exiles who's in charge."

I ignored Igliss, though I'd heard every word, and looked steadily at the king. "Wouldn't that undercut the work you've done, sir?" I heard Igliss inhale, prepared to interrupt. But Nebuchadnezzar raised his hand and nodded for me to continue. "People do best when they have some security," I said, "a place they belong. Your Babylonia benefits, as you've said, from the skills and expertise of many different people."

"I've ordered up troops to quiet things down."

"Any means necessary," Igliss said.

I closed my eyes, trying not to imagine the cruel punishments Igliss intended.

"We're deploying them to outlying areas – Igliss's suggestion. Nabonidus and Belshazzar are already on their way to Nippur. Troops can catch up before they arrive."

Igliss scoffed. "Who'd think a bunch of scholars –"

"Nippur is a scribal center," Nebuchadnezzar explained. "Lots of Jews. Some time ago, Belshazzar volunteered to fetch a palace scribe from there, someone who can handle dialects for the Lands Beyond the River." I remembered the argument I'd heard when I first arrived. "It's a good idea," the king said, "and now's the time. Troops will restore order, and we'll get a scribe, too." This was my chance.

"Let me go," I said.

"To Nippur?" Nebuchadnezzar said.

Igliss snorted.

I could feel the stray lock of hair against my cheek and neck. "I'm not from Babylonia," I said. "Everyone knows it." Both men were listening closely now. "My presence in Nippur would demonstrate," I glanced at Igliss, "that foreigners can have a respectable place in Babylonia, too." Igliss's face was like stone. I tried not to let his disdain get under my skin. "I'll take Bushu's nurse with me." I pointed to Rachel through the doorway. "She's Jewish."

"Nabonidus and Belshazzar are already on their way."

"Then they can see to our safety. *Without* the troops. And I have another, one who can drive us." I pointed at Shalam, standing next to Rachel.

"That's a prestigious position," Igliss said, his voice snapping back with its customary edge.

"He's the best," I said. "And..." I swallowed hard. "I'll take Bushu, too, our son, Nabu-shuma-ukin."

"No," Nebuchadnezzar said. "It's too dangerous."

Igliss's eyes narrowed.

"That's the point," I said. "By going unarmed, we show that we are all together – foreigner and native – here, in this one empire, Babylonia." Nebuchadnezzar's leaned forward. I knew he wanted to use the foreigners he'd taken to Babylonia to their best purposes, and insurrection hardly suited that. But he was right. It was dangerous. So I wasn't surprised when Igliss's demeanor changed.

"Ah, yes." A grin played at Igliss's thin lips. "The boy prince, himself Median... It's a good idea. But surely, you won't take the dog."

CHAPTER 14

I didn't take the dog. Gulash was so big, and protective, too, that I feared he might be seen as a threat, even a weapon, just when we needed to show alliance. I tried not to imagine all the ways this could go wrong but dug instead into the confidence I'd had in Media, keeping Mandane safe in all sorts of circumstances. Still, those were dangers of the wild. This was different – from people. I hoped that these people in Nippur could see that we were not so different, the Jews and I, Bushu too – foreigners seeking dignity and respect in a land not home.

I found myself wishing for Khai's steady presence, remembering how, now years ago, he'd been assigned to "keep the dowry safe," on that fateful journey from Media to Babylon. I remembered the assistant priest's hungry eyes while I was subjected to that humiliating massage ritual and how Khai had suddenly appeared when the man approached, and nothing ever came of it again. I remembered being left alone on that journey for so much of the time and wondered now how much of that was Khai's doing, in how many other moments he might quietly have deflected danger – not from the land, that I could handle, but from people. And I remembered with a pang of regret my anger and misunderstanding – how Khai had tried to protect Bepti and failing in that ensured the stallion's lineage endured. I wished I could tell him: the young mare, Bepti's daughter, was now white.

I pushed thoughts of Khai away and my worries to the side and got ready to go.

The distance between Babylon and Nippur was too far to travel in one day but easily accomplished in two, so I figured that if we didn't catch Nabonidus and Belshazzar right away, it didn't matter. We'd meet up wherever they camped. Nebuchadnezzar said that after several miles across the desert, they'd follow the Chebar canal, which goes directly to Nippur, about thirty-five miles southeast.

Kara looked anxiously after us when our carriage drove away.

I was surprised when we pulled up alongside the men, only a few miles down the canal. I explained our presence in the briefest way. Belshazzar slumped over his horse. "I would have thought you'd be a bit farther by now," I said.

"He's not feeling well," Nabonidus said.

Belshazzar was morose but hardly looked ill. "I can feel sweat between my shoulders blades," Belshazzar whined. "I'm dripping."

"Drink some water," I said.

"I have."

Nabonidus rested a hand on his horse's mane. "When is the last time you traveled in anything but a litter, Shazzi?"

"Haven't we gone far enough?" Belshazzar ran his arm across his forehead.

I took in his flushed face, his soft hands and fine clothes. And I looked at his father – his skin leathery and tough, at ease. A rush of pity, or was it sadness, disappointment maybe, blew across Nabonidus's face like wind through river grass.

I hopped out of the carriage. "Ride with Bushu," I said, taking the reins of Belshazzar's horse. Resentment flickered in his eyes, but it didn't outweigh the desire for comfort. He slid off the horse. No one said anything when I threw a leg up and over the saddle. It felt good to be on a horse again.

We arrived at Nippur's outskirts before midafternoon the next day. Even at this distance, we could hear the sound of shouting, things breaking... I'd managed to keep my anxiety at bay until now. I glanced back at the carriage. How many times had I protected someone else? But Mandane was not my child. Was this yet another of my impulsive mistakes, an excuse to get out of the city, even to ride? No, the stakes were too high. Bushu's well-being, but also Rachel's and her people, exiles undeserving another military attack despite their uprising. If I could show that I was both foreign and a respected member of the royal family, here to show the same respect to other foreigners, to conduct the business of hiring an intelligent and well-trained member of their community for a task to which he was uniquely able, I hoped to bring if not peace, then some calm. The alternative, proposed by Igliss, would be a massacre. I wasn't sure how to do this except take the next step.

"We'll walk from here," I said. Nabonidus shrugged and dismounted. "Shalam, wait with the horses. We'll be back by dark."

"Are you sure?" Shalam said, worry in his voice.

Not trusting my voice, I nodded.

Nabonidus silenced Belshazzar's inevitable protest with a look.

I took Bushu's hand, so trusting, in mine. The clamor grew louder as we approached. Through the gates, I could see stones flying, people scurrying. Had I made a mistake taking Bushu into this melee? I clutched his tiny hand more tightly. Men at the gates scrambled to attention when they saw us coming. I didn't give them long to wonder. The simple gold band that I wore around my head, the fringed robe, and hair coiffed in the Babylonian style – the best I could do alone that morning – marked my station. For once I was glad for the fine, decidedly Babylonian clothes that Bushu wore.

"We are here on official business, to fetch a scribe for the palace. Where is your governor?"

"In his house, ma'am. Says he won't come out for anything." The guards glanced at each other. "If you haven't noticed..."

I waited.

"... It's dangerous here, ma'am. You should leave immediately. The revolt in Jerusalem emboldened these damned Jews." I felt rather than saw Rachel slip behind me and imagined her gentle head dropped in fear, shame. "Good Babylonians will set them straight. But it's no place for... for such as yourself."

I raised my chin. "It's exactly the place." Bushu's hand lay warm in mine. "We'll go in ourselves," I said.

Belshazzar's jaw dropped. "They'll kill you."

"Who?"

"Jews, people fighting the Jews... Does it matter?"

"Well, they'd better not." I glanced down at Bushu. He was staring a question back up at me. I gulped. This gamble must pay. I looked Belshazzar in the eye. "You can stay."

"Impossible," Nabonidus said. Belshazzar glared at him. "He's coming with us."

I took a deep breath. Then I drew Rachel up beside me. "Who are the Jewish leaders?" I asked.

Her voice quiet, "Rabbis," she said. With a tiny smile, she took Bushu's other hand. "And elders."

A woman approached, her dress dusty and thin, carrying a basket of figs. Eyes down, she tried to slip past us at the gate. "You." I caught her arm. The woman froze. "Can you tell us where the school that trains scribes is?"

Bafflement replaced fear. She glanced at Rachel, who nodded encouragement. "There are many," she stuttered, "a whole section of town. Inside the gates, look southeast. There's a hill. Go there."

She shifted the basket to her other shoulder. "We call it 'Scribal Hill.'"

"Thank you. Are you selling those figs?"

The woman looked warily at the gate and nodded slowly. "It's my only way..."

"We'll buy them. All of them."

Nabonidus handed the woman a silver piece and gestured to Belshazzar to take the basket. The woman turned the piece over and over, her eyes wide. She said, "I'll lead you there, ma'am."

I took a deep breath and walked through the gate.

"There!" a high voice called. Half a dozen youths scraped up stones from the street. They cocked their arms and froze, staring. "Hey, come and see this!" someone called.

"Belshazzar," I said, eyes straight ahead but my heart pounding, "pass out the figs."

I saw Nabonidus give Belshazzar a discreet shove. Hesitant at first, he stepped forward, extending the basket in front of him. It's hard to throw things when you're reaching for a sweet. Young men dropped their stones. Gradually, the street quieted. People gaped at our tiny party. Crowds filled along one side and down the other. People whispered behind hands. And so we went, a spectacle through ever quieter streets, to the base of a small rise.

"All along here," the woman said, "are schools. That one," she pointed to a door pock-marked by the stones that lay around its base, "they say is the best." Then, she seized my hand and bent her head, her lips brushing the faint scar I'd brought from Media. "The gods bless you," she said and darted away.

Behind me, Belshazzar said, "Let's get this over with."

I knocked. Waited. Knocked again. Finally, the door opened a crack.

Nabonidus stepped forward. "We're looking for the school's master."

"Closed today."

I put a toe in the door. "I understand," I said, "under the circumstances."

"No." The door opened further, revealing a young man. "For Jews, it's the Sabbath."

"You're not Jewish?"

He poked his out and glanced around nervously. He shook his head. "But I didn't want to get involved out there. Come in."

We did, one behind another.

"Our teacher is Jewish, the best," he said as we entered. "Every year, Rabbi ben-Isaiah accepts a limited number of non-Jewish students." The young man shut the door firmly, pulled out a long bench and gestured for us to sit. "I got lucky. If you could call it that. He's tough on all of us. I can't believe you came here. It's so dangerous."

I felt Bushu wrap an arm around one of my legs. "We want peace," I said.

"The rabbi believes that some day we'll all come together, all the nations under one God, that we'll learn together peace and justice."

I bent and hugged Bushu to me. "That's what he teaches?"

Belshazzar scoffed. "'One God'? How can you possibly –"

I stood quickly, knocking Bushu off balance. Rachel caught him. I glared at Belshazzar. "We are here in peace." I glanced at Nabonidus, who nodded me to go on. "We are here to listen. Now, please, continue."

"One of the poems that the rabbi makes us rewrite talks about that - peace. He learned it from his teacher who learned it from his teacher, who was a prophet in Jerusalem over 100 years ago. Would you like to hear it?"

"No," Belshazzar said, even as I said, "Yes."

Belshazzar nudged his father's arm. "Time?"

Nabonidus said with a force hard to miss, "We are, as Amytis said, here to listen."

The young man looked from Nabonidus back to me. "Well, my favorite part is the end.

'And they shall beat their swords into plows

And their spears into pruning hooks:

Nation shall not take up

Sword against nation;

They shall never again practice war.'"

I leaned toward Rachel. "Do you know that?" The girl shook her head, no.

"So you memorize this poetry as part of your education?" Nabonidus asked.

"All kinds, and stories too. *Gilgamesh*, the *Enuma Elish*, of course; quite a bit from his people. The rabbi says that it helps us to learn not just grammar and diction but the music of language. Writing serves to keep records, sure, but he says that it can also shape the ways that people think and feel. It can be almost holy. Rabbi ben-Isaiah teaches all of it, the mundane and technical as well as the mystical and lofty."

"Where is he?"

"He doesn't like to be interrupted on the Sabbath..." He looked from Nabonidus to me. "It's not far."

The rabbi's house was, as the student described, the smallest of the row fronting onto a winding alley. Its blue door was distinctive. Next to it, a small brass box hung fixed to the plaster wall.

At our knock, the door opened. A young woman looked anxiously from one visitor to another, surprise softening when her eyes landed on Bushu. "Bubby," she called behind her. To me she said, "I assume you're here to see my father."

Giggles and scuffling drew my attention to a low doorway. The rabbi entered, bent in tickling play with a little girl who bobbed ahead, staying just within his reach. Seeing us, the man straightened. Gray streaks, kinked and curly, in thick dark hair and eyebrows so bushy they had wings lent an air of mad dishevelment to an otherwise well groomed man.

The little girl, still laughing, ran up and took the woman's hand. She stared at Bushu.

"Rabbi ben-Isaiah," the student said, "This is the king's wife Amytis, the prince Nabu-shuma-ukin –"

"Bushu," Bushu said, staring back at the little girl.

" -- his nurse, one of our own, and... other people from the palace."

"My name is Nabonidus. This is my son, Belshazzar."

The rabbi turned to the young woman. "Tell your mother that we have guests." He looked at Bushu's nurse and smiled. "For dinner."

"I'll get back," the student said. "The school's untended for now."

The rabbi nodded, and the young man trotted away.

I explained our errand – that we were looking for a scribe, a student from his school that he might recommend.

"Is it customary that the king would send his wife and child on such an errand?" the rabbi asked. He gestured toward the door with a sparkle in his eye and said, "They're all out there, wondering – a prince of Babylon and his mother, the king's wife no less, behind the door of a poor old rabbi." His expression sobered. "In this of all times."

"For that, for peace, we chose to come," I said. "Fellow foreigners. And to retrieve a palace scribe, we hope."

"Dinner," the young woman said from a doorway and disappeared again.

I'd forgotten how hungry I was. The fragrance of a hot meal made my head swim.

"Please stay," the rabbi said.

"It's an honor." I'd barely gotten the words out when a boisterous group of young men burst from another door. Seeing us, they fell silent.

After a moment, the youngest stepped forward. He hesitated between Nabonidus and me, then said to me, "I trust that my family has welcomed you." This, from a boy of no more than twelve or thirteen, caught me off guard.

"Yes," I said.

The boy had the same fine, almost Egyptian features as the young woman. His shoulders and jaw still had the round edges of a child, and his eyes were bright and lucid; but he looked at me with the steady gaze of an old sage.

"My sons," the rabbi said. He introduced the eldest two – son-in-law, son. "And this," he drew the boy to his side, "is Elnatan, 'Nathan,' for short." He took his hand from the boy's shoulder. "Before more talk, dinner." The rabbi gestured for space while the girls shook out a broad cloth and let it fall lightly to the ground. He stepped onto a corner. "The rest of the week, we might not have much. But on Shabbat, we are wealthy, rich with the best things - time, family, and tradition. Come. Sit."

The young woman and little girl deposited in the middle a platter of fresh greens – parsley, mint, and spring onions, their tiny white bulbs anchoring long strands of deep greens. Belshazzar frowned, looked around, and then finally sat with the rest of us.

The young woman placed an ornate chalice of pounded bronze atop a plate in front of the rabbi.

I leaned in to Rachel, sitting next to me. "Do you do this, have this practice, in Babylon?"

"No. And the people who do... near us, anyway... they keep it quiet."

I said, "We've been told that your school is the best."

"I don't know about 'best,'" the rabbi said. "But I do know: anyone can train a monkey to record onions, the barley required by a temple, or the dowry of a wealthy girl." He absently adjusted the chalice on his plate. "But only a scribe who has mastered grammar and syntax, analyzed rhythm and sound, memorized great songs and stories, *and*," he looked from one visitor to another, "cultivated a spirit of compassion as wide as all humanity," he smiled at Bushu, "can become the conduit of art -- the beauty," he opened his hands, "of God."

I didn't ask, what god. I simply had never heard such a thing, had never considered... stories as art, and this business of writing. The beauty of God, indeed.

A cough from the doorway broke the silence. Grinning, the rabbi clapped his hands together. "My wife!" A plump woman, her cheeks flushed sashayed in carry a steaming pot. The ends of her headscarf swayed with her steps. A heady savor wafted through the room. My mouth watered.

CHAPTER 15

"The great second meal." One of the young men leapt up to take the pot and lower it onto the cloth. "On this day," the rabbi said, "we do nothing to impose on the Creator's creative prerogative." The young woman lowered a stack of plates. The girl followed with a platter of flat bread. "Our women invented this stew assembled before the Sabbath begins that cooks its way until now. Nothing is better," the rabbi said, as he scooped up a fragrant ladleful of beans and barley, speckled with herbs and glistening with translucent rings of onions, then found a small hunk of meat so tender that it fell from the bone as he laid it atop. He passed that plate to me, serving each guest before his family and himself last.

The rabbi stood. He lifted the carafe and began to pour wine into the goblet. His lips moved silently as the wine filled the glass. Wine rose to the top but still he poured. When it began to run over, Nabonidus started as if to help, but no one else seemed alarmed.

Finally, the rabbi set the carafe back down. He lifted the dripping glass with both hands and said, "Long ago, the prophet Moses charged us never to forget. Once we were slaves in Egypt.

Yet Yahweh-God liberated us and brought us to the land God had promised to us. Now, here, so far from home, we remember too how God created the entire universe, Babylonia as well as Judah, and all with order and goodness."

I had so many questions – the Judean "Yahweh-God," "Creator," "made *Babylonia*,"?! But I kept my mouth shut. Clearly he had more to say. I could hardly believe the others also remained silent. I looked at Belshazzar, daring him to interrupt. He didn't. He was staring at the food.

"Then God rested – a seventh day, made blessed and holy." The rabbi closed his eyes and said, "Blessed are you God, King of the Universe, Creator of the fruit of the vine."

The rabbi swiped the bottom of the goblet with a cloth, took a sip and held it out to me. I could feel people hold their breath. I thought about the gods of Media – my gods back home – of the gods of Babylon, so demanding. Each in his or her own country. But the Yahweh god could be here, could *choose* to be here?

I took the cup. I sipped from it. Then, I passed it along. Belshazzar refused, but not Nabonidus. So each except the smallest drank as the cup passed around the group. Then the rabbi picked up a piece of bread, scooped, and everyone began to eat.

When the last person finally leaned back from his plate, the rabbi said, "Before we leave the table, it is customary to sing a song of hope and praise. This is new. We call it 'a song of going-up' because it tells about the heart of the home that we are so far from today – the mountain of God."

Belshazzar cleared his throat.

Nabonidus spoke quickly. "We're here to listen." repeating my words, and looked meaningfully at Belshazzar. Belshazzar pinched his lips closed.

The rabbi began a mellifluous tune. He shut his eyes, hummed, then sang, "When Yahweh-God brings us home, we will laugh and sing for all our joy. Those who sow in tears today will reap in gladness. They will come back singing by the time of the sheaves." The rabbi bent his head and said, "Blessed are you, merciful one, who is everywhere, always, creator of this bread."

Belshazzar snorted and pushed to his knees. When I raised my head, my eyes were wet.

AFTER THE FAMILY had dispersed again, the rabbi said, "Now, what is your business with me?"

Belshazzar said, "We need a scribe. Someone to serve in the palace."

"I have a student or two. Perhaps the young man you –"

"He should be a Jew," I said. "With the ongoing trouble in Tyre, Jerusalem, too…"

Impatient, Belshazzar said, "Let's go." He stood. "There's a community just south of Babylon. A certain Ezekiel -- prophet or priest or something – plenty of Jews."

"Sit." Nabonidus said.

Glowering, Belshazzar lowered himself again.

The rabbi watched him. "I was once full of fire like you," he said. "I couldn't believe that our God who had promised an ever-lasting kingship to David and chose the temple, would ever let Jerusalem fall." He sighed. "Then it did… at the hands of your King Nebuchadnezzar."

He looked at me, then back at Belshazzar. "I had thought that only the magnitude of our collective sins over generations could justify such destruction and humiliation. Now I'm not so sure. Of the greatness of our God, I do not doubt. I cannot."

Belshazzar slapped his thighs. "That's –"

I said to the rabbi, "Go on."

"I know it's dangerous to say," the rabbi went on, "But the particular holiness of Jerusalem, I don't doubt that, either. Still. What exactly is the meaning of our destruction and what are the plans God has for us now, I don't know."

I wasn't surprised to see Belshazzar roll his eyes. How could this complacent Babylonian courtier wonder about purpose, about pain and loss, when he'd never suffered a bit of it?

The rabbi shrugged and opened his hands. "Maybe our future, the future of our faith, is in words. We are stewards of a past that defines our present and informs the future even as it is infused with mystery. We keep asking, adding, passing along..."

The boy Nathan stepped out of the shadows behind the doorway. "I will go to Babylon, Father."

The rabbi's eyebrows took flight. "No!"

Nathan walked forward. "I've learned well. You've said so yourself. And I know enough of our own dialects – Judean and Israelite, modern and old, too – to know the way the Phoenicians, the Philistines, the people of Gath,Tyre, and more speak and write."

"'No!" The rabbi struggled to his feet.

We all stood.

The rabbi gestured urgently for Nathan to leave the room.

The boy stood still.

The rabbi tipped his head back, and closed his eyes. "Adonai, you trickster." He raised his hands and lowered his head. "I should have imagined this boy might be the one you seek." He looked from me to Bushu and back again. "In our tradition, it has always been so: the youngest, the least likely, who is chosen. Yet we're surprised every time. Come here, child." The rabbi bent his head to meet the boy's eyes. "Your mother may never forgive me." He put his hands on Nathan's shoulders, just beginning to fill out. "God goes with you."

I pulled Bushu to stand in front of me, the warmth of him against my thighs.

The rabbi said in a heavy voice, "We'll send Nathan to you just as soon as he's ready."

Belshazzar stamped. "We take him now."

The rabbi, stricken, looked at Nabonidus.

"It's true," I said as gently as I could. "We have a horse. He doesn't need to bring anything."

The rabbi put his head into his hands. "It's too much. Adonai, you ask too much." I didn't argue.

When he raised his head again, the rabbi, his eyes red and throat ragged, asked simply, "Can you wait until dusk? Give us until the Sabbath is over?"

I nodded yes.

NATHAN'S MOTHER did not see him off. The rabbi apologized for her absence. "She –" but he couldn't finish. My heart ached for him, for her. Nathan held a satchel of personal things in one hand; in the other, a sack that the rabbi said was food. "Enough to share," the rabbi added. The boy stepped forward with his things. Nabonidus lifted the food sack. "Does your wife know it's just the four of us, plus a guard?"

"It's her way," the rabbi said shrugging. "Two other things before you go. Nathan has never been on a horse before."

"Father!" the boy protested.

"They'll help you."

I asked, "And the other?"

"There is a Hebrew scribe – an old priest from Jerusalem, something of a sensation -- who was settled with other Jews on the Chebar canal. I think it's just outside the city. Belshazzar mentioned him earlier. Ezekiel. I would like Nathan to meet him. Please, if it is possible, stop there on your way through tomorrow? Or another time?"

"No," Belshazzar said, "His work will be in the palace and commence immediately."

The rabbi winced. Then he stepped close to his son, took the boy's face in both hands, and bent his head. "May the Lord bless you and keep you. May the Lord make his face to shine upon you and be gracious to you. May God give you peace." The boy blinked and swallowed hard. The old rabbi stood in the doorway until we couldn't see him anymore.

The streets were quiet as we walked back.

WE REACHED the gate without harassment. "Tell the governor he can come out now," I said to the guards. "And if he doesn't maintain this peace, the king will find someone who can." I adjusted the golden band around my head, took Bushu's hand and walked toward the carriage. Although it would be full dark soon, I was eager to put some miles behind us before sleeping for the night.

As we approached Shalam, from whom we'd left under a cloud of anxiety only hours earlier, I realized that my fear was gone. I had breathed freely from the moment I'd stepped inside the rabbi's home.

Nathan's fear however, had just begun. The boy's face drained its color when he looked at the horse he was to ride. So, with my hand on the carriage door, "Nathan," I said. "Here."

The boy cast a furtive glance back at the horse before he walked quickly to the carriage.

"Get in," I said.

He hesitated a moment and then stepped up, clearly relieved. I shut the door and walked over to his horse. I took the reins, hitched up my over-robe and tunic, and swung onto the horse's back. Belshazzar, back on his own mount, hissed something to Nabonidus. But Nabonidus urged his horse forward to follow me. Belshazzar didn't once complain about the heat or the effort of our journey as we rode back toward Babylon.

When we stopped for the night, I asked Nathan, "Do you really think your god is here, in Babylonia?"

"God is everywhere."

"Maybe the gods," I said. "But I mean your god in particular."

"Yes, our god," Nathan said. "Our god is the only god."

I caught my breath. "That's blasphemy. For my part, I don't care. But be careful who you say these things to."

Nathan sighed. "I can't explain like my father. Or like Ezekiel. Do you know, they say that Ezekiel actually *saw* God's throne come from Jerusalem to Babylonia – flying through the air. Our god is here with us in exile."

It was more than I could accept. Had we fetched a young man as sick in the head as Crown Prince Ean? Still, I wanted to know more. "If your god is invisible, how do you know, god or goddess?"

"God is both male and female," he said. "Or neither. Some priests are writing a story, another story of creation."

"Another?"

"It's not like they presume to record exactly what happened," he said as though such a thing were obvious. "No one knows that. So, the stories tell angles, different perspectives on origins, purpose, even images of God. They don't have to agree."

"Of course," I said. Because I couldn't think what else to say.

But Nathan wasn't done. "Like Ezekiel's teaching that God can even be here in the land of our captors, that new creation story tells of God actually creating the whole world – from the beginning – in a poem."

"Of course," I said again, completely bewildered.

NEBUCHADNEZZAR WAS PLEASED by the results of our mission – Nathan's knowledge and skills could be put to use right away. And there hadn't been any more trouble from Nippur. Our success (specifically, the king's recognition and appreciation of it) appeased Belshazzar somewhat, but he clearly disapproved of my method – highlighting my and Bushu's foreignness. I overheard him complaining of it to Igliss, a sympathetic audience, for certain. But I didn't dwell on it. I had only a few weeks left with Bushu before he'd be taken from me to begin his formal training.

At the time, I didn't appreciate how important that step from boy-in-the-palace to prince-in-line-for-the-throne would be. After Bushu came of age, it would be no ordinary crime to hurt him. It would be a crime against the gods. Before then... Well, he had guards, sure. And he had me and Gulash, of course. But until he reached that milestone to be formally recognized as a Babylonian prince belonging to the gods, he was just another boy-child. Little. And vulnerable. In my desire to have him for as long as possible to myself... and to wrest Kassiya from Igliss's isolating clutches, I was blind to this window of danger.

CHAPTER 16

I knew I wouldn't see Khai at the feast for Bushu's coming of age – five years old! He was brokering some kind of an agricultural deal for prestigious Babylonians, I'd heard. I tried not to wonder, not to ask about him. My disappointment was mitigated only by knowing that Kassiya would be there, though, for certain. I asked if we might have a day, the day after the feast – Bushu and I – without guards.

It would be Bushu's last day entirely with me, and I wanted to enjoy it fully, with Kassiya, too. I'd come to suspect that it was Igliss who had prohibited me from visiting their mansion and had made it impossible for her to accept my invitations. I figured he couldn't do that to my face, not while Kassiya was right there.

I made sure that Kassiya was seated next to me for Bushu's big day. She looked wan, drawn, and shockingly thin. "I'm sorry we haven't seen much of each other," I said,

"I've been so preoccupied, with Bushu and all…"

"We hope that my wife will know what that's like before much longer," Igliss said. He put an arm around her shoulder and pulled her toward him awkwardly. "She's had a difficult time lately. Another baby, months along this time." Igliss pushed Kassiya upright again. "But no real loss. Just a girl." Kassiya's eyes were wet. "Next time, a strong son." He pinched her cheek so hard that it left a mark. Under the table, Kassiya grabbed my hand. So, I bit my tongue.

"Come to the palace tomorrow?" I asked. Kassiya gave me a little smile that withered as quickly as it had come. I heard Igliss huff a rebuke as he took the seat next to her. Under the table, Gulash stirred. I said, "A day just us, down by the quay..."

Igliss followed our conversation with attention. Kassiya nodded, barely, but it was enough. And Igliss didn't forbid it. But his eavesdropping got on my nerves.

I caught the cloudy eye of the Sippar temple shatammu. "Igliss, you two know each other, don't you?" I knew full-well that they knew each other. I also counted on the fact that Igliss would be pleased to talk with someone in so prestigious a position, though the man was old, frail with some long illness, and quite deaf. "Managing such a large temple estate, that must a lot of responsibility." I hoped my hostility and sarcasm wasn't showing through. "Nothing I could possibly understand, for certain." Igliss took the bait and turned his attention toward the shatammu.

With him distracted, I put my hand on Kassiya's arm. "How are you?"

She looked down at her lap and shook her head. Gulash nuzzled her hands.

"Tomorrow," I said. "Tell me everything."

Suddenly, the room was quiet. Igliss cut off his conversation and looked toward the far door, his expression as dark as a winter storm. I felt Gulash stand and turn under the table. My throat tightened. There in the doorway Bushu stood, dressed like a noble little man.

Nebuchadnezzar called him forward. He looked so small, my boy. I watched as Nabonidus respectfully directed Bushu forward. He had inherited my hazel eyes and light brown hair in big, loose, waves. Otherwise, to my sorrow, he looked every bit

the Babylonian prince. He had been excited to wear the luxuri-
ously ringed robe and golden belt criss-crossed over his chest, a
child-sized scabbard hanging at his side. His fine leather sandals
flapped lightly as he continued alone to take the other chair next
to the king. I grinned to see that a lock of hair had escaped the
thin gold band around his head. Oh, how I hoped that my son
wouldn't forget my lessons about home – Media – that he would
remember its extraordinary value precisely because of its vast
wildness.

GIVEN how hard it had been to get together with Kassiya, I was
surprised when she really did show up the next morning,
dressed for a picnic. As for Igliss, he'd want to be with
Nebuchadnezzar. The Sippar temple's shatammu had died in the
night – right there in the palace. Given how important the position was – powerful and prestigious, too – I figured Igliss would
be at Nebuchadnezzar's side as the king deliberated his
successor.

But Igliss was not with Nebuchadnezzar. He was with here,
with us.

Kara crossed her arms over her chest, briefly blocking the
doorway when they arrived.

I hugged Kassiya as Igliss strode in. His presence was
unnerving.

Gulash stepped to my side, drawing Bushu closer, too.

"Aren't you just a prince of a fellow?" Igliss said bending
down, one arm behind his back. Bushu stared at the mustachioed
lips drawn back to reveal big teeth and shrank back against my
knees. Gulash stepped between the man and the boy with a low
warning rumble. Igliss stepped back, his smile morphing into an
anxious grimace.

"You remember your uncle Igliss, don't you?" I asked, trying to
be friendly.

Bushu rested his hand on Gulash's back and nodded slowly. The dog, quiet, sat.

Igliss said, "You seem like the kind of boy who has a lot of toys. You probably don't want any more."

Bushu brightened. "Um, I do." He stepped forward.

Gulash tilted his head back to look at me. I tapped my side, and he came back to me.

Bushu said, "I mean, I do want more."

"Well good," Igliss said. "Because this is for you." He drew a ball out from behind his back. Made from a sheep's bladder blown up taut with air, it was somewhat lopsided. "You can play catch with it." He glanced warily at Gulash and handed the ball to the boy. Then he gestured for Bushu to toss it back to him. I nudged Bushu, and he tossed it shyly.

I caught Kassiya's eye. She shrugged, as much in wonder as me. We'd neither of us seen this side of Igliss before.

"Or you can kick and roll it, like this," Igliss said. He put the ball on the ground and eased it forward with a narrow foot. The ball rolled almost within Bushu's reach and then swerved sharply to the right. Bushu laughed and darted forward.

"Thoughtful of you," I said.

"It's nothing." Igliss brushed off his hands.

"Well, he likes it."

Just then, the rest of our party arrived – a boy clutching a kite, and his slave, a swarthy man with a serious disposition.

"What is your name?" I asked the man, ignoring Igliss's disapproval.

"Bariki-ili, my lady."

I don't know who was more surprised, the slave because I asked his name or me, that he called me "lady." No one, not even Kara, called me that.

"He's a Hebrew," the boy said.

The boy, the same age as Bushu was the citizen son of a distinguished elder, here to discuss the Sippar temple replacement. The boys would participate together in some of the same physical training over the coming years. But I didn't want to think about that then. I simply wanted to enjoy this last full day with Bushu and Kassiya. From the corner of my eye, I saw Igliss speak to Bushu, who nodded vigorously. Kara urged the noble-boy, shy at first, into the room. Gulash swiped his tongue across the boy's face, which sent him into giggles. Bushu, the ball tucked under one arm, grabbed they boy's hand, and they took off out the door. "When we play, we can hide, for real!" I heard Bushu say to the boy.

We passed out of the palace and walked the broad road to the quays. I turned my mind from the absence of trees lining the road and the dust we stirred and focused on the pleasure of Kassiya and Gulash by my side, and the simple joy of the boys up ahead. Because Nebuchadnezzar had commissioned a big reno-vation of the city's main river wall, the near quays were out of use. A temporary system of quays served upriver from the city, which made the day even more of an adventure. There would be all sorts of men working the docks in activities I predicted would be of great interest to Bushu and his friend.

It was a beautiful day, the best that Babylon had to offer, I'd learned. Heat and humidity melted the city most of the year. But almost worse were the winter weeks of dreary gray cold, with wet chilling rain – never the clean brisk blessing of snow. In between, the gods would grace us with days such as these – clear with a warm breeze. And no guards. Just us. I would savor every minute. Winter was coming.

We talked for a while of small things. Gulash bounded between the boys ahead and us, walking at a pace Kassiya set. Slow. "Finally, I asked, "Tell me. How are you? Really?"

"Igliss is determined that I should bear a son."

"He can be as determined as he wants. It doesn't matter."

"You know about Ean. That he refuses to marry. He's still not well."

"Yes, but we were talking about you." I did want to know the details of Ean's not-ill-ness; but right now, I wanted hear from Kassiya about herself, if Igliss kept her also from company with the elite Babylonian women, what had happened with the miscarriages. In the early months and years of my living in Babylon, she reminded me over and over again of Mandane. Now, she reminded me again of my sister, but this time with a pang that maybe Mandane could have helped her with pregnancy, with the babies. "Not Ean," I said, "but you."

Kassiya shook her head. "Ean – That's why Igliss is so… forceful." I couldn't follow the logic. Kassiya stopped. "Sometimes I'm afraid of him."

"Well, no matter what Igliss wants, you are the king's daughter," I said. "He cannot hurt you." Then I realized that of course he could. He could hurt Kassiya in all sorts of ways that she would never tell and no one might ever know. I determined to visit Kassiya at their mansion whenever I knew him to be at the palace and simply not accept a servant's rejection at the door. I stopped to look her in the eye.

"You can count on me," I said.

I wish now that I hadn't.

"Stay with us," I called up to the boys. We were close to the quay now, and it was just as busy with boats and barges, boxes and sacks and other merchandise loaded and off-loaded... as I'd expected. And as they'd hoped. The boys tossed the ball between them, occasionally setting it down to kick along. Gulash cocked his head this way and that.

Kassiya squinted at a figure just ahead. I looked just as he stepped behind a tower of boxes. "Hmm." She shook her head, dismissing it.

Gulash whined. I ruffled his ears.

On the water, a heavy barge prepared to dock. Just then, the boys' ball rolled close to boxes. They dashed toward it. Shiny metal or gems or something caught the sun as a sandaled foot from behind the boxes kicked the ball away. The ball flew toward the water. Oblivious to the barge, the boys oblivious ran straight for it.

"No!" I cried. Bariki-ili caught his charge, sweeping the boy up under one arm, but Bushu kept running. And the barge kept coming. "Stop, Bushu!" Gulash leapt from my side, I close behind. Gulash intercepted Bushu, knocking him back away from the water just in time. The barge slammed the dock, popping the sturdy toy like an insignificant bubble.

Gulash licked away Bushu's startled tears.

"My ball," he wailed. Kassiya hugged him close.

"That could have been your head." I was shaking.

Bariki-ili set the noble-boy down and tickled Bushu until he giggled. Then the slave picked up the kite. "Let's see how this flies." He nodded to me with a look of sympathetic understanding. "Over there." He pointed to a quiet rise far from the docks. A group of palms cast shade on the bank.

Bariki-ili showed the boys how to get the kite aloft and hold its string. Slowly, I relaxed, the near disaster behind us. Kassiya and I watched and laughed as the boys tugged and pushed for turns. When the kite tangled in a tree, the boys ran, tagging each other around and behind the trees. Gulash lay in the shade. I stroked his head and neck.

"Remember when you got him?" Kassiya said, smiling. "I couldn't believe it when I heard." She laughed. "What you did!"

"I couldn't believe it, either," I said. "Reflex, I guess."

Gulash rolled onto his side with a satisfied groan.

"You have such courage."

"Thoughtless impulse, rather. Headstrong stupidity. Naivete at best," I said.

"You'll be glad to have Gulash's company with Bushu gone so much."

I nodded. "But I'm going to visit you at your grand mansion on the canal. All the time."

"I'd like that," Kassiya said quietly. "Very much."

I called to the boys, "Stay close so we can see you."

Bushu called back, "But we're going to play hide-and-seek. No one is supposed to see you!" I looked at Kassiya, grinned, and shrugged.

"Gulash." The dog raised his head. "Go with Bushu." He heaved himself up and trotted toward the boys.

Bushu whined, "But he'll give away my hiding place."

I scowled. "Well, don't be long. Gulash, come here." Bushu ran to his friend, who dropped Bariki-ili's hand with a whoop. As they ran toward the docks, I felt a familiar twinge of unease. Gulash returned and lay next to me, his head between his paws, watching the boys go. Kassiya said something, but by now the boys were out of sight, and I didn't like it.

I stood. Gulash alert next to me.

"Mad dog!" a cry went up from the docks. They sprung into even more chaotic action as some fled and others scrambled for weapons to find the dangerous dog.

"Bushu!" Frantic, I ran toward the melee, Gulash at my side.

Bariki-ili emerged from the crowd. But it was the noble-boy, not my son, in his arms.

I grabbed the elbow of a merchant fleeing the area. "Have you seen my son?" I begged him. Wide-eyed, he didn't answer. I let him go. "Gulash," I said, "Back." He hesitated, but I waved him away, fearing for his safety, too. He loped back toward the quiet hill.

"Hey!" a voice called.

Near the docks, I could just see... yes, it was! Khai. And in his arms, he held a frightened, soaking wet, but alive Bushu. I ran to meet them. "Gulash!" I called. The dog dashed to my side, passed me, and ran on ahead, tongue lolling out the side of his mouth as long loping strides closed the distance to Bushu and Khai. Suddenly, Gulash groaned and tumbled forward. A crude spear quivered in his side, darkening with blood. "No!" I fell on the dog. He gasped for air. Saliva ran pink from his mouth. I looked up. A man, I squinted. It couldn't be. He dashed behind a wall of goods. But not before I saw. It was him. Igliss. Rage made it hard to see.

Khai arrived with Bushu just as Gulash drew a last gurgling breath, then lay still. Tears smarted in my eyes. I rested my hand on Gulash's still warm shoulder and struggled to my feet. Khai looked at the dog, then at me as he handed Bushu to me. Only my son's warm body in my arms and the surprise of Khai's presence kept me from howling and seizing the spear in pursuit.

"Careful here," Khai said, cupping the back of Bushu's head. "I think he knocked it against something." I grabbed my son and buried my face in his wet hair. Kassiya caught up. She knelt beside Gulash. I steadied my breath. Kassiya. Igliss's wife. I needed to be careful, indeed. Bushu whimpered against my shoulder.

"What happened?" Kassiya asked.

"I was loading my boat," Khai said. "Out of the corner of my eye, I thought I saw something falling. Then, everyone was looking for the dog." To Bushu, Khai asked, "Do you know what happened?" Bushu shook his head.

Bariki-ili said, "And I had been watching this one." He jostled the boy, who wriggled to get down again.

I set Bushu down. He stood unsteadily next to Gulash's body. I crouched and pulled my boy close, one arm around his waist, my eyes swimming on the dog.

Gulash, my dearest friend. To him I had never been an imposter, a foreigner. He had never judged my background, my clothes, my speech, or my hair. He'd never advised that I be anything other than exactly who I am. I ran my palm along the dog's muzzle and rested my hand on his cheek. Across the back of my hand the thread of that jagged white scar shone bright in the late-day sun. He would have protected us from anything. But I couldn't protect him. I stroked his heavy head, leaned over and rested my forehead on his dove-gray shoulder. I raised my head. Tears had darkened his fur.

Khai bent over Gulash. "I'm so sorry. Whoever did this must have thought –"

I stood. Igliss knew exactly what he was doing. And this death wasn't his first choice. I hugged Bushu more tightly to me.

Khai offered to carry Gulash back to the palace and to bury him in the gardens. In his dark eyes was something deep. His voice soft, "You'll know the place," he said.

I thanked him, vaguely wishing for more – what I didn't know.

I kissed Bushu's head and shivered. What I did know was chilling.

WHEN WE REACHED MY ROOMS, Igliss was there, waiting outside. In fine sandals, gems across the toes, golden buckles at the heel, I noticed. He grabbed Kassiya's elbow. "You're late," he said.

I thrust Bushu into Kara's arms, seized Igliss's arm, and yanked him away from Kassiya. "Let her go." Everyone froze. To a waiting guard, I said. "Take my son to his rooms." I shot Igliss a scathing glance. "From now on, guards all the time. And the gods, too." He'd know what I mean.

Igliss glared at Kassiya. Then he strode off, Kassiya hurrying behind.

I inhaled, trying to steady my quivering body.

"What was *that*?" Kara said, shutting the door.

I caught myself bracing for Gulash's boisterous greeting. I gulped. "I saw it," I said. "Him. Igliss killed Gulash."

Kara gasped.

"That's not all," I said. "I think it was Bushu he wanted dead."

Kara reached behind herself, caught a chair's armrest, and lowered herself into it.

I walked to the window. "He's always hated me. He hates that

our country, Media, with all its rich 'resources,' is not in Babylonian control. And I finally understand… " I looked down. All
those people – different clothing, different languages – busy in
the streets, in the palace, in the temples. Foreigners, no matter
how many generations they might be here. I turned. "He hates
that *my* son, a foreigner in his eyes --"

"-- could be king." Kara nodded, "diluting their ideal of a pure
Babylonia." She inhaled deeply, thinking. "Many Babylonians are
hostile to foreigners, especially those in power. They wouldn't
kill a prince, though."

"Right. But for Igliss, that's not all. Kassiya said something…" I
paced, my shoes slap-slapping the tile floor. "Sure, Ean seems
healthy, but something isn't right with him, *and* he won't marry,
give them an heir. So if he dies, it's Bushu who would become
king and his heirs after him, something Igliss could not abide.
But if Bushu were out of the picture and Kassiya had a son, the
throne would go to her child. Igliss's son would be king." I
groaned in frustrated fury. "He wants Bushu dead."

"But now… as of tomorrow, to kill him would be a crime
against the gods."

"Yes," I said. "But things can happen. And the more I think
about his position, his motivations, the more certain I am that
Igliss wants nothing more than to get rid of my son, the half-
breed prince."

"What are you going to do?" Kara asked.

CHAPTER 17

The next morning, I asked Rdiya for help getting ready. It took all the time we had. Then, I joined Nebuchadnezzar on a litter taking us to some newly completed building project or other. When we arrived, I watched my foot step out as if it were someone else's. A foot so clean it was almost pink, the nails buffed and oiled to a clear shine. I had hardly recognized myself in the mirror when Rdiya finished. Gone were the loose waves in my hair that I had insisted on retaining. Rather, every piece was tightly wound, brought under severe control and fixed with the bejeweled golden band of Nebuchadnezzar's primary wife. And where my natural complexion had been my only coloring, save a light line of kohl around the eyes, now I was the picture of dramatic royalty, Babylonian royalty. Berry stain reddened my lips and blushed my cheeks. The hazel green of my eyes flashed out from an intense liner of kohl. Gold powder radiated from my lids. From my toes to the top of my head, I knew I was the picture of elegant, *Babylonian*, refinement. Well, I'd act the part, too. Maybe one day, it would feel natural. Right now, I was just looking for an opening with the king...

He walked ahead. I let a young priest usher me to the place

where I'd watch Nebuchadnezzar and the priests call down the gods' attention and blessing. I tried to focus, to be an appreciative queen.

Nebuchadnezzar raised his arms. "Marduk, you created me and made me king. I, more than any king before me, have made your city beautiful. Even as I honor your supremacy with love and awe..."

My eyes climbed up the high wall – brick like everything else here – mud underneath it all, I thought.

"Look kindly upon my uplifted hands. Hear my prayers!..."

Above, a hawk glided on currents of wind.

"For truly I am the keeper king..."

I watched the hawk circle north.

"...Your careful servant," Nebuchadnezzar droned on.

I shuffled, craning my neck, then lost the bird to clouds. I looked down and sighed. Dust clung to my oiled toenails.

"GETTING MORE PIOUS, ARE YOU?" Nebuchadnezzar asked when we were underway again.

"I'm sorry I haven't done more before now." I waved an arm to take in the canals, the walls, the roads. " All this work. The gods must be pleased." I hoped it sounded genuine.

"The gods wish I'd find a shatammu for Sippar."

I started. This would be easier than I'd thought. "About that."

"It's a very prestigious position, political."

The litter rocked and rolled with the men's trotting steps.

"I have an idea," I said. I had wracked my mind for alternatives but could think of only this. "Just the person." I tried to keep the ambivalence from my voice. "Someone you trust... I wouldn't presume, of course."

Nebuchadnezzar was listening now.

Now or never. "Igliss, sir, your son-in-law." There. It was out.

And I knew it would cost the young woman who'd become so dear to me.

Nebuchadnezzar snorted, amused, his attention gone. "But I want him here." He shook his head. "And I like having Kassiya nearby." He looked at me again. "I thought that you and Kassiya were friends." The litter stopped. Still he scrutinized me. Could he see how awful I felt for the betrayal waiting on my tongue?

I brushed my palms across my lap to steady them. "I'm afraid I've already mentioned it," I said, hating the lie. "I'd miss her of course." I swallowed. "But Kassiya is very excited."

Nebuchadnezzar stepped out and turned. "She is?"

I was grateful to have to look at the ground as I followed. "I just hope she hasn't said anything to Igliss. I didn't –"

Nebuchadnezzar frowned, thinking. "He *is* a good choice… And if Kassiya wants to go, too…" Nebuchadnezzar walked away.

Back in my rooms, I ripped the crown from my head and the clasps from my hair. I knew I should feel happy, relieved at least. I'd gotten Igliss out of Babylon. He'd be a day's ride to the north and so besotted with his new position and – yes – busy with its myriad important demands (basically the city's entire religious and business life) that he couldn't very well plot or orchestrate my son's demise. But what was that I'd said to Kassiya? That I'd visit frequently, be there for her, that she could count on me? Instead, she'd be even more at the mercy of that cruel man. I threw my shoes across the room. I felt sick.

A eunuch at the door announced a visitor's arrival.

When Kassiya approached, her face was pale. "Igliss is going to be the new shatammu of the temple at Sippar." She sat down, dazed. "He's so proud of himself, so excited. How can I ever..." she looked at me with haunted eyes, "I'd hate that."

I put my arms around the only woman friend I'd had in this court, one I loved like a sister. The sister I had left. I looked over Kassiya's head at Kara, whose mouth was a thin line. I felt sick with betrayal. One day, Kassiya would learn what I had done. And she would hate me for it.

Kassiya and Igliss left the next day. I don't know when. I made myself busy playing the game of Ur with a noblewoman whose husband had been a client of Igliss's. I lost. I filled the following days with invitations extended and accepted, visits to the myriad temples, and lessons in Babylonian literature – I could read fairly well now – and music. I even tried to pick up Mandane's embroidery, from where she'd left off so many years ago. I rarely saw Bushu, of course, who had his own rooms now, thankfully a team of guards, and was deep into the rigors of his training. When I could bear it, I visited Gulash's grave – there at the base of the sweet cornelian tree.

SOMEHOW, the years passed, and quickly. I would have thought that after Bushu left my care, time would slow for me to the pace of the wide Euphrates. Instead, it lurched and tumbled by. I thought of Khai more than I cared to admit. Every now and then, I'd hear about another of his entrepreneurial endeavors – successful, each one. But I never saw him, not once.

Meanwhile, Nebuchadnezzar seemed never even to age. He continued with the same vigor and power of determination as ever, managing the regions he'd conquered, and building as if each brought him that much closer to the gods.

Kassiya and Igliss remained without an heir. And she said nothing to me. I continued to hope that I could reconcile with her, explain why I took the action that I did. But even on the rare occasions that brought Kassiya to Babylon, I could never manage a word with her, much less a moment alone together. Still I tried. Even in this, it was as with Mandane - no word. I feared Mandane was as angry as Kassiya at my perceived betrayal. And I couldn't figure out how to correct that without seeing her in person. I hoped: one day.

. . .

AFTER ENDURING YET another wet winter that chilled me more than any Median blizzard, I welcomed the distraction that would be the Akitu.

"Any news about Ean?" I asked Rdiya.

She shook her head. "They got him as far as Uruk's outskirts this time. Then –" Rdiya shook her head. "I'm told the king executed an apprentice of the temple. The boy had been sent to the king's quarters -- some last minute need before the festival. The boy rushed in, didn't await the king's invitation." Rdiya shrugged. "Nebuchadnezzar had him killed on the spot."

I shuddered, remembering my first day in Babylon.

"He's always disappointed when Ean... can't attend."

It took years for me to accept how crucial the New Year festival was. It was a sustained spectacle, yes, but it had import for Babylonians far beyond the visual. The course of those days confirmed Marduk's priority among the gods, the king's divine mandate to lead, the complex hierarchy of Babylonian society, and the supremacy of Babylonia among the nations of the world. Though it was Almost two weeks long, everyone who could come did. I knew with alternate dread and excitement that I'd see Kassiya then. And I hoped, as always, that this time we could talk.

Drying mud left cracks that disappeared into dust beneath the feet of merchants, priests, animals, and cars. The Euphrates bustled even more frenetically with preparation for the barges of the gods and their entourages, coming from all points in the empire to convene the annual conference of deities. Over the years, I had learned the ritual of days. So I was there on the first day with Nebuchadnezzar and the rest of the court – Bushu with his tutors across the way – to observe the high priest's unlocking of the temple, and on the second to witness his bathing at the river. The third was a highlight – the ceremonial preparation of wooden effigies. Still, I couldn't find Kassiya in the crush of people and jostling crowds. I told myself that on the fourth day, when people gathered in discrete arrangements – with the court designated a dais for listening to the priest's bilingual reading of Babylonia's creation story, the *Enuma Elish* – I would at least see Kassiya, if not speak with her.

In the temple courtyard, I stepped onto the platform next to Nebuchadnezzar. The bench on his other side was still empty. Over the well-oiled heads of noblemen (Belshazzar always among them), I saw Bushu with a pang of longing. He was taller than the last time I'd seen him. And more Babylonian. He stood, sober and conscientious, with a tutor and a bevy of guards.

A breeze carrying what I now knew was the last hint of cool for months to come ruffled the wide sleeves of my over robe. It teased at my hair, but Rdiya's work gave the breeze no purchase there. I didn't notice it for long. Kassiya had come. I caught my breath. That once bright young woman walked like an old lady, skeletal and far too pale, to take her place next to Nebuchadnezzar. I tried to catch Kassiya's eye, but Igliss stepped in next to her. It was he who returned my look with a sneer. All through the long reading, Kassiya never once looked at me. Her attention on the priest was as dutifully pious as Igliss's. Then, in the break before we would reassemble on the docks to see Nebuchadnezzar off to Borsippa where he'd retrieve the statue of Nabu, I lost sight of Kassiya altogether.

Nebuchadnezzar was in higher spirits after returning from Borsippa, pleased with renovations "to the temple of the seven spheres," I overheard him report. He had eaten from the twelve loaves of bread, the roasted meat and honey, all served to Nabu's statue on a golden tray. "seven tiers," he said, " brilliant blue all over. Each brick might as well be pure lapis lazuli." Might as well, but wasn't, I thought with grim satisfaction. Media's freedom, purchased with my exile, still held. And Nebuchadnezzar lived on. Until I could bring Bushu back to Media with me, it was his welfare and Kassiya's, too, that I worried about.

On the fifth day, I watched the animal sacrifice, the pure goat and the perfect white bull. I hadn't gotten used to it, exactly, but the years had dulled the memory of that awful day they killed my horse. I never would have imagined I'd still be in Babylon. I looked across the pit at Bushu, his fourteen-year-old frame hinting at a handsome man yet to be. He'd excelled in his training, even in the face of the hostility some of his Babylonian tutors and cohort held for the half-Median prince. I watched the slain bull fall into the oil-soaked reeds and smelled it burn while the king and priest sang their song to Marduk, the bull who burns in the heavens. Grief over my beautiful steed had diminished even as his offspring added to the Babylonian stables.

Memory of my own gods had also faded in the years I'd inhabited with the Babylonian gods. I wondered at the Jews' determined hold on theirs. Some Jews had of course assimilated, simply become Babylonian. Many youngsters knew no other home than Babylonia. But there were those who wouldn't give up. Nathan, the young palace scribe was one.

The next day, I tried to walk with Kassiya into the temple for the ritual humiliation of the king. But Igliss kept between us. So I ended up standing next to Igliss when Nebuchadnezzar walked forward to relinquish the signs of kingship and kneel before the priest. Other than this occasion, no one ever saw Nebuchadnezzar cry, of course. So this moment, when it was crucial that he show tears, was always suspenseful. The priest needed to deliver a very strong slap.

But when the priest raised his hand to strike the king to initiate the ritual that reenacted Nebuchadnezzar's divine selection, I felt Igliss beside me flinch. I stole a glance at him. He stood transfixed, enraptured. Though his hands lay at his side, they were open and out as if it were he, not the king, receiving, welcoming the blow. The smack resounded through the small shrine. Nebuchadnezzar showed the crowd tears in his eyes, and a cheer went up. Marduk had accepted him again. Beside me, I heard Igliss sniff. I turned to see him wiping his eyes.

Kassiya never returned my look. I tried simply to throw myself into the festivities. It wasn't over yet. The next day's spectacle of the gods' arrival, each statue with its attendants, brought people swarming to the river's banks even before the sun had fully risen. Everyone wanted a view of the seven fate-decreeing gods pulling into Babylon, each aboard his or her own barge fashioned for the occasion and attended by an entourage of priests and priestesses, oblates, servants, and slaves. I couldn't even see Kassiya for the crush of people.

Then the final day, the culmination of the festival, arrived. The gods, after a night spent in their individual shrines, would be washed, fed, and dressed for their formal recognition and brief journey out the Ishtar Gate to the Akitu House. There, they would convene under the leadership of Marduk to determine the world's fate for the coming year. It was my last chance to talk to Kassiya.

I knew Rdiya hadn't spoken with Kassiya, either, and it bothered her at least as much as me. Yet we didn't share our concerns. All these years, all those moments of intimate exchange – this Babylonian "manager of the queen's household" was in my bedroom, my bath, attended my meals and prepared me for every obligation to the gods. Still, the undercurrent of hostility remained. At least I'd made my peace with it – it had nothing to do with me, or nothing I could change. I was Median, to my pride and her rancor. I looked out the window while Rdiya finished my hair. In the streets below, as far as I could see, Babylon's disparate masses extended. I knew that Nebuchadnezzar was deep in the temple of Marduk, even now getting dressed in his best regalia, shining bracteates, necklace, wrist cuff, arm bands, and crown – all representing the wealth of the gods and greatest of those, Marduk.

I no longer thought I could be next to Kassiya for the event.

But maybe I'd have an opportunity before or after. In truth, I hated to admit that I'd seen enough. Even if she'd wanted to talk to me, Igliss, whose hostility toward me was both nationalistic like Rdiya's, and personal – he hated me – wouldn't let her have anything to do with me. And she wouldn't fight him for it. It was just as well. Kassiya was clearly pregnant. I hoped for her sake that she could bring this baby to term. I tried not to think what a son would mean to Igliss. As for Kassiya's own health, it didn't look good. For the thousand thousandth time, I wished it were Mandane with her gentle skills and not me, ignorant and awkward, in this place. Seats all around me in the royal section were filling quickly with palace administrators and high-born citizens. Kassiya finally arrived, Igliss holding fast to her elbow. She shuffled heavily into a seat some distance from me.

The temple's bakers had won the honor this year of carrying Marduk's platform. They'd better be strong and many, I thought. The float was covered in beaten silver. The dragon on which Marduk stood was covered in lapis lazuli and bronze, and the god himself glittered with jewels and gold. Then there were the gods' priests, temple officials, and all of their accouterments. What's more, they'd carry Nebuchadnezzar standing atop, clasping the god's hand to display Marduk's regal choice. The weight was unfathomable.

The pageantry was stirring, I could see that; but the dramatic suspense was lost on me. It wasn't as if Marduk – the frozen statue, that is – could possibly seem to reject Nebuchadnezzar. Surely, we all knew the outcome of this charade.

I heard the scratch of a stylus. Nathan sat behind me.

"They've got you working the Akitu?" I asked.

He nodded. "To translate and transcribe the proceedings for Semites in the empire."

"Such great gods," I said quietly over my shoulder. "You'd think they could speak for themselves."

A barely audible snort – I could hear him smile.

People around me pointed, and the crowd craned forward to see the first, towering carts. Oxen, their horns tipped with gold, strained against the burden – an ostentatious display of the wealth and bounty of conquered nations. Ivory carved furniture, fine painted porcelain, linens and wool, candelabra fashioned with exquisite whorls and figures, instruments – lyres, drums, and horns – each a work of art distinctive to the lands from which they came. All that silver and gold. Basins and cups over-flowing with gems. There were embroidered fabrics, exotic birds, and yet more gold.

"One day the world," I heard Igliss say.

Slaves tattooed for the gods they served came next. Only the finest – strongest and most beautiful were on parade, their skin oiled, shaved, and naked to the sun. The titters and approving grunts I heard all around me were, I knew, repeated with crude remarks in the streets below.

The crowd grew louder when after a pause, the empire's conquered kings, the defeated monarchs, appeared in the road. Each had been dressed in the regalia of his country. Each bathed and primped. But the men, once the most powerful in their coun-tries, were strung together, one behind the next with a rough rope draped like a noose around their necks. Each head and face was shaved and bare as a stone. They walked without looking left or right. And they walked, as required, with their hands in the air – hands displaying amputated thumbs.

I could never bring myself to join the jeers. I noticed that Nathan, too, was quiet behind me, his stylus still. Igliss saw and jabbed his finger toward Nathan's tablet. "Shirking already?" he asked.

"He's thinking," I said. "Or maybe *you* can give him the proper Hebrew to use."

Igliss turned away and joined a collective cheer. One of the kings had stumbled, and the man's misstep jerked the others in an awkward, choking dance. The crowd waited eagerly for moments like this. I heard Nathan catch his breath. Finally, to my relief, the defeated kings passed through Ishtar's Gate and out of sight.

A hush fell as the first of the gods' chariots appeared. Nabu's, covered in beaten bronze, caught the sun in blinding flashes as it moved. Marduk's son, Nabu the god of writing and wisdom, looked out serene from his pedestal over the heads of the priests and oblates riding along. The crowd also dipped and swayed, focused as they were so intently on how the statue moved. Each shift meant something. When the god tipped one way, the people in its path cheered or put hands over their mouths in happy affirmation of the god's attention.

It was the same for each of the successive gods.

The chariot of Shamash-of the-sun was of the brightest white. Covered with glittering glass, the vehicle itself earned its own worship nearly as fervent as for the god, resplendent as the sun, his face in the sky. The goddess Ishtar's float, bedecked in stars and trembling with the steps of a dozen priestesses, was led by a team of leopards, leashed and managed by a woman wearing sheets of beaten silver over a blue linen robe. Nitocris. I squinted in an effort to see this bastard daughter of Nebuchadnezzar's, wife of Nabonidus and mother of Belshazzar. I caught the float's complex smell of roses, cloves, and crushed juniper instead.

Finally, the great god Marduk, his golden "skin" shining in the sun, appeared at the end of the road, taller than tall atop his bronze dragon pedestal on the flowers-bedecked platform. Nebuchadnezzar rode at his side, the scepter of kingship in one hand; with the other, the king held fast to the god's hand. The noise was so great it was all I could do not to cover my ears. People angled for the god's attention, focusing on how Marduk leaned, stared, and bent with the steps of the bakers.

I glanced back at Nathan, scribbling again. "What does it say?" I asked, nodding at his tablet. He looked around furtively, but everyone else was captivated by the parade.

"It's about what kind of a god needs to be constructed and carried..."

I leaned in.

He read, "Marduk bows down, Nabu stoops, carried as burdens on weary animals." Nathan scribbled some more and then read that in a whisper so low I could barely hear. "They hire a goldsmith to make a god and lift it here and there." Nabu's float disappeared through the Ishtar Gate. More scribbling. "Where they set it down, there it stays," Nathan said. He spoke as he wrote, "But Yahweh says, 'Not so with me.'" I watched Marduk's statue bob and roll on its shining platform even as I listened to Nathan reading aloud, "Yahweh says, 'I carry you. From your birth I have carried you.'" Sweat poured from the brows of the platform-bearers. "And when you are old and gray," Nathan slowed. "I, your god, will be there, still carrying you."

CHAPTER 18

Kassiya and Igliss left for Sippar first thing in the morning. I never got a chance to talk with her. As usual. I tried to put it out of my mind. But concern for Kassiya must have clung to some thread in my mind because that night, I dreamt Mandane, light and laughing, like she'd been when we were little girls. But in the dream, Mandane became Kassiya, and the laughter turned to weeping. I ached to reach out, to comfort her. But Mandane – or was it Kassiya? – kept moving, and my body felt as heavy as bricks. It took all of my strength to lift a hand. Just as I was finally about to reach her, to stop Kassiya and fix what was wrong, she disappeared. Mandane evaporated. I woke, bereft. I sat up and drank some of the mint tea that had cooled beside my bed. Stars shone in the night sky. All those gods and goddesses. The brightest – Ishtar's. When I finally slept again, the same strange and disturbing dream came. But this time, Kassiya was the happy one, who became a weeping Mandane.

As soon as the festival was over, Bushu left for Ur to learn about the ancient temple there and how Nebuchadnezzar's team of builders planned to make sensitive repairs. Or something like that. I rarely ever saw him now. I could only hope he remembered all I told him of Media. But I imagined, I feared, that with Babylon the only home he'd known, and now growing into the privilege of a prince, that when we could finally go home to Media it would be hard for him to leave. He might not want to. That thought was as painful as anything I'd felt. Besides, Nebuchadnezzar seemed only to be getting stronger. Ever since those early months, after which Igliss and others had kept me from Nebuchadnezzar's bed (fine by me), we were married in name only. Still, as long as he was alive and my son a prince, I had to be here. As the years passed, I missed Media only more. And it seemed there was ever less to keep me here. My missing and its sense of lack – purpose, place, people – took on a chronic tone. I ached, and I could no longer say exactly what for. I didn't dare plumb the longing that echoed of Khai. He'd been a friend to me when I hadn't even realized it. Once, I mentioned it to Kara – my missing Khai. But she reacted with such dismissal, such displeasure of my interest in the commoner that even though she was the slave and I a queen, I felt rebuked. I didn't bring it up again. That didn't stop me from learning what news I could get, occasional at best, about him. And I visited the daughter of my stallion whenever I could.

The days, then weeks passed without news of Kassiya and how she was doing in Sippar. My inquiries got vague responses and always from Igliss – that she's busy with the new household, socializing with the elite citizenry of Sippar... I didn't believe any of it. She would never forgive my betrayal. Neither could I, necessary as it had been. I worried about her. The worry was real, but it also gave me an excuse.

I'd heard that Khai was back here, in the Old City, fixing up a dilapidated house in an off-street in the Kumar neighborhood in order to rent it out. So, one morning, with as much nonchalance as I could muster, I asked Kara, "Find out where I might find Khai?

Something about my question, uttering Khai's name, lifted a weight inside me, brightened the dark.

Kara tilted her head. She didn't have to speak her disapproval.

"I'm worried about Kassiya."

"And the Egibi? What does Khai have to do with that?"

"He does business in Sippar sometimes. He could check on · her for me." I held my ground despite Kara's look. Finally, she left.

Kara returned with the information an hour or so later. She held out a robe with a hood so wide it was almost another cape. "I'll show you," she said, as if I'd asked for her company. It was just as well. We struck out, back along the roads and lanes of inner-city Babylon then wandered into ever smaller lanes.

"I got directions," Kara said, "from the slave who used to summon him for the king. I hope they're right."

"Much farther?"

Just then, Kara stopped in front of a wooden door whose fresh red paint stood out against the doors around it. "This should be it," she said. Kara glanced down and snorted at the dust that clung from the road to the spatters on my robe. I lifted my hand to knock, then jumped in surprise. Before I could rap my knuckles on the door, it opened.

Khai's face was lined, his expression tight; but seeing us, it broke in happy surprise. He smiled at me. Again, that smile. Something quickened in me. "And Kara, yes?" His looked from me to her and back, his smile fading. "I hope everything is all right. The horse?"

I nodded quickly and glanced down the street.

"Right," he said. "Come in. Qudashu, visitors!" Khai called through the arched entryway. "Don't trip," he said, pointing to short stacks of gleaming tiles along the floor at the edge of the entryway.

We entered a courtyard open to the sky. A woman emerged from a low doorway and patted her hair – shiny black and neatly

tucked up high in a ring of clasps so bright that I winced when
one caught the sunshine and threw it in my face. Her clothes
were simple, but she wore them with the pride of a noblewoman.
Beautiful, and again I felt the bumbling rube.

"You honor us," Qudashu said unsmiling, her tone at odds
with the words. "Tea," Qudashu said to a young man whose face
appeared in a far doorway.

Conscious of a stray hair that had worked loose under the
hood and my robe dirty from the street, I said simply, "I have a
request," hoping now to get out as quickly as we'd come.

"I'm afraid we don't have all the amenities of home here. As
you can see." Qudashu gestured to a pile of freshly cut reeds
neatly laid along one wall. "We are in the process of renovating...
again." Her voice was smooth if a little sharp, with no trace of
hurry or stumbling to suggest that she didn't entertain royalty
every day. "But we can offer you a seat."

I let Qudashu direct me to a makeshift bench. Khai disappeared into one of the doorways. The elegant lady sat on a limestone slab as if it were a cedar throne. "You have a request, you
said."

I folded my hands in my lap, one over the other, and then
again, aware of old scars that didn't seem so invisible anymore. I
lifted my chin. "It's for Khai. My request."

"My husband? There he is now."

Khai spoke with a young man as they walked, side-by-side
into the courtyard. The youth, his face upturned, spoke with
animation. Khai nodded, attentive.

"Our eldest," the woman said as they approached. "Iddina –
the same age as yours, I believe."

"So I've heard," I said.

"Have you?"

Before I could answer, the boy flashed a smile so like Khai's
that my heart tumbled. I watched him walk around to Qudashu.
He stood, relaxed behind her.

Khai grabbed a wooden bucket, tipped it, and sat. Qudashu looked away as if embarrassed by his disregard for finer things.

"I came on confidential business." I cleared my throat. "Something that needn't trouble the king."

Qudashu raised her eyebrows.

"Nor anyone else," I said, hoping for some time alone with Khai.

Qudashu turned to Iddina who bent his ear to her mouth. She whispered something, but only he left. I watched him step aside before passing through a doorway to make room for a slave approaching with a tray. Three cups jangled on the tray.

"Here," Qudashu patted a small wooden table. On an embossed plate in the middle of the cups were several crescent shaped pastries dusted with crushed almonds.

"Please help yourself," Qudashu handed a cup to me, "and do go on." She took another for herself, and then sat back, waiting. Khai handed the remaining cup to Kara. "One more, please," he said to their servant.

I inhaled. "It's been a while since I've heard from Kassiya, my step-daughter." I looked from Qudashu to Khai. "I believe you travel frequently to Sippar." I lifted the tea to my lips and felt the cool mint in my nose. "Would you bring a message from me to her?"

The slave returned with a cup for Khai.

"For certain." Khai drained his cup and set it back on the plate. "I'm heading there in the next couple of days. I'll see Igliss then."

"Please tell Kassiya, or tell Igliss to tell her… I miss her. And come visit soon."

"That's all?" Qudashu asked. "It's hardly enough to merit an errand like this."

I focused on Khai's warm eyes, "Tell her that it could be a surprise for the king." I shifted. "Do you ever see Kassiya when you go?"

Khai frowned. "Now that you mention it, never." Then he

brightened. "Igliss tells me that she's busy with her duties, friends... Not that it would matter to me."

"Truth is," I glanced at Qudashu, "I don't – "

"Don't wish to concern the king," Qudashu said. "As you mentioned. Or spoil the surprise. Have a sweet," Qudashu said, gesturing to the pastries on the table.

"Thank you." I nibbled at a corner. Tender crust yielded to a dark, sweet filling redolent with spice. Delicious, but I was having a hard time swallowing.

Qudashu looked at Khai, "I trust this won't interfere with your work," she said sharply. "It's an important contract."

Khai nodded. "Also this, for the king..."

"So Amytis here claims."

I clenched my jaw. Did Khai's wife share the anti-immigrant sentiment I'd seen among some Babylonian nobility? I stood. I didn't begrudge her her pride but refused to forsake my own. "Thank you for your time."

"You're welcome," Qudashu said.

Khai stood.

Qudashu brushed a crumb from the corner of her mouth and remained on the bench.

Khai walked me and Kara toward the door. "I'll be sure to pass along your message," he said. Something in his tone told me that he meant it. That he understood.

I stopped in the hallway and glanced back toward the court-yard where Qudashu directed the slave. "I'm sorry we imposed. Your wife –"

Khai lifted one shoulder and tilted his head in a quick half-shrug. "She'd like nicer –" Khai stopped. "Qudashu was raised with certain expectations. She deserves more." He hung his head briefly, then raised it again. "But the work is picking up..."

We continued to the door. I could feel Khai's presence behind me, almost sense his breath at my neck. Before I passed through and into the street, I turned. Khai stopped just short of bumping into me. Our eyes met. And held, for a moment.

Khai glanced behind him to a now empty courtyard, then back at me. "Something else?"

Kara's elbow caught my side as she stepped onto the street.

I shook my head quickly. "No." I turned to follow her.

"Wait," Khai said. He stepped up close. I watched his hands reach toward my face.

I held my breath. With fingers light as linen, he drew my hood over my head. "Don't forget that." A smile on his face, he tucked a stray hair under. "Lest anyone else see who you are."

I pulled away, exhaled suddenly, then turned and hurried back out onto the street.

Kara and I didn't speak of the visit, of my request, or indeed of Khai or Kassiya, either, all along the walk back to the palace. Indeed, not until Khai had returned from Sippar.

IT WAS some days before a eunuch came to my rooms and reported that the Egibi was here to see me. I worked to keep my voice level, calm. "I'll meet him in the administrative wing, central courtyard," I said. "Tell him to wait there."

I dodged Kara's look. I tried not to hurry Rdiya's fixing my hair, tried not to lose the composure of my station – the king's primary wife, tried to keep my steps to a leisurely pace... But when I stepped into the wide space, bustling with all kinds of people going this way and that, and saw him there, my breath still came shallow and fast.

Khai stood near a bench in the corner. He leaned against the palace wall as though he had all the time in the world and nothing more desirable to do than watch all the goings-on. I stopped, smoothed my over-tunic, and walked toward him. He straightened when I approached. It seemed to me that his contentment fell away, too. He frowned.

With that, grateful as I was to have an opportunity to talk with this friend, the purpose of his errand – my concern for the young woman so like Mandane, the girl I'd betrayed – came rushing back like an ill wind. "How was she?" I asked.

Khai shook his head.

I found my way to a bench, suddenly tired.

"Igliss wanted to talk." Khai grimaced. "Under other circumstances, I would have liked to hear his thoughts on the uses of bitumen, about lending at interest, even about architectural adjustments to the Entemenanki." He looked down. "I didn't see much of Kassiya."

"Tell me about it." I gestured to an empty footstool some feet away. "All of it."

Khai drew the seat close and sat facing me. He took a deep breath and nodded.

Then Khai told me everything, just as I'd asked. It was as if I had been there with him.

It took Khai some time to find Igliss at the temple complex. Entering the sprawling grounds, Khai first asked a man herding sheep into an enclosure where he might find the temple's second-in-command. The frazzled man shouted quick directions over the animals' bleating to the bakery. The aroma of fresh bread, savory and sweet, and the image of them cooling there -- golden brown loaves in generous rounds -- reminded Khai that the last he'd eaten was a cold bite at dawn.

Not seeing Igliss, Khai approached the woman overseeing girls grinding barley and emmer wheat. She stepped away from the figures, crouched over the rough stones, their sleeves rolled high as back and forth with a soft thud and long crunch, each pushed and pulled granite cylinders over the grain. The woman batted away a cloud of chaff and stepped with Khai back into the doorway. "I think he went to the brewery commissioned for this month." She pointed to the gate leading into the street and bent her wrist. "Straight out. First one after you take a left."

Seeing Khai hesitate, his eyes on the loaves, the woman said, "I'd give you some, but Igliss would have my head for it." It was useless to pretend that he wasn't hungry, so Khai nodded. "But here." The woman reached into the deep pocket of her apron and thrust a heel of bread into his hand. Khai ate hurriedly. At the gate, a woman leading a donkey loaded with neatly tied parcels of the gods' fresh laundry said that she'd just seen Igliss in the weaving room.

Khai ducked under a low lintel. Finally, he recognized narrow shoulders under an elegant robe.

"What kind of a weaver would let yarn like this out of her keeping, and for the gods no less? Shame on you. Unravel the thing and re-spin this yarn. We'll talk about pay after that."

"Terribly sorry, sir."

"Apologize to the gods. Such shoddy work."

The woman flinched. "We may have to dye the yarn again."

Igliss leaned into her face as she leaned away. His voice was low. "Then dye it again."

The woman stepped back, her eyes wide. "Yes, sir. My daughter will be here soon. We'll work til it's done." Red-faced and trembling, the woman scrambled to take the cloth that Igliss held pinched disdainfully between thumb and finger.

Igliss turned. Seeing Khai, he brightened, leaving the distraught woman forgotten behind him. Khai gave her a sympathetic look.

"You're a busy man," Khai said.

"It's a great temple," Igliss said. He gestured to the complex's busy expanse as he marched across it, Khai matching his stride, "which depends on so many things going just right." Igliss slapped a donkey out of his way. "I pride myself on high standards, managing all the little people." Igliss stepped through an archway between courtyards. Khai followed. "They must do their part of course, in providing for the gods – the agriculture, the husbandry, jewelry and garments, bronze and silver smithing… and all of them expect to be paid."

Khai stepped quickly to dodge a man bent double with a sack on his back.

"Barley and dates, sesame oil, even silver." Igliss raised thin eyebrows. "Very expensive. Someone has to do it, though. And the king did ask me. Such responsibility. But how could I say no?" Igliss steered Khai toward the gate. "Well," he clipped. "The king could tell – I'm very good at it." They stepped into the street. "You know," Igliss leaned in conspiratorially, "there is precedent for the qipu of the temple, a position that I've been assured could be mine, to advance to governor of Babylon."

"I didn't know that," Khai said, "But that doesn't mean anything -- my ignorance."

"As well as I've done here, I expect I'll be managing things in Babylon… when Nebuchadnezzar acknowledges my fitness for advancement, of course."

"For certain."

They walked through the sprawling complex, the plaster walls emanating heat from the setting sun. "If only Kassiya would hurry up and bear me a son." Igliss's jaws flexed as he clenched and unclenched them. "The empire deserves better than a half-breed prince in line after a fool."

I flinched when Khai reported that, then nodded him to go on. He did.

"I'll gladly manage for Ean," Igliss continued. "But gods forbid he dies. That scare a few years ago –?" Igliss huffed. "Babylonia needs someone who knows who we are – best in the world, a beacon of order -- and cares about keeping us strong." Igliss looked at Khai. "If Ean should actually die… The other, Bushu?" Igliss spat the name and waved a hand as if swatting a fly. "And his mother, regent? Babylonia needs a Babylonian."

Khai shrugged. "What do I know of matters of state?"

Igliss nodded, his lips turned down appreciatively.

"But in business," Khai said, "I've found that dynamism and diversity pay off."

Igliss wasn't listening. "Now, Media. If we could just find a way…" He turned to Khai as if seeing him for the first time. "You saw it. Such potential," Igliss raised his face to the sky, "just begging for Babylonian development." They turned in at a heavy wooden door set with ornate bronze detail. "You said you had something for me?" Igliss asked.

"A simple request. From Amytis. She'd like Kassiya to visit – a surprise, though, for King Nebuchadnezzar."

"So she's lonely, then," Igliss said with a smirk, "that woman."

"Amytis misses Kassiya. She even came to my house."

"Really." A glint passed through Igliss's eye. "I hope she didn't bring that dreadful dog."

Khai frowned. "Gulash? No, he's dead – killed a while ago."

Igliss smiled, nodding. "Ah, that's right. Then I suppose she *would* be lonely." He fixed his eyes on Khai. "So she visited *you*."

Khai stiffened. "As I said… as she said, she would welcome a visit from Kassiya."

"My wife is very busy," Igliss said, turning away brusquely. "Then again." He turned back around slowly, musing. "Pity the Medess. Still and ever a foreigner. Her boy, that prince?" He drew out "prince" as with a spit and a hiss. "Doing well, is he?"

"Too early to say, but word is, he'd make a fine king." Khai glanced behind him toward the door, now closed. "Could… if it came to that."

"Isn't that wonderful." The sarcasm was impossible to miss. "Well. Maybe Kassiya and I can visit Babylon soon, after all." Igliss's lips pulled up in a cold grin. "I would so like for Kassiya to see how satisfying it is for a woman to bear a son. I'm growing impatient. You people wouldn't know what that's like, multiplying like flies as you do."

Khai inhaled sharply. He unclenched the fists at his sides. "I should get back."

"You're staying the night, surely, with Nanna-Suen a mere crescent, and clouds, too."

"Yes, it's too dark to travel. Besides, I need to pick up cargo on the way back, and suppliers are long gone by now."

"Where do you stay?"

"On the docks with the men and the merchandise."

"You'll stay with me."

Khai opened his mouth to protest.

"I insist."

Khai left Igliss's house the following morning at dawn. Against Igliss's urging, he insisted on walking. It was only a mile or so to the docks and mostly downhill from the grand mansion. Despite the hustle on the docks, Khai walked slowly. During the return trip downriver, Khai said little to anyone, addressing matters of logistics and questions about procedure for the goods only.

"We docked in Babylon," Khai said to me, "and I came straight here."

WHEN HE FINISHED, I sat quiet, unsure what to say. Khai stayed, simply sitting quietly as I gathered my thoughts.

"So you did see her – Kassiya?"

"Yes. Igliss said she's quite the social hub among Sippar's elite –"

I snorted. "How did she look?"

Khai opened his mouth, blew out a breath. He squinted at me as if weighing how much to say. "Smaller," he said.

I put my hands on my hips. "I want the truth."

"She's had some trouble, woman-trouble."

So she'd lost that baby, too.

"Probably why she's so thin. And pale."

I sat down again. "Please, just tell me."

Khai pulled his chair closer and took a deep breath. "She looked awful, ancient, her spine all stooped like her eyes hadn't lifted from the floor for years. Against such colorless skin the girl's lips looked like a wound."

I leaned back and wrapped my arms around myself. And I had done this to her, getting Igliss that position in Sippar.

"When she reached out to fill my glass, her sleeve… her wrists were as fine as a songbird's."

I dropped my head. I didn't notice a lock of hair fall like a plumb line along my cheek until I felt Khai lift and lay it over my shoulder. I looked up.

His eyes were kind. "Igliss said that she may be pregnant again and must not travel."

I gritted my teeth and blinked back tears long enough to watch Khai pass through the courtyard gate and out of my world again.

That night, I had again the strange and disturbing dream about Kassiya and Mandane. But this time, Mandane was the happy one, who became a weeping Kassiya. Still, I couldn't make things right.

It was Kara who brought the news.

From Media, the word had come. My sister Mandane was dead.

CHAPTER 19

*M*andane, dead. It couldn't be. What's more – we'd both honored Astyages's "no contact" command – she'd been dead for years. It hit me: Mandane probably died when I'd first had that dream.

Kara delivered the news with all the compassion she could bring. It wasn't enough.

"You're wrong," I said. I staggered backward, knocking a lyre to the floor where it clanged discordant notes. "No." Not Mandane, the sister I'd protected all our lives. "No," I heard myself say, But Kara's twisted face told me otherwise. "No!" from down some long, dark tunnel. I caught myself falling against a wall. Kara bent over me. I pushed her away, drew up my knees, and covered my face with my hands. I must have made noise that brought eunuchs running. Rdiya turned them away.

Still I sat.

Late morning breezes surrendered to midday stillness. The air grew heavy with its ordinary burdens – the smells of temple sacrifice, the strident call of street hawkers, late-day prayers.

How could all this go on with Mandane dead? How could anything go on? I had spent my life for hers. Yes, for Media, but for so long that the place and the person had become one to me. All these years, years when I'd assumed she was well, that she'd come, with Harpagus's help to understand my taking her place in Babylonia. I'd assumed she was happy, content in Media. Even after I'd learned she married into humble Parsa, far from both Media and from me, I'd supposed she was well, imagined her raising princes and princesses of her own, midwifing for the area women. Safe and secure. I just couldn't understand...

Finally, when the sun abandoned me again and night settled like a blanket, I raised my head. My voice came out ragged and torn. "How?"

Kara startled. The scars across her face were pale. I felt her slide down to sit next to me on the floor. Rdiya, her expression like stone, watched from across the room.

"They say that your father brought her to Ecbatana – "

"From Parsa?"

Kara nodded. "To give birth there."

"She was pregnant?" I looked into Kara's eyes, the bad and the good. She knew the awful irony as well as anyone. I choked it out, "Died... like her mother? No one to help?"

Kara shook her head. "She had the baby, a boy. Dead."

I slumped back. "Then Mandane died, too?"

"She couldn't bear it." Kara pinched her lips together. "He was the only baby she'd been able to bring to term. She wanted to name him Cyrus for her husband's father, so proud to be king of Anshan." Kara took a deep breath and continued. "When they told her the infant was dead, she drew a dagger from under her pillow..." My head swam. The dagger I'd left behind. "... and killed herself."

I felt my mouth open and close. My throat seized in a scream that wouldn't come. I tore at my tunic, ripping it neck to waist. Kara caught my hands and pinned me tight until exhaustion left me limp again. "It should have been me," I managed. "She was supposed to be here."

"They would have killed her here," Kara said, glancing up at Rdiya.

Rdiya said nothing.

"And that dagger," I said, remembering the tiny weapon I'd thrust to Harpagus – I groaned – when he gave me her golden jackal robe. "Dead. Her baby, too." I couldn't be consoled, try as Kara did, and later even Rdiya, in her way.

I DIDN'T SPEAK for days, which turned into weeks. Every morning, I let Rdiya dress me, fix my hair... as though I might go out. I didn't. It was as though all the energy of my life had drained away. Finally, I let Kara lead me out my rooms. Dawn. We were going to the river.

MY FEET MOVED SLOWLY. I had to stop more than once along the way. I was so weary, so weak. Upriver from the quays, it was quieter. Kara sat on the bank. "Here," she said patting the ground beside her. "We can watch the sun rise."

I shook my head. I couldn't possibly sit still. I walked to shore and stood alone, looking out over the slow water. The sun had crested the horizon and begun to burn away the haze. The morning star, an unblinking white orb, hung low in the sky. A young couple stepped down from the bank across the river, holding hands. They looked up at the star, then stooped to put something into the water. Their tiny raft caught on fire. I'd heard of this – a tiny reed bed with two figurines, lovers looking for the goddess's blessing.

"Always flowing it is," a man's voice startled me. "The river." Khai stepped down next to me. "Even when it doesn't seem to be." Something about his presence cracked the carapace of grief that had grown around me. A glimmer of life apart from my own troubles seeped through. We stood side-by-side.

"I used to come here every day," Khai said, "back when I was a palace scribe."

Khai didn't seem bothered by my silence. Nor, as usual, by my station.

"People asked," he continued, "why in the world a commoner would give up such a position."

I remembered wondering the same, once I came to know how rare such jobs were.

"Always my family have been farmers, always the same plot," Khai said. "There was never enough. So to give up my position as a palace scribe, and after all that training..." It felt good to hear him talk. "No one could understand." Khai bent and picked up a fistful of stones. "But I saw that with all the king's building, renovating... There was opportunity." He let the stones tumble from one hand to the other. "Besides, palace life –" Khai glanced at me – just a moment, but straight into my eyes. "It's just not me." He picked one stone out from the others, then angled his body just so, and let the stone fly. It skimmed the water before sinking out of sight.

Khai looked at me then. He took his time, appraising my hair piled high and glittering I knew with tiny gems and golden clasps, the fringed robe, down to my jeweled sandals. Under his gaze I felt more pointedly than ever the costuming of it all. "It's good to know who you are." He turned back to the river and skipped another stone. "And why." We stood silent, unmoving.

"Foolish," I said, my throat cracking from disuse. "Me. When everything was more complicated." I swallowed hard. "I thought I knew why, why I was."

"Rebellious," he said, "when I first met you. Foolish, maybe in a way." He nodded. "But in your case, the worst was for the best." I looked my question at his face. It didn't make sense. "You challenge authority for the good of others than yourself." He skipped another stone. "Or did."

I was about to say, "Not good for Mandane." Yet if I hadn't

chosen to take her place here, not only would the treaty never have terms so vital to Media, but Mandane would certainly have been killed for presuming to do the gods' work. And that would have been the end of any treaty, the end of Media as it is and should be. *And* Mandane would be dead.

But what was that other part he said – that I *did, in the past* champion others' welfare. I imagined what Khai saw, right now, when he looked at me – a woman of royal privilege, withdrawn even in grief into the luxury – and expectations – of her station.

I looked down at Khai's hands – big-knuckled, clenched now. I lifted one in my own. He let me turn his hand over, open it again. One stone remained inside.

"There's another reason I left the palace," Khai said. I could feel his eyes on me as I plucked the stone from his calloused palm.

I stepped forward and looked out at the water. Then, with muscles remembering past time and miles, ever so slowly I lifted one foot. Steady on the other leg, I raised it higher, knee bent in front. Then, like so many years ago, when I was a sure, strong girl careless of anything except the conviction of her affections – an identity defined by love – I cocked my arm and sent the stone skittering across the river's surface.

He didn't say more. I didn't ask. And when I turned, both feet on the ground again, Khai was gone.

But his words stayed with me.

Before returning to my rooms, I told Kara I wanted to walk through the gardens, which had gradually filled in over the years with more Babylonian plants than Median. I supposed that was as it should be. Still, I scoured the tiers for what Mandane might have liked and plucked some fenugreek from one of the few Median plants still struggling to survive. Its smell, sharp and sweet, followed us back to my rooms. There, I removed the Baby-

Ionian sandals, fringed robe, and under tunic. Instead, I pulled on my trousers and the loose blouse of a Median summer. Clasp by clasp, I let my hair back down. I plucked out the sparkling gems and ran my fingers through. I settled a simple gold band around my brow. Kara watched me silently. I caught myself waiting for Rdiya's rebuke. I didn't have long to wait, though the rebuke never came.

Rdiya flew in the door, "It's Kassiya," she said. "The baby is coming." Rdiya was frantic, shaking with distress. "But this morning, her face and hands..." Rdiya put her hands, fingers wide alongside her face, showing how Kassiya's had swelled. "And they say her water – it's foamy. All wrong!"

I shut my eyes against the news, as if that could keep it out. But it only made the memory and its implications stronger. This was how Mandane's mother had died. This was exactly what Mandane had spent her life trying to prevent from happening to other women. When we were five or six, Kara had finally given in to Mandane's persistent questions, had told us the details of what exactly had happened on that fateful night. That was the beginning of everything – Mandane's obsession with figuring out how her mother could have been treated, Mandane's insistence on treating birthing women in distress... and ultimately Mandane's disqualification from marrying Nebuchadnezzar. It was the reason for my taking her place here. So in a way, it was also the reason for Mandane's death.

Kara said, "Isn't Igliss handling it, with his bevy of priests, sacrifices?"

"Yes, but Kassiya is no better and getting worse." Rdiya cried, "I raised her like a daughter. Please," she seized my hands, her eyes wild. "I would do anything." Rdiya ran toward my dressing table, seized the small box that held what remained of the things Mandane had packed. She put it into my hands. "I know what this is."

A rush of images – Mandane with her satchel busy at the side of countless women – played across my mind. It's true. Even though I wasn't always in the room, I couldn't help but learn some of what Mandane knew. I was with her on all her medical errands, after all. But I didn't have her touch, and I didn't ever try.

"She'll die," Rdiya pleaded.

Kara snatched the box from my hands. To Rdiya, she spat, "They'd kill Amytis for trying to help."

But a desperate urgency grew in my chest.

Kara begged me, "Think about Media. If they claim you've presumed to priestly work, they'll say the treaty is broken."

"Please," Rdiya whimpered. "There's no other hope."

My heart sank. Dear Kassiya, so like Mandane to me.

"They'll kill you," my old slave's voice was pinched with anguish. Her scarred eye quivered.

I groaned. There really was no choice. "Kara," I said. "I cannot *not* help Kassiya."

Rdiya jumped a tiny leap and squeaked, her hands over her mouth.

Kara crumpled.

"But –" I said to Rdiya, "I need you to do something for me."

"Anything!"

"Whatever happens, request that I be given leave to visit Media, to pay my respects for my dead sister."

Rdiya hesitated. I knew I would do what I could for Kassiya whatever she said. But, "for certain," she said.

I quickly gathered some things. The fenugreek – why had I picked that on this day of all days? – I stuffed into my sack. I kept packing, rifling through what I could find.

I felt Kara's hand on my arm. "You'd do this for Igliss?!" she whispered.

"For Kassiya." I laid my hand over Kara's. "And listen. The doctor-priests have already been trying. So maybe they'll let me help without accusing me of presuming to do the gods' work.

That is, *if* I can help." I resumed packing so I wouldn't have to look at Kara's anguished face.

Suddenly, Kara threw her arms around my neck. "The goddesses Gula and Ninmah, too, go with you." I couldn't remember if she'd ever held me quite like this, as if it were the last, as if....

I hugged her back, then said, "If they kill me, promise you'll make sure Bushu loves Media that he'll continue to protect it as well as he can."

I searched Kara's good eye, filled with tears. She bit her lip and nodded agreement.

I swallowed hard. "Now, I have to go."

IN THE STABLES, I grabbed a bridle before the astonished stable boy could stop me. It didn't take long to find the daughter of my stallion. Her coat was white as snow, and there was fire in her eyes. I slipped into her stall, steadied her with my voice, and then we flew out of the barn, clattered across the courtyard, and blasted out the palace gate, my hair loose behind me. I held her back long enough for a guard catch up to us to explain my errand as we galloped. Then, I flew on alone. We stopped once, along the river for me to fill a sack with the hawthorn's red berries that grew along its bank while the horse caught her breath and drank.

When I arrived, Kassiya was too far gone to recognize me, but the priests there did. I urged them to stay, since I'd hoped they could claim any benefit was their or the gods' doing. But it was useless. With Kassiya's condition near death and Igliss absent (probably in the temple performing gods-only-know what sacrifices), the doctor-priests couldn't leave fast enough. They were gone within minutes. They didn't have to explain: they didn't want both the king's daughter and Igliss's heir's deaths on their hands. Same as Media, I thought. Women's problems ultimately became the problems of women. I tried not to worry what accusations they might bring against me – whether I succeeded or failed – and focused on Kassiya, trying to remember what Mandane would do.

Kassiya's eyes, even deep in a puffy face and unfocused, were big with fear.

"I'm here," I said. My grip, light as it was, left indentations in her skin.

I crushed seeds in a mortar with shaky hands. Their earthy sweet smell brought memories of Mandane rushing back. Through swimming eyes, I added berries and water. I swiped my eyes and brushed a hair from Kassiya's forehead, her own eyes staring out to some distant point. I pushed the bowl to her lips, closed tight.

"Come on," I pleaded. The room was empty but for us. I tipped the bowl. No response. The sweet slurry ran down her chin. "Please." But Kassiya wouldn't drink. I settled back on my heels. "I'm sorry," I said. I rested my forehead on the edge of the bed. "For what I did." It was quiet, so quiet. I reached up to clean around Kassiya's mouth. She turned her head slightly, with effort. Her eyes seemed to settle for a moment on my face. Then her lips brushed my hand. I threw my arms over Kassiya in a hug, until her body spasmed again in pain.

I leapt up and opened Mandane's box, the one that had accompanied me from Media so long ago. I peeled back the linen inside. There lay the demon god Pazuzu. Mandane must have known he was Babylonian, too. I hated his wild eyes, the scaly winged body and serpentine penis. But I took him from the box and laid the bronze form beside Kassiya's head. She stared at it in fear but didn't demand its removal.

I forced myself to say the words.

"Pazuzu," I said, "Keep ahold of your claw-footed wife that she leave this young woman alone. Don't you take Kassiya. And give the baby to us, too." The figurine seemed to leer back with its hybrid face, half snarling dog and half hissing cat.

With that, Kassiya opened her mouth. I poured the medicine in.

She coughed once. I waited. There was nothing more to do.

Just when I'd begun to doubt that it would have an effect, Kassiya grimaced and arched her back. I held her hand lightly in mine. She relaxed, then tensed again, gripping my hand with surprising strength. Contractions. Finally. My heart quickened.

"It's coming," I said, "almost there."

Suddenly, Igliss burst into the room. "Get out!" he yelled.

I jumped, knocking Pazuzu to the floor. Igliss stared at the bronze image in horror, his face splotchy with rage. The last thing I saw was his arm, bigger than I'd remembered. I heard Kassiya groan, and the next thing I knew, I was on the ground. The right side of my face pounded in pain. Igliss came after me again. He yanked me to my feet. I looked over my shoulder at Kassiya. With a surprisingly strong backhand, Igliss sent me smashing against the wall. I slid down. The room narrowed to a tunnel sparkling with flecks of light. Then Igliss had me by the shoulders. I tried to gather myself before he slammed me again. But a boisterous, protesting cry stopped us both.

Igliss dashed to the bed. "A boy!" he roared, pleased beyond imagining. He held the squalling infant high as a trophy and pulled his lips back in a toothy smile. "My son." For the moment, to my relief, it seemed he'd forgotten me.

A line of blood running down my scalp and dripped onto my shoulder. My whole body ached, and I could barely see out of my right eye, already nearly swollen shut. But I eased myself off the floor and went to Kassiya. Her eyes were closed. I held her wrist and exhaled in relief. It was only in sleep, her heart beating on, weak but steady. Igliss swiped at the baby's mouth, pulled off the cloth covering Kassiya, pushed the child to her breast, and pulled Kassiya's arm up to brace the nursing child. Then, he turned back to me. I ignored his ugly scowl.

Igliss watched as I began to wrap Pazuzu in his linen shroud. I could almost feel the engine of Igliss's machinations grinding away at my body, grinding their way to Media. I had to stop it, and this one tiny window was closing fast. I folded the cloth this way and that.

I spoke as calmly as I could. "If you believe that I presumed priestly work." I spat the blood from my mouth. "Or otherwise called on malevolent forces to deliver this baby..." I set the figurine back into the box. "Then surely you believe this: If you kill me..." I looked Igliss straight in the eye. "... then your son will die."

Igliss blanched and stepped back. It worked.

His thin lips quivered. "Get out."

I didn't need him to say it twice. The ride back, though excruciating on my body, gave me time to think. The treaty remained secure. Igliss was too superstitious to threaten me again. But he finally had the heir he'd wanted. The son he wanted to put on the throne. I shivered. Could Bushu ever be safe?

BACK IN BABYLON, Kara fussed over my injuries while Rdiya wrung her hands. "You're sure she's all right?" she asked.

"Yes," I said. "Tired, weak..." I couldn't tell Rdiya how relieved I was not only for Kassiya's survival but also for her forgiveness. I thought about the power of love received. How maybe it could heal something in a person.

"You should go to her," I said.

Rdiya's expression was confusion, disbelief. "But –"

I waved her away. "And stay. She needs you more than I."

Rdiya smiled. "You would do that?"

"You've taught Kara what needs doing here. We'll be fine, and –" I didn't need to say anything more. Rdiya was a whirlwind of activity and at the door before I could have finished my sentence. At the threshold, she turned. "Thank you," she said to me. Then again, with the slightest dip of her head, a whiff of respect that I'd long ago given up ever receiving from her, "Thank you."

Kara harrumphed in grudging acknowledgment. Then Rdiya was gone.

In the silence after she left, Kara asked, her voice tight with anxiety, "And what of you?" I felt her hands stop in their ministrations, loosely clasping my head. "Will Igliss come after you?"

I remembered his face when Igliss held the infant and I thought how this baby – Kassiya's baby, King Nebuchadnezzar's grandson – was so much more to Igliss than simply a son. I remembered with satisfaction his accepting the superstition I'd sown. "No," I said.

For now, I spared Kara the other part – how the lives of both Bushu and I, foreign imposters in the eyes of some to a pure Babylonia and occupying such high positions, were at even greater risk now.

"No," I said again. "He won't dare to press charges."

Kara drew me back against her breast. I felt it heave once, before she resumed her distance.

CHAPTER 20

I don't know what Rdiya said on my behalf, but my request that I be allowed to go to Media to grieve after learning of Mandane's death – Bushu, too – met no resistance. Media! I held my breath in those days before we left, waiting for someone to tell us that the prince really shouldn't go. Still, no one said anything.

Finally, I bade Kara goodbye, promising to bring news. Then, we were off. My son and I would travel with Shalam and another guard, no carriage and no baggage save what the journey demanded. My only regret: that we couldn't take the white mare. But she'd become a prize steed in her own right – well cared for – and had been conscripted to some particular service.

I confess that I traveled the first fifty or more miles looking over my shoulder and insisting that Bushu stay close (though by now he was at least as skilled as me with a sword and more). What harassment we encountered was only after we'd passed into Media. Yes, the land was still just as wild and open as when I'd left. But with each mile we could see that poor leadership had taken its toll. Bandits terrorized roads that had been safe all my life. What towns and settlements we passed through showed signs of deterioration, even impoverishment.

"This is new to me," I said to Bushu as encountered yet another village, its houses in various states of decay. Skinny children played naked in the dirt outside.

He was quiet. I looked over. Bushu's cheeks were ruddy with sun and wind. His hair hung loose but for a small band, like mine. His eyes, when he looked back, were bright. "Sorry," he said. "Did you say something?" He didn't wait for an answer. "It's just so – so wonderful." His sat up. His arm swept wide to take in the hillsides of diverse trees. A herd of mountain goats grazed high above a granite outcrop. A kettle of hawks circled in the sky. Some small animal chattered its commentary from thick shrubs along the road. "It's exactly like what you've been trying to tell me all my life. Wild, and... and... so much!" He sat back. "The air is so clear my eyes almost hurt. But I can't stop looking." He shook his head and grinned. "I can't even imagine what the mountains, real mountains, will be like."

I smiled and kept the other observations to myself.

MY FATHER'S mental state had worsened, which explained the deterioration and criminal danger I'd witnessed along the roads. Harpagus reported rumblings of rebellion against him, secession, which had only made my father more paranoid, more cruel. Harpagus himself, the way he told me these things – his eyes evasive, his words guarded – it was almost as if he'd suffered it personally, directly. But the warmth he showed to me and to Bushu, too, was if anything even greater. The old Harpagus was still there.

And even that news couldn't dim my delight at seeing Bushu so utterly entranced. He loved everything about Media. I took him to the grove where I'd prayed that last day before leaving, and I showed him the river –Anahita's strength and revitalizing power. We watched the half-wild horses from the backs of our own and climbed rocky heights simply for the view. Each day in Media was precious, so I spent precious little time in the palace, much less with my father.

IT WAS FROM THAT CLIFF, the day before we were to leave, that Bushu said, "I remember when I was little how you told me to treat other foreigners with respect, even kindness, to appreciate their differences and that they might be struggling in ways I couldn't see." We had sat to catch our breath on a rock over-looking the valley and Ecbatana below. A wind whistled up the cliff. "You told me not to mind when powerful people looked at me askance or ignored me altogether simply because I wasn't pure Babylonian." I nodded, remembering. "I thought I knew what you meant," Bushu continued. "But I didn't totally under-stand until now. I *couldn't* until now, until I knew what it felt like to live without that hostility, without that judgment. Here, I feel -_"

In the distance a golden jackal howled.

Bushu looked at me. "Home."

With that, I could have sailed with eagles or run with the wolves. In my joy, I could hardly sit still. Bushu's face, rugged from our days in these mountains, swam in my eyes. I put my arm around his shoulder so he wouldn't see my tears.

But Bushu wasn't done. "I want to stay here," he said. I nearly fell off the cliff. "There isn't anything more for me in Babylon. You've said that Grandfather, Astyages, needs clearer vision for Media, a steadier hand in leadership. I may not be able to do everything, but I could help."

What was it the rabbi said, when his son Nathan offered to go to Babylon? God, as some kind of trickster – surprising us with our children...

"It wouldn't affect the treaty," Bushu said. "You've made that clear. I'd simply forfeit any right to the throne. It doesn't matter..." he gazed out past Ecbatana to Mount Alvand and the range beyond, "... I'd marry a Median woman, maybe have children of my own. We'd live here the rest of our lives."

I had never even dared hope to imagine anything like this. "Are you sure?" I had to ask. "You wouldn't regret it?"

Bushu laughed. "I can hardly wait." I could hear the relief, even jubilance, in his voice. "I'll send word. Maybe one day, travel back to Babylon, collect some things. Or we could have them sent."

I wanted to agree to every bit of it, keep Bushu in Media from now on. But there was one thing. "This is something you need to do in person," I said. "In Babylon. It's too great a concession, and people might suspect you'd been put up to it. They might worry that one day you'd return and – I don't know – take back your position, push more 'Media' on them..."

Bushu stared out over the forest and rivers. Then he nodded. "All right," he said.

We agreed that we wouldn't say anything on the journey back. Nebuchadnezzar should be the first to hear. In truth, like Bushu, I couldn't see any downside or any reason someone would oppose his decision. Instead, especially those who hated having a half-foreign prince in line for the throne, would be happy to see him go. As for me, I was overjoyed. When Nebuchadnezzar died, making me free to leave Babylon, it would be to join my son in Media. I couldn't have wished for more.

We would leave for Babylon at dawn the following morning.

HARPAGUS WOKE ME. My eyes were scratchy, still tired. "Is it time?" I asked.

"You need to see something before you go," he said.

I was too sleepy to resist. The shock of cold morning air finally woke me and stirred a primitive thrill I thought I'd forgotten: happy simply to be alive in this place. The sky was dark, the air still.

Harpagus led me to the horses. "Where are we going?" I asked.

"I'll explain as we ride." His tone sobered me.

The gate guards didn't stop us – the palace steward and the king's daughter. The older guards nodded, remembering how fond we'd been of each other when I was a little girl. There was nothing to ask, nothing to challenge.

We headed west, along the valley with its string of humble houses. This is where the palace slaves who raised food for the king's table, tended the orchards and fields, and kept the animals lived. Harpagus's voice was quiet but urgent. "Some time after you left those years ago, your father, King Astyages, had a troubling dream. He woke, desperate with worry and demanded the magi interpret it for him. They told him its meaning was that Mandane would have a son who would take his throne."

"A son of Mandane? You're sure?"

Harpagus nodded. "So, to neutralize the threat, he married her to a man far away, so poor that 'king' in name only, he could hardly have been called a prince. But he was. So she went."

"Parsa."

"Yes. Some time after that, he had the same dream. Astyages inquired, and we learned that Mandane was pregnant. Astyages told her to come back to Media to have the baby. Conditions in Parsa were... primitive, he said. He said he worried about her health and the health of the baby."

"Of course, she of all people," I said, "knows – knew – how dangerous pregnancy can be." It made a kind of sense. "But you doubted his motives?"

Harpagus nodded. "Still, all those other attempts to have a child... And he was forceful, persuasive about it. So your sister came back to Media."

"I heard what happened," I said, thinking I'd spare him the report and me the hearing. "Kara told me that because the baby was born dead, Mandane –" My throat caught, "killed herself." I swallowed. "With the dagger I left behind."

"There was that." Harpagus pulled up his horse. "Not your fault."

I stopped next to him.

"But you didn't hear the whole thing, the true thing." Harpagus held my eyes and fidgeted with his reins, clearly struggling for words. Finally, he simply looked ahead and urged the horse on. I kept abreast. "Only four of us know." Harpagus didn't look at me again until he'd finished the story.

"While Mandane was in labor, the king dismissed the midwives. He said Mandane knew how to birth a child." Harpagus hesitated. "And she did," he said. "The baby was fine."

"What?! But I thought –"

Harpagus shook his head. "Your sister bore a healthy baby. A boy. Perfectly fine. But before the child could even fill his lungs, Astyages took the infant out of her room. The king handed him to me." Harpagus's voice lost all inflection. "He told me to take the baby," Harpagus reported reported in a dull monotone, "into the mountains and kill him."

"You didn't!"

"I didn't know what to do."

I shivered. From the morning chill or Harpagus's tale, I couldn't tell.

"I was so distraught. My own boy was just a baby." It sounded like a plea. Harpagus looked at me then, his eyes haunted. "I told my wife - I couldn't do it."

I was speechless. The horses' footfalls were a welcome beat, solid and steady while my mind and heart were anything but. Fury at my father, of course. Deep down, I'd always known that Astyages didn't care about anyone except himself. And such a weak man – so inept a king and fearful of losing power – was dangerous. Any perceived threat – real or imagined – had to be destroyed.

Still. That Astyages would want to kill his own grandson. *And* make Harpagus party to his murderous scheme...

Up ahead, I recognized the hut we visited the day the Babylonians came to fetch Mandane. It belonged to shepherd slaves, a childless couple. What was it that Mandane said they called the woman...?

Harpagus cleared his throat. "My wife had an idea."

We'd arrived at the hut.

"I told a shepherd slave, the man who lives in this cottage..." Harpagus's shoulders slumped. The back of my neck pricked with alarm. "...To take your sister's son –" Harpagus's voice splintered like dead wood underfoot, "up into the mountains. I told him that *he* had to kill the baby – to leave it exposed."

A new fury flashed through me. "You brought me here to tell me that?!" I wheeled my horse around intending to flee. But Harpagus had grabbed its bridle. We scuffled. As I tried to wrest free, Harpagus said, "When I got home, my wife told me that the slave's woman..."

Spaco, I remembered, who couldn't seem to bear a living child.

"She also had just given birth." The woman Mandane said they called Dog.

"But their baby was dead." Harpagus watched my face as I put together the implications of all he'd told me. Then, he released the bridle.

I stayed.

A light flickered inside the cottage. Still trying to make sense of it all, I glared at Harpagus. But he was looking at the door.

It opened, and a man peered out. Seeing Harpagus, he turned and called out behind him. Spaco stepped to his side and from behind them stepped a boy. He couldn't have been more than nine or ten years old. My breath caught in my throat. I hardly remember getting off my horse. I approached, transfixed. The child's eyes were dark-lined like mine. No one moved when I crouched before the child and reached my hand to his face. His lower lip, red and full, bore an unmistakable dip, the spit-distance image of Mandane. I stood again, my eyes swimming.

"They call him Bartatua," Harpagus said.

He led me, stunned, away from the little family.

"But his name," Harpagus said, "chosen for him by Mandane and Cambyses, is Cyrus."

PART III

CHAPTER 20

I hardly noticed the journey back to Babylon, so preoccupied was I with everything that had happened. I told no one of Cyrus, of course, and was grateful for Bushu's chatty exuberance. Out loud, he was working out how he'd be able to formalize his forfeiture, say his goodbyes, and pack to leave Babylon, all within only a few days.

As for me, my mind was already back in Media, joining Bushu there. For the treaty's sake, I'd have to stay in Babylon until Nebuchadnezzar died. But he was an old man. Gods willing, it wouldn't be long. So I also played out the many ways I might come to know little Cyrus. Harpagus and the shepherd slaves had kept their secret close. Even Cyrus – Bartatua – didn't know. To him, Spaco and her husband Mithradates were his mother and father, and that was that. I supposed it was just as well. Harpagus assured me that they were good people, hard-working and honest in every other way. And I supposed that the gods got some pleasure out of the strange twist: Mandane, who had attended Spaco's failed pregnancies years ago would herself bear their only child. Mandane, my sweet sister. I would honor the secret, not reveal my relationship to Cyrus. But I liked to think that maybe one day...

When it came to my father Astyages... Well, I did everything I could not to think of him at all. Mentally, I had tossed him aside. I had to. My initial anger was so blinding that I nearly revealed the vital secret. Revenge wouldn't bring my sister back and would only endanger the baby she'd left behind. Besides, nursing my anger at Astyages's horrible actions only poisoned myself. Instead, I relished the wonderful surprise – Bushu's desire for Media. The wonder of it was so great that it was finally able to eclipse my father's murderous intent.

The days of travel gave me time gradually to let sink in a truth I'd barely dared hope for all my Babylonian years – that Bushu and I would really both live in Media. Nebuchadnezzar's continued good health belied his years. I thought he'd never die, that I'd never be free again. But this – that Bushu himself would finally make it happen. It seemed too good to be true. All those years I had tried to foster a love in my son of the home he never knew. It had seemed impossible. The glory of Marduk's Babylon under King Nebuchadnezzar was so real, so immediate. And he had grown responsibly into a proper prince. He had excelled at the studies and skills his Babylonian tutors demanded and participated in public life precisely as expected. Their traditions had become his own.

But Media! Bushu had slipped into her wild wonders as easily as if he had known and loved this country his entire life. Now, if he wanted to leave Babylon to the Babylonians, there was no reason it couldn't be so. And he did want that. One thing I knew for sure: Igliss and Babylon's elite, the ones so concerned about foreigners in important positions would be happy to pack our things and see us out.

Babylon's city walls rose up off the land. It had been over fifteen years since I'd first arrived, but that moment – seeing Babylon's walls for the first time – came back in a rush. I had to stop a moment, to catch my breath. Bushu was eager to press on, to get there, to tell them his news, his plans. So, even though the city was still far away and it was late, we traveled on despite the growing darkness.

We arrived in the middle of the night. In the dark, guards at the gate couldn't identify us until we were close. But even when Shalam called out for them to let us pass, they rushed to attention, swords and shields clanging at their sides.

"What is this?" I asked.

"Haven't you heard? The crown prince Ean is dead." The men dropped before Bushu in deep bows. "Gods keep crown prince Nabu-shuma-ukin!"

Bushu's face paled so white I feared he would fall off his horse.

"Marduk look with favor upon him!"

I dismounted onto wobbly legs of my own. People came running. Attendants bowed and scraped their way to Bushu. I was grateful for Shalam's reflexive protection. He wouldn't let them touch my son, no matter how groveling their behavior seemed. Nabonidus came with other palace officials to hustle Bushu away. I noticed that neither Igliss nor Belshazzar was among them. "Stay with him," I said to Shalam and rushed inside.

The palace was in chaos. Adad-guppi caught up with me in the hall, animated and bright despite it being the middle of the night. She told me that since Ean's death, her son Nabonidus and the other palace officials had been scrambling to manage what they could. Or tried. Nebuchadnezzar was inconsolable. The king was so lost in grief over Ean's death that he couldn't see to even the most basic administrative details. He wouldn't even leave his rooms. At my door, I bade the old woman goodnight and told her to get some rest.

As it happened, Ean had killed himself on his way to Babylon. For all the years that I'd been in Babylonia, the only time Ean had been pushed to leave the comfort of Uruk for the capital city was on the occasion of the annual Akitu. And every time, he succeeded in staying in Ur. This time, it was Igliss who had pushed Ean to leave Ur.

Igliss had requested that the crown prince attend the naming ceremony for Igliss's son. Nebuchadnezzar had agreed, of course, with delight. The king always wanted to bring Ean, the son he loved beyond reason, back to the capital, back to the palace. This time, what Ean's mother had called illness and others blamed on her witchcraft's demon possession got the better of the man-boy. Somehow in an odd lapse of attention during his transfer in Uruk from the sick house to the carriage, the crazed prince got ahold of a knife and opened his throat. There was nothing anyone could do.

Report was that the naming ceremony had had a decidedly grim mood.

Igliss called his son Labashi-Marduk. A Marduk name, of course.

Kara told me these things as I went through the motions of readying for bed. Despite the drama and the details, what I heard was that Igliss had succeeded in removing one of the two heirs who stood between him and the power of the throne. And he hadn't had to bloody a single hair on his own body. I knew I wouldn't sleep. There were yet hours of darkness before morning, hours to lie awake, ruing my insistence that Bushu return, and thinking what next.

Igliss wouldn't outright kill Bushu. Now that Bushu was crown prince, it would be a crime against the gods – something even Igliss wouldn't commit. Thankfully, for the time being anyway, Igliss was back in Sippar. But he certainly wanted my son dead. And he wanted Media. Always Media.

I tossed and turned on the bed as I tossed and turned in my mind, trying to figure a way to extricate Bushu from Babylon. Assuming that Bushu still wanted to forfeit his royal position... I'd ask him tomorrow. But with Nebuchadnezzar in this state,

Igliss would assume the reins of state. And with Media.... well, given the frayed, even volatile condition of the empire, in no small thanks to my father's crippling narcissism and paranoia, how could I ensure its protection without being there? No matter how I turned the options and possibilities, I finally recognized that no matter what, there was nothing to do until after the official mourning period ended.

Somehow and after some time, I did fall asleep because Kara woke me in the morning to say that Igliss was in my public rooms, drinking mint tea and nibbling pastries.

"Sorry. I know you would have preferred to meet him elsewhere – anywhere else," Kara held my trousers out for me. "I just didn't expect him."

I grabbed a Babylonian tunic and robe instead. "Do up my hair?"

She set to work.

"Do you know what it's about?" I asked as her fingers twisted and tugged in my hair. "Igliss's visit?"

"I can guess," she said. "Power, wealth. Did I say power, already?"

Turns out, what Igliss wanted was for me to help him convince Nebuchadnezzar to go with Igliss to Sippar. Igliss claimed that Kassiya and the baby would be good company for the bereaved king and getting away would afford him a break from the stress of the palace. "But," Igliss whined, "Nebuchadnezzar seems to think he should stay in Babylon."

I couldn't imagine what Igliss had in mind with his request except that it would be self-serving. Maybe somehow way up in Sippar, with distance from the court, Igliss thought he could take advantage of Nebuchadnezzar's weakened state... But I still couldn't see what gain that would give Igliss. Neither could I agree to the request, given who was asking. "I'll honor the king's wishes," I said, "that he stay here."

Having yet to see the king, I couldn't know how discordant

the notion was. Nebuchadnezzar had no reasonable wish in the world.

The death of Ean, on whom he had pinned all affection and hope, plunged Nebuchadnezzar into a mourning so severe that he became unrecognizable. Even after the official period had ended, Nebuchadnezzar remained locked in grief. He refused to cut his hair or nails and insisted on eating only vegetables, like the Jewish courtiers he had brought from Jerusalem – a kind of penance in Nebuchadnezzar's case.

I had to get Nebuchadnezzar better, back to reason, back in charge. There were things only the crown could do. I hated to admit it, but until Nebuchadnezzar resumed those duties, Bushu could not walk away from the throne. Turns out, Bushu had come to the same conclusion, though to my relief, Bushu assured me that he wanted more than ever to leave Babylon. For a bit longer, then, we had to stay, and stay quiet about his plans to leave until Nebuchadnezzar was himself again.

THE DAY that Babylonia recognized Bushu as the crown prince was a non-event. An official missive, composed by Nathan under the supervision of the king's legal agent, circulated through the empire. But there was no feasting, no royal speech, no celebration. Bushu was simply informed by Nebuchadnezzar's steward that he should show up in the throne room in a few days for that week's audience. He, the crown prince, would sit beside the king on the dais when Nebuchadnezzar heard the cases of aggrieved Babylonians. Frankly, I was relieved that there wasn't more hubbub around Bushu's promotion. The less attention his station drew from jealous nobility, the better, as far as I was concerned.

Indeed, Bushu's first official act came before that and left him more determined than ever to get out of Babylon. It was a minor matter, something to do with priests of some temple or other.

Bushu went as expected in order to participate in this new royal role.

Kara was trying to get me to use some Egyptian ointment – a plant butter – on the new wrinkles around my eyes and forehead (I couldn't have cared less about it), when Bushu stormed into my rooms.

"He turned his back on me," Bushu said, throwing himself into a chair. The bracteates along his fringed robe clattered in protest. "The priest. He would never do that to the king. And Nebuchadnezzar, *my own father*, it was like he was asleep. I did everything right. I have studied the steps, learned every – I don't even want to be here. But I can't say that, either."

"You've faced this prejudice all your life, in one way or another." I resisted the impulse to placate him. So, I just stated the obvious. "The only difference now," I said, "is that you're the crown prince."

"So it's worse."

"Ignore it," I said. "Tomorrow is the king's audience –"

"*King*'s." Bushu spat.

"Maybe it will jar Nebuchadnezzar back into his right mind."

Behind me, Kara tsk'd. We both looked at her. "Careful about that," she said.

"About what?"

"Suggesting the king *isn't* right of mind."

THERE WAS a third throne on the dais now. For the queen mother. For me. Unlike Bushu, I was not required to attend the king's audience. I hadn't planned to. There was already enough antipathy by some of the powerful native Babylonian elite toward foreigners in respectable positions, much less the royal family. But then, Adad-guppi had questions about making space for more antiques in a room displaying the king's collection. As I was heading to the palace's public section, I saw a familiar form up ahead – broad shoulders in a simple coat. Despite myself, my heart beat faster. As he turned a corner, Khai saw me, stopped, and grinned.

"I'm surprised to see you," I said. "Here. 'Palace life...' I remember you saying."

"After I left, I realized –" His inscrutable eyes settled on mine. "It has its charms."

I felt my face warm. I cleared my throat. "I heard you were off to Susiana, north to Assur..."

"Business is good," Khai said.

I looked into Khai's face, always so open. "I'm glad to see you."

He smiled. Then, "Sorry," he said. "I shouldn't keep you. You'll be at the king's audience tomorrow?"

I must have looked confused.

"Renovating the gardens...?"

"Oh! Then, yes. Good." I hated how I felt flustered. But I realized what I'd never wanted to admit. This man. I wanted to be near him, to see him, to hear him again. To feel his touch, even if it were only to tuck away the hair from my face as he had so long ago. I made myself turn away even before he disappeared down another hall.

WHEN THE GUARDS opened the door to the king's rooms, the sharp features of Igliss was the first thing I saw.

I pulled back. I asked the guard, whose straight hair and dark skin suggested foreign descent, "What's he doing here?"

"Just arrived. 'To comfort the king,' he says." The guard rolled his eyes. "Brought the baby, an awful little thing."

"And Kassiya?"

The man shook his head. "Only the boy's nurse. Igliss says Kassiya won't leave Sippar. She grieves the dead prince, 'her brother, after all'." He said these last words with Igliss's nasal lilt.

I clenched my teeth, then nodded my readiness to enter. But

as the guard prepared to announce me, I had second thoughts. I put a finger to my lips and shook my head. The guard grinned and gestured to a spot just inside the door where I could watch unseen, hidden by a post. And listen in.

Igliss said, "We all do wish the late Eanna-šarra-utsur, the estimable Prince Ean, could have succeeded you to the throne." He shook his head in slow, exaggerated arcs and gave a sigh so loud that it was audible where I stood. "Your first-born, beloved son."

Blind to the charade, Nebuchadnezzar dropped his hands as if weighted with iron gloves. "I could never find a way to release him from that curse." His gaze passed right through the far walls. "I failed him."

Igliss shrugged. "It's the way of the gods, or the evil of demons."

I watched Nebuchadnezzar hang his head in defeat. I fought the urge to rush forward and shake the king by his shoulders, to say, "Do you care nothing about your son Bushu, the crown prince, the one who is alive?!" But I clamped my mouth shut and kept to the shadow, the pillar cool against my skin.

"You know that I and Kassiya will do anything to help you," Igliss said. "You have so much to worry about these days. To be king," Igliss stretched out his arms, gave them a little shake, and watched the wide sleeves fall around the chair's armrests as if it were already a throne, "of the greatest nation, greatest empire, in the world... It must be exhausting. I don't envy it of you for a single moment."

I bit my tongue.

"I *am* tired," Nebuchadnezzar said.

"So much to do. Tyre unsettled, diplomacy in Egypt..."

I left before I lost control. "Don't envy it." Right, I thought, sarcastically. It's all Igliss has ever wanted. I could have screamed at Nebuchadnezzar's blind complacency.

. . .

NATHAN CAME by my rooms in the morning to drop off the docket for that day's audience.

"Anything in particular that I should know?"

"The gardens," Nathan said, "some kind of maintenance - is on the agenda."

"That much I do know. It's why I'm going." Nathan had grown into exactly the kind of young man he'd seemed as a boy that he would – forthcoming, confident without self-congratulation, an intelligent scribe whose disinterest in palace affairs reflected a sense of self and purpose apart even from this prestigious work.

I looked at him. "The name Cyrus."

I heard Kara catch her breath. I'd told her, of course. And that his identity was a secret only we few knew.

"Do you know what it means?"

Nathan shook his head, no. "Except..." He considered. "It may be like Kurash – Elamite,

meaning something like 'protection, care.' It usually appears with a god's name – 'so-and-so will

protect, or look after.'"

Kara gave an audible huff and muttered, loud enough for my ears only, "Just like a nephew of yours, not to have a god's name attached."

I ignored her.

"Have you ever been into the gardens?" I asked Nathan.

"No," Nathan said. "But I can smell them. I hear the birds that come and see other things – bees, butterflies... We have a tradition –"

I grinned.

Nathan caught it. "A tradition for everything, yes." He paused. "That's all we have left."

I took the sheet and nodded for him to go on.

"It's one of the oldest of our stories..." He tilted his head, "that human beings were created for the purpose of caring for the garden of God. That we are made of earth and created in order to keep it with reverent care. Our sole purpose and perfectly satisfying."

I sat down.

"But we… grew up." Nathan looked past me toward the window. "That's in the stories, too. We made the work drudgery and found that the world we inhabit is imperfect and unfair." He looked at me again, shrugged, and walked toward the door.

"Wait," I said. "Your tradition, that story..."

Nathan turned.

"Is that all?"

"That's just the beginning."

CHAPTER 21

"You have to keep still, if I'm going to finish this in time," Kara said.

I'd been putting on and taking off one bracelet after another. I rifled through my dressing table and looked behind the vials filled with perfume and ointments and shells of eye shadow and lip color. Kara was in the midst of trying to arrange my hair in the formal up-do style, but loose, too. She had already run black kohl in a heavy line all around my eyes and applied a powdered highlight to the lids. My lips were stained a deep red with kermes, a Phoenician cosmetic. There were times to embrace the Babylonian-ness of my condition. I figured that this, the king's audience was one of them. I reached for a golden eye-stone bracelet that Nebuchadnezzar had given me years ago. Stone inlay created a circular pattern of genies in pairs around a stylized sun-burst tree. At the center was an eye stone itself surrounded by a many-petaled pattern. A curl that Kara had tucked behind the crenellated crown slipped free. She huffed.

"Leave it."

Kara laid gnarled, fire-scarred hands on my shoulders and held me at arm's length. She looked me up and down, her good eye sharp as ever, then fixed a final golden bracteate, embossed with the face of Ishtar's lioness, to my shoulder.

I took Kara's hands in her own. "We've come a long way, Karadara."

"Watch your tongue in there."

As I NEARED the great hall of the throne room, I wondered if it was too late to turn around. I'd never wanted to sit on a throne, and there were plenty of people who didn't want me there, either.

"My lady."

I started. Speaking of not wanting me there...

Belshazzar emerged from an adjacent hall. A shine of hair-wax betrayed the effort to tweak his Aramean locks and beard into the tight rolls that marked Babylonian male fashion these days. I took in his fine clothes.

Igliss stepped out from the darkness behind him. It felt like an ambush. I reminded myself of my station. "Our queen mother." Why did Igliss always have to sound so sarcastic? His beady eyes scanned me, crown to bejeweled sandals. "Indeed." It didn't sound like approval. But it made me more determined. I would attend this audience. Yes, as the queen mother. I walked on, the two courtiers falling into step behind me.

"I understand that reinvigorating those..." Igliss's nasal voice drilled the air, "...shall we say, ambitious gardens are on the agenda. Medes," Igliss confided loudly to Belshazzar, "You simply can't take love and loyalty to their country out of them." He had no idea how right he was. It almost made me want Bushu to stay, remain as crown prince, just to spite Igliss. Almost. But not enough. Bushu's leaving – and mine as soon as Nebuchadnezzar died – would thrill Igliss beyond imagining. That was fine with me, if it put Bushu out of danger and back in Media. Restoring Media's tranquility and prosperity – out of Babylonian control – would be revenge enough. We just had to get Nebuchadnezzar back in charge. Maybe this audience would see to that.

The throne room seemed even larger than before. Nowhere in Media or Babylonia, for that matter, was there anything to compare. Today, entering to take a seat on the dais, its magnificence struck me more than ever. Its span was immense, dwarfing any individual person inside, and its elegance breathtaking. Golden lions embossed in glazed tile strode above a line of rosettes. Above them, a register of yellow and white lotus flowers, linked by graceful arcs of pale blue were the foundation for blocks of tall, stylized palm trees above which three more registers of flowers delighted the eye with color and order. I stepped inside and awaited the king's invitation.

In the middle of that long stretch of open hall, atop the dais, on the throne so long empty sat Bushu. His modest crown caught the light from high windows and shot it back out in long, golden beams. If I didn't know how much he longed to be elsewhere, back in wild Media, I'd say he looked every bit at ease in this role, a prince in line for the throne, confident and capable – a bright young man ready to do whatever the task required. My throat tightened to think of him as a baby, a little boy... and how happy I was that he had grown to love Media as I did. We nodded a greeting to each other.

Next to Bushu, the king looked even more old, shrunken. I saw with dismay that he still hadn't washed or trimmed his hair. His toenails curled around the ends of his sandals. The horror was magnetizing. I forced myself to look away. I'd hoped that conducting the king's audience would bring him back to his senses. But to look at him now... it was hard to imagine that events here could transform this derelict back into the fiercely ambitious, power-focused king I'd always known Nebuchadnezzar to be.

I tore my eyes away to settle instead on the chair waiting for me. I'd never seen the queen mother's throne before. I'd been told that Syrian exiles had carved it of imported hardwood. It was simply beautiful. Its back depicted the goddess of the animals standing on a stylized mountain, arms outstretched and holding fronds from which gazelles, standing on their hind legs, nibbled. The chair's arms, wide and smooth, each ended with the neck and placid face of a lioness. Its feet were hers – broad feline toes ending in ebony claws.

At a small table to the side, Nathan prepared his tools to record the day's proceedings. A few courtiers milled against the far wall. I could hear one of the king's managers in the hall organizing the people who had come with cases to be heard. We waited in the doorway, I, with Belshazzar and Igliss behind me.

Finally, at the king's barely perceptible invitation, I walked forward. I could hear the swish and step of Igliss and Belshazzar behind me. The gentle slap of my sandals on the limestone was a simple comfort. Without looking at Igliss or Belshazzar, I took my place on the queen mother's throne, resting my hands on the lionesses' heads. It fit as if made for me.

NEBUCHADNEZZAR CALLED for the first visitor. Guards swung open the great doors in the middle of the room. Escorted by a eunuch guard, a man strode in wearing an ostentatious bronze clasp with Marduk's spade emblazoned across it to fix a tunic that despite a broad belt couldn't hide his portly frame. I recognized him as the husband of one of the women I saw occasionally among the citizens. The man started when he saw Nebuchadnezzar's state – unkempt and haggard—and stumbled back a few steps. He recovered himself, bowed to Nebuchadnezzar from a safe distance, and nodded to Bushu and to me. Igliss prompted him to begin.

The man cleared his throat. "Among the peoples in Babylon, it has come to my attention that some insist on continuing to honor their defeated gods as if superseding even the great and most high Marduk..."

From behind the king, I heard Igliss sniff derisively. I thought of Adad-guppi, devoted to Nanna-Suen despite her position in court. Her grandson Belshazzar stood behind the scribe, as Babylonian as could be; but I'd never forgotten the argument I'd overheard some years ago. And I was acutely aware of Nathan, recording the proceedings a few feet away.

"I've heard rumors that they wish to repatriate the deities, smuggle their statues out."

"Rumors." Nebuchadnezzar sighed. "Tell Nabonidus if they turn into action."

Nabonidus, I thought, as devoted as his mother to the moon god of Harran... but dutiful, too. He wouldn't undermine the throne.

The next person was an elderly woman. She cringed at the sight of the king's state and never again lifted her face from the floor. In a tremulous voice, she complained that her husband had died leaving behind debts that she had no knowledge of or any part in accruing. They were due to a neighbor from whom her husband "had rented slave women." Nebuchadnezzar passed it on – "for the court judges," he mumbled.

Someone came complaining about immigrants – people moving to Babylonia from unrest in the north. I heard Igliss shift, probably trying not to say what he was thinking – that it was Media's fault. Nebuchadnezzar muttered, "Let them come."

"But sir," Belshazzar said, with a look to Igliss.

Before Igliss could reinforce Belshazzar's concern, Bushu raised his voice. "There *is* plenty of work," he said. With Nebuchadnezzar's disinterest, that ended it.

Case after case. I listened and watched. It was striking. Without fail, each person retreated when confronted with the king's state. As for Nebuchadnezzar, he hardly made an effort, even to listen, and deferred decisions with the briefest comment, whenever possible.

Next on the agenda, the gardens.

When the guards opened the doors again, there stood Khai. I hoped no one else could hear the rings of my necklace clang softly against each other. My heart beat stupidly hard. Nebuchadnezzar waved the eunuchs back, leaving the commoner to cross the space alone. Khai walked with neither hesitation nor haste, as always, his back straight, his body relaxed. His clothes were simple, the sleeves of his robe a little frayed at edges, well-used, but clean. He, too, had accumulated lines around his eyes. Gray streaked the hair at his temples.

Khai stepped up to Nebuchadnezzar, closer than any person had before. "My lord. My lady –" Khai's eyes warmed. Or maybe I imagined it. "Prince. Gentlemen," he said bowing, each time less deeply than the last.

The room was silent. I shifted, anxious and curious what he might have to do with the gardens, now. Khai stood loosely, waiting for an invitation to present his case. Unlike any before him, he held his place.

On his throne, Nebuchadnezzar straightened with a creaky effort. Slowly, he leaned forward. He fixed Khai with rheumy eyes. "Have you ever lost a son?"

I started.

"Every child my wife has born lives still," Khai said, his words steady and clear. He was the only one who didn't seem shocked by Nebuchadnezzar's question.

"Yet you are not afraid of me, your king, a wretch?" Nebuchadnezzar asked, shaking his stringy hair and waving bony fingers with their talon-like nails in Khai's face.

Nathan lowered his stylus.

Khai held Nebuchadnezzar's gaze. "I am not, my lord, though sorry for your loss."

I couldn't imagine how Khai kept his composure. Or what

Nebuchadnezzar was thinking now. Despite my hoping and the prayers of countless Babylonian priests, Nebuchadnezzar was no better. If anything, this public audience had demonstrated the tenacity of his grief and confirmed how weak and out of touch he'd become.

Bushu stirred on his throne, coughed into his hand.

The sound brought Nebuchadnezzar out of this strange interrogation. He sat back. Nathan lifted his stylus again, ready to resume recording the business at hand. "The gardens." The king's voice dropped, weary again. He waved a hand to go on, as if forming words was too great an effort.

"Yes, sir." Khai looked at me, then back at the king. "I'm here to petition for the position of the gardens' manager."

I caught my breath. That would put him on the palace grounds nearly every day. I tried to squash the eagerness I felt rising in my chest.

Igliss scoffed. "That is a citizen-class role."

Nebuchadnezzar nodded agreement.

A wisp of defeat passed across Khai's face. He dropped his eyes.

Emboldened, Igliss sneered. "Whatever made you think –?"

"*I* think –" My voice broke a little. Khai lifted his head. That look was all I needed to speak out clearly. "He is the perfect fit." I turned to Nebuchadnezzar. "After all, he is the one who first selected, secured, and transplanted the specimens we have."

Igliss's face reddened with anger. "It is a citizen-class, position," he repeated slowly, loudly.

Belshazzar added loudly, "And this man is nothing but a commoner."

"Sir." Bushu slid forward on his throne. Nebuchadnezzar didn't look, but the prince continued anyway. "We have defeated peoples," Bushu said, "filling other such positions, according to their talent, training, and skill." I tried not to smile. He was right, and it was Nebuchadnezzar's own choice that had made it so.

Choosing my words carefully, I said, "Years ago, this man brought a variety of plants from abroad to introduce into the gardens. Some have adapted and even continue to flourish." I let my eyes wander over Khai's face. The beard cut close, barely covered the strong line of his jaw. His neck was a deep brown where it disappeared into the border of his tunic. I remembered my son's arms wrapped around that neck, the relief of finding Bushu alive. And I remembered Khai carrying sweet Gulash to his grave. "But some of the plants have failed to establish themselves," I said, "and others need replacing. The whole requires singular and ongoing oversight." Nebuchadnezzar tipped his head back and closed his eyes. "It can be a place of great solace," I said. Igliss's eyes narrowed with hatred, and was it suspicion? So I added, "And as you yourself have said, this is a great contribution to the beauty of Babylon, heart of the empire, heart of your heart." I couldn't be sure, but I thought I saw a flicker of amusement in Khai's eyes. Still, he listened, arms at his sides, unmoving.

Nebuchadnezzar lifted his head. "Go," he said to me, "show him, this new manager."

I stepped down next to Khai.

"Sir," my son tried to get the king's attention. "Why don't you go, too?"

Igliss slithered a little closer to the king's throne. I stiffened, seeing Igliss's interest. I had never told Bushu about that day, my suspicion that Igliss had tried to kill him as a boy.

"I can attend the rest of the day's audience," Bushu said. "I can manage the details."

Nebuchadnezzar hesitated, then dipped his head and heaved himself up.

"I'll stay here," Igliss said, "to advise the young man."

A chill ran down my back.

But the prospect of being in the garden with Khai, even with Nebuchadnezzar's glum presence beside us overrode my anxiety.

We'd only been in the gardens for a few moments – I'd

pointed out the medlar, its limbs stripped by some insect or another – when the king begged off. "Tired," he said, "too tired." To my surprise, Nebuchadnezzar left, taking his attendants with him, which left Khai and me.

Alone.

FOR A MOMENT, among the trees, the flowering shrubs, and vines, while bees thrummed the air overhead and birds called to one another, Khai and I simply stood. I could feel his eyes on me; but I couldn't turn mine to meet them. Not without giving myself away.

Finally, I chose a path and stepped forward. I tried to carry on as if this were any other day and he any other prospective garden manager, asking Khai for his opinions on this or that failure to thrive or site issue among the plants. But the warmth of his body, so near mine, the timbre of his voice both gentle and clear was too much. I found myself angling toward the cornelian tree under which Khai had buried Gulash, so long ago. It was in full fruit – bright red berries hanging from their delicate greens threads.

I plucked one. "They're tart at first." I held it by its stem, "then sweeter than you can imagine." I looked at Khai for the first time since we'd entered the gardens.

Birds trilled from a near branch. But neither of us tore our eyes from the other. With a single, quick lift of his chin, Khai gestured for me to give it to him. I held out the fruit. Instead, with a small smile, he opened his lips. Heart pounding, I leaned forward, my eyes searching his, and put the berry into his mouth.

Suddenly a sound, a rustle – not of animal nor of bird, not wind or rain – disturbed the branches of a bush nearby. I pushed Khai away. From the corner of my eye, I thought I saw the sweep of a robe, the heel of a sandal. My breath caught in my throat.

Beside me, Khai exhaled. "A lizard," he said. "Look, there –"

Sure enough, flicking its spiny tail atop a boulder, a buff colored reptile as long as my arm waggled its head.

Still, I was shaken beyond recovery.

I knew in the animal of my body that within another moment, as if the land in its fecund richness had opened up, I would have closed any distance between myself and this man. I shuddered. Were anyone to witness such a breach of the contract I'd given my life to make and keep, all I'd ever sought to keep would be lost. The treaty would be broken, my son judged a traitor, and wild Media subjected to a Babylonian domination without mercy. And all so close to the time when all I could ever hope would come to pass: Bushu forever in Media, and I just as soon as Nebuchadnezzar was dead to join him there. All I could ever hope… but for this.

I raised my eyes to Khai's only to say, "Go. You know what these gardens need. Fetch what you can, all the way to Ecbatana. Just go."

"And when I return?"

I memorized my beloved's eyes, the shape of his chin, his nose, his face. "You'll not see me again."

Khai, stricken, nevertheless nodded assent.

"Now!" I said with all the urgency that burned in my chest. Khai's stepping away was like tearing a limb from my body. Still, to his back I called, "Promise me –" For a moment, the words stuck in my throat. "That unless it were to save Bushu's life – again – you will never come back to the palace."

Khai voice was husky. "I promise."

I couldn't look at him any longer. When I raised my eyes again, Khai was gone.

Gone. Lost to me forever. I had ruined what hope there was for us to share time and place. A gardener and his employer. It would have been enough. Now even that was lost.

. . .

I FORCED my feet to move back toward the palace.

As soon as I reentered, Nathan met me at the door, breathless.

"A shipment of tribute and gifts from Egypt just arrived," he said, panting. "Adad-guppi asked if you could sign for them?"

"Where is Bushu?"

"He's already there, at the courtyard."

I fell into hasty step beside him. "Did something happen?" I asked, dreading – what, I didn't know.

"There's a woman among the goods."

I couldn't understand the problem, but I trusted Nathan. So we hurried on.

Sure enough, standing barefoot in the late winter sun, just in front of the crates and boxes was a girl, barely the age I was when I first came to Babylon. But this young woman was a slave. Her lips were painted red with ochre. Wide eyes, heavily etched with kohl, caught mine then flashed about, taking in her surroundings. Loose curls brushed a delicate neck. The woman's skin was as smooth as burnished bronze. A painted blush colored her cheeks. Bracelets jangled off her wrists and anklets of gold and abalone circled strong legs. Most striking to me: the robe she wore was Bushu's. She clutched it tightly closed. It was easy to guess that she was otherwise naked.

Near her, Bushu was in an animated discussion with Adad-guppi. Igliss stood to the side. Seeing me, Adad-guppi broke away and hurried up.

"Oh good," Adad-guppi's bright face cleared in relief. "You're here."

"What is this?"

"Someone needs to sign –"

"But Bushu –"

"Someone," Adad-guppi said, "who is not *invested*." She raised her eyebrows and nodded her head in their direction.

I followed her gaze. Bushu was talking now to the girl. Even from a distance, I could see what I'd never seen on my son's face before. And I ached for him, as I ached for myself – gaining and losing Khai all in a moment. For what I saw there was love.

Igliss could see it, too. The smirk on his face as he looked from the girl to Bushu and back told me everything I needed to know. Igliss would use this.

I didn't know how or when, but, "Have Silla meet me in my rooms," I said to Adad-guppi. The manager of the king's women could fetch her there. To the girl I said, "You'll come with me." I cut off Bushu's protest. "Stay, record the items and formulate a proper response for the Egyptian king." I gave him what I hoped was a meaningful look. To my relief, Bushu stepped down. He gestured to Nathan to prepare the document but not before gently insisting the girl keep his robe for now. Igliss grinned.

As I signed to take the things into my management, I realized that the only way to get Igliss away from Bushu – until Nebuchadnezzar was fine again – was for the king to go with Igliss to Sippar.

I would agree to Igliss's request.

CHAPTER 22

They left that same day. Bushu and I joined the small group of palace officials and administrators to see the king off to Sippar. The king's absence would only be for a little while, maybe mere days. "The rest will do him good," I overheard someone say.

I hoped so. We needed the king back on his throne, back in his normal state so we could leave for Media.

Before Igliss stepped into the carriage to join Nebuchadnezzar, I watched him take Belshazzar aside and whisper something that made Belshazzar pull his round shoulders back and nod with determined pride. Seeds of doubt settled in the fertile ground of my imagination.

I DIDN'T HAVE long to think on it. Hardly had Igliss and Nebuchadnezzar left through the gate than Bushu turned to me. "I need to know if Shiyati's all right."

"Who?"

"The girl who arrived with the Egyptian goods." Bushu walked beside me.

"So you know her name." A blue bird with a rose-colored chest flitted over a wall, out of sight. A wall meant nothing to a bird.

"We talked. Before Igliss got there."

Igliss. I shivered, remembering the scare I'd felt with Khai there in the gardens. But Igliss hadn't said anything, hadn't let on. Besides, he was with Bushu. It must have been that lizard.

"Please. Can you arrange for me to see her again?"

I stopped. "You need to put her out of your mind," I felt the cold hardness of those words in my own heart. "She is one of the king's women now."

Bushu's mouth was a thin line.

"Shiyati." I kept walking. "That's not an Egyptian name."

"She's from Parsa."

I stopped.

"Yes, from where your sister lived."

And the country of Cyrus's paternity. How I wanted to know about that place!

I took Bushu's hand in mine. "I'll invite her to my rooms," I said, "and I'll tell her that you asked, that you care how she's doing." I watched Belshazzar approach.

"Let me be there," Bushu said.

I waited for Belshazzar to pass – barely acknowledging us – before saying, my voice low, "You know how dangerous... a man... taking the king's women."

"The same as usurping the throne." Bushu nodded. "But this is different. You and Kara would be there. And it's not as if I'd be in the concubinage."

Some yards away, Belshazzar turned back. He looked at us one more time before going through the gate back into the palace.

"It's too dangerous," I said. "And with Nebuchadnezzar gone –"

Bushu pulled away. To my surprise, he scoffed. "*You* –" The scorn on his face stopped me cold. "You didn't even wait for him to leave before..." Bushu looked around then stepped closer, his voice low. "I know about you and the Egibi."

As if hit in the stomach, I folded as I exhaled. So it had been my son there in the gardens. Relief turned to anger. Bushu was using that... I straightened. My son's face was soft again, pleading.

I sighed. "All right," I said. "Meet me there in an hour."

I RETRIEVED THE GIRL MYSELF. Silla had given the girl proper attire. But Bushu's robe still draped her shoulders. We walked in silence for a while. I thought about what had brought this young woman – barely older than a child – to this place, and couldn't help but remember my own arrival... The girl hugged the robe more tightly to her.

"My son tells me that your name is Shiyati," I said. The girl braved a quick look my way and nodded once. "And that you're from Parsa."

The girl slowed her steps and straightened her back. "... of the Maraphii."

"You say that with pride."

Shiyati looked at me then. "It's one of the noble tribes." Her dark brown eyes were clear. "My father is the chieftain."

How with such a pedigree had the girl happened to become a slave? Kara met us at the door, Bushu was already there. He stepped aside, a grin on his face. Color rushed his cheeks.

"Did you know a Median princess?" I asked as we stepped inside. "Mandane?" My voice caught on my sister's name.

A flash of recognition brightened the girl's face. "Yes, the king's wife."

Kara stared, her eyes wide in the disfigured face.

"The girl is from Parsa," I explained.

Shiyati was sober again. "Her death is when the troubles began."

"Sit," I said. "Kara will fetch us something to eat and drink."

Kara scowled but shuffled off. Bushu followed us into my public room.

"What happened?" I asked. "These 'troubles'? And to you?"

"Our family," Shiyati sighed. "We were told that we had to make our farm into poppy fields. The king's official, who enforces the edict –"

"The order came from the palace?"

"Sort of." Shiyati nodded. "There's no real palace. Not like here. Anyway, the steward, a horrible man, said that I would have a better life in the city." She looked at the ground. "We were starving. There was no choice."

"The king of Parsa is growing poppies?"

"More and more, grown for milking. They say Parsa is vulnerable for take-over by Susa or tribes from northern Media. They promise that opium will bring profit to make weapons and stronger defense. Maybe it will..." She looked down at her hands. "For those who are left."

Throughout the hour or so that we talked, Bushu never once took his eyes off Shiyati. She told us that after Mandane's death, Parsa declined in wealth and order. Meanwhile, my father Astyages had been making threats to tax and subdue Median tribes, who as Bushu and I had seen, were growing restive. Violence had already broken out here and there.

As she spoke, Shiyati never looked at Bushu, but she was clearly aware of his attention. Her honey-brown cheeks even under the make-up blushed a pearly red. When Silla came to bring Shiyati back to the women's quarters, Shiyati gave Bushu a smile. "Thank you for lending me your robe," she said as she handed it back to him. "No one has been so kind to me, since... " her eyes swam, "... I left home."

.   .   .

AFTER SHE LEFT, Bushu turned to me, his eyes shining. Before he opened his mouth, I said, "There is nothing we can do until Nebuchadnezzar has returned."

"But –"

"Shiyati will be fine until then."

Bushu's face fell.

"Now," my voice softened, "we have work to do."

Bushu rose, then stopped at the door. When he turned to me, his face was bright again with hope. "You know, Nebuchadnezzar married a slave."

I bit back the correction on my tongue – I was never a slave, not exactly... Then I realized it wasn't me Bushu was talking about. "You're right," I looked at how Bushu's shoulders had filled out. "When Nebuchadnezzar is back – it should be soon – I'll speak with him." The angles of my son's face had lost their childish softness. "It's time we found a girl for you."

Bushu hugged the robe he'd lent to Shiyati to his chest. "I already did."

A WEEK PASSED. Bushu didn't raise the issue of Shiyati again, but I could see by an occasional quietness, a dreamy gaze, that she was on his mind. And I understood. How often I had thought about Khai, asked myself where on his Median expedition he might be now. It would be cold there; but a good time for getting plants – digging and transporting them during their winter rest – provided the snow wasn't too thick or the ground too frozen. I imagined his warm smile, his attentive interest, as if I mattered...

Meanwhile, we carried on. While Bushu and I made the rounds to assess Nebuchadnezzar's diverse construction projects around the city, from the Ishtar Gate to the temples in the neighborhoods west of the river, from the bitumen project on the walls at the northern moat to the fortified citadel, I noticed with pride that Bushu made sure both to praise the Babylonian citizenry for their leadership, and to note the exiles' contributions and developments. Meanwhile, Nabonidus and his seemingly ageless mother Adad-guppi helped keep the logistical details on track. Palace life was again on an even keel.

Except, that is, for the king's absence.

Word from Sippar was that the king's condition remained unchanged. Another week passed. Adad-guppi approached me. "Some cases simply can't wait any longer," the old woman said. "The king's audience may not have been busy before he left, but the docket has grown unwieldy. Would you join the crown prince in holding a surrogate audience, just to assure people, maybe handle whatever is critical? I'm sure you can delay many of the cases." Reluctant, I agreed.

WE WALKED TOGETHER, Bushu and I, through the halls toward the administrative wing. As our feet tap-tapped a steady pace along the stone floor, I stole a look at my son from the corner of my eye, and then again. Bushu was quiet, thoughtful. He seemed older, much older than his fifteen years. He caught me looking at him.

"I hope," he said, "that Nebuchadnezzar will agree to it." He didn't have to say that it was marrying Shiyati he meant.

"It would strengthen Parsa's alliance to Media," I said, happy that his intention to return to Media seemed unchanged.

At my implicit blessing, Bushu grinned as widely as I'd ever remembered.

I nodded. "Meanwhile, let's show Babylon that they have nothing to fear from a queen of Median descent and their half-Median crown prince."

We entered through the king's door. Several courtiers lounged against a far wall, waiting with an idle curiosity to see what would happen without Nebuchadnezzar present. Among them stood Belshazzar.

A eunuch, one of those I had noticed served as a kind of page, approached. "The roster is incomplete," he said. He gestured toward the double doors closed to the public hall outside. "There are far more here."

I glanced at Bushu.

"I've heard that people were frustrated with the king's behavior," Bushu said, "They probably saved up their complaints for --."

"When he's back." I tried to sound definitive. "Well, it should be soon. In the meantime –" I told the eunuch to have the guards open the doors and invite everyone in.

"Everyone?" The eunuch sputtered.

I looked around the hall. It was enormous. "Don't tell me they won't all fit."

"It's not that –"

"Then bring them in."

I could feel Bushu's eyes, incredulous, on me.

At first, the din was deafening. A flood of people from all walks of Babylonian life – citizens and non-citizens alike, slaves and foreigners, too -- surged into the hall, people asking their neighbors what did this mean, will their cases be heard, how could this work...? I knew that some among the crowd were born here but of foreign descent and some were new immigrants, people from Media and from elsewhere – including Parsa, I'd heard – looking for work and a better life. Belshazzar's company straightened, muttered to each other, and watched the unprecedented masses, quieter now, swaying and humming into the hall. When the doors cleared again (and the room still only a quarter filled), I stood.

Their faces were attentive. Some reluctantly, some openly sneered, but each waited, curious at the least for how we, Bushu and I, might handle the unprecedented circumstances.

I cleared my throat. "King Nebuchadnezzar determined to make a brief trip to visit his daughter and grandson," I said, "to enjoy a brief period of recreation. He'll be back any day now." I looked around as I spoke, hoping that the thrum of doubt in my mind didn't weaken the confidence in my voice. "You'll be best served by the king, of cour–" It had been years since I slipped up like that. I quickly corrected, "For certain." A disgruntled murmur rose from the floor. I wasn't sure if it was what I'd said or how I'd said it. "If however, your situation cannot wait, I and the crown prince will manage it as well as we can." The hum grew decidedly brighter. Apparently, in this case it mattered less where I was from than whether or not the people would receive the justice they'd been waiting for. When it died down again, I said, "We'll give some time now for those who would prefer that King Nebuchadnezzar hear their issues to leave." No one moved. "Or whose cases can wait –" still no one moved, "to leave the room."

The hall was silent now and still. People looked around, looked at the door, looked back at the dais. Some shuffled their feet. "People whose cases can wait," I repeated, "may leave the room." No one left.

I took a deep breath. "You," I said to the eunuch. "Fetch another scribe." The crowd made room for him to reach the door. "We'll begin with the existing roster."

We worked through the cases together as swiftly as possible. I saw with relief and pride that Bushu was at least as competent an arbiter as I. When we were into our eighth or ninth case, the eunuch returned with the scribe.

I stood again. "The crown prince will take some there," I gestured to one side, "while I take others here." The scribe set up near Bushu, and for the rest of the afternoon and well into the evening, we heard cases simultaneously. Occasionally we sought each other's advice, and occasionally, a defendant would protest and demand the other's attention. But for the most part, it went smoothly. And gradually, the crowd thinned.

When horns from the city walls reported the midnight watch, Nathan scratched notes for the last of the cases. The hall was finally empty.

I stood and stretched my arms high over my head, twisted my stiff back this way and that. Bushu slumped forward, resting his elbows on his knees. When he looked up again, he was smiling. "Good practice," he said. I nodded, smiling back. When he got to Media and I finally could join him, together my son and I would get the country back in shape, strong, secure, and prosperous. For now, though, we would take care of Babylonian needs so that when Nebuchadnezzar returned – and none too soon – we could leave without crisis.

Bushu said, "Maybe hearing that we held an audience will provoke Nebuchadnezzar to return, resume his work. Then..." He didn't have to say more. Bushu's eagerness to leave for Media – with Shiyati –was hardly his alone. I hoped he was right.

I sent to Sippar detailing what we'd done and how things were going in Babylon with respect to official and national business. And I asked if the king might return, refreshed, within a day or two. There was no reply.

IT WAS during our public audience on the third week that a courier interrupted proceedings with news from Sippar. I read the note quickly, sighed, and passed it to Bushu. I could almost feel him deflate. The people waiting quieted. I stood.

In as strong a voice as I could muster, I said, "The king has been detained in Sippar." I swallowed. "Indefinitely."

As demanding and stressful it was keeping up with the nation's affairs, I considered how it could nevertheless be a panacea to grief, a distraction really. I'd hoped the king would return and experience that for himself, finally making it possible for Bushu to abdicate and us to leave for Media. On the other hand, maybe carrying the burden of the empire really did make Nebuchadnezzar's condition worse.

While I was thinking, I watched Belshazzar at the back of the room confer with another courtier, citizen class. The man nodded, then called out toward the dais, "and what about the Akitu?"

The Akitu, the single most crucial event in the Babylonian calendar.

A murmur went up from those gathered.

"What about it?" I asked, trying to sound unconcerned. "It's still weeks away."

"Will the king be back for that?"

"For certain." I said. I glanced over at Bushu. His jaw was set tight. Sometimes I could see Bushu's father – King Nebuchadnezzar, who had conquered peoples and nations, built an empire, reveled in the cosmopolitan court he had orchestrated -- in the set of my son's eyes, the strength of his chin.

"The king will take Marduk's hand," Bushu said, "here in Babylon, just as it's always been done."

As the crowd settled, I leaned in to Bushu. "We have to get him back," I said.

The next day, I visited Bushu in his quarters. "From now on," I said. "We spare the king everything. Let's hope that either the rest or the restlessness of hearing nothing –

"Will get him back more quickly," Bushu finished, nodding.

"And I've been thinking," I said, "the king's audiences have returned to normal numbers. You should take them all." At this, Bushu stifled a grin. "You handle requests better than me, anyway," I said. "Whatever you do, don't call on Nebuchadnezzar for counsel or attention to state matters." He sobered. I walked back and forth across his floor, thinking. "Welcome advice but tell people that as much as you value their opinions, you'll make your own choices and take full responsibility for decisions. Whatever happens, don't send to Sippar for help." Bushu's face reflected a good mix of anxiety and confidence. I laid my hand against his cheek. Stubble tickled my palm. "You really are ready to do the king's work, aren't you?"

"Yes." Bushu lowered my hand with his own. "And to forfeit the throne."

So we kept on. And by all practical accounts things went well.

Yet on more than one night, I bolted out of sleep, sweating and breathless with the dream-ghosts of murder and destruction – Bushu impaled, his body morphing into a bleeding Gulash's; wildfires decimating forests and forcing Media's animals onto Babylonian swords, while I watched helplessly entangled in chains of jewelry; mountain paths I knew by heart paved wide and flat for armies from the south dragging logs back to Babylon – each orchestrated by Igliss behind a dead-eyed Nebuchadnezzar.

I'd wake, heart racing, and go to the window. I would train my eyes on the Euphrates, steadying my breathing on its slow and sturdy flow. I'd imagine tracing its line upstream all the way to where Nathan said Media's Eden might be. I'd think of Cyrus, Mandane's son, secreted away to grow strong with the shepherd slaves. And I'd think, every time with a lift in my heart, of returning there one day. I tried not to think about the commoner I'd never see again, the man whose breath on my cheek, his hand on my neck, his lips... I longed for with a taut hunger. I couldn't help looking for Khai down every hall, in every room I entered, every courtyard I passed through. But just as he'd promised, Khai was never there. He was gone.

By contrast, Belshazzar seemed to be everywhere. He watched and listened. But he was a courtier. It was normal, I told myself. I knew he took special note each time Bushu asked someone with business in Sippar what they could tell him about his father: Is the king still eating only vegetables? Has he cut his hair or nails? Is he conducting himself any more like the man he once was? In private, Bushu told me he didn't know how much longer he could wait. He yearned to fetch Shiyati, leave for Media and never come back. I urged him to be patient. We had to do this right.

But the days and weeks added up. We oversaw preparations for the upcoming Akitu until it was only a week away. Still, Nebuchadnezzar, who was so critical to the ritual proceedings, had not returned.

Bushu and I continued to fulfill what duties we could without troubling Nebuchadnezzar with any of it. We didn't talk about it – no one had imagined Nebuchadnezzar would be gone for so long – but Bushu was growing anxious. And impatient, too.

CHAPTER 23

$\mathcal{N}$athan told me later, "The crown prince asked me to do some research, to figure out how Nebuchadnezzar's grief became so debilitating. 'See if you can find out if my father angered a god and how, or if this is the product of an evil spell?' Bushu asked me. He provided me with a temple pass so that I could look at the books of the priests, consult with exorcists…. 'Are there witches in the temple or nearby community who wish my father ill or are in alliance with some enemy? Even if we can't locate the person who cursed him, there should be some way to reverse or override it.' The prince was adamant," Nathan said.

"It sounds reasonable."

Nathan nodded. "But-" He hesitated, perhaps anticipating how absurd what he was about to say would sound to me.

"I told your son that only the true God, Yahweh, can defeat the powers of evil." Even after all these years, Nathan still believed. "Whether God will or not, who knows? We cannot control God." Nathan shrugged. "Anyway, I promised to do the research and also to pray. 'But the help you seek,' I told your son, 'only comes from the Most High. There is no god above ours.'"

Absurd indeed. "Didn't Marduk defeat your God," I asked, "when the Babylonians defeated Judah and destroyed the temple?"

Nathan pursed his lips. "Yahweh allowed it to happen." His voice was at once quiet and clear. "Yahweh used Babylonia against us."

I'd never heard anything like it – one people's god controlling a totally different people with their own gods, Babylonia no less. This Yahweh, and the faith of his people, people such as Nathan and that prophet-priest Ezekiel, baffled me. "But Yahweh is your god," I said, "and if he is as powerful as you say, then why didn't Yahweh defend your country, your people?"

Nathan took a deep breath, as if his answer required everything he could bring to it, and still it wouldn't be enough. "Some prophets say that our history shows a consistent failure to do the things that we had promised to God. We failed to protect the vulnerable. We neglected our relationship to the creator of heaven and earth, failed to recognize the interconnection of thought and deed, of heart and purpose. They say that God forgave and forgave until finally Yahweh determined that, as per our agreement, we would lose the land that God had given to us. Some say that God even allowed the holy temple to be destroyed. Ezekiel, others too, believe that God will restore us again and punish the arrogance of nations such as Babylonia, in order that everyone knows the full identity of our God."

"Do you believe that?" I asked.

"I don't know." Nathan's shoulders slumped as if all the confidence and clarity he had just mustered were so much air, now escaping a deflating bladder. "Yahweh-God selected us out of all the peoples of the earth, they say. But for what? Not for favor, I can tell you that. Or if so, it's a kind of favor that I for one could do without." He gave a wry smile. "I have a lot of respect for Ezekiel. He was a priest, a man of extraordinary learning, vision, and creativity..." Nathan shook his head. "I come from a different prophetic tradition. My father was trained in a school of thinking that goes back another 100 years to a prophet who counseled kings – Isaiah. I do believe that we've misused our freedoms from time to time, failed in certain responsibilities..." Nathan let his eyes pass around the room, glanced down at the tablet in his hands, the thin sandals on his feet, then back at me. "Ours is a God of novelty, renewal, and creation for the whole world. Somehow, human beings are to be involved in that. But I also I believe that this, this last punishment – Babylonian assault and exile -- is greater than we deserved – double for all our sins."

THAT EVENING, I walked along the city walls, my golden jackal robe loose over bare shoulders. The fur had survived the years of storage with surprising grace. I wished I could say as much. Especially on these days of late winter, when Babylon's gray seemed never ending, longing for the clean snows of Mount Alvand, the icy wind of its slopes cutting through dizzy-bright air tore at my heart like a ravenous lynx. All these years in Babylon, and still there were moments, breath-snatching and devastating, when I missed Media as acutely as when I'd first arrived.

I saw a familiar shape ahead -- Bushu, trailed by two guards. I picked up my pace. Closer, I heard Bushu's voice. But he wasn't talking to the guards or anyone I could see. His head was tipped up. Closer still, and I recognized the prayer. Babylonian. My heart sank. It was one thing to ask Nathan to interceded with Nathan's god; it was another to pray the prayers himself.

"O Wagonstar," Bushu said, "built of the gods -- Ninurta the farmer, Marduk the king, and the heavenly daughters of Anu, most ancient. Give me a dream-sign that my father Nebuchad-nezzar will become healthy and well."

Over the years, it hadn't bothered me, Bushu's observance of the many prayers and rituals honoring Babylonia's deities. I did them myself. It was simply part of the roles we played. But this was a private matter, his praying electively to this land's gods. And it bothered me now. After all this, had Bushu's loyalties finally aligned with Babylonia? What if, having tasted what the kingship could be, Bushu had changed his mind about abdicating? What if the thing I'd hoped above all – Media's wild integrity secure for all time, and Bushu living there – wasn't as fixed as I'd thought? My belly ached with dread. This appeal to the deities of Babylonia. Had Bushu dedicated himself to Marduk, as a future king – committed to the priority of Babylon – would do?

Now that Bushu was the crown prince and acting every bit the king, had he changed his mind about abdicating the throne to live in Media? I thought a moment. As long as Shiyati was in Babylon, she might remain among the king's women – the *king's*, Nebuchadnezzar's for now. The only way Bushu could only be certain Shiyati were with him was if Nebuchadnezzar released her to leave with him, away from Babylon. From what I could see of Bushu's feelings – love – that would be enough for him to want to leave. I determined to break my silence. I would reach out to Nebuchadnezzar in Sippar.

I FOUND Bushu in his rooms. He had been working through a stack of documents, some regarding the endless architectural renovations Nebuchadnezzar had started, some legal reports from the public audiences and more I hadn't seen yet. I knew he worked hard to preoccupy his mind while we waited. In the privacy of Bushu's quarters, I told him that I had requested the king release Shiyati into Bushu's care. The message would go out with a rider that evening. Bushu was thrilled. As soon as Nebuchadnezzar returned, Bushu could abdicate, and be on his way to Media, with the girl.

"One last thing," Bushu said. "I must ask Shiyati if that's what she wants, what she'd wish."

Bushu's concern for the girl's feelings moved me. "But," I said, "no one must know our plan, not yet. You cannot tell her until it's time to go, not a moment before."

"I won't go unless she wants to."

I would have reassured him – Shiyati would certainly want to leave Babylon, and stressed again that he should *not* try to talk to her before abdicating before Nebuchadnezzar returned– but we were interrupted.

So, I was in Bushu's public rooms when the chief official of Marduk's temple came by.

"WINTER IS PASSING." The shatammu's eyes measured me, then settled on Bushu in a way not unkind but not exactly charitable, either. Accusing, almost. "The New Year Akitu festival is nearly upon us."

"Yes, it is." Bushu didn't seem to notice the edge I heard in the shatammu's voice. Bushu pulled a document out from under one of the piles. "Orders for Ishtar's provisions came in just yesterday."

The shatammu shifted on his feet as if searching another angle. "We have made inquiries to Sippar, sent respectful requests..."

"Tell me. I'll handle it."

The shatammu raised his eyebrows. He stepped up closer. "Will the king be present for the Akitu? We have not heard."

I leaned forward. "You sent messengers?"

"Yes. Written queries, too."

Bushu and I shared a quick look. "Delivered to the king?"

"Through our temple associates. I understand that the king went to Sippar to get away from the stress of the capital." He fixed Bushu with a stern look. "But Babylonia's king, as you know, plays a central role in the festival, especially the culmination." The shatammu's voice was tight, urgent and anxious. "It is the definitive moment for an entire year. If Nebuchadnezzar is absent, the festival cannot be satisfied. He must make the walk, hand-in-hand with Marduk." His voice rose. "It is then that the great god renews his covenant with the city and its ruler. If there is no king... the welfare of the empire... Marduk may turn his glorious face away and withdraw every benefit." The shatammu slapped the table. "The gods may leave us utterly bereft!"

Bushu laid his palms flat on the desk and stood. His voice was steady. "My father is fully aware of the significance of the day. We all are. He is not well, it is true. But the festival will proceed, and proceed with a king."

"But --"

"I will take care of it." Bushu's tone cut off further discussion. Good for him, I thought. Still, the exchange left me troubled.

The shatammu made a shallow bow. "Thank you, my lord, for your assurance."

When the door opened, I saw Belshazzar waiting.

I SAID a quick goodbye to Bushu, but he was already deep into some document or other. He didn't notice when I went to the door the shatammu had just exited, stepped to the side, and peered around its opening.

When I saw Belshazzar intercept the shatammu, I slipped my sandals off and held them in my hand.

"Belshazzar of the king's court." Belshazzar introduced himself with a little bow.

"I recognize you," the shatammu said, "a regular oblate in the temple of Marduk."

The tile-paneled hall gave their voices just enough amplitude for me to catch every word.

"Our great god is well served by your conscientious management," Belshazzar said.

The shatammu's mouth twitched at the praise, resisting a smile. He hadn't caught the obsequious tone.

"What a surprise," Belshazzar said, "to see you in the palace. You must be busy, with the Akitu festival so soon."

Belshazzar adjusted his robe. He'd begun to develop a paunch.

"Very, indeed."

Belshazzar fell into step beside the temple official. I followed, my bare feet quiet on the stones, and kept to the shadows.

"I can only imagine," Belshazzar said, "what madness it must be gathering the gods, making everyone comfortable, negotiating last moment requests..."

The shatammu puffed out his chest. "'Negotiating' is the word, all right. Every god and every member of every staff expects to be the center of all attention. Each need is a crisis."

"I hope that the palace is helping."

"Helping? Hah. This has nearly undone me."

"Why is that?" Belshazzar asked.

The shatammu stopped and looked at Belshazzar, assessing. "Well, you are a courtier of rank." He leaned in. "We're simply not sure that King Nebuchadnezzar will be back in time."

I caught my breath. I had hoped that only Bushu and I worried about that – that people trusted Bushu's word that the king would be present.

"No!" Belshazzar feigned astonishment. He fiddled with his beard. "That is a terrible problem. You talked to the prince about it?"

The shatammu nodded and walked on again, Belshazzar keeping pace. "He did not promise that Nebuchadnezzar would be there. Neither did he say that he would ask the king himself. Yet he made very clear that there would be a king participating."

So that was it.

Belshazzar stopped and inhaled dramatically.

The shatammu turned back to look.

"Do you think," Belshazzar asked slowly, "that the crown prince doubts his father's fitness to rule?" He let the significance of his words hang like swords. I wished that they were – I felt my blood rise – so that I could fight them back. But this wasn't the time. I forced myself to remain still, quiet.

"He did say that Nebuchadnezzar is sick."

"Hmmm." Belshazzar drew it out.

The shatammu stopped. "Do you think there's more?"

Belshazzar pressed his lips tightly together and squinted. "Do you?"

"I hadn't considered it until now." The shatammu waved his finger in the air thoughtfully, "But, you know... Couldn't be." He shook his head, "No, no."

I exhaled. It was all right, after all.

"That's a relief," Belshazzar said, "Because I've had some concerns... too serious to contemplate."

Thankfully, the shatammu was already looking ahead toward an exit that would take him to the temple complex's main gate, busy with parties coming and going.

"If I can help," Belshazzar said, "or lend an ear, a discrete ear."

The shatammu looked back at him.

"And you can expect additional daily offerings from my family, in light of the demands of the season. As we do every year, of course."

"Marduk sees the pious," the shatammu said, "and the temple thanks you for support."

As soon as the shatammu had passed through the gate one way and Belshazzar after him another, I hurried back to Bushu's quarters to finish what I couldn't do earlier. He repeated, "I won't go unless she wants to."

"Then you understand that you have to wait to talk with her," I said. "We cannot let anyone know these plans until Nebuchadnezzar is back and restored. You cannot tell her about Media, until you're ready to leave." We both knew that if Bushu left with Nebuchadnezzar in such a state, Igliss would find a way to blame

Media and void the treaty. Bushu slumped. "It won't be long," I assured him (and myself, too). "When Nebuchadnezzar returns for the Akitu, I'm sure he'll give you permission to marry Shiyati. Then you can ask her. Now," I said. "Make sure that everything is ready for the king's return. Check with Nabonidus – the military should be in its best shape... There are other things, too."

"I know," Bushu said. "I checked with Saradan – he was inspecting fields of winter wheat." It was a relief to hear again the practical and competent young man Bushu had shown himself to be. "I was assured that the kitchen, including baking the festival's sacred loaves, is all in order."

"And Sebi," I said, "that Susian bodyguard..." My mind ticked through details specific to the king's return. "Oh, and the steward should make a final check of the king's rooms..."

Bushu cleared his throat. "I've got it," he said firmly. "I'll take care of that."

I didn't think much of his tone at the time, of the decisiveness of his answer. I just said, "Nebuchadnezzar will be here tomorrow." He had to be. The Akitu would begin two days hence.

THAT NIGHT, as I lay staring out at the Babylonian stars, I thought again about Anahita, Mithra, and Mazda, the gods of home. I hoped that they would find in Bushu a devotee worthy of blessing and aid. It was easy to imagine, but hard to believe that in a couple week's time, after the king had returned to resume his duties – for surely the Akitu would accomplish that – my son would be riding north. My son, a prince *of Media*. After all those years teaching him about the wild mountain land that I loved and after his seeing it for himself, it had worked – that's what Bushu wanted most of all. Even now, despite the promise of ruling as king of Babylonia, the most powerful empire in the world, he would settle in a weakened and compromised Media. But prepared to restore its strength. And that he'd bring with him a wife from Parsa – a noble chieftain's daughter, no less... I took a moment to savor the sweet truth of these things, still hardly believing it and just as soon as I could, I would join Bushu. At home.

So, I didn't see Belshazzar converse with a rider at the Adad Gate and hand him a scroll. I didn't watch the horse canter north, a gray apparition in the clear moon light. Neither did I know that early the next morning, well before light, the king's carriage pulled up in the palace courtyard.

From it, Igliss stepped out. Alone.

CHAPTER 24

I woke, restless with a buzzy kind of energy. I had barely risen from bed when a messenger appeared.

"A parcel from the Egibi," Kara reported as she laid the linen bundle into my hand.

The papyrus note attached to it explained. "My spade uncovered this just off the road south of Ecbatana. For you. Beautiful."

For a moment, I savored the ambiguity of that last word, what – or whom – it modified before turning back the wrapping. I heard Kara gasp with me. In my hands lay a tiny gold-plated dagger, its ornate sheath identical to the one I'd left behind, the one with which Mandane had ended her life. I hardly dared look but ever so slowly I drew the weapon from its sheath. Sure enough, that little notch. It was the very same dagger.

Kara and I looked at one another, equally astonished, equally bewildered by how this particular object came to be lying in the dirt somewhere off that road in Media.

I shook my head. "I doubt we'll ever know." I handed it to Kara. "To put with my Median things. One day..." I said. Kara nodded. We both knew it wouldn't do to display until we could finally return to Media. For good.

· · ·

BUT ITS ARRIVAL at my door - from Khai - gave me just the excuse I needed.

"Kara," I said, slipping my feet into simple sandals, "If anyone comes by -" we both knew Nebuchadnezzar had to return today to prepare for the Akitu, "tell them that I'll be right back."

She narrowed her eyes until only the good one remained open. "It's the Egibi, isn't it?"

"A quick visit. Tell anyone who asks that it's about the gardens, or the Akitu barge contract... international trade. I don't know," I said, getting flustered. "There's a lot to discuss."

"There'll be plenty of time after the Akitu," Kara said, "to visit with him *in the company of others*."

I thought how Kara had been with me for as long as I could remember, how she knew me better than anyone, and how I had not yet told her about Bushu's plans to abdicate. Now here she stood, aware that I was keeping something important from her. But I held my ground.

"Then, I'm coming with you," she said. The set of her mouth defied argument.

I selected a robe with embroidery at the cuffs that swirled like flame.

"Now sit," Kara said. I let her put my hair up into a loose knot and waited, hiding my impatience, while she wound invisible threads beaded with carnelian chips through the headdress. "It's just Khai," I said. Two ivory combs held brown curls off my face. "He knows who I am." Kara hooked a necklace matching gold filigree earrings behind my neck.

"He should be reminded of your position." She stepped back. I took the chance to stand, slip my feet into shoes, and head out the door.

Kara caught up to me. In her hands she held out a scarf.

It was a conciliatory gesture, and we both knew it.

"Thank you," I said, laying it over my head, grateful to be less conspicuous.

"Do you remember the way?" Kara asked, when we were on the street.

Like the back of my hand, I thought, its white scar nearly invisible now.

We left the palace through the Sippar gate and turned onto Nanna-Suen-the-Kingmaker Street. We hustled through ever more narrow streets, this way and that, until...

In front of the house with the red door, a man stood balanced on swaying scaffolding two stories high, a heap of reeds over one shoulder. He held the roof with one hand. With the other he grasped fistfuls of reeds and cast them in wide arcs onto the roof.

Kara leaned toward my ear. "Khai?"

I felt the scarf slip off my head.

His thin linen tunic was soaked so thoroughly that I could see the darkness of his skin beneath. Having exhausted the bundle, he grasped the scaffolding with both hands and swung, his body falling away below him. Next to me, Kara gasped.

I laughed, remembering my own exploits in Media's high tree branches, as Khai's feet found purchase on the beam beneath. He glanced down, saw us, and grinned. Then perched on his hands, he let his body fall again, this time to the ground just in front of us. A scent like cardamom and fresh earth followed him down.

"These old houses..." Khai gestured helplessly. "You remember the place."

"The gardens are doing well," I said.

"And thank you for giving Amytis the object you found in Media," Kara said. "Now, we should go."

"Come in." Khai smiled.

Kara glanced around. "Is your wife here?"

Khai shook his head. "Qudashu talked me into buying a home on Prosperity Canal. We live there now, in the winter anyway. I've been renting this one."

"And your son?" Kara peered in the doorway.

"I'm on my own today." Khai brushed his hands together. "Iddina would rather manage the books and such." He laughed a little. "He's a creature of comfort, luxury. Like his mother." He looked back up at the roof. "But no matter. I like doing this kind of thing."

I followed Khai through the doorway. Flecks of dry reeds, like specks of gold leaf, caught in Khai's hair. I resisted the urge to brush them away. I heard Kara's steps shuffle behind me.

"Thank you for giving Amytis the object that you found," Kara said. "We should go."

Khai nodded. "I'll just wash my hands –" Then I saw criss-crossed through Khai's palms, scratches and cuts. Nothing serious, but –

"Oh, my," I exclaimed, feigning horror. "You're bleeding."

From their faces, neither Kara nor Khai believed that I, of all be people, would be concerned over so minor an injury. I dropped the pretense but maintained a serious tone.

"Kara, hurry back to the palace and get some of that ointment. You know, the paste in the alabaster jar, the short square one."

Kara tilted her head and scowled.

"You'll be quick," I said, all but pushing her out the door.

Kara huffed dissent but left anyway.

Khai nodded for me to follow him to the stone basin where he bent to rinse his hands and arms in the fresh water. I recognized the courtyard, but the tilework, fruit trees, and graceful doorways were new. My eyes grazed a faded floral mural on one wall before returning to Khai's, contemplating me. He dried his hands and straightened again.

"I'd hoped you'd come." Khai lifted a rough palm to my cheek.

I leaned into his hand. Khai's eyes followed my face as I remembered his defending Kara on that long ride from Media so many years ago, the horrible murder of my horse, his help with the gardens, rescuing Bushu, burying Gulash, and reporting on

Kassiya, walking the gardens.... In the dark of Khai's eyes I saw reflected every feeling: relief, surprise, warmth, friendship, longing, and... I caught my breath.

His eyes, both soft and hungry, searched mine. In my ears echoed the golden jackal's cry. I don't know which of us moved first after that. Our bodies collided, mouths and hands seeking and finding and wanting. More. We stumbled through the courtyard, still kissing through a dark doorway. Khai tore me away from his body. His eyes searched around wildly. He groaned. "There's no furniture." His voice was low, his breath heavy. I pulled at the belt around his waist, and we dropped to the floor. There, in a tangle of limbs and heat and cardamom-earth, the rest of world evaporated. Even time, with its normally relentless march, suspended, one moment hanging breathless in the forever of nothing but us.

Finally exhausted, we fell apart. I smiled up at the beamed ceiling. Never had I known such absorption into another, such dissolution that nevertheless left me feeling so full. I turned my head to see Khai gazing at me, his eyes soft, his face a gentle smile. I let my fingertips find the damp skin of Khai's chest, a hair twine round my finger. "Come to me," I said.

Khai grinned, rolled over, and pulled me close. "Yes!" He kissed my neck, held an earlobe with his teeth.

"Come to me in Media," I said, serious now. "One day."

Khai held my eyes, in his was a sadness deep as mine. He gathered me to him again. Neither of us needed to say that he couldn't. He stroked my back, found my lips with his. Both of us knew that such a thing could never be.

Both of us knew that *this* could never happen again.

But tenderly moving his lips to my cheeks, to the lids of my eyes, "One day," he said. And I was grateful for the kindness. I inhaled deeply, willing myself again to savor this time, this stolen moment of bliss. Khai here, beside me, our lovemaking, however illicit, something no one could ever take away.

Khai leaned on one elbow. With a fingertip rough from his labor, he traced the old scars that tracked across my hip, my shoulder, my ribs. "For your sister," he said. I nodded. "Those," he said, "are the wounds that heal."

My eyes filled. Some injuries, some cuts we bear for life. And in this moment, Khai had no idea how deeply I needed to cut him from me. I must have whimpered. He locked his eyes to mine as if to give me strength. Why was it that a person's wantings could be so at odds – that to have one was to lose another? How does a heart bear these things?

The creak of a far door opening, the brief rush of street sound, and closing again heralded Kara's return. It brought me back to the danger we were in and the urgency of this time.

I sat up, reached for my under-tunic. Khai watched me rise, then stood. I pulled on my robe, fastened its bracteates, and stepped to the bedroom's doorway. Naked and unself-conscious, Khai turned me to face him. He brushed the hair back from my face, tucking strands back up, his fingers tender, meditative.

I swallowed hard. "This –" I shook my head. "I –"

Khai put a finger against my lips. "I know," he said, his own eyes swimming. Khai cupped my face in his rough hands, "always wild Media." Then he let me go.

It wasn't until I saw Kara in the arched entryway, her face stricken and heaving for breath, that I thought to wonder why she hadn't returned sooner. It took one word. "Igliss," she said. And I flew out the door.

As we hurried back to the palace, Kara's exhaustion keeping me to a pace that wouldn't arouse suspicion, she told me what had happened.

It started when Belshazzar told my son that he was expected in my quarters. Thinking he'd find me, of course, Bushu went and our faithful guard Shalam with him.

But I wasn't there. Igliss was. And he had a hold of Shiyati, her arm in a tight grip. Bushu leapt forward, enraged. Igliss pushed Shiyati away.

Even as Shalam held him back, Bushu spun on Igliss. "What are you doing here?" Bushu demanded. He shook off Shalam's grip.

"I've been commanded..." Igliss steadied his voice. "...to retrieve a slave or two." He paused. "For your father's pleasure."

Bushu exhaled in a ragged growl.

"She's a feisty little thing."

"Why is no one else here?" Bushu asked. He shook off Shalam's hold.

"I too was surprised to find your mother absent." He shrugged. "Maybe she was restless for 'fresh air.' You know how she is. So," Igliss crooked his finger at Shiyati to draw her to him.

Bushu stepped between them. "Leave her."

"Hmm," Igliss said, feigning indecision. "But the *king* says, 'Take her.'" He glanced up to the ceiling as if summoning an answer. But when he looked back at Bushu, his narrow eyes were flinty black. "I answer to Nebuchadnezzar, not you." To Shiyati he said, "we leave tonight."

"Shalam intercepted me," Kara said, "as I was entering the royal wing. About here." We hurried down the hall. "He told me what had happened. He didn't have to tell me to find you."

As soon as we got into my rooms, heavy footsteps and the clattering of metal brought me back to the door. I felt Kara brush carnelian chips from my shoulders. I opened the door, and two guards stepped into the gap.

"What's going on?" I pulled my robe close around my body.

"Trouble in the concubinage, my lady."

"What kind of trouble? Where is the prince?"

"He's fine. Under guard in the prince's personal quarters." The guards looked at each other. "Possible insurrection."

I felt the blood drain from my head. It was a crime punishable by death. I mustered a breath. "Nonsense! Let me pass."

But they stood like a wall in front of me. "Orders are to keep you here."

"Whose orders?"

"Nabonidus's, my lady. Well, Belshazzar's, but he says his father --"

"I am the queen mother. You will let me pass. My son is the crown prince and Babylon's standing regent. "

"The prince *is* the problem, my lady."

As it happened, when a eunuch summoned Shiyati back to the women's quarters from my room, Bushu had whispered to her, "Meet me at the king's door."

Bushu himself went straight to the king's quarters, ostensibly to ready it for Nebuchadnezzar's return. So that is why he was so eager to do it himself – to see Shiyati, originally intending to ask if she would come with us to Media. Bushu had crossed through the king's audience rooms, into the private quarters, and through the sumptuous bedroom. He walked to the door leading to the concubinage and drew back the ornate iron bolt. It was unusual for Bushu or for any man except the king to be at that door, but not impossible. He pushed open the doors. On the other side stood two eunuchs. Shiyati was nowhere in sight.

Startled, "Where is the new girl," Bushu asked, "the one from Parsa? I'm making final arrangements to the king's rooms," Bushu explained. "Fetch her for me?"

The eunuchs conferred, then shook their heads. "There's no one from Parsa."

Bushu scowled. "From Egypt, then. She came by way of Susa, I think..." Growing more and more agitated, Bushu tried to peer around the men's shoulders.

One of the eunuchs nodded. "I know the one. Wait here."

But after a time the eunuch returned alone. He shook his head. "I'm not sure –"

"Remember?" The other eunuch said to his companion, "the king's... ? Igliss. That's him. He was here, and he said something about –"

"No," Bushu said. "You have to find her!"

The eunuchs stepped back in surprise. "*You* have to wait here." They hurried off.

Bushu didn't wait long. Haunted by what he'd already seen of Igliss's treatment of Shiyati, Bushu couldn't take it anymore. He charged in.

Bushu threw open doors, dashed in and out of rooms. He grabbed the arm of a woman standing in a doorway. She jerked away, leaving her robe in his hand. He shoved it back at her. "Where is the new slave?" Bushu demanded.

She looked at him, mouth gaping and clutched the robe against her breasts.

"The one from Susa, from Parsa," he said angrily.

"Susa?" she said, "I not Susa. I, Tyre. Tyre."

Bushu pushed her away and ran on.

He grabbed another woman. "The Parsan." He shook her arm. "Where is she?"

"I think the king called for her."

Bushu loosed a heavy groan and ran on. "Shiyati!" he called.

A eunuch, alerted to an unaccompanied man other than the king in the women's quarters, called "Guards!"

A woman pulled Bushu into a room and shut the door. She covered his mouth with her hand and signaled for him to be still. "You need to get out. She's gone."

"No!" Bushu tore her hand from his mouth and smacked the

wall. "He has her. I know it. He has her in one of those rooms and is abusing her as we speak."

"There is no man here but you, my lord."

"How do you know that?"

"You know yourself," the woman said. It is a capital offense. Listen, if you do as I say, I will take you to her room. You can talk to the women whose rooms are nearby." Loud voices echoed from the courtyard. She laid her hand on his quivering arm. "It is not safe for you to be here."

"Take me there."

Shiyati's tiny cell was tidy but empty. The woman slipped away.

Two girls sashayed past the prince and slid onto the bed. "So you're the king now?" Sheer tunics clung to every curve. Their eyes were lined with kohl, lids colored in bold blue. Both girls wore the same ruby lipstick as the woman who escorted Bushu. Their perfumes melded into a heady combination.

"Where is Shiyati?" Bushu asked.

The girls looked at each other and giggled. "She's probably just busy."

The shouts of eunuchs rang through the courtyard and halls.

"With a man?" Bushu hissed.

They shrugged, one after the other.

Bushu ran back out. A eunuch stepped in front of him. "My lord."

"Where is Igliss?" Bushu shouted in his face. "Where has he taken Shiyati?"

"Sir?"

"Igliss. Where is he?" Bushu craned to look. A guard seized his arm. "I must detain you." By now five or six other guards, all of them eunuchs, had arrived. They stood silently barring the prince from any exit.

CHAPTER 25

I had to pass only one sleepless night before the king returned. Not the best way to get him back, I thought. But Nebuchadnezzar will straighten this out, and all will be well.

Bushu and I each wore our best Babylonian finery to meet the carriage. I'd even had Kara put up my hair in deference to local tradition. We stood on a dais, prepared for the Akitu but hastily decorated for the king's return. A dozen guards stood at attention around the base.

It was a day oddly bright for this time of year, and dry, too. Fitting, I'd thought, for the relief I felt at the king's leaving Sippar. If this is what it took for him to escape Igliss's manipulative grasp, so be it. Soon everything would be set right again. I looked around. Shalam was nowhere among the guards. I hardly had time to wonder before clatter and tumult signaled Nebuchadnezzar's arrival. He roared into the city like a storm.

The wheels of the king's light war chariot churned up a cloud of dust through which his mounted bodyguards rode unflinching. A closed carriage followed at some distance reinvigorating the dust, and luggage carts rolled in behind that. Nebuchadnezzar stood tall beside his charioteer. His hair was cut to his shoulders, beard neatly trimmed. Golden bracteates on his king's robes cast light like arrows from his person. A silver pectoral covered his chest, and the crenellated gem-studded crown encircled his head.

"Finally," I said under my breath. The king was back.

Heavy rings flashed from Nebuchadnezzar's fingers in the afternoon sun, though he did not wave to the people cheering along the road and flanking the gate. Nebuchadnezzar looked neither left nor right but fixed a granite gaze straight ahead. Before they passed through the Ishtar Gate, the king took the reins to drive the team himself through the arched entryway and into the palace courtyard.

"Seize him!" Nebuchadnezzar shouted, even before he slowed the chargers. The horses halted in a furious, whinnying clatter.

I watched in horror as the king's guards dismounted, and joining those on the ground, stormed the dais, rushing for the prince. This couldn't be happening. It didn't make sense.

I threw myself in front of Bushu. "No!"

Guards tore him from my hands. They shoved him off the dais, face-first onto the stone yard. Others yanked him, nose streaming with blood, to his feet and hurried him stumbling to stand before the king. I flew off the make-shift platform, but Nebuchadnezzar's guards pushed me aside. Suddenly, Kara was beside me, urging me to my feet.

"You!" Nebuchadnezzar glared at my son with eyes like iron pikes. "Have you forgotten that I," he slapped his chest, "I am the king of Babylon? I and I alone, by the favor and grace of the great god Marduk! Guards, bind and bring him to the great hall."

Two men, arms as thick as tree trunks and faces equally hard, grabbed Bushu's arms, wrenched them behind him and tied his hands.

"You're wrong!" I called. Bushu winced as they jerked the knots tight. "He has done nothing!"

Nebuchadnezzar narrowed his eyes at me. "Escort that woman to her quarters."

"Keep still," Kara warned as the men approached to take me away.

I straightened my shoulders. "I will stay," I said. "That is my son, our son –"

Nebuchadnezzar turned his head in disgust and threw out his hand as if to erase me from the scene. Unmoving, I glared at the guards and back at the king.

"She might as well see," Nebuchadnezzar said. "But if she so much as opens her mouth, drag her to the dungeon."

Kara sidled close. Trembling, "Not a word," she whispered.

GUARDS STOOD at attention as the second carriage pulled up. Two eunuchs hurried forward and opened the doors. Kassiya stepped out gingerly, her eyes fixed on the ground, holding the infant Labashi-Marduk. After another moment, a man's narrow feet in brushed leather shoes unfouled by the dust of the road emerged. Igliss leaned out, looked up at the sky, and smiled. He stepped down and bumped Kassiya aside without acknowledgment or apology. Kassiya raised her head then. She caught her breath, eyes wide, at the sight of Bushu.

I was grateful for the iron grip that pushed me forward again. I could feel Igliss's gaze burning into my back. I wanted nothing more than to gouge out his eyes, then his cold, ugly heart. Bushu let himself be jostled and dragged by the guards toward the audience hall where he had so recently issued the orders of the empire. Bushu spoke to the man on his right. I thought I recognized the word "Shiyati." But the man, his eyes straight ahead and lips firmly closed, only gave Bushu a harder jerk forward. Where was Shalam?

A flash of fabric, a profile -- I thought I saw Nathan ahead. As soon as we had passed into the hall, the men assigned to me pulled me to a stop. I heard Kara shuffle in behind me. The crowd closed in around us. Only Nebuchadnezzar's throne was on the dais.

The king himself still hadn't arrived.

"Remember," Kara said, "Not a word."

THE CROWDS MADE SEEING Bushu difficult, but a few inches this way and that afforded me a partial glimpse. Bushu's nose had stopped bleeding, but with his hands bound behind him and no sympathy from his handlers, the blood had dried on his face into a grim and jagged beard, where he'd not yet grown one. Time passed, but no one mounted the dais. With all these people, the heat grew stifling, the air stale. Sweat loosened the blood on Bushu's upper lip and darkened his tunic.

Suddenly, Bushu began to sway. His face paled. I lurched forward instinctively, bumping against three people in front of me. The guard behind me pulled me back. I stood in his fierce grip, biting my lip and willing Bushu to bend his knees. He did. He lowered his head for a time. When he raised it, his color was normal again. I winced to recognize in his face what looked like resignation. "Fight," I whispered under my breath.

Finally, Nebuchadnezzar entered. He blustered into the hall from the door to his rooms, barking orders right and left as he strode, every bit the powerful king again. Seeing Igliss in fresh clothes to the king's right, I clenched my fists at my side and shut my eyes for a long moment. One breath, two. I kept my mouth closed. A judge and two scribes hustled along behind. Nebuchadnezzar took the throne. Igliss, standing just behind the king looked down his beak of a nose at the prince and let the bud of his red tongue wet thin lips. Igliss tapped his manicured fingertips together, his eyes narrowed to slits. My throat tightened, muted and furious.

Bushu looked away.

The judge brought the crowd to attention. He called for "the trial of Nabu-shuma-ukin known as 'Bushu,' son of Amytis of Media and King Nebuchadnezzar; Babylonia's crown prince, entrusted with the reins of state during the king's mourning and absence," to commence.

Nebuchadnezzar sat easy on the throne. Deep lines crossed the king's forehead and others ran like old battle scars down his cheeks. His face was peppered with tiny bumps and had the strong red cast of skin freshly scrubbed. Nebuchadnezzar was much thinner now than when he had left, stripped of anything soft or extraneous.

I studied Bushu, also looking at the king. I squinted against the improbability. The prince's face was full of compassion. It was as if Bushu were trying to imagine what kind of grief could so go to work on a man as to carve and chisel him away like living stone, sympathizing with the monarch – his father, after all – who had bound him and prepared to try his own son for insurrection, punishable by execution. Then I saw Nebuchadnezzar, probably feeling the prince's eyes, look at Bushu, this son very much alive. And curl his lip.

I inhaled sharply. Whatever warmth of pity, longing, or familial piety Bushu may have felt for his father turned in that moment to ice. Bushu stiffened. Only the muscles of his jaws moved, grinding over and over again.

Igliss leaned in and whispered in the king's ear. And the trial began. The judge called one witness after another – a courtier, regularly present in the audience hall (I recognized him as a friend of Belshazzar's); an elder, manager of some building project on which Bushu had instead deferred to a foreign expert... Each with some suspicion, some twisted observation, some damning accusation. I held my tongue.

The judge called for the leader of Marduk's temple.

"He said with assurance," the shatammu reported, "that there would indeed be a king present for the Akitu festival. That all would be in order when the time came for the great god, praise Marduk, to take the king's hand and walk with him in public procession."

"Did he name that king?" the royal judge asked.

The shatammu glanced at Igliss, who raised his eyebrows and tilted his head at Bushu. Kara took my hand and squeezed so hard that my knuckles ached. I forced my mouth closed tightly and bit my tongue. The prince continued to stare at a distant spot that held his gaze without interest.

"Not that I recall," the shatammu said.

The judge opened his mouth. But Igliss asked, "Did the prince say that he knew when his father, King Nebuchadnezzar, would return?"

"No one knew, sir," the man said.

Igliss looked pointedly at the judge, who started with a jerk and cleared his throat. "So," the judge said, "the prince declared that there would be a king for the upcoming festival even though no one knew when King Nebuchadnezzar would return to Babylon."

The temple official glanced at Bushu, who remained as still as the Euphrates' surface on a mid-summer day. "Yes, I suppose so. I imagine that he was..."

"We are not asking you to imagine," Igliss interrupted. "Just tell me what you know."

I could hardly see Igliss for the white dots of rage that danced in front of my eyes. With Igliss directing the witnesses and line of questioning... Bushu shifted his feet. It was wrong, all wrong.

Suddenly, all color drained from Bushu's face again. He swayed. Igliss barked to the guards on his either side, "Step away," as Bushu crumpled to the ground. I stifled a cry and pushed forward. But the crowd was too thick. I couldn't see. Bushu was on the floor, out of sight. The low hum of uncertain voices stopped at the resounding crack of a palm across skin. The sound of the crowd rose, then went silent again as Bushu was hauled again to his feet, head lolling on his shoulders. Another moment, and Bushu shook off his captors. He bent his knees, then straightened them, raised his head, and squared himself. His nose was bleeding again. One eye was quickly swelling shut.

I willed him strength.

Belshazzar took the place of the witness.

"State your identity," the judge said.

"Belshazzar, son of Nabonidus. Honored to serve my lord Nebuchadnezzar in the name of the king of the gods, Marduk," Belshazzar said, with a deep bow to Nebuchadnezzar.

I stole a glance at Kara. She was as still as stone.

"What have you seen and heard concerning the defendant?"

Belshazzar looked at the prince, then back at the judge. "Quite a lot, sir."

Bushu snapped his head, looking more closely at the plump courtier.

"Most recently, I learned that he had given orders to prepare the military and that he was planning to spend time in the king's private bedroom. He insisted on being the one to ready the space for the king. I assumed that meant King Nebuchadnezzar. But when he forced his way into the women's quarters... Well, it pains me to say but it seemed a clear, public display of sleeping with the king's women."

A disapproving gasp went up from the crowd. I groaned.

Igliss said, "I believe that speaks for itself."

"And how exactly did you come to know about the young man's plans for the military and intention to move into the king's bedroom?" the judge asked.

"He summoned my father to oversee the military's preparations and directed the palace steward about his plans to resume affairs as though the king were already present."

"I see," said the judge.

One of the door attendants leaned over and whispered something into the judge's ear. "My lord," the judge said to the king. "Another witness."

"Bring him in," Nebuchadnezzar said.

Belshazzar bowed and began to leave.

"Stay," Nebuchadnezzar said.

Belshazzar glanced at Igliss, who gave a light shrug, then cast his eyes to the space at his right. Belshazzar stepped over to him.

"Meshach," the attendant at the door called out.

Nathan appeared in a far doorway. His lean frame cast a short shadow as he walked into the audience hall. His face was sober but without twitch or tremor as he dipped his head briefly to Nebuchadnezzar. He did not look at Bushu but nodded to Igliss. He acknowledged Belshazzar with a small smile. My heart sank. Would Nathan betray Bushu, too?

Belshazzar glanced up at Igliss, shuffled his feet, and winced a smile back at the Jewish scribe.

"Belshazzar," King Nebuchadnezzar said, "You know this man?"

"One of the royal scribes, my lord." Belshazzar hesitated. "From among foreign exiles repatriated in Nippur," he added. "Worked recently for the accused."

Nebuchadnezzar nodded to the judge to continue the questioning.

"You know him how?" the judge asked.

"I, and… others, brought him to Babylon some time ago."

"Did you select him or simply retrieve him?"

It seemed ages ago when I and Bushu – then just a boy – had traveled to Nippur, had shared a Sabbath meal, and met young Nathan for the first time.

"We selected him, sir."

"How?"

Belshazzar cleared his throat. "We visited his family and talked to them at length. His father runs a scribal school and is a well-respected leader within that community. The boy, a Jew, seemed fitting to serve the palace and king."

"Honest and discreet?" the judge asked.

"Of course, sir."

The judge nodded slowly. "The conversation with your father Nabonidus, in which the accused expressed his desire to ready the palace for the king, this scribe was also present, was he not?"

"I don't know, my lord." Belshazzar's forehead glistened.

The judge turned to Nathan. "Were you there?"

"I was."

"Is it true that the prince requested that the military be prepared?"

Nathan hesitated. "Yes, sir."

My shoulders slumped.

"He began our meeting, however, by --."

I straightened.

"I will ask what I need to know," the judge said.

Nathan shut his mouth, but I felt a bud of hope in my chest. Maybe --

"At this meeting, did the prince indicate that he would attend to the king's bedroom?"

"Yes, sir."

Igliss said, "Even with a full palace staff charged with such matters?"

Nathan looked at Igliss then back at the judge. "But you should know --"

"I know what I should know," the judge said, his high voice rising higher. "Only the king may direct my questioning."

Nebuchadnezzar said, "Go on."

The judge asked, "What did the prince want with you?"

"I am a scribe, which in my trad--"

"What did he want with you in that meeting?"

"To investigate the king's condition, sir," Nathan answered.

Hushed whispers vibrated through the hall.

Igliss leaned forward, a smile flitting across his face. "So *that's* where the rumors started." His voice echoed against the tiled walls.

I felt my stomach drop. This was all twisted and wrong.

Igliss nodded. "There was talk... and I believe that Belshazzar can confirm this..." Igliss stroked his chin with long fingers, "nasty rumors of the king suffering... well... a *madness*," he let the word sink in, "like his dear departed first-born."

Whispers turned into a buzz as people exclaimed each to his neighbor.

Igliss looked at Belshazzar. Beads of sweat ran down from Belshazzar's temples.

Still I kept my tongue. Speak, Nathan. Speak, I thought.

"But, sir." Nathan stepped forward. "His concern –" A sudden hubbub at the back of the room overwhelmed Nathan's voice.

"Eunuchs from the women's quarters are here, my lord," a runner announced.

"Bring them in," Nebuchadnezzar said.

"You may go," the judge said to Nathan.

The young scribe stood still. "But sir."

"Now," the judge said to him.

Nathan dropped his head as guards escorted him to the door.

I watched him disappear, my hope with him.

The eunuchs arrived in a swirl of brightly colored robes and bustled into the hall. They shared their observations. And the scribe dutifully recorded their testimony: The prince had forced his way into the women's quarters, a final act leading many to believe that he was now king.

Nebuchadnezzar's hands gripped the lion's heads of his armrest so that the muscles of his forearms flexed. When the testimony's report was done, the king spat words, low and rumbling.

"That boy is no prince, no son of mine, but an ungrateful bastard. To the prison!" Palace soldiers grabbed Bushu.

Nebuchadnezzar stood. "Guilty of attempting to usurp my throne, this criminal's execution will follow the Akitu."

"No!" I cried out. Kara tried to cover my mouth, but I wrenched free. "He's innocent!" I ducked around Kara and pushed forward, but I was no match for the armed guards. One seized my arm roughly and pulled me into the aisle.

Nebuchadnezzar quivered with rage. "And her! To the prison!"

I struggled against the hands that held me. I felt my shoulder pop as the guard yanked me around to leave. With one last lunge, and wincing against the pain, I wrenched to face the king.

With Bushu so convicted, the treaty was void. I saw Kara lurch to the side as someone shoved her to make way for the prisoners. The old woman fell down into the crowd, disappearing in the clamoring mass.

My heart broke For Kara, for Bushu, for Media. "No!" I cried out. Everything I had tried to do. My entire life. Failed. And my son, my only son, the baby I didn't want but now couldn't imagine living without, condemned to death. The guards yanked me along.

I could hear Bushu somewhere behind. I tried to slow, to wait. But the men were strong and Bushu was too far behind to catch up. Judging from the sound, they were dragging him inert, feet scuffing and banging along the floor.

Then I heard his voice, ragged with despair. "Shiyati!"

The guards turned, I with them.

"Where is she?" Bushu croaked.

Igliss bent to whisper in Nebuchadnezzar's ear.

"The slave you requested," Bushu's tone was weary with defeat, "from Susa, Parsa."

"The girl is dead," Nebuchadnezzar said. "Killed, of course."

Bushu slumped against his keepers' arms.

"Guards! To the prison."

.   .   .

My heart dropped with every step as palace soldiers escorted me toward the northeast corner of the palace beneath which I knew the palace prisons lay.

"My son," I said. "Please. Let me see him."

The guards heaved me forward. I couldn't hear Bushu anymore.

We stopped at a heavy door. The guards drew back its iron grate, then down we went in single file, down the narrow, stone stairs. I strained to see by the wan and waving light of the soldier's torch. The air grew increasingly heavy and dank until I could hardly breathe without either gagging on the smell or drowning in its humidity. I knew that on the other side of the wall lay murky waters – the palace moat, diverted from the Euphrates in a slow dark band, dirty and deep.

At the bottom of the stairs, the soldiers jerked me to a halt.

"Bushu!" I called.

"Shut up," one of the men said as he plucked a set of keys from a hook on the wall.

The other gave a punitive jerk to my aching shoulder.

"Where is my son?"

They laughed.

They continued down a hall and stopped again. Without loosening their grips on my arm, one guard held his torch while the other dragged back an iron-enforced door that ran from the stone floor to the dripping ceiling. In the wavering glow, horrified, I glimpsed an emaciated man with long, scraggly gray hair huddled against a rough wall. I recoiled. What I had taken at first glance to be odd patterns of clothing, I now saw were scars, matted streaks, and patches of blood. But for this, the man was naked.

"No," I managed through my revulsion.

But the guards tossed me inside, shut the door, and let the iron lock fall into place.

CHAPTER 26

*W*ithin minutes, they were gone, and the light with them. I stood in the darkness, afraid to move. I listened but heard only the slow drip of water onto stone. I took shallow breaths through my mouth in the fetid air. Then I heard it – the shuffle and slap of steps coming closer. Silence again. My heart hammered. My hand went to my hip. But it had been years since I carried a knife and scabbard. I hoped my eyes would adjust before the man reached me. I took a small step backward. The iron door stopped me. A hand on my arm, I stifled a scream.

"Who are you?" foul breath whispered in my ear.

I pulled away and slipped on the grime-slicked floor. When I threw out my arms, I felt my hand brush through the man's greasy hair. I choked on a cry and righted myself again.

"Who are you?" the voice repeated.

I shook out my hand as if to fling away the filth and stood still again. Who am I? The humiliation of my failures; the loneliness of being different, foreign, never fitting in; my homesickness for a wild Media that would soon be gone, whipped into service to domineering Babylonia... At eight years old, at ten, at twelve, I had been indomitable – of no account, but tenacious as a willow whip. Of no value, but then... The treaty that would protect wild Media had depended on me. But here? Now? In the dark, I squared my shoulders. "I am – " My shoulders slumped again. "Was... wife of Nebuchadnezzar, mother of the crown prince of Babylon."

"Ah," the man said. I could hear him shuffling away again. "A dangerous position." I heard him sit with a sigh. I exhaled, slowly, steadied my heartbeat.

"Do you deserve to be here?" The voice, soft as it was, still rang round against stone.

I groaned. I had taken Mandane's place. And for what?

"A hard question," he said, "subjective."

Lost. All lost. "I am the daughter of Media."

"A charge?"

"In its way. Please, do you know where they have taken my son?"

"You couldn't hear him?"

"Not after we reached the stairs."

"Solitary," he said. "If you think it's bad here –"

"Don't tell me," I said. "At least he's alive." I gingerly swept first one foot and then the other along the floor in front of me.

The man was quiet.

I wondered if some spot here might still be dry. "Who are you?" I asked.

The man exhaled sharply through his nose, as if to laugh for a sardonic second. "God only knows," he said. "Harmless to you." Something about his tone made me believe him. He began humming, a slow and rolling tune. The song, then another, and another after that, let me know he remained at a distance. The music managed also finally to begin to soften the edges of my nerves. When the man spoke again, it was simply to ask, "What's going on out there?"

"Madness," I said. "Nebuchadnezzar's son-in-law..."

The man waited.

"Too much. I'm not sure where to start." I took a deep breath. "When Nebuchadnezzar's son Ean the former crown prince died, the king was so overcome with grief that Igliss talked him into going to Sippar. Igliss –" I spat in the direction of the door.

"I know the man," my cell mate said. His tone was tired.

"He set everything up. And now, Media... My son. Agh!"

"Take your time," the man said. "These things are never simple."

"I love Media, my home, the land that I have given everything to preserve. But my father, the king of Media, is incompetent, paranoid. Igliss used that, used Nebuchadnezzar's weakness, my son's strength... While Nebuchadnezzar was gone, my son took care of things." I put my hands over my face. After a moment, I lowered them. "And I... There was a man..."

"Ah," the man said.

"So when Bushu fell in love..." I shook my head.

"Love. That's enough to land a person in prison."

I squinted through the darkness. "She was a slave. From Parsa." My voice cracked. "Where my sister... used to be."

"Dead, isn't she?" the hidden man asked.

I let out a jagged breath. "Yes. Both. My sister, and the slave. My sister, years ago. I tried to save her." Now it was my turn to laugh sardonically. "That's how I ended up in Babylon, Nebuchadnezzar's wife to satisfy an old treaty. All along, I've been trying to save Media." I hung my head. "But because of me, because of my foreignness, my failures, my frustration in love..." I dragged a sleeve over my cheeks. I could hear the man's breathing – a regular rasp, not asleep. "Who are you?" I said. "Why are you here?"

"I don't know, anymore. I tell you the truth on that."

I sniffed. "Who were you before... this?" I dabbed at the base of my nose with my sleeve.

"A king."

I waited.

"You're not laughing?"

"Why would I laugh?"

"You saw me, I think. You can smell me, I'm sure."

"Where were you king?"

The man's voice was thin but steady. "A tiny nation to the west, a beautiful country of rugged hills, some covered in trees others soft and smooth as the curves of a woman. The hills flatten as you go toward the coast of the sea."

I felt around for a place to sit, recoiling with each damp and slimy touch.

"There my people grew all manner of lovely and delicious things. We called it the land of milk and honey. Judah. Israel."

"I know of it," I said, "Judah."

"The god of heaven and earth, of all that was, is, and will be gave that land to us." The man snorted. "So the stories go. But we forgot, some prophets said, whose land it always is -- God's -- so Yahweh-God took it from us. Other prophets said whatever the people wanted to hear." There was a shuffle and a sigh as the man shifted his position. "A long time ago, when Nebuchadnezzar was young, he tried to control us. We resisted. I had been king for only three months when Nebuchadnezzar's army swept down and took a lot of us away. I've been here since then. My uncle became king in my place. Judah answered to Babylon. Was supposed to, but my uncle revolted. Nebuchadnezzar, Igliss with him, destroyed everything."

"I heard about that time." That day came rushing back, when sopping wet and wounded, I'd kept the log from sweeping Mandane downriver, the day Mandane would marry Nebuchadnezzar, how my father had berated me that Babylonia not conquer Media like it had Judah. A sob escaped my throat as I imagined the fate of Media now that the alliance was broken.

"They dragged my uncle away, forced him to watch the execution of his sons, then blinded him. I saw him here, beaten and humiliated. They made him grind grain like a common woman. They say that he died of an injury; I say it was a broken heart."

Tears pricked behind my eyes – tears for that man, for my mountain home, for Bushu alone somewhere.... I bit my lip. If I gave in, I'd never stop. I lifted my head and swallowed hard. "Yet you survive," I said.

"If our god needs a whipping boy, I'm it. I endure for our people, trying not to die, though I hardly live. Crazy, maybe. But it gives me purpose, a sense of who I am and why I'm here -- to be the lightning rod of Yahweh's anger." He paused. "Name's Coniah, short for Jeconiah. My throne name was Jehoiachin."

The man fell silent. I stood still. The occasional scuttle of a rodent echoed, amplified. in pitch black, I stepped slowly, my hand out, toward where the voice had been. I touched the wall, clammy and uneven. Then I brushed against the old man's hairy head. This time, I didn't flinch but rested my hand on the man's shoulder. The skin was papery, the bones beneath as sharp as the stench in my nostrils. "May I sit here with you?"

"It's all yours," the man answered. "Or was." He coughed lightly. "Sit if you like."

I pulled my hood up and slid down, trying not to imagine what slithering creatures may be watching, waiting. "Does 'Jehoiachin' have some special meaning?"

"'Yahweh establishes,' but it doesn't say for how long... or for what purpose." The old man sucked breath between his lips, making a smacking sound. "After thirty years in this place, I wouldn't appear to be much of a candidate. But enough. It's been a long time since I've had a companion. Tell me more of what's going on outside this horrid place."

I gave in to the wetness at my back, my bottom. I could feel it soaking up through my leather soles. "What do you want to know?"

"Anything. Everything. Doesn't matter. Make it up if you want. Just talk."

did. I talked and talked – about how amazing Bushu had become and how I had hoped that he would love Media as I did. I told how he did indeed love it so much he'd live there if he could. I told about the gardens that Nebuchadnezzar constructed – right next to the palace – to try to mimic Media's mountains, and how we filled them with plants from home and here. I talked about Khai, how he had built a business from nothing and a family to be proud of. Yes, I answered, the man I'd fallen in love with. I told him of my sister's death. My voice hitched again when I told about Kara, the slave who had been with me my entire life. Call it hope, but I didn't tell the secrets I'd been keeping – about Bushu wanting to forfeit the throne and return to Media, about Cyrus alive...

But I told about delivering Kassiya's baby with the little knowledge I had gotten from Mandane's obsession for healing. And I told about the journey to Nippur years ago, quelling the ricocheting violence of revolt.

I told about Igliss's attempt to kill Bushu on the one day that he had a chance, and I told about Gulash and about my Nisean stallion, killed in brutal sacrifice shortly after I'd arrived. I made

Coniah laugh, a broken hack, when I told how, there in the stables, I'd wrung equitable terms for the treaty from Nebuchadnezzar. And after a pause, I told that my half-sister was the princess, the one born for Babylon -- that I, Amytis, was the daughter of a slave woman, bastard to Astyages; and that until that fateful day, I had had only one purpose: to protect Mandane long enough for Mandane to marry Nebuchadnezzar.

"I had thought I'd always live as wild and free as anything in Media's mountains and hills," I said, "and that that place, and all its creatures, would be protected from harm by the alliance with Babylonia. But," I explained that when the Babylonians came to fetch Mandane, I learned that the terms of the treaty had never been established and that Igliss seemed to assume they could strip Media as they wished for Babylonian purposes. "Then, I saw the danger to Mandane – that they would kill her for the doctoring work she couldn't help but do – and how it would threaten the treaty. So I took Mandane's place... " My voice dropped away. Then, as I told this Jewish king about Media, relating details of its wonders, I felt my voice regain energy and intensity as if in the telling I could protect it again, preserve its wildness, keep the sophisticated balance of nature in all its myriad and incalculable value alive and well.

At some point, I must have fallen asleep, talk merging into dream. I was back in the palace in Babylon, curled up in the gardens. It was cold. But Khai was there. He'd found me, and now he was tugging on my robe. I started awake. Pleasure turned to horror. The old man's breath was foul on my face.

I jerked away.

"You have such nice clothes. It's been a long time since I touched such things." The man's voice moved away. "Besides, you were tipping over. Sorry if I woke you."

I pulled my robe more tightly around my shoulders, stiff but wide awake.

"There was a time," Coniah said, "in my kingdom when

fineries like yours were common at court." He sighed. "Generations ago, our nation was a great alliance of tribes. We were
called simply 'Israel' and extended through fertile lands north of
Judah, from the Great Sea to the desert."

"I suppose your god gave those to you, too?"

"It's a long story."

"I've got time." I thought about the comfort my own recollections had brought to me. "Tell me," I said. "Everything."

I heard him take a long breath. "Singers tell that many generations ago, a shepherd boy by the name of David son of Jesse from
the tribe of Judah was selected by Yahweh-God to lead our
nation. We have many stories about this David, remembered not
only as a great king, but a poet and musician, too. It was his
tunes, passed down over nearly five centuries, that I was
humming earlier. Oh, David also had faults and shortcomings --
comforting, perverse maybe, to know that even the great King
David was no image of perfection. Anyway, when he died, one of
his sons, Solomon -- not the eldest -- succeeded him to the
throne. No one could know, then, that those were to be the most
glorious years of our nation.

"Under Solomon's rule, we finally built a temple – in
Jerusalem. Cedars from Lebanon, golden utensils, tapestries of
the finest woven wool... well, you know nice things. It was
magnificent. But most importantly, it was the place where our
god, who had wandered with us, could settle in sacred holiness
and be for us strength and blessing. Forever, we thought. Zion.

"We gained an international reputation under Solomon's rule,
though the prophets tell that it came at ultimate cost. Solomon
facilitated the worship of his foreign wives' gods and goddesses.
Too tempting -- we had been charged by our god to have no
other gods ahead of Yahweh.

"When Solomon died, the son who succeeded him pushed the
people to work even harder with big buildings and all the
external trappings of nations. In the process, he so alienated

tribal families to the north that they defected, forming another kingdom. This, they called 'Israel.' Our Judah is what remained, a smaller, poorer nation by any standards. But it was Judah that had Solomon's temple, the golden city of Jerusalem, and the line of kings who inherited Yahweh-God's original and supposedly enduring promise to David.

"And it was Judah that survived, some two hundred years later when Israel succumbed to the ravenous engine of Assyria. Judah continued to hobble along for decades, some better than others. Some times even hinted of a full recovery. But whatever Judah's condition, even in the worst times, we believed that Jerusalem could never be defeated on account of Yahweh's promise and protection-- David, the temple. Assyria's defeat without conquering us seemed to confirm that. But then the Babylonians – your husband – came along." He snorted. "And here I am.

"Some days I believe with our sages that it was all Yahweh-God's doing, that our guilt brought us here. And I've heard rumors of hope that our nation, even I, would be restored again once Yahweh's anger has passed. O come, o come Immanuel, and ransom captive Israel. Most days I don't know what I believe. But the songs of David and the stories of Yahweh-God's mercy and grace; of God's choosing us, regardless our merit or worth, they keep me going. I've heard people out there are collecting them, putting them together on scrolls. In writing." He was quiet. I imagined him shaking his head, maybe; or maybe smiling a little in hope? I couldn't tell.

"I'm not always in a room this bad," Coniah said. "I have been in spaces with light and a bed, company too. But just when I feel I'm recovering -- that the sores are healing, on the outside at least -- some guard decides to entertain himself by requiring me to bow down and pledge obeisance to Nebuchadnezzar. I won't. At first it was simply because our traditions forbid it. God alone is lord."

"I've heard that, from a young Jewish scribe."

"Good for him. For me, it's now just a point of pride, my tiny act of resistance. But what energy it gives me... until they whip and beat the energy back out of me again. More often than not, I end up back here. Alone."

I tugged my robe loose to spread next to me. "Come." I patted the fabric. I felt Coniah lower himself stiffly beside me. "How do you do it?" I asked. "Here, alone?"

"Not well. There are times when I would give anything for a way to die. But I know that my people attach hope to me. Sometimes that thought makes me want to live, out of sheer spite. I recall stories, sing the songs of my ancestors as well as I can. They help me to be human. Every so often, shortly after the Akitu, when I'm still clean, I'm granted a conjugal visit. I have several children, or so I'm told. My wife was a beauty and enjoyed clout in her own right. I don't think Babylonians allow women much liberty..."

"Citizen women can own property and do with it what they like, for the most part. Of liberty, never enough," I said.

"Our women have, or had, their own seals with which to issue requests, finalize legal documents and the like."

"Women in Babylon, whatever their rank, have no legal clout, no personal seals. The elite have a lot of jewelry, I can say that." I let myself wonder about Kassiya, gentle Kassiya, powerless in the face of Igliss's intimidations and cunning. "Tell me more about Judean women. Or anything you like."

"Forgive me," Coniah said. "So much excitement today, and I'm tired. Go ahead, though. Talk, if you wish. I like to hear your stories. Besides, it made you feel better, didn't it?"

I nodded. Then, remembering that Coniah couldn't see me, I said, "Yes. Thank you. Talking took me into dreams. But --" I wrapped my arms more tightly around my legs, wondering how I could sleep much less live. "The charge against Bushu – usurping the throne. It's a capital offense." My voice broke.

The man only said, "There'll be no executions until after the Akitu."

I tucked my forehead between my knees, bone on bone and groaned.

"Listen to me." Only the lack of teeth softened Coniah's voice. "Don't you give up."

I rocked back and forth. "The Akitu begins tomorrow."

I TRIED NOT to think about each of the days passing as one closer to Bushu's death, or to wonder if the Babylonian army had already reached Media. But when the guards hauled Coniah away to be paraded with the conquered kings – the festival's ninth day – I was alone with my thoughts. I could not bear them. In three days, they would kill my son. I couldn't stop imagining Bushu's execution -- slowly, publicly as a traitor, pretender, usurper of the throne. And I, like the Judean king after Coniah, would be forced to watch. Only three more days.

Alone, I beat my head against the stone until finally, blessedly, I fell into darkness.

When I came to, I pushed myself up slowly to my hands and knees. My head ached with a fierceness I hadn't felt since childhood injuries. I ran my tongue over my lips, spitting blood and grit from my mouth. I flopped against the wall and groaned. There was no answering sound, no shuffling of Coniah's bony frame, no touch of his thumbless palm on my shoulder. Loneliness crushed me like a collapsing cave. I gasped for air, for hope, then cursed myself and my body for breathing still.

It couldn't have been even a full day. Yet the mania of solitude in a misery without answers dashed me against the stone again, this time without mercy.

I came to to the sound of footsteps in the hall, their beat growing louder, closer. I struggled to my feet and clung to the iron rails of the door. Guards returned Coniah to the cell. In the torchlight, I could see that the old man's hair was trimmed close, His skin glistened with oil, and he smelled... He didn't smell at all. His dark eyes flashed in the torchlight. The guards stripped a pale blue robe from his shoulders as they shoved him back into the cell.

I nearly wept to have him back, my tears checked by guilt at such happiness. I held my arms stiffly at my sides, resisting the desire to embrace my shining friend.

"Tell me," I said, as the guards disappeared with their torches.

"Shame and sunlight," Coniah said, "a heady combination."

"Was Igliss there?"

A snort and silence told me all I needed to know. "Right beside the king."

"And the army?"

"They've moved out."

"Media." I sat down. "I couldn't save it," I shook my head. "Such arrogance."

"Yours or theirs?"

"Both."

At some point I fell asleep, dreamless and dark. I didn't know for how long. The whisper of a grating – iron on stone? – brought my head up, ears reaching for the sound. Sure enough, distant voices grew louder accompanied by the torches' yellow light. The guards had returned. They opened the door. One took my arm and pulled me up on shaky legs.

"Where are you taking me?" They didn't answer but led me, limping toward the door. "Wait," I turned back. In the dim light, Coniah's eyes glimmered wet. "Please," I struggled to reach the collar of my robe against the weight of the guard's arm. Finally, the guard loosened his hold enough to allow me to remove my robe. I handed it to Coniah. I grimaced to see my fingernails and knuckles black with grit. The old king took it, draped the robe carefully over his arm, nodded to me, and stepped back into the far reaches of the cell. As I submitted to the direction of the guards, I heard the strains of a tune that Coniah had taught me, "Doe of the Dawn," the melody for a Hebrew poem, "My god, my god, why have you forsaken me?"

I remembered its ending of rescue and praise.

I hoped he'd keep singing.

WE HAD JUST REACHED the bottom of the stairs when the glow from another corridor caught my eye. The guards hesitated.

"Bushu?"

Coughing met my call.

I leaned away from the stairs with all my might, pulling the guards back toward the dark. Curious themselves, they let me stand but didn't release their hold on my arms. Light from the other party grew brighter. Another pair of guards appeared with a heavy form between them. I gasped. "Bushu," I whispered. They held him up. His head, the hair dark and matted straight, lolled between them. His feet dragged. I struggled, but the guards held me firm. "Bushu," I said again. His head flopped up and his mouth hung open, swollen and bloody. One eye was swollen shut, the other rolled up and back, finding me and losing me again.

"What have you done to him!" For the first time, I looked at the guards holding him. I caught my breath. Shalam. "You!" I said, devastated and accusing.

"He'll take your place with the Jew," Shalam said sharply. The other guard jerked Bushu forward and cast his partner a silencing glare. Shalam pinched his lips tight as he carried Bushu on down the prison hall.

I fought against the guards, but I was weak. The men pulled me forward. I heard the keys drop onto the hook on the wall. Then they hauled me up the stairs. I shouted for answers, but they remained resolutely silent. As we passed into the palace, I could tell from a softening of the darkness that it was just before dawn.

.   .   .

THE GUARDS DEPOSITED me in my former rooms. Kara hurried to me, her arthritic legs jerky with haste.

"You're here?" My voice sounded hoarse.

"Where else would I be?"

"House arrest," one man said. They shut the door behind them, and I could hear them take up places on either side. Kara fussed over my tunic, muttered how dirty I was, how thin, the bloody lumps and abrasions on my head...

"Bushu?" I let Kara push me toward the washing room. "Do you know anything more?"

Kara fetched a papyrus scroll off a small table. "Shalam left this here."

"Shalam?" I sat and read it eagerly. At first.

"What does it say?" Kara asked.

"I..." I shook my head. "I cannot," was all I could manage. Next to Bushu's death and Media's loss, well, this felt like those wrapped up together. Worse than I could imagine.

CHAPTER 28

$\mathcal{K}$ara didn't push for answers. Instead, she stripped off my clothes and eased me into the bronze tub of warmed water. She buttoned her lips as she sprinkled and then poured a jar of rose water into the bath.

"Please," I said. "Leave me."

After Kara left, the room felt as silent as a tomb. Two more days, I thought, and the festival is done. I scooped up water and let it fall, running down my face. I have done everything wrong, I thought. I splashed another scoop against my face, then wiped it angrily away. Why couldn't I have kept my head down, conformed? I slid down until the water rose over my chin. And Khai – if only I hadn't... Bushu would have lived to succeed Nebuchadnezzar, and Media would be safe forever. But no. I stared at the ceiling, my voice a whisper, felt flat and dead. "All is lost."

I slipped under the water and closed my eyes. I let the air out of my lungs slowly. Slowly I heard the bubbles rise and disappear. Then I rested – no movement, no breath, no sound. Nothing. It would be like this. Soon, I would take a breath, a wet and watery breath, flood my lungs with it, let it keep me under. I would not see Bushu executed, Media ravaged. I wouldn't suffer Igliss's victory or a shameful return to my pathetic father. I opened my mouth wide to welcome my final breath - water. Suddenly, hands under my arms hoisted me to the surface. I sputtered. Still alive, I sobbed.

Kara let me cry.

Kara rubbed soap into my scalp with slow, strong fingertips, then poured water over to wash it out again. I shook with tears. Kara wrung a linen square, soaped it, and scrubbed my back and arms. Then she firmly pressed the linen into my hand. I cried as I rubbed it over my body until gradually, finally, the spasms of grief and fear and regret that clinched my belly and hunched my shoulders subsided to nothing.

I stared at the water, watched it silently accept the prison's filth and horror, let it take the terror and despair from my body, suspend, and float it down into a quiet layer of grit below. Kara ran a comb slowly from my head to the ends of my hair, working gently through every snarl and knot. She continued to comb my hair long after it was smooth, until, at last, I was still.

When I finally stood, Kara wrapped me tightly in clean, brushed linen. For an instant, the old woman held me, swaddled like an infant, tight. Then she briskly rubbed me dry. Kara reached for a fresh under tunic.

"No," I said. I walked over to the cabinet and pushed the Babylonian clothes aside. From the back, I drew out the rough trousers I had worn on the day I had left Media. "You cleaned them."

"For certain," Kara said.

I held them up. The tear at one ankle had been mended and the belt loop repaired. I pulled them on, the legs billowing from my hips with a familiarity that felt like yesterday. Kara retrieved and handed me the belt, camisole, and over-shirt. Dressed, I ran my fingers up and through my hair, fluffing it out to dry with all the wayward curls, thick and loose, that it was inclined to have.

. . .

THERE WAS no announcement of a visitor, no respectful inquiry from eunuchs at the door that someone was waiting for me in my public audience room. Instead, harsh voices and the scraping of a table across the floor brought me to the curtained door. Behind it, I could see a tray of fresh bread, fruit, and yogurt on the table. My mouth watered. It had been a long time since I'd eaten anything so fresh. I pushed the soft cloth aside.

There in a chair beside the table sat Igliss.

Blood pumped behind my eyes. "Release my son at once." My hands clenched into fists at my side. I marched up to him.

Eyes wide, Igliss froze for a moment, staring at me. It was all I could do not to attack, and he knew it. Warily, he gestured to another chair, pushing it away from the table with a carefully clad foot. "Oh, do sit." Then, his tone sardonic again, "You must be famished after all your... time."

I refused to let my eyes follow his hand to the food and ignored the chair he pulled.

"This certainly does compromise that silly treaty." He tapped his fingertips together. "Breaks it, actually."

"I heard." I laid my hands on the table and leaned toward him. "You're attacking after all. Admit it."

Igliss tilted back, feigning to be aghast. "Oh, no. We're simply settling in, making Media more habitable. Establishing outposts, roads for the transport of goods, military... Your father has been eager, begging actually, for vassal status."

"What?" I stood again.

"He's always been an amenable fellow. Smart - ish. But you and that treaty..." Igliss's jaw ground briefly then relaxed. "Well. All that's over now. Civilization for Media. You'll see. For certain, Media will have to pay taxes and tribute, like everyone else."

"My father is a fool."

"All the better, then, for his country to bow to Babylonia's leadership. Crown Prince Labashi-Marduk. Such a lovely ring that has."

"Bushu is wrongly accused, and you know it."

"Your son is a traitor..." Igliss stroked his chin absently and looked up at the ceiling, "if an outsider could be a traitor..." He looked down again, rested his arm on the table, and reached for a grape. "Well. At best a usurper. Couldn't wait for throne."

"Not true!" I swept my arm across the table, sending the tray clattering to the floor.

Igliss jumped back but quickly got a hold of himself again. "What a mess," he said, waving a long finger over the food scattered on the floor. "Yet –" He let his eyes travel over her, head to foot. "To look at you there..."

I planted my feet defiantly, letting the trousers fall around my legs.

"I suppose you're accustomed to it."

Good thing I didn't have my scabbard. Much as I wished to cut this snake down then and there, that would only have worsened things for Bushu and for Media, too. I crossed my arms, the sleeves of my short over-shirt billowing wide, and tossed my head. "Remove him," I called.

But the guards at the door neither looked at me nor took even a step from their posts.

"Not so important now, are you?" Igliss shrugged. "Merely an unwelcome foreigner awaiting deportation. After the execution, of course."

"Agh!" My hands shook with fury as I yanked the chair away from Igliss. "Say it. Whatever you came here to say."

"The charges against your son are dire." Igliss cracked his knuckles slowly. "The worst. If it were up to me, you'd die together. But the king, in his great mercy..."

I heard Kara mutter some snide retort.

"Bushu will die of course. But!" Igliss brightened with exaggerated cheer. "You'll be spared." Igliss walked to the door. "The scaffold's ready," Igliss hesitated, musing, "though there's talk of the pike. A man on a stick, now there's a warning. Flayed, first."

I felt the blood leave my face.

"Gods forbid such a criminal die with his skin on. At least you'll get to watch. It'll be the last thing you see."

I couldn't help the shudder that passed through my spine. Remembering how Coniah's successor's eyes had been ripped from his head after he'd been forced to watch his children killed. "Get out!" I yelled.

But Igliss wasn't done. As he stepped through the door, he turned. "After that, you'll go with the army's next wave. Back to Media, just like you've always wanted. Too bad you won't be able to see Babylonia finally put those resources to good use." Igliss grinned, then swept out the door. Guards pulled it shut.

"Agh!" I flung the chair across the room. Its back of carved mahogany shattered. The parade of animals lay in pieces on the floor. The gold gilded chain that had run along the top was snapped in two.

At my feet, Kara got to her knees and began to pick up the food, sweeping with an old linen. She was stiff, slow.

"Stand up," I said.

Kara rose awkwardly. Her eyes – the good and the bad – deep in her burn-marred face, were soft and wet.

"I am nothing," I said. I took the cloth from her and let it drop. "You, then, are no slave."

Kara stiffened and squinted at me. She raised her eyebrows, brushed her hands against her rough robe briskly, and said, "Well. I can hardly leave."

I hung my head. Even in this, simply liberating the old woman who had served me all her life, I had failed. Kara wrapped her arms around me. The depth of my failures seemed bottomless, and when I didn't think I hadn't anything more to lose, I lost again. I leaned into her familiar embrace. Oh, the horror awaiting

Bushu, all of Media, and me too... Finally, I pulled away and dried my eyes.

I walked back into my private rooms. I walked all the way through to the bank of windows at the palace's northeast corner. The city went about its business as if this were any other Akitu, any other year of celebration and renewal. The river flowed as if it were any other day, and the sun's bright rays filtered through the sky to earth as if it were any other moment. The piney scent of cedar and rosemary drifted up from the gardens, winning out for a moment over the blood-meat smell of sacrifice.

I felt Kara step up next to me. We stood there silently for several long minutes.

"We have two days," I said, "to get Bushu out of prison –"

Kara whispered, "How?"

The plan was simple. I retrieved the sack I'd stuffed with valerian after seeing Khai for what I had believed was the last time. I had thought to use it to help myself sleep, never imagining the intervening days would be spent in prison.

"I'll lace the palm wine on my tray with valerian and leave it outside the door. Hopefully, the guards will be tempted to finish it and fall asleep at their post," I said. "I may be under house arrest, but you're not. Once the guards are asleep, you will slip out and make your way to the dungeon on the pretext of delivering one last message from Bushu's mother before he dies. Hopefully, you'll find enough sympathy to get through." I thought of Shalam, certain that he'd betrayed me, betrayed Bushu. But it was he who delivered that letter from Bushu... a missive I hated.

"Hopefully," Kara repeated, nodding.

As I spelled out the steps we'd take to free Bushu and return to Media and there we'd raise the Median army to revolt against Babylonia, Kara's expression changed from hope to pity.

I talked anyway. "Listen carefully now. You have to steal the keys from the bottom of the steps so that no one sees you. Come right back here."

As I talked, I could hear the determination and clarity of my voice lapse into a flat despair. I paused. Kara nodded for me to continue. I took a deep breath.

"Together," I said, "we'll set up a distraction, find the cell where Bushu is held with Coniah, open it, and we'll all escape."

"The Jewish king, too?" Kara asked. The whole thing was already so hare-brained. Why not make it even more unlikely?

"Yes," I said. "Thanks to the festival, there will be horses hobbled outside each gate, waiting for riders who are at the festivities. Once we're out of the city –" I didn't need to talk about how we'd get that far unseen much less past the gate guards. I went on anyway. "We'll make for Media. And once inside its borders, we'll raise alarm along the way to Ecbatana to summon an army in revolt against Babylonia."

"Nothing to it," Kara said.

I pursed my lips. "Nothing *but* it," I said.

Kara looked at me for a long moment. "That girl," she said, "so rough, so scrappy, who left the woods and wilds of Ecbatana over fifteen years ago…" She smiled. "A queen. Elegant, refined. Yet under it all, always the same fire, the same defiance, the same raw allegiance." Her smile disappeared. "You know it's impossible," Kara said. "And you could be killed. We could be killed."

I dumped the sack of valerian on the table and spread out the dried roots.

"Will you help me?"

"Will I help you?" Kara took my face in her chapped hands. "Of course I will."

CHAPTER 29

That evening, I watched Kara's gnarled fingers gather the twelve beads of power -- carnelian, lapis lazuli, yellow obsidian, jasper... She purified the stones with holy water and incense and strung them on a linen thread. When it was full dark, the old woman laid them on the window sill and faced the dog star. "O Bright one, O Gula, exalted Lady. You who grants both food and fortunes, be present. Give me, your weary servant, justice. Let the evil of Igliss, his plotting, his sorceries, his spittle and spatter, turn back against him. Do this, and I will sing your praises forevermore."

Kara's piety brought to mind the gods of Media and with them the forests and rivers and mountains, all the wild things that lived fierce and shy and sly and loyal. I thought of the responsibility and privilege of being human within it all, of both our insignificance and our agency, our weakness and our power. And sent up my own wordless prayer.

We waited. Evening passed into night. Nothing had happened. No news, no sign, no change. Finally, I handed Kara the tray. "You remember the way?"

Kara nodded toward the window. "I'll be back before Nanna-

Suen comes into view." She knocked on the door. When a guard cracked it open, she held the tray up, "Too much wine for my lady tonight. She can't drink such a fine beverage while her son suffers. May I put it out there?" The guard grunted, took the tray, and shut the door again.

Kara and I stood silently, listening. After a few minutes, we were rewarded by the sound of the vial lifted and poured, low voices cheerful, then quieter, and then the muffled clatter of armed bodies lowering themselves to the floor. Kara lifted her hood over her head and eased the door open. Quiet snores greeted her. Limbs lay akimbo. As she slipped out, one of the guard's arms dropped across the threshold. We froze. The snoring resumed, and Kara hurried down the hall.

I retreated into my private rooms to wait. I looked at my lyre, and picked it up, plucked a few chords. Where was Kara now? I tried to find the tune that Coniah had taught me, coming back again and again to it. But I couldn't concentrate.

Kara should have the key by now.

I hung the lyre against the wall again and went to the window. The streets bustled with activity. People passed in and out of homes, sharing food and drink as the gods feasted in the Akitu house during the festival's final days. Most of Babylon would be drunk or so full of rich fare, I hoped, that my party could slip out of the city undetected and unmissed until we were well on their way.

Still, no Kara.

After a time, the moon filled the window.

So much had to go exactly right, and already it was late.

A figure passed below and glanced up. For a moment, my heart jumped. Khai? No. I though back to the moment we had shared, body and soul. It felt a lifetime ago. I wondered what he had heard, what he thought. The moon had moved out of view again, taking with it the only light. I walked back into the room on heavy feet and stood for a long time, dread and despair erasing time. Street sounds came seldom now. It was the middle of the night.

At first, I feared that Kara would get caught, even killed. But by now, if that had happened, I would have known. I would be back in prison. But still the hall was quiet, empty but for the sleeping guards.

I finally admitted: Kara was gone. Fled. Who could blame her? I'd run, too, if I were her. Still, my heart broke at this last betrayal. I had depended on her more than I'd ever known. And I realized that I loved her. I lowered myself onto the padded stool of my dressing table where Kara had so often and for so long tended to my hair, readying me for this Babylonian world. I picked up the eye stone bracelet that Nebuchadnezzar had given to me after we married, opened the drawer, and shoved it to the back. My hand bumped a soft package.

Slowly, I took it out. The kerchief that Mandane had given to me a lifetime ago, still stained with the blood of that girl who wouldn't stop fighting for Media. I put a finger to the cheek that had long since healed, then laid the cloth on a table and drew back the linen's corners. There in the center lay the feather hair clasps and below them, the bone-white talons. "Oh," I whimpered, the grief. I laid my head on the table and closed my eyes.

Darkest night began to yield a muddy dawn. I squinted into the first hint of sun, raised my head. What else was there to lose? From a hook, I took one of Kara's rough robes. Better to die this way. One by one, I lifted the feathers to my hair and fixed them in place. I drew back the hair from my left temple, pulled it up, and clipped it fast. The talons swung from their threads against my neck.

The roll of papyrus, Bushu's letter from prison, still lay on the table. I glared at it, then snatched it up. I held its edge over an oil lamp. But this, hateful as it was, had come from my son's hand. I blew out the first licking flame, crumpled the document roughly and shoved it into my belt.

The hall was empty, quiet but for the guards' heavy breathing. I raised my hood and stepped over the guard's arm. I looked around, crouched, and from the sheath on a guard's hip, I slid his short sword out. He shuffled, bringing his hand toward his waist. But he let it drop before touching the leather. I stood, tucked the sword into my belt, and glided into the hall.

I WOVE my way through the palace. Servants had begun their rounds, bleary-eyed from the revels and too intent on their tasks to pay my small, hooded figure any mind. I retraced the steps I'd last walked. Finally, around the corner I could see a dim hallway. At its end was the iron gate blocking access to the dreadful stone staircase that dropped down into darkness. Two guards conferred lazily. I moved forward even as the stench emanating from the stairwell repulsed me, reminding me of the horrors below. Shadows streaked and spotted the walls.

I put my hand on the sword. I tipped my head back against the wall and took a deep breath. Then, like the shy mountain lions of Media, I stepped from one shadow to another. A tap-tap behind me made me freeze. I exhaled so quietly that I got dizzy. Then, slowly, I brought my head around to look. No one. I focused again on my goal, assessing and evaluating the best way. I might be able to cut down one man before they could react. But both of them? I studied the guards' movements. One man made the other laugh, low and gritty. They didn't sound drunk. I'd just have to move quickly – stab one before either could react and then dash down the stairs, hoping to catch the other as he followed. He'd have the upper stair advantage. But what choice did I have? I stepped quickly into another patch of shadow, nearer the guards and the gate.

Behind me, a susurrating -- fabric against plaster? – again stopped me cold. Again, I looked. Again, I saw nothing. I stepped into another shadow. Almost close enough now to strike. Close enough to be caught. My robe brushed against the wall, and the guards snapped to attention, hands on the hilts of their swords. They peered into the dim light. I froze flat against the dark wall and held my breath. After a few minutes, one shrugged to the other. They relaxed again. I tightened my grip on the short sword, hoping that the years hadn't been too long to trigger the muscle memory I needed. I leaned forward, coiled my body to jump.

Suddenly, "Sirs!" a voice called.

I pulled back into the shadows, heart pounding.

"Hold!" The guards drew their swords.

Out from the darkness across the hall from me stepped Kara.

"Hold!" the guards called again.

Kara halted. Behind her, a spot of light danced on the wall. Kara's good eye found me, still hidden, and darted to the sword at my hip.

When I put my hand over the weapon's hilt, the bouncing light disappeared.

Kara walked forward. "Has the prince come out yet?"

What is she doing? I thought. This is not our plan.

The guards conferred. "What?" one called back.

"The prince. His release."

For a moment, I let myself believe that it was true, that Bushu's innocence had been discovered, that he'd been freed. But I knew Kara's voice too well. It was a bluff.

"For certain not." They shared a laugh, and my fantasy died.

"He will be soon. I am Karadara, the queen's servant, and wish to attend to the prince before the queen sees him."

"Prince, you say." They laughed again. "Funny."

"I'll wait around the corner, here," Kara said.

"Wait if you like. But come any closer," they weren't laughing now, "and we'll have to kill you." The threat was real. I could hear it in their voices. I willed Kara to retreat.

Kara took a few steps back along the hall. Relieved, I retreated behind her. As soon as we'd turned the corner out of the guards' line of vision, I whispered, "I thought you'd run away." You should," I said, urgent now. "Go now, go north, back to Harran. Maybe you still have family there..."

Kara shook her head. She put a hand on my arm. "Go to the king in his quarters."

"What?!" I recoiled. "I'll be killed on the spot." A horrible realization seeped into my mind. "You want me dead."

Kara pursed her lips. "After I left you in your rooms," she said, "I realized that there was a way – there *is* a way... So I did what I could. Now, there isn't much time." She took my face gently between gnarled hands. "You dead is the last thing I could ever want."

I looked at the twisted and scarred face of my old nurse, as familiar as the lines and veins across my own hands.

"Do you trust me?" Kara asked.

As I looked into her eyes, one bright the other cloudy, I thought of Kara's constant presence in my childhood, her attention for me as much as for the true princess Mandane, her risking alienation and rejection to follow the litter that bore me to Media, her counsel and care and ministrations all these Babylonian years....

I heard my voice, in wonder, say, "You set yourself on fire... You, disfigured beyond recognition..."

The guards coughed. "Hey, old lady!" one called.

"And then you came back," I said, tears running down my cheeks. I threw my arms around this woman, who so many years ago, had nursed the infant, motherless Mandane. And me.

For a sweet moment, she held me close. "Now, go, my darling daughter. Go!"

Then, before I could protest, the old slave, my mother, my own, stepped back out into the hallway, back into the guards' view.

"Here!" Kara called, in her smoke-scarred voice. She ran straight at them.

It was one last, terrible diversion.

I knew what I had to do, the only thing that would redeem her sacrifice. The ensuing noise – armed guards rushing with a roar, men thirsty for the clash, the beating, the blood – covered my flight. Choking back sobs, I dashed down the hall, forcing myself not to look back, not to see. I covered my ears as I ran. Even still, I couldn't help but hear the swish of swords unsheathed, the clang and grunt of armored men throwing themselves forward, the crack and smack, the awful slurping schwoosh of blade in flesh.

Kara never cried out. I gulped for air.

IN MY MOTHER'S poor robe – my mother! – the hood pulled over my head, I got through the palace hallways without drawing attention. Finally, I was at the king's door. I gasped for breath, for calm, struggling to rise above the flood of emotions that threatened to swamp what fortitude I could muster. Lapis lazuli tiles overhead made the ceiling seem even loftier. The doors – imported cedar with great iron studs and rings for handles – were tightly shut. What was it that Kara had in mind? Go to the king in his quarters, she had said. It was madness, but –

At my approach, the king's guards stepped in front, feet wide, arms crossed.

"Open it," I said and threw back my hood. I caught my breath.

It was Shalam who stood before me, blocking my way. So he was one of the king's guard, now. His face was blank. I ached with the betrayal. Slowly, ostentatiously, I pulled the short sword from my belt. The other guard lurched forward, but I let the weapon clatter to the ground. I raised my hands, empty. "I must speak to the king."

I expected them to deny me. With Bushu so accused and sentenced, the king would hardly permit me an audience,

But Shalam nodded to his companion. They opened the doors. I stepped inside. The doors clanged shut behind me with the finality of a tomb.

Nebuchadnezzar sat in a chair, looking every bit as he had before Ean's death – a capable king, strong and uncompromising. Igliss was there, too. Of course. "Wh-?" I heard Igliss exclaim. "House arrest," he hissed in the king's ear. I fixed my eyes on Nebuchadnezzar's. Cold. He didn't invite me forward.

I shrugged off the coarse robe and let it fall to the floor.

Nebuchadnezzar made no move. No matter.

I thought idly, maybe it would be Shalam's sword that killed me. And if there were a life after this, as Kara believed, if there were a place where the dead gathered again, I would see my mother this afternoon.

I took a breath, lifted my chin and stepped forward. I would die as the Median bastard that I was born. My short Median over-shirt caught the air. I felt the feathers in my hair lift and spin. How clean the air feels, how pure, I thought, and I so empty. My trousers waved loose against my legs.

"Seize her!"

With each step, the talons clicked near my ear.

"Kill her!" Igliss's voice came as though through a tunnel.

"My son is innocent," I called.

I didn't turn to watch the guards surge forward. I just drew back my shoulders, opening my chest to welcome the blow that would cut me down.

"A sword!" Igliss called.

So it was Igliss who rushed forward, his arm extended. I turned my head, then, following Nebuchadnezzar's gaze. I turned around. Behind me, Shalam red-faced with the effort, restrained his partner. With one arm, its old muscles ropey from the strain, he pinned the man's arms to his sides. With the other arm,

Shalam prepared to stop Igliss. Igliss skidded to a halt and whipped around back toward the king, sputtering, aghast. And then I could see: behind Shalam the doors were thrown open. A throng of people poured in.

Igliss spun back into the room, rushing to the king. "Insubordination!" He waved his arm. "This must be stopped."

But on the people came until finally they stood and quieted. Out of the silence in the now crowded hall, a voice called out, "Release the prince."

What had I heard? My eyes smarted. Not everyone believed him to be a usurper.

"Release the prince," another joined, and another after him. Their voices grew.

Now I understood. Kara had mustered these people – people of all kinds, some I recognized, many I did not, people whose cases Bushu and I had heard, whose work he had praised, whose humanity we had championed – people who now came to my aid, to Bushu's defense.

Nebuchadnezzar stood, his eyes sparking with anger.

"Kill them all!" Igliss yelled.

Don't let them die because of me, I thought. Not that.

But there were too many. The chant grew, "Release the prince!" until it drowned out Igliss's stammering outrage.

Nebuchadnezzar raised his hand for quiet. The cry died down, but it left a silence even more charged.

Nebuchadnezzar called out. "He's right, you know," nodding toward Igliss. "Death." The king fixed me with cruel eyes and gestured the guard forward. The younger man twisted out of Shalam's grasp. The guard drew his sword and strode forward.

"Go ahead." I offered him my chest. "You have taken my son," I said to the king. "You have taken my land. I am already dead." I felt cold as stone. "But you'll be killing your own son. An innocent man."

"Wait." Nebuchadnezzar raised a hand. The guard lowered his

sword, but he didn't sheath it. I heard its iron tip rest on the stone floor. Nebuchadnezzar leaned back.

Igliss huffed, incensed.

"On what grounds," Nebuchadnezzar asked, "this 'innocence?' His case has been heard." He strummed his fingertips on the arm of his chair. There was no other sound.

I swallowed hard.

"Bushu is guilty," a clear voice said from the back. I didn't need to see. The speaker was Khai. Another betrayal?! But he went on, "Only of falling in love." Footsteps, steady and sure.

"Stop him!" Igliss called.

Then Khai was at my side, and in the air a hint of cardamom earth. I felt my body still. Warmth returning to my icy bones.

"How do you know that?" Nebuchadnezzar asked Khai.

Khai's shoulder brushed mine. "Look at what he did."

Igliss sputtered, "Made a show of sleeping with the king's women!"

Ignoring Igliss's glare, Khai looked only at Nebuchadnezzar. "Bushu is a young man, who still thinks," the warmth of Khai's shoulder dissipated as he stepped away, stepped forward, "that the heart must have its love at any cost." I watched Khai's broad back tightened, as though he were drawing himself inward. "The prince hasn't yet learned to wait." He glanced at me, then back at the king, moving his body between me and the hostile, royal dais.

"To wait, you're right." Nebuchadnezzar leaned forward, his voice rising. "He tried to take my throne --"

"No," a voice rang out from the back.

Nebuchadnezzar scowled.

There was some scuffling as the speaker worked his way forward. "The prince sought your health." Nathan emerged from the crowd, brushed off his robe, and without looking for the king's invitation, stepped forward.

Igliss waved frantically to the guards at the door, "A travesty!"

Nebuchadnezzar inhaled loudly. "Explain yourself, scribe."

With neither hurry nor hesitation, Nathan stepped up next to Khai and told how Bushu had asked his help in discerning the cause of Nebuchadnezzar's prolonged grief, a grief, Nathan said, that had required Bushu to take the reins of state. "He was looking for a cure."

I opened my mouth, ready to defend Nathan's observation, but Nebuchadnezzar said to Nathan, "And did you?" He held out his arms, displaying his now perfectly fine state of being, "find the cause? the cure?"

"I tell you what I told the prince. Only Yahweh-God could make you well." Nathan gestured lightly at Nebuchadnezzar's person. "He has."

Nebuchadnezzar laughed. "Well, thank you, Yahweh," he said in a voice laced with sarcasm, "for being so gracious and magnanimous as to allow me to rule this great empire, for returning to me my sense and good reason. Let's all praise the King of Heaven, the source of justice, who puts us in our place, and keeps us all in line."

Igliss leapt forward. "Blasphemy!" He brought his voice back down. "I know that you are joking, my lord, but I cannot stand by while we trade Babylonia's greatness for lawlessness, chaos, and discord. With all respect, and sharing the joy of your recovery, the gods of Babylonia are sufficient unto the world. And Marduk, who presides over all in this city, 'Gate of the Gods,' and beyond is greatest of them all. This rabble," Igliss swept his hand over me and the people beside and behind me, "would have us squander the traditions and principles that make Babylonia what it is. They are nobodies. They have no clout, no right to speak on matters of law, the gods, or Babylonia's future. Nor should they ever."

"Go on," Nebuchadnezzar said.

Igliss, his eyes bright with self-righteousness, squared his narrow shoulders. "The accused, an imposter prince, led *citizens* -- Babylonians of status and position to believe that he would steal the throne. That is what his rightful trial determined. Such criminal, traitorous action happens when someone with foreign blood presumes to Babylonian royalty. It is unacceptable." Igliss dropped his head for a moment, and then lifted his face, shining with the passion of certainty. "Babylonia, with its long-standing citizens of tradition and power – pure Babylonia - is a light to the world. These foreigners, these immigrants cannot understand, much less lead us and all nations, to a better future." He flung out his arms and let the echo ring. "Babylonia is civilization itself."

Lowering his voice and arms, Igliss said to Nebuchadnezzar, "You, my lord, have conquered far and wide, building and expanding without precedent to the betterment of all." He shot me a look of disgust. "That former alliance," he spat, "does no one any good. Media needs Babylonian development and management. Not vice versa. Yet the deposed and disgraced Bushu has been informed and influenced by..." Igliss pointed at me, letting his hand open to take in my hair, my blouse, my trousers... and curled his lip. "He has not embraced the gods. The youth has heathen inclinations, following in his mother's ways. Surely, it is better that he be killed for his crime. Babylonia deserves better. The world needs better than a foreign usurper on this throne."

A small cough broke the silence. I turned to look and felt Igliss behind me coil in anger. Kassiya, so thin as to cast barely a shadow, stood holding her son, a pouting baby. She took a few steps into the room, caught Igliss's glare, and stopped. In a voice barely audible she said, "I don't know Media except that it's different from here." Labashi-Marduk twisted in her arms, but she held tight. "And," she glanced at me, "Amytis is different, too, in ways I don't always understand." She looked down at Labashi-Marduk, then up again. "But Amytis saved my life. She saved the life of my son, of our son, *because* of her foreignness."

I heard Igliss growl. Kassiya buttoned her lips and looked down.

Igliss said, "Irrelevant."

Nebuchadnezzar's eyes lingered on his daughter Kassiya and the boy – his Babylonian grandson – a brat of a boy already, but Babylonian. Nebuchadnezzar gave Igliss a definitive nod – unmistakable – understanding and respect. Nausea roiled me. That was it. I had done everything that I could. Igliss looked at me and grinned, the same toothy grimace that I remembered from the first time I saw him. He knew he had won.

My knees buckled. Khai rushed to steady me. Regaining my footing, I heard the crackle of papyrus against my hip. Its sharp snap reminded me of this one, last thing. Much as I hated it. I nodded a thanks to Khai, hoping he could read in my face everything I read in his, and tilted my head to release him back into the crowd. He went.

Alone, I faced the dais again. Igliss, his expression smug; Nebuchadnezzar, in disdain. I hated every bit of this, my mouth bitter with what I had to say. "Justice," I spat. "Truth and fair dealings are a Babylonian king's responsibility? Even your gods would kill an innocent young man." I reached into my pocket.

The guard leapt forward, but I produced no weapon, merely the small scroll of flimsy papyrus. "A prayer. From your son." I held it up.

CHAPTER 30

*N*ebuchadnezzar waved for Nathan to take the scroll from me and read it aloud.

"The Lament of Nabu-shuma-ukin," Nathan read, "a prayer, of the weary and bound person."

A hush fell.

In the perfect quiet Nathan read aloud from Bushu's schooled stylus. He read of the prince's pure motives and earnest commitment to the welfare of king and country. Nathan read, not looking up to see Nebuchadnezzar's attention and immune to Igliss's shifting feet, of the injustices the prince wrote that he had suffered, of the misunderstandings and lies that had landed him in such an abject and hopeless place. The prince told of his innocence. And he prayed a lament, a plea, and a promise.

I knew the words that my son, a poet, had composed. The language – its prose at once elegant and poignant – had music. I could hear the beauty of it, even though I knew how it ended.

"I have been caught in the snare of an evil man. A crafty enemy tricked me. He captured me in a net of his making." Nathan paused. "Great Marduk - " Nathan looked at me.

I dreaded hearing it – out loud, in this place.

Nebuchadnezzar waved the scribe to read on.

"Once long ago..."

If only I could have rescued my boy...

"You, Marduk, overcame resistance and rejection to become the highest god..."

… freed Bushu from the snakes' nest of Babylonia.

"… the god of Babylon, the god of the world." Nathan shifted his feet. "If you release me from prison, I will devote myself as a loyal slave for the rest of my life to Marduk's will and command. Through this prayer to Marduk may I be freed to serve him and Marduk's Babylonia all of my life. No higher god, no greater land."

I heard my breath, a groaning sigh.

"So writes the weary and exhausted son of Nebuchadnezzar." Nathan lowered the papyrus, its brush against his robe the only sound.

I closed my eyes, feeling all the losses I'd ever suffered converge in my chest. And then this. In Bushu's final days, he would turn his back on Media. For him it would be Babylonia, above all.

When I opened my eyes, Nebuchadnezzar hadn't moved. He sat, staring out at nothing, it seemed. Then he took a sharp breath, glanced at Igliss, and held his hand out for the scroll. Nathan stepped forward and handed it to him. Nebuchadnezzar looked it over, his eyes retracing the words. Then he rolled it up again. He tapped the scroll against his palm, once. Twice. Finally, he spoke.

"In Marduk's name," Nebuchadnezzar said, "Free him."

A great roar went up.

"My son," Nebuchadnezzar said, "servant of Marduk, the crown prince of Babylonia."

The crowd outside whooped in deafening acclaim.

I closed my eyes again. Relief and gratitude swirled with tremendous grief. Oh, how one's wantings could vie. I was dizzy with the mix.

Bushu restored, gods be praised. And pledged by the gods to Babylonia forever. Damn them.

Tears coursed down my cheeks. I felt Kassiya's arm on my shoulder and Khai's steady presence beside me. Then I turned, and with a strong back and sure steps, I walked out.

So it was that when the Akitu festival ended and Babylon gathered at the river to bid farewell to the gods for another year, Bushu was present and standing next to King Nebuchadnezzar. Ringing the prince's dark brown hair, lay a crown of gold studded with color. Inlaid gems formed insignia of the visiting gods– Lady Ishtar's rosette, Nanna-Suen's crescent moon, the sunburst of Shamash…. In the middle of the prince's forehead, Marduk's spade rose from the band and glittered in fragments of red cut glass.

Standing next to him, I felt my son radiate a kind of heat, the warmth of a power hard-won. Maybe it was just the spring sunshine. Imagination or not, he would be king one day, king of Babylonia. I wished the thought didn't make me so heart-heavy. As per his promise to the gods, Bushu would never leave Babylonia except for war. And there'd be no war with Media. So, he'd never again know Media's air, smell its pines, or see its snow-capped mountains. Bushu did reassure me, in confidence, that he would protect and sustain Media. I couldn't ask for more.

So, I hadn't protested when he insisted that I, like everyone else, call him Amel-Marduk instead of Nabu-shuma-ukin. He was to be "Servant of Marduk," not Bushu. Amel-Marduk, or Evel-Merodach, as the Jews said. I didn't know if I could ever really get used to that. Then again, I had gotten used to a lot of things.

Igliss and Kassiya took Labashi-Marduk back to Sippar. They were among the first to leave. Igliss's anger at the way things had gone was mitigated by an ego-boosting promotion. Nebuchadnezzar made him governor of Sippar. With the status of this lofty post, Igliss had become more powerful than ever before. I took some comfort from seeing how the smug satisfaction of Igliss's new title softened his manner toward Kassiya. I hoped it held.

In the spring light, shimmering off the slow river, everything felt new. With Bushu restored, the formal terms of the treaty between nations were reinstated. I had ridden with the courier as far as the city's distant outskirts, to hurry the messenger on to call back Babylonia's troops. Wild Media was safe again.

My hair hung loose, bound with Babylonian gold... for now. Notwithstanding the vigor on display with Nebuchadnezzar's return, he was an old man. And the period of his sickening grief had taken a toll. The tiny gold-plated dagger remained hidden; but quietly, I planned for the day I could wear it again, planned for my return to Media. In the meantime, I embraced my foreignness as asset, advocated for Babylonia's outsiders, and tended my garden. Alone.

Nathan continued to serve as a palace scribe and was entrusted with all of the most sensitive correspondence. And I made sure that he was free, once a week, to spend Shabbat with other Jews from greater Babylonia, even traveling on occasion to see his family in Nippur. We became friends.

It was still hard for me to think of Kara as my mother. But when, in the quiet of my rooms before sleep or walking along the city's wall, I recalled moments – something Kara did or said – that had seemed so odd then, and now made perfect sense, they shone like beads of water strung along a line. Some made me cringe, moments when I'd treated Kara as the slave she was. But most were good for one reason or another. I'd always miss her.

I caught myself looking every so often for Khai's grin, listening for his voice, or found myself staring, heart pounding, at the broad back of a young man down the hall. Each time I was both devastated and relieved to find that it was not Khai. Shortly after we had met alone at his house, he resigned his post as manager of gardens. They were fine, even if I wasn't.

CHAPTER 31

hen Bushu took the throne, uncontested, as Babylonia's King Amel-Marduk, he was twenty years old. Bushu never grieved Nebuchadnezzar, never forgave him. When I asked, he said only that just as Nebuchadnezzar had rejected him as a son years before, he rejected Nebuchadnezzar as his father forever. Fair enough, I thought.

Among the first things that Bushu did as King Amel-Marduk was to release Jehoiachin from prison. He gave the exiled Jewish king the highest place at the king's table and consulted him as a trusted advisor and friend. He even made Coniah's son, Shesh-bazzar one of the city administrators. Nathan's people pronounced Bushu's new name Evel-Merodach and thought of him well, an entirely different man than his father, the king who had destroyed Jerusalem.

Most of the positions—administrators, priests, judges, bakers, and managing officials -- Bushu left with the Babylonians who had held them during his father's reign. And despite my reservations and concern, he allowed that Igliss would continue to lead the temple and administration of Sippar. Bushu knew as well as I that from that position, Igliss maintained and cultivated relationships with the conservative elite of Babylonia's oldest families and prestigious citizens. Then again, I told myself, it might be worse were Bushu to demote him and Igliss return to Babylon... dispossessed and angry. So, perhaps it was best that Igliss remain some distance from the capital and happy in his role. Of course he doted on his son, Labashi-Marduk, making no pretense that Igliss had grandiose plans for the boy who according to rumor was growing into an insufferable little person. I hated to imagine how it affected Kassiya.

I hardly did. I hardly thought of anything other than the fact that I would finally be able to return to Media, finally able to return to the place I'd never wanted to leave those many years ago. It was bittersweet – I'd leave my only child here, and he wedded to Babylonia. Better that than dead, I told myself. And I knew that he loved Media still, wild Media, my Media. With Bushu now Amel-Marduk as king, Media was safe. To ask for more would have been too much.

AT DAWN, on the morning of my departure from Babylon, I asked the scribe Nathan to walk the city walls with me. While most people couldn't help exclaiming from such a vantage point over the magnificence of the city's streets, the enormous temple tower, the city's new walls, renovated quays, and breathtaking gates, we walked in silence.

We stopped at the northeast end and stood there, side by side. Just above the horizon, a bright star – Ishtar's – still shone against the lightening sky.

"There's a poem circulating among the Jews," Nathan said, "about Nebuchadnezzar."

"Tell me?"

"It's a taunt."

"All the better," I said.

Nathan tilted his head and raised his eyebrows.

"Go on."

He took a deep breath. "How you have fallen from heaven, O morning star. You thought in your heart, 'I will climb to the sky. I will match the Most High.' Instead you are brought down to the place of the dead, to the bottom of the pit."

"Is that what they believe?"

"Look around." Nathan stopped and swung his arm, taking in the city's wonders. "All these monuments. All these..." he patted his chest, "- lives that his own dictated. Yet he died," Nathan shrugged, "like any other man." We walked on. "Like any other man, each of us is answerable to the expectations of God."

"And what are those?" Amytis asked, "those expectations."

"To do justice, endear kindness to your heart, and go along always humbly with your god." Nathan said. "Not my words, someone else's."

I laughed. I was tired of Babylonian religion's many daily duties, the rituals and anxieties over this god or that's wishes and desires, the details of temple practice and prayer and appeasement. How refreshing, how wise, this simple demand.

"That's it?"

"As for the details," Nathan shrugged. "Not mine, either."

I looked around, my eyes traveling over sprawling Babylon. I undid the few gold clips I'd affixed to my hair in deference to my son, the king, and tossed them up and down absently in my palm. "It's time for me to go."

I looked into the distance, toward the north. I lifted one foot, cocked my arm, and with a single sweeping toss, I cast out the gold, watching it skim the morning air like stones on the river. Then I looked at Nathan.

"In Media there are people who share your history. Israel." I smiled. "Come along?"

Nathan stepped back in surprise. Then he stepped forward again. "A wandering Aramean was my father... Why not me?"

The next morning, I rode into the courtyard astride the white mare, that Nisean charger, descended from the stallion that had come with me from Ecbatana so many years ago. When she tossed her head, I could feel the feathers in my hair catch the eager energy rippling through the horse's neck and mane. Nathan had already boarded the carriage that he would ride. An ox-cart loaded with provisions and driven by a single armed servant was our only other vehicle. Bushu, or rather King Amel-Marduk, stood at the gate, Shalam beside him. We had said our goodbyes. As long as Bushu was in Babylon, and another too, so too would be a bit of my heart. We cantered out. I looked back only once. From the top of the city wall that spanned the gate, I could see through a swimming gaze a man, broad-shouldered and relaxed. He raised one arm, its palm open to me, steady and high, for as long as I could bear to look.

CHAPTER 32

*B*ack in Media, I had expected to see unrest such as Bushu and I had witnessed in Media years before but not to the degree I saw now. It would take a long time to restore security. I got to work right away. In the coming months, I worked to restore trust, dignity, and peace to Media's population, visiting tribes and commissioning trade. I found that I liked to visit, and I liked to go alone. The people trusted me more easily that way, and their trust made me safe.

As for Cyrus, it was my father, of all people, who told me – and with pleasure, no less – that the boy had been discovered alive. Astyages thought him a regular princeling and had returned him to Anshan in Parsa, to his father Cambyses there. Harpagus said nothing except to confirm that that was indeed the case. Unfortunately, the cottage of Mit and Spaco had burned. It was thought that they perished in the fire. He was tight-lipped about the details. Given his role and his unfailing obedience to my father, I didn't think much of it. I was too busy to wonder at any of it, merely happy that Astyages had welcomed the boy alive, after all.

The business of Media kept my mind from thoughts of Khai.

Mostly. My heart was another thing. Still, to think of him hurt less now than when I'd dismissed him from his post, hurt less than when I left Babylon, and I hoped would hurt less another month, another year from now. Meanwhile, I heard regularly from Bushu, whose messages carried news of the empire – projects completed, festivals observed, Nabonidus's capable management of foreign territories, new music inspired by the cosmopolitan court... – and always something about Sippar, always benign, always (I assumed) composed to put my mind at ease. And if I dreamed a nightmare of Igliss stalking my son or couldn't shake recollections of the man's hard hatred, I would ride.

AT THE STREAM, flashing with current and quick-darting trout, I pulled up my mount. If I squinted just right, I could almost see Mandane's form in the water, reaching, reaching for that plant she insisted on taking with her to Babylon those many years ago. I blinked, and she was gone. But I remained. There on the bank I thanked Anahita for sending me, for setting me on a journey I could never have imagined. Wild Media protected. I couldn't ask for more. Though I would. And I begged forgiveness from the life of this land for all I'd done wrong. One day, maybe for some of it, I could forgive myself.

But for now, the alfalfa in the valleys was as tall as the bellies of the stout horses who grazed there, and I turned my horse toward the fields. When we reached them, I galloped my mare into a herd of those four-legged warriors. She whinnied with fierce joy. Bent over her neck and squinting into the wind, I tied off the reins and let them fall loose into the white, whipping mane. Who was I? I was someone who knew Media's value lay not in exploiting her material resources but in wise management and restraint. I knew that respect for, not control of, her wildness would serve us better than subjugation and ignorant domestication. I who had had jewels and cushioning luxury nevertheless knew true privilege. For what was it if not to live with no want in the presence of wonder and beauty? Who was I, indeed?

The mare lengthened her stride, stirring up the herd to join the race. There, in the midst of the galloping horses, I lifted my face, raised my arms and held them out. There, matching my horse's thundering gait, I let them fly up and down like wings. In the distance, a golden jackal howled. From somewhere near, another replied.

THE END

CAST OF CHARACTERS

A few things to note: Even for historical characters, there may be some question or disagreement regarding specific details – see "Author's Note." I do not provide here dates of death or other details that don't transpire during the course of this particular narrative. With the exception of Iddina and Coniah, nicknames are my own. An asterisk (*) denotes non-historical characters, people that I've made up.

Adad-guppi: Aramean (from the defeated Harran); attendant in the Babylonian courts of Nebuchadnezzar and Amel-Marduk; mother of Nabonidus, grandmother of Belshazzar.

Amel-Marduk (Bushu): son of Amytis and Nebuchadnezzar II; born Nabu-shuma-ukin; becomes King of Babylon in 562 B.C.E. In the Bible, his name appears as Evil-Merodach.

Amytis: daughter of Astyages, king of Media; sister of Mandane; wife of Nebuchadnezzar (and according to legend, the woman for whom he built the Hanging Gardens of Babylon because she missed her mountain home so much); mother of Amel-Marduk; aunt of Cyrus II.

Astyages: son of Cyaxares; king of Media; father of Amytis and Mandane; grandfather of Cyrus II.

Bariki-ili: Hebrew slave who (historically) earned a reputation for seeking his freedom, running away and getting caught over and over again.

Belshazzar: son of Nabonidus and Nitocris and so the (illegitimate, I imagine) grandson of Nebuchadnezzar.

Cambyses I: King of Anshan (Parsa); husband of Mandane; father of Cyrus II.

Cassiya/Kassiya: daughter of Nebuchadnezzar; wife of Neriglissar; mother of Labashi-Marduk; (half-, I imagine) sister of Nitocris and Eanna-sharra-utsur (sharing the father Nebuchadnezzar).

Cyaxares: (d. 585 B.C.E.) king of the Medes; father of Astyages; grandfather of Amytis and Mandane. (Some say he was the father of Amytis).

Cyrus II: son of Cambyses I and Mandane; niece of Amytis; grandson of Astyages; raised by Median slaves Spaco and *Mit(hradates) who called him Bartatua until he was ten years old, then returned to Parsa.

Eanna-šarra-utsur (Ean): son (I imagine eldest) of Nebuchadnezzar with his first wife; in 587 B.C. receives rations in a sick-house in Uruk (historical). I imagine he suffers schizophrenia.

Egibi: family name of Babylonian entrepreneurial family that becomes a powerful corporation beginning with **Nabu-ahhe-iddin (Khai)** and endures for several generations.

Harpagus: palace steward to King Astyages.

Itti-Marduk-balatu (Iddina -- this nickname is historical): eldest son of Nabu-ahhe-iddin (Khai) and Qudashu; heir to the Egibi estate.

Jehoiachin (historically also Jeconiah/Coniah): King of Judah removed by Nebuchadnezzar in the first deportation mid-March, 597 B.C.E. and imprisoned in Babylon. He was eighteen years old at the time and had been king for only three months.

*Karadara (Kara): Aramean commoner from the defeated

Harran; slave in Astyages's court; wet nurse to Amytis; slave to Amytis in Babylon; finally revealed (spoiler alert!) to be Amytis's mother.

Mithradates (Mit): Shepherd slave to Astyages's palace who with his wife Spaco raised Cyrus II (whom they called Bartatua) from infancy until Cyrus was ten years old.

Mandane: (legitimate) daughter of Astyages, hence princess of Media; half-sister of Amytis; wife of Cambyses I; mother of Cyrus II; I imagine that she commits suicide upon being told of her newborn's (Cyrus's) death.

Nabonidus: Aramean from defeated Harran; son of Adad-guppi; courtier in the Babylonian courts of Nebuchadnezzar and Amel-Marduk; husband of Nitocris; father of Belshazzar.

*Nathan: from Nippur, Jewish scribe for Nebuchadnezzar; son of *Rabbi Yakov ben-Isaiah and *Michal; moves with Amytis to Media.

Nabu-ahhe-iddin (Khai): son of Babylonian farmer Shula Egibi; scribe, entrepreneur; husband of Qudashu; father of Itti-Marduk-balatu (Iddina); founder of the Egibi family corporation.

Nebuchadnezzar II: (634 -- Oct. 8, 562) son of Nabopolassar, king of Babylon/Babylonia; husband of Amytis; father of Nitocris (illegit, I imagine), Eanna-sharra-utsur (Ean), and Cassiya by an Ishtar temple slave from Uruk (I made up this unnamed earlier woman/wife). Father of Amel-Marduk by Amytis.

Neriglissar (Igliss): probably served with Nebuchadnezzar on campaign against Jerusalem in 587 B.C.; husband of Cassiya (so, Nebuchadnezzar's son-in-law); father of Labashi-Marduk.

Qudashu: wife of Nabu-ahhe-iddin (Khai); mother of Itti-Marduk-balatu (Iddina).

*Rachel: Jewish wet nurse in Babylon for the baby Amel-Marduk (Bushu).

Rdiya: head of Amytis's Babylonian household; based on the historical Ardiya of Nebuchadnezzar's court staff.

*__Shiyati__: Parsan woman enslaved in Susa and taken to Babylon; love interest of Amel-Marduk's.

__Spaco__ (probably itself a nickname; means simply "Dog"): Shepherd slave to Astyages's palace who with her husband Mit(hradates) raised Cyrus II (whom they called Bartatua) from infancy until Cyrus was ten years old.

CITATIONS OF QUOTES

Earlier versions of these novels include footnotes citing sources, yet more information, and sometimes my own thinking about what I was learning, mainly to help myself remember what led me to make the narrative decisions I did. I've had illusions of making those footnotes available to readers. But they're terribly unwieldy (in the hundreds), and the research keeps coming. Likewise, any bibliography would number in the hundreds, probably over a thousand. Yikes. So, I include here only those sources (hopefully all) from which I have drawn direct quotes. It feels incomplete. But then, such is life. Oh, and for details about the Akitu ceremony, I've drawn heavily from J. Bidmead, *The Akitu Festival: Religious Continuity and Royal Legitimation in Mesopotamia*, 2004, Gorgias.

"**Something about the west... Jerusalem, maybe**" See the Bible, Jeremiah chapter 39. Nergal-Sharezer is widely believed to be this Neriglissar.

"**To the Land of No Return**," Kara began..." Ancient Mesopotamian stories rarely had titles. This title is a modern one, based on the Sumerian version's first line. See Erica Reiner, *Your Thwarts in Pieces, Your Mooring Rope Cut: Poetry from Baby-*

lonia and Assyria, 1985, Michigan Slavic, 29-49 for a discussion of the poem and its versions.

"**'To Kumar,' Rdiya barked...**" The description of Babylon here is informed by Andrew R. George, "A Tour of Nebuchadnezzar's Babylon," in *Babylon: Myth and Reality,* 2008, British Museum, 54-59.

"**Sing us one of the songs of Zion**" See the Bible, Psalm 137.

"**I looked at the heavy doors as I passed ...**" D. J. Wiseman, based on other scholarly sources tries to make sense of the ancient Babylonian documents that list these woods. I don't know what color the wood from Magan was, but it may be the same as sissoo -- not ebony (D. J. Wiseman *Nebuchadrezzar and Babylon,*1985, Oxford, 55) but a Pakistani rosewood (Daniel Potts, *Ancient Magan: The Secrets of Tell Abraq,* 2000, Trident, 67).

"**Birth-prayer of gratitude to the midwife goddess Ninmah...**" See Erica Reiner, *Astral Magic in Babylonia,* 1998, University of Pennsylvania, 22.

"**A tiny reed bed with two figurines...**" Erica Reiner, *Astral Magic in Babylonia,* 1998, University of Pennsylvania, 23.

"**Marduk, you created me...**" *The India House Inscription,* col. IX, lines 47-65.

"**A golden eye-stone bracelet... many-petaled pattern**" Such an item was discovered at the Assyrian Kalhu worn by queens and courtiers (Michael Roaf, *A Cultural Atlas of Mesopotamia and the Ancient Near East,* 1990, Checkmark, 165).

"**That evening, I watched Kara's gnarled fingers... praises**" Erica Reiner, *Astral Magic in Babylonia,* 1998, University of Pennsylvania, 127-128.

"**If our god needs a whipping boy...**" It is possible that the "suffering servant" of the Bible, Isaiah 52:13-53:12, as it was composed, was Jehoiachin (See also Michael Goulder, "Behold My Servant Jehoiachin," 2002, *Vetus Testamentum* 52:175-190.

"**'Well, thank you, Yahweh,' he said...**" See the Bible, Daniel 4:29-34.

"'The Lament of Nabu-shuma-ukin,' Nathan read..." I am convinced by Irving Finkel's argument that the Nabu-šuma-ukin who composed a lament from prison was this person, who later changed his name to Amel-Marduk. Nabu-šuma-ukin may have been a common name as it appears in reference to scribe and priest in ancient inscriptions, too. Irving Finkel, "The Lament of Nabû-šuma-ukîn", in *Babylon: Focus mesopotamischer Geschichte, Wiege früher Gelehrsamkeit, Mythos in der Moderne*, 1999, Saarbrücken, 323-342.

"He gave the exiled Jewish king the highest place..." Amel-Marduk is the Evil-Merodach of the Bible's 2 Kings 25:27-30 and Jeremiah 52:31-34.

"*Karadara (Kara)" The ancient Iranian Kāradārā means "having work," which Tavernier observes is "a good name for a slave." See Tavernier, *Iranica in the Achaemenid Period (ca. 550-330 BC): Lexicon of Old Iranian Proper Names and Loanwords, Attested in Non-Iranian Texts*, 2007, Peeters, 226. The Indo-Aryan influence in Media at this time makes it feasible that such a name might be given to an acquired slave. A child might shorten it to "Kara." The word *kāra* in Old Persian means "the people, army" (Prods Oktor Skjærvø, *An Introduction to Old Persian*, 2005, online pdf, 25), which I also find provocative.

For details about the Akitu ceremony, I've drawn heavily from J. Bidmead, *The Akitu Festival: Religious Continuity and Royal Legitimation in Mesopotamia*, 2004, Gorgias.

A few of the resources I leaned on for details about the looks and layout of ancient Babylon include Andrew R. George, "A Tour of Nebuchadnezzar's Babylon," in *Babylon: Myth and Reality*, 2008, British Museum, 54-59; Joachim Marzhan, "Koldeway's Babylon," in *Babylon*, 2009, Oxford, 46-53; and Marc Mierhoop, "Reading Babylon," in *The American Journal of Archaeology*, 2003, 107:257-275. The following description of the Akitu festival is heavily dependent on J. Bidmead, *The Akitu Festival: Religious Continuity and Royal Legitimation in Mesopotamia*, 2004, Gorgias.

SOME OF MY SOURCES FOR
INFORMATION

I am tremendously grateful to those scholars of ancient Near Eastern history and literature who have made troves of information available and keep adding to what we know and how we think about the people, the places, and times that these narratives so lightly brush. I'm deeply sorry not to provide exhaustive documentation for all the research that informs these books. In lieu of even a bibliography, here is a list (itself incomplete) of some of the hundreds of scholars, past and present, whose work informed the story I tell.

Abraham, Kathleen
    Abusch, Tzvi
    Ackerman, Susan
    Ackroyd, Peter
    Adams, Robert McCormick
    Ahn, J. J.
    Aiken Littauer, M.
    Albenda, Pauline
    Albertz, Rainer
    Albright, William F.

Alexander, Robert L.

Algaze, Guillermo

Allen, Lindsay

Al-Rawi, F. N. H.

Álvarez-Mon, Javier

Amiet, P.

Aminzadeh, B.

Anthony, David W.

Ataç, M. A.

Austin, M. M.

Avigad, N.

Axworthy, Michael

Bahrami, B.

Bahrani, Zainab

Baker, H. D.

Balcer, Jack Martin

Bandstra, Andrew J.

Barkworth, P. R.

Barnett, R. D.

Barr, James

Basham, A. L.

Basirov, Oric

Beach, Eleanor F.

Beaulieu, Paul-Alain

Beckwith, Christopher I.

Bedford, Peter Ross

Berman, Joshua

Betlyon, John W.

Bidmead, J.

Bivar, A. D. H.

Black, Jeremy A.

Boardman, John

Boda, Mark J.

Bodi, Daniel

Bongenaar, A.
Bottéro, J.
Boucharlat, Remy
Boyce, Mary
Pierre Briant
Brosius, Maria
Browne, Edward Granville
Calmeyer, P.
Cameron, G. G.
Carter, C. E.
Castle, W. E.
Chalmers, C.
Choksy, Jamsheed K.
Cohen, Andrew C.
Crowell, Bradley L.
Curtis, John
Curtis, Vesta Sarkhosh
Dalley, Stephanie
Dandamaev, M. A.
Davies, Malcolm
Davies, W. D.
de Miroschedji, Pierre
De Souza, Philip
Dever, William
Dick, Michael B.
Dillery, John
Dougherty, Raymond P.
Draycott, Catherine M.
Drews, Robert
Dubberstein, Waldo H.
Dusinberre, Elspeth R. M.
Dvornik, Francis
Eilers, W.
Elgood, C.

Errington, Elizabeth
Eshel, Esther
Eskenazi, Tamara Cohn
Farazmand, Ali
Farrokh, Kaveh
Finkel, Irving L.
Flattery, David Stophlet
Fleming, D. E.
Foltz, Richard
Forsyth, Neil
Foster, Benjamin R.
Foster, Karen Polinger
Fried, Lisbeth S.
Frye, Richard N.
Fuchs, Esther
Gabrielli, Marcel
Galil, Gershon
Garrison, Mark B.
George, A. R.
Gese, Hartmut
Gopnik, Hilary
Goulder, M.
Grabbe, Lester L.
Gray, Louis H.
Grayson, Albert Kirk
Green, Anthony
Green, Jack
Griffiths, A.
Guliaev, Valeri I.
Gurney, O. R.
Hallo, William W.
Handley, Morrison
Harmatta, J.
Harris, Rivka

Harrison, Thomas
Harvey, D.
Head, Duncan
Hedrick, Larry
Henkelman, Wouter
Hirsch, Steven W.
Hoglund, Kenneth G.
Holtz, Shalom E.
Horsley, Richard A.
Houston, Mary G.
Huff, Dietrich
Ibrāmī, Hūshang
Ivantchik, Askold I.
Jackson, A. V. Williams
Jacobs, Bruno
Japhet, Sara
Jawad, Laith A.
Jennings, Justin
Joannes, F.
Jong, Albert de
Jordana, Xavier
Jursa, M.
Kaptan, D.
Katz, Steven T.
Katzenstein, H. Jacob
Kawami, Trudy S.
Kessler, K.
Kessler, John
Killick, R. G.
Kleber, Kristin
Knapton, Peter
Knoppers, Gary N
Knowles, Melody D.
Kratz, Reinhard

Kriwaczek, Paul
Kuhrt, Amélie
Lacocque, André
Lambert, W. G.
Landes, David S.
Lang, Mabel L.
Langdon, S.
Lavī, Ḥabīb
Leach, E. R.
Leiden, W. H. C.
Leloux, Kevin
Lemaire, André
Lerner, G.
Lincoln, Bruce
Linssen, M. J. H.
Lipiński, Edward
Littman, Robert J.
Liverani, Mario
Lloyd, Alan B.
Lloyd, Seton
Lucas, C. J.
Luckenbill, Daniel David
Lukonin, Vladimir G.
MacGinnis, John
Machinist, Peter
Malandra, William W.
Malbran-Labat, F.
Marzhan, Joachim
Master, Daniel M.
Matsushima, E.
Mattila, R.
McGovern, Patrick E.
Meier, S. A.
Middlemas, Jill

Miller, M. C.
Mills, Lawrence Heyworth
Mierhoop,
Miroschedji, P.
Moorey, P. R. S.
Muscarella, O. W.
Mukherjee, Siddhartha
Nashef, Khaled
Nefiodkin, Alexander K.
Nejad, Hadi
Nesbitt, M.
Neumann, C.
Neusner, Jacob
Newman, Judith H.
Nodet, Etienne
Noll, K. L.
Novotny, Jamie
Nylan, M.
Nylander, Carl
Ogden, Graham S.
Olson, J. S.
Oppenheim, A. L.
Page, Hugh R., Jr
Pallis, Svend Aage
Parpola, Simo
Parker, Richard A.
Panaino, Antonio
Paspalas, Stavros A.
Pearce, Laurie E.
Pedersen, O.
Pelikan, Jaroslav
Peradotto, John
Pettinato, Giovanni
Pham, Xuan Huong Thi

Pinches, T. G.

Poebel, A.

Polosmak, Natalya

Pongratz-Leisten, B.

Potts, Daniel T.

Powell, Marvin A.

Pritchard, James B.

Oeming, Manfred

Rainey, A. F.

Reiner, Erica

Rolle, Renate

Röllig, W.

Rollinger, Robert

Root, Margaret Cool

Roth, Martha T.

Sack, Ronald H.

Salonen, A.

Sancisi-Weerdenburg, Heleen

Sanders-Goebel, P.

Sandison, AT

Sarraf, M. R.

Sarshar, Houman

Sasson, J. M.

Schaudig, Hanspeter

Schauensee, D.E.

Schmid, H.

Schmidt, H. P.

Schwartz, Martin

Schwemer, Daniel

Scurlock, Joann

Seymour, M. J.

Shahgolzari, SM

Shea, William H.

Shiff, L. B.

Simpson, St John
Skjærvø, P. O.
Soudavar, A.
Stadter, P. A.
Stausberg, Michael
Stein, Gil J.
Stevens, Marty E.
Stol, Martin
Stolper, Matthew W.
Stott, Katherine
Stronach, David B.
Sumner, William M.
Suter, David W.
Tavernier, J.
Thomas, D. R. A.
Thureau-Dangin, F.
Trotter, James M.
Tuplin, Christopher
Ulansey, David
Ungnad, A.
Vallat, F.
Van de Mieroop, Marc
Van Driel, G.
Vargyas, P.
Vaughn, Andrew G.
Veen, J. E. van der
Vogelsang, W. J.
Waerzeggers, C.
Waters, Matthew W.
Watts, James W.
Weiershauser, Frauke
Weinfeld, M.
Weisberg, David B.
Weiss, L.

Weitzman, Steven
Widengren, G.
Wiesehöfer, J.
Wiggermann, F. A. M.
Williamson, H. G. M.
Winter, Irene J.
Wiseman, D. J.
Wunsch, C.
Yamauchi, E.
Yavari, A.
Younger, K. Lawson
Zaccagnini, Carlo
Zadok, Ran
Zawadzki, S.
Zevit, Z.
Zimansky, Paul E.
Zimmern, H.

AUTHOR'S NOTE

Without Cyrus, we may never have had a Bible. And without Amytis, we may never have had such a Cyrus. But few people have heard of Cyrus much less of Amytis. And the role of Babylon in biblical development remains largely the purview of scholars and academics. I excuse our collective ignorance in part because the relevant facts are few, hard to come by, and riddled with uncertainties. That doesn't mean, however, that they can't make for a good story.

This book (begun over fifteen years ago) – and the others in what has become a multi-volume (and could be many more) saga – happened because I started making things up. I had intended to write a nonfiction tome about a momentous period in human history (the transition from Babylonian to Persian rule) and the figure who stands at its center (Cyrus II, a.k.a. Cyrus the Great). But the more I learned, the more intriguing the women became. And the more I learned, the more I was forced to accept what all the experts say: we know very little... concretely, that is. But oh, so much was possible.

I threw myself into the research. At some point, what I was learning reached a critical mass and slipped its academic bonds.

Turns out, the research had been seducing my imagination all along. Finally, I had to face it: they'd eloped. I found myself filling in the long blanks between certainties with imagining what might have been. Ancient characters had become real people. Events and places began to take the shape of a novel. Also, I have a terrible memory. In all that research, I was finding associations and connections that no one seemed to have made before, and I didn't want to forget them. My best vehicle for keeping track was story.

I agonized. My agent at the time pointed out the cold truth. We simply could not sell a book of nonfiction with, er, fictional elements no matter how extensive the disclaimers. So, I ordered the facts back into their house, and tried to send my imagination packing. Alas, the two would not be parted. Finally, a friend of mine who had herself recently made a shift from nonfiction to historical fiction confronted me. "Why are clinging to nonfiction?!" she said. "Accept it. It's a novel."

Once I did, the project became pure delight... and a full-blown series with Amytis, my tree-hugging bastard princess, their through-line. That said, this particular book stands (or falls) on its own.

How much of the book is true? I understand the question, I do. And my best short answer is: all of it and none of it. This is a work of fiction. I made it up. That said, it is entirely based on huge amounts of hard-core research undertaken over the many years that this particular project has demanded and over decades before that as a student of the history and literature of the ancient Near East (what today we call the Middle East), earning a Ph.D. on the topic and a tenured appointment as a professor of it.

The question deserves a longer answer. First, a warning: the information here is best read *after* the novel itself for a couple of reasons. Most obviously, it will spoil the suspense. Equally serious, your brain might break. There are so many odd names and potentially unfamiliar references below that without having a story to hang them on... well, consider yourself warned.

Second, a quick note about sources. This story takes place 2500 years ago. Many relevant records, such as they ever were, are long gone. But many remain. Sources for modern researchers are wildly diverse, some primary and many derivative. They range from ancient histories to modern archaeological excavation reports, from the list of wages due to workers in a Babylonian temple to the Bible's Psalm 137, from an ancient world map drawn on clay (now housed in the British Museum) to a palace gate in stunningly beautiful tile (now housed in Berlin).

No one knows it all. Much about the period and its people is still in question. Hints and rumors abound. Ancient histories followed different rules than what we might wish. For such as Herodotus, one of our most important sources, reporting absolute fact was not always as important as telling a good story. And not all of the sources, ancient and otherwise, agree with each other.

Take Amytis, this book's main character. That she is historical we can agree. But exactly who she was, not so much. Even her lineage is in question. Was she the daughter of Cyaxares or of Astyages? The (very few) records differ, and her mother is consistently nameless. That she is remembered as marrying Nebuchadnezzar II to satisfy the treaty established by Cyaxares and (Nebuchadnezzar's father) Nabopolassar allows me (almost) to have it both ways: I represent her as the daughter of Astyages, married to Nebuchadnezzar only because Cyaxares did not have any daughters. (I don't know if the historical Cyaxares did or didn't have daughters.) There is no record of Amytis being a bastard.

As daughter of Astyages, Amytis would have been sister to Mandane, Cyrus's mother. Herodotus tells the story hinted at here about Astyages's paranoia leading him first to get Mandane married off to Cambyses of Parsa and then of attempting to kill

Mandane's infant son (the newborn Cyrus). I made up Mandane's subsequent suicide.

Herodotus tells that Nebuchadnezzar built the Hanging Gardens of Babylon for Amytis, homesick for the forested mountains of her beloved home, Media. There is reason to believe that such Hanging Gardens never existed, or if they did that they refer to gardens far north of Babylon built by an earlier monarch. But the legend was enough for me, and enough to imagine a young woman committed to protecting (by virtue of Nebuchadnezzar's honoring the historical treaty) her native land from Babylonian development.

Ancient Media (in modern Iran) was indeed a wild, biodiverse, naturally rich and beautiful place, even more so than I could describe in the novel. And ancient Babylonia (in modern Iraq), especially under Nebuchadnezzar had a reputation even greater than I show for destroying places in the course of conquest and building like mad. It is hardly a stretch to imagine the clash between what we now call environmental preservation and "development."

The other great conflict in the novel, Babylonian discomfort with a foreign presence, which drives the tension between Amytis and Igliss, is likewise timeless and human (anti-immigration, xenophobia...). We know that Nebuchadnezzar's policy in war was to take from conquered nations the best and brightest, to bring them back to Babylonia and put their smarts and skills to work. Babylonian exiles such as those from the defeated nation of Judah were given positions throughout the empire, including the palace, as important tradespeople and intellectuals. Nebuchadnezzar's court was cosmopolitan, and not all Babylonians were happy about that. Some native Babylonians, especially of the higher classes and with a stake in the nation's face and future would have had issues with such integration. That a foreign woman might bear the crown prince, as in this story, may have been intolerable for some people.

We don't know for certain that Amytis was the mother of the historical Amel-Marduk (my Bushu). But among other things (timing, e.g.), it appears that after the historical Amel-Marduk succeeded his father, Nebuchadnezzar, to the throne of Babylon, there was a wave of Median immigrants. Many Babylonians didn't like it. Some of this bears on (and could spoil) the sequel's drama and suspense; relevant here is evidence that Amel-Marduk was sympathetic to these Medians, which supports the possibility that he was (half) Median himself.

I follow the scholar Irving Finkel in believing that a document recovered from this time, "The Lament of Nabu-shuma-ukin," is Amel-Marduk's. (Some of that historical text is in this novel.) Its composer, a finely trained poet, calls himself the son of Nebuchadnezzar and says he was wrongfully imprisoned. He promises to devote himself to the god Marduk, if the god would only secure his release. Hence, the name-change to Amel-Marduk, "servant of Marduk." In ancient Hebrew (transliterated), Amel-Marduk is Evil-Merodach and shows up in the Bible as the Babylonian king who released the Jewish king from prison and accorded him an honorable place "at the king's table." (Because of how easily English-speaking readers might confuse the English "evil" with the Hebrew "Evil," the transliteration [not to be confused with translation] of a name meaning "servant of," I chose to spell it differently [erroneously] as Evel.) This Evil-Merodach, nee Nabu-shuma-ukin, may well have met the Jewish king in prison.

Jewish legend also lands Amel-Marduk in prison (and furious with Nebuchadnezzar ever after). We do not know why the prince was imprisoned, but the most likely reason would be an attempt to usurp the throne. Sleeping with the king's women would have demonstrated such an effort. I made up the love story that supports it.

I also made up the love story between Amytis and Khai. But I didn't make up Khai and admit that I fell a little in love with the historical man myself. As I note in the character list, Khai is based on a Babylonian by the name of Nabu-ahhe-iddin, from the family Egibi. Nebuchadnezzar's near manic building – walls, temples, palace, quays – surely created a lot of work and opportunity. Babylonian society was stratified, with "citizens" (from among which politically powerful elders came) at the top. But for industrious, intelligent, and entrepreneurial people, advancement was possible.

The historical Nabu-ahhe-iddin (my Khai) was such a person. We have a remarkably large repository of records from his businesses spanning generations and including some family information. From humble beginnings with a small family farm, this man developed a full-blown corporation with holdings in transportation, real estate (including rentals), banking, and of course farming. We know that he served for a time as a palace scribe and may well have had close dealings with Amytis during the course of a long and dynamic career.

The historical [Khai] also worked for the historical Neriglissar, whom I call Igliss. As per this story, Neriglissar appears to have participated in the Babylonian campaign against Judah (see below). Neriglissar was a member of the prominent Babylonian Nur-Sin family and did marry Kassiya (or Cassiya), daughter of Nebuchadnezzar, to become the king's son-in-law. His son with Kassiya was indeed Labashi-Marduk for whom [Igliss] had lofty ambitions. Their story continues in the next book, so I won't say much more here except that I'm confident that the conflict that drives this narrative was real.

The family of Adad-guppi, Nabonidus, and Belshazzar is historical. I found the historical Adad-guppi to be so intriguing and her name not too difficult that I decided not to call her anything else. No one but a handful of scholars knows about Adad-guppi, so I wanted to give her a chance out in the wider world. Adad-guppi is sometimes called a priestess. Indeed the historical record of her devotion to the moon god of her native place, Harran, is striking. Also, we know that she secured and maintained an important position in the Babylonian court lasting through several kings. Adad-guppi had been taken by the Babylonians along with her son, Nabonidus, from Harran, when the Babylonians and Medes together brought the Assyrian empire to its knees. Without, I hope, giving away what's to come in the next books, Adad-guppi lived, according to an inscription that we still have, in good health until the ripe old age of 104 years old.

Incidentally, those familiar with the biblical narratives might recognize the place name of Harran and maybe even link it with Ur. A whole lot of the greater biblical story begins in those sites. Abraham (then Abram) departs from Ur with his family, including father Terah, wife Sarah, and nephew Lot and settles in Harran, where Abraham is said to have heard God's call to "Go... to the land that I will show you." Ur and Harran were the two cities of the moon god. I'm not sure what to make of these connections, but there's yet another story in there somewhere. Oh, and Abraham's leaving Ur and then Harran appears in the Bible right after the Tower of Babel story. (Babel/Babylon – not a coincidence. See below.)

When I first began this project, I was ill-inclined toward Nabonidus, having accepted the ancient propaganda against him. With a whole lot more learning under my cap, Nabonidus has become admirable and even dear to me. Ultimately, his story (only a tiny bit of which appears here) strikes me as a classic tragedy. Historically, he was the king of Babylonia whom Cyrus defeated. But I'm getting ahead of myself. The historical Nabonidus relevant for this book was indeed a person of Nebuchadnezzar's court and the father of Belshazzar.

The biblical book of Daniel, set during the period of the Babylonian exile but dating from centuries later, occasionally conflates or switches Nebuchadnezzar and Nabonidus. (Notice "switches" not "confuses," because it could have been intentional.) The Bible is a great resource for information about the ancient world, including the history of the ancient Near East. But it does not report things exactly as they happened, and we mistreat its narratives when we expect them to report facts like modern journalists should do. This does not make the Bible "wrong," but rather our reading of it. And we miss what may be of most interest and value in the biblical texts by requiring them to conform to our expectations. Stepping off my soapbox... The biblical book of Daniel portrays Nebuchadnezzar as enduring a period of madness from which God heals him. That's too delicious to ignore.

Many scholars, myself included, believe that the decade that *Nabonidus* (Babylonia's king at the time) spent apart from Babylon lies behind that story, at least in part. I nod to the fact that the Bible chooses to tell the crazy-guy story as Nebuchadnezzar's madness. There certainly was plenty about Nebuchadnezzar that could justify such a representation in the eyes of the people responsible for Daniel-the-Book's final form.

That Belshazzar is sometimes wrongly called Nebuchadnezzar's son makes more sense if they were otherwise related. I make the historical Nitocris the mother of Belshazzar (and so Belshazzar is grandson of Nebuchadnezzar). This is not historical but not impossible, either. Contrary to popular (Bible-based) belief, Belshazzar was never the king of Babylonia. He did however, perform kingly duties (and I suspect would have been delighted to be confused as king for real) when his father Nabonidus, then king of Babylonia, was absent from Babylon for those ten years mentioned above.

Nebuchadnezzar did have a son, Eanna-sharra-utsur, the basis for my Ean. And that son is indeed historically remembered for having received sick rations in Uruk. I made up the rest of his story in order to reconcile the timing. Eight of Nebuchadnezzar's historical sons have been identified. Amel-Marduk appears to have been the eldest. But the sick-house rations document dates from before my dating for Amel-Marduk. My imagination took over from there.

Kara is fictitious; slavery in the ancient world is not. It *is* complicated, though. (Try this on: slaves could themselves own slaves.) People regardless of race or creed could become enslaved in the event of war. And the conditions of their servitude ranged from torturous brutality to virtual autonomy. (A great resource for understanding slavery in Babylonia is Muhammed A. Dandamaev's *Slavery in Babylonia*, translated by Victoria A. Powell.) Finally, whatever the status and conditions of a slave, the basic denial of personal liberty would have been, then as now, dehumanizing and unacceptable to those who experienced it.

The Jews. Next to Amytis, my favorite part of this whole story. Some background in super-brief: The nation of Israel, which gained international attention during Solomon's reign in the tenth century B.C.E. when the temple in Jerusalem was built, fractured into two after Solomon's death. The northern kingdom, confusingly also called Israel, was defeated by the Assyrians toward the end of the eighth century B.C.E. Many of those Israelites were removed to places within the Median empire, hence my reference to Jews in the capital, Ecbatana.

Judah, the former Israel's southern kingdom, with its capital of Jerusalem endured. But it was subject to the vicissitudes of politics to the east. Ultimately Babylonia's rise made Judah a vassal state. In 597 B.C.E., Nebuchadnezzar took issue with Judah's Egyptian alliance, laid siege to Jerusalem, and removed Judah's king of only three months, Jehoiachin/Coniah (the guy in this novel) and some of Jerusalem's best and brightest, including the prophet Ezekiel, and took them to Babylon. Ten years later (587 B.C.E.), Judah's effort to rebel was met with devastating punishment. Nebuchadnezzar's Babylonian troops, including the historical [Igliss] utterly defeated the nation, destroyed the Jerusalem temple, brutalized its king, and took another wave of people to Babylon. It is possible that the "suffering servant" of Isa 52:13-53:12 was composed with Jehoiachin/Coniah in mind.

I think that the single most important event in the Bible's development is the Babylonian exile. It's important in two ways: for how it affected the theology and literature already circulating, and because it served as the catalyst to assemble and collect as well as compose what would become biblical texts. There was no "Bible" before this time. For all intents and purposes, there was no Judaism, either. That is, the religion recognizable to us today as Judaism largely grew out of the land-less, temple-less condition of exile. It was a painful and a fruitful time.

Among many biblical texts, some of which I cite in the novel, the biblical story of the Tower of Babel was probably written or informed by Jews living in Babylon who had occasion to observe the many and grand building projects undertaken by Nebuchadnezzar. One of those projects was a huge and seemingly endless renovation of the temple of Marduk in the center of the city. People from many different nations, no doubt speaking diverse languages, worked in Nebuchadnezzar's Babylon. (Hence the biblical story's "confusion of tongues" and what Jews saw as an arrogant effort to reach the heavens.) Nebuchadnezzar's policy concerning conquered peoples was to take advantage of their skills and learning, putting such to use wherever they served him best.

It cannot be understated – the enduring effect of efforts to make sense of the chaos and destruction of Babylonian control and the nature of God and God's relationship to people that the exile generated among the intelligent, devout, and literate Jews taken into Babylon. Those efforts and the diversity of their answers permeate the Hebrew Bible and shaped a multi-faceted theology that many centuries later could (not necessarily but by interpretation) identify a Jew, Jesus, as the redeeming incarnation of a fiercely loyal and loving God.

I have tried to show a little of that here. Judean exiles, whom I call simply (and not quite accurately) Jews, permeated Babylonian society. We know of Bariki-ili, the slave desperate for freedom; and we know that Ezekiel exercised a liberty to preach and gather with Jewish elders in Babylonian exile. We know that a community of Jews lived and worked at literary pursuits in a district of the town of Nippur; and we know that many of the exiles from Judah and their descendants ultimately adopted and integrated into Babylonian society.

The Babylonian pantheon was multi-faceted, with gods and goddesses gathering in Babylon once a year from their respective cities in the biggest annual festival, the Akitu. I chose to use the archaic Sumerian name "Nanna-Suen" for the moon god of Harran/Ur rather than the Akkadian "Sin" lest English readers misunderstand the name as some modern moral judgment. The gods and goddesses so named in the novel and many more besides were part of a complex pantheon. The massage ritual is real, as is the practice of reading divine messages in animal organs. The prayers I cite are based on extant documents of the time, and the biblical texts (not yet biblical of course) may have circulated or been composed under circumstances such as I depict.

A few miscellaneous notes: I have made up the "for certain" vs. "of course" idioms to give Amytis a way of sounding different from native Babylonians. Description of the furniture, clothing, and architecture reflects archaeological and scholarly research as much as possible. Media was known for its war horses, which were an international sensation, the product of careful breeding and what some called the magical grass on which they fed. The fields of Media grew exquisitely nutritious alfalfa.

Finally, for a story originally rooted in the historical Cyrus II, Cyrus is barely a rumor here. That changes in subsequent books. Of Cyrus's birth and even lineage, we cannot be sure. We don't know the date of his birth, whether he came from royal or peasant parentage, or even what the name Cyrus means. As to the latter, I follow the logic represented in the novel – that it is Elamite and connotes protection. Concerning his parentage, I follow Herodotus and others in naming Mandane as his mother and Cambyses I as his father. Both Cambyses I and Cyrus II called themselves kings by the Elamite title "king of Anshan" not "of Persia." I understand Anshan to have been a city (the modern archaeological site of Tel el-Malyan) within what was a relatively small and loosely confederated country of Parsa, itself arguably within the greater control of Media (and so of Astyages). In this fiction series, I follow Herodotus's dramatic and gruesome tale of Cyrus's birth and rise.

As for Amytis as she appears at the end of this novel, there is historical precedent for locating her back in Media. I doubt we're too far off by imagining her return to have carried terribly mixed emotions –heart-broken for what she left in Babylon: her son, of course, and maybe a lost love; and happy to be back in the wild and beautiful land of her birth, protected in its wild integrity by the sum of her actions.

But that, too, is for another story.

ACKNOWLEDGMENTS

I'm guessing that any project that spans more than a decade from inception to completion represents the support, goodwill, and contributions of all kinds from more people than a book's "Acknowledgments" can cover, no matter its author's efforts to be exhaustive. That's certainly true here. My apologies to those I've missed. Thank you.

And thank you, each and every named below. I've had illusions of providing detail to describe the nature of the contributions each person or group (libraries! my students! professional organizations!). But just as I bailed on providing an exhaustive list of specific sources and a more exhaustive Author's Note, finally I provide only the barest list here. Its notice – meager – is inverse to my gratitude – great. Thank you.

Finally, a special thanks to my dad, Richard Swenson, and my (late) mom, L. Cecile Swenson whose support of my work has been so unqualified that I might almost take it for granted. I don't. And to my husband, Craig L. Slingluff, Jr., a huge thanks for being so ceaseless a cheerleader of this project. I'm not sure I ever would have sent these books out into the world without your unflagging enthusiasm for the saga and the needling to publish it, such as only a person sharing one's life, day in and day out, can do.

Thank you sincerely also to the following, in order simply by alphabet: Richard Abate, Khooshe Aiken, Lindsay Allen, Hanadi Al-Samman, Gigi Amateau, American Academy of Religion, American Schools of Oriental Research, Willis Barnstone, Bennington Book Club, Biographers International Organization,

Bodleian Libraries of Oxford University, Christiana Brenin, Laura Browder, Ellen Brown, McKenna Brown, Theo Calderara, Bethany Carlson, Jamsheed Choksy, Susann Cokal, Meredith Cole, Jonathan Coleman, Michael Cordell, Rob Crawford, the cadre of Cville Women Writers, Stephanie Dalley, Cliff Edwards, Robin Farmer, Louise Finger, Greg Fontana, Jeannie Fontana, Donna Freitas, Shirley French, Kathleen Gacek, Brad Graff, Martien Halvorson-Taylor, Kate Hamilton, Sandy Hausman, Stacy Hawkins, Paul Hilding, Stephani Hilding, Historical Novel Society, Doug Hoffman, Denise Honeycutt, Kate Hunter, Molly Ill, James River Writers, Eric Jarrard, Gretchen Kainz, Andrew King, Dean King, Chris Park, Eva-Marie King, Amelie Kuhrt, John Kutsko, (late) "Boots" Mead, Meg Medina, Manny Mendez, Alex Nagel, Jen Pearson, Stephanie Pearson, The Porches (Trudy Hale), Debby Prum, Ginny Pye, Emilie Raymond, Dianna Rostad, Charles Shields, Guadalupe Shields, Society of Biblical Literature, Maya Smart, Patty Smith, Jack Spiro, Devon Sproule, Beth Stefanik, Matthew Stolper, Jon Swenson Tellekson, Linnea Swenson Tellekson, Deb Swenson, Nigel Tallis, Sandra Treadway, University of Virginia library, Rachel Unkefer, Virginia Commonwealth University library, Virginia (Foundation for the) Humanities, Claire Wachtel, Pat Watkins, Jon Waybright, Anne Westrick, Vera Wilde, Mark Wood, Women's International Study Center, Writer House, and Irene Ziegler.

MAP

This is a map of the Median Empire, Egypt, Lydian Empire and Neo-Babylonian Empire in the 6th century BC (1024 px; there are other sizes available).

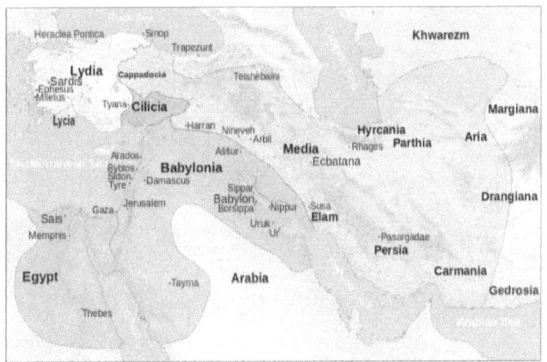

Date: 30 April 2013.
Source: File:Median Empire-hu.svg
ETOPO1 topographic data from NGDC (http://www.ngdc. noaa.gov/mgg/global/global.html).
Author: Original: User:Szajci; English: User:WillemBK

(page URL) https://commons.wikimedia.org/wiki/File:Median_Empire-en.svg

(file URL) https://upload.wikimedia.org/wikipedia/commons/b/bd/Median_Empire-en.svg

Attribution: Original: User:SzajciEnglish: User:WillemBK, CC BY-SA 3.0 <https://creativecommons.org/licenses/by-sa/3.0>, via Wikimedia Commons

ABOUT THE AUTHOR

Kristin Swenson, Ph.D. writes across genres. Tenured professor of religious studies with speciality in the history and literature of ancient Israel (Hebrew Bible), she is passionate about the natural world and loves a good story. All the better if a story connects the disparate threads of women and lesser known persons with what history we have. In addition to her writing, Swenson has developed an eco-grief practice to help people continue to advocate for the wild with equanimity and joy. She also maintains a website celebrating (and advising for) the eco-friendly kitchen. Swenson lives and works in Charlottesville Virginia and Duluth, Minnesota.

ALSO BY KRISTIN SWENSON

FICTION

Genie of Pasargad (Babylon/Persia #4; PGB)

Beat the Kettledrum (Babylon/Persia #3; PGB)

A Falcon Takes Flight (Babylon/Persia #2; PGB)

Howl of the Golden Jackal (Babylon/Persia #1; PGB)

NONFICTION

A Most Peculiar Book: The Inherent Strangeness of the Bible (Oxford University)

God of Earth: Discovering a Radically Ecological Christianity (Westminster John Knox)

Bible Babel: Making Sense of the Most Talked About Book of All Time (Harper)

Living through Pain: Psalms and the Search for Wholeness (Baylor University)

What is Religious Studies?: A Journey of Inquiry (with Esther R. Nelson, Kendall Hunt)

POETRY

Haiku 365 at www.kristinswenson.com